These bastards [illegible] are. Keeping some of [illegible] h it seems as though [illegible] the table. If that's a M[illegible] ple mil-spec fangs that [illegible] or were retrofitted by whoe[illegible] her title, then she's got even more energy output that she hasn't touched yet. Her designers put in enough power plant capability to drive her at full speed while also powering her beam weapons. So when her commander pushes the power plant to those higher gigawatt levels—

Damn it. "Schendler, raise Bloodhound One right now. Secure channel two."

"Sir, Magee is responding on secure two."

"Bloodhound one, this is Doghouse."

"Reading you five by five, sir."

"Good. I need a fast report on the ship's systems."

"Yes, sir. Inconsequential small arms damage throughout. Minor damage to control elements on the bridge; can't know functionality unless she was up and running. But the biggest problem is that someone took a sledgehammer to the containment rings."

"Alignment is shot?"

"Again, can't say without trying to start her up, sir. She's running off batteries, right now. And if the rings are messed up just enough to allow fusion to begin before finally losing containment—"

"That's sufficient, Captain." Wethermere looked at the respective position of the blips in the holotank. The bogey could start firing any moment now. "Bloodhound One, prepare to abandon ship."

"Sir?"

"Did I stutter, Magee? I said 'prepare to abandon ship.'"

ALSO IN THE STARFIRE SERIES

BY DAVID WEBER & STEVE WHITE

Crusade
In Death Ground
The Stars At War
Insurrection
The Shiva Option
The Stars at War II

BY STEVE WHITE & SHIRLEY MEIER

Exodus

BY STEVE WHITE & CHARLES E. GANNON

Extremis

BAEN BOOKS by STEVE WHITE

The Prometheus Project
Demon's Gate
Forge of the Titans
Eagle Against the Stars
Wolf Among the Stars
Prince of Sunset
The Disinherited
Legacy
Debt of Ages
St. Antony's Fire

THE JASON THANOU SERIES

Blood of the Heroes
Sunset of the Gods
Pirates of the Timestream
Ghosts of Time
Soldiers Out of Time

BAEN BOOKS by CHARLES E. GANNON

Fire with Fire
Trial by Fire
Raising Caine
1635: The Papal Stakes (w/ Eric Flint)
1636: Commander Cantrell in the West Indies (w/ Eric Flint)

IMPERATIVE

A Starfire Novel

STEVE WHITE &
CHARLES E. GANNON

IMPERATIVE

This is a work of fiction. All the characters and events portrayed in this book are fictional, and any resemblance to real people or incidents is purely coincidental.

A Baen Books Original

Baen Publishing Enterprises
P.O. Box 1403
Riverdale, NY 10471
www.baen.com

ISBN: 978-1-4814-8243-1

Cover art by Dave Seeley
Ship models by John Douglass
Maps by Randy Asplund

First mass market paperback printing, May 2017

Distributed by Simon & Schuster
1230 Avenue of the Americas
New York, NY 10020

Pages by Joy Freeman (www.pagesbyjoy.com)
Printed in the United States of America

Maps

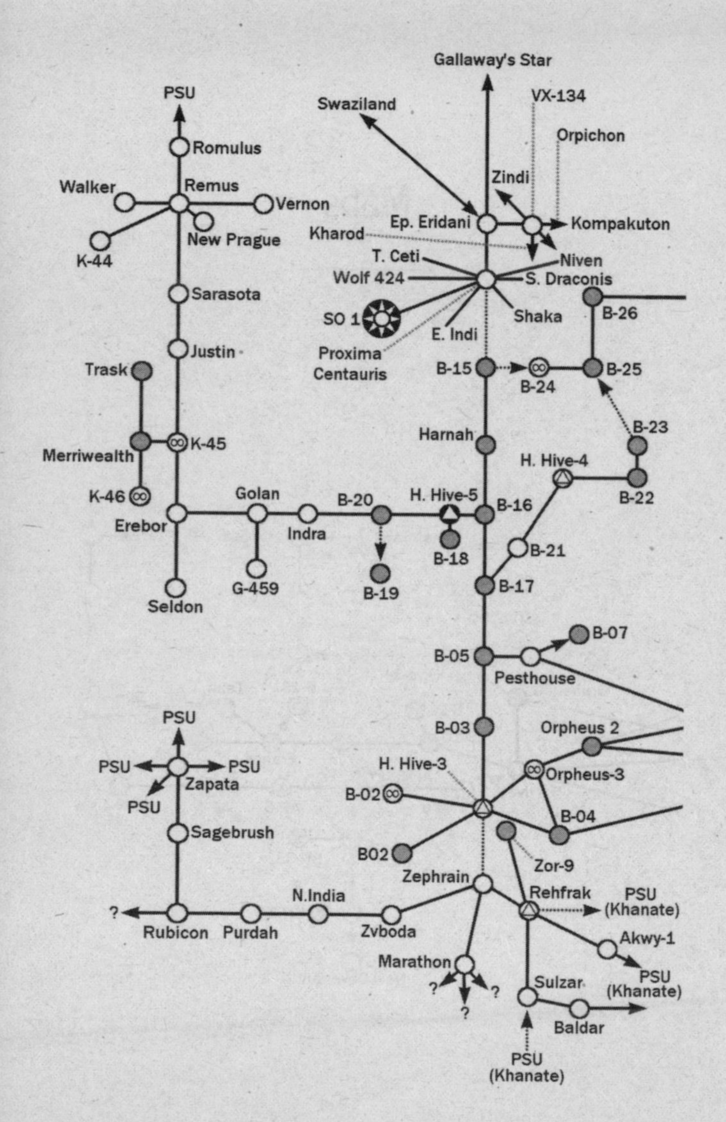
Gallaway's Star
PSU
Swaziland
VX-134
Orpichon
Romulus
Zindi
Walker
Remus
Vernon
Ep. Eridani
Kompakuton
New Prague
Kharod
K-44
T. Ceti
Niven
Wolf 424
S. Draconis
Sarasota
B-26
SO 1
Shaka
E. Indi
Justin
Proxima
Centauris
Trask
B-15
B-24
B-25
B-23
Harnah
K-45
Merriwealth
H. Hive-4
K-46
Golan
B-20
H. Hive-5
B-16
B-22
Erebor
Indra
B-18
B-21
G-459
B-19
B-17
Seldon
B-07
B-05
Pesthouse
PSU
B-03
Orpheus 2
PSU
PSU
H. Hive-3
Zapata
Orpheus-3
B-02
PSU
B-04
Sagebrush
B02
Zor-9
Zephrain
Rehfrak
PSU
(Khanate)
N.India
?
Rubicon
Purdah
Zvboda
Akwy-1
Marathon
PSU
(Khanate)
?
?
Sulzar
?
Baldar
PSU
(Khanate)

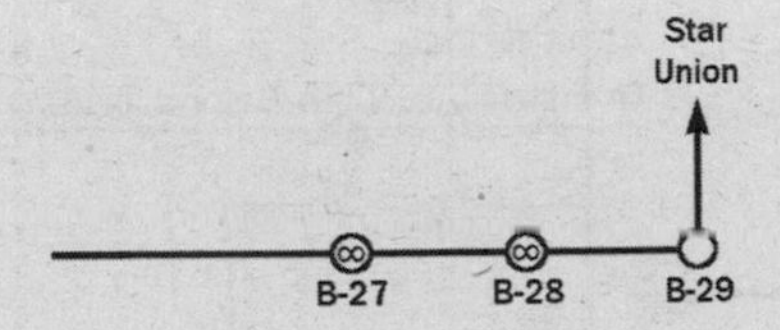
Star
Union
B-27
B-28
B-29

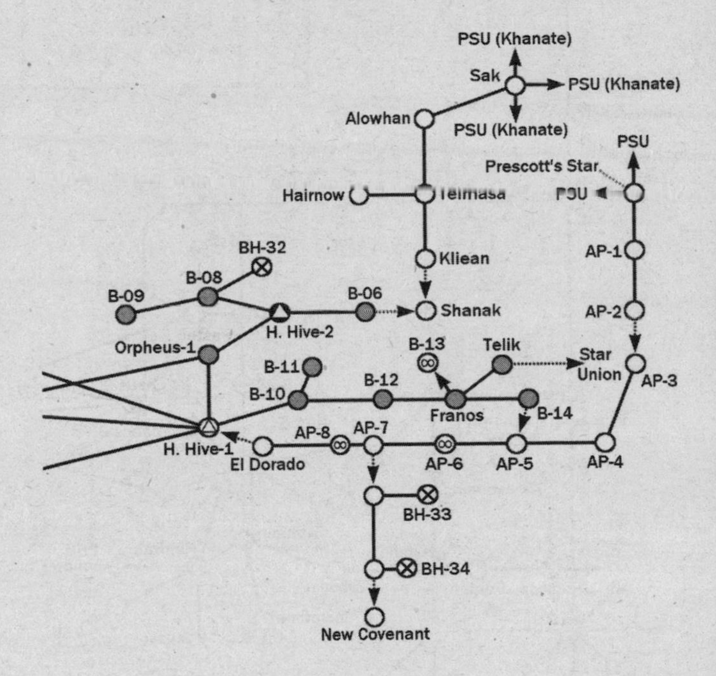
PSU (Khanate)
Sak
PSU (Khanate)
Alowhan
PSU (Khanate)
PSU
Prescott's Star
Hairnow
Telmasa
PSU
AP-1
Kliean
BH-32
B-08
B-09
B-06
Shanak
AP-2
H. Hive-2
Orpheus-1
B-13
Telik
Star
Union
AP-3
B-11
B-12
B-10
Franos
B-14
AP-8
AP-7
H. Hive-1
El Dorado
AP-6
AP-5
AP-4
BH-33
BH-34
New Covenant

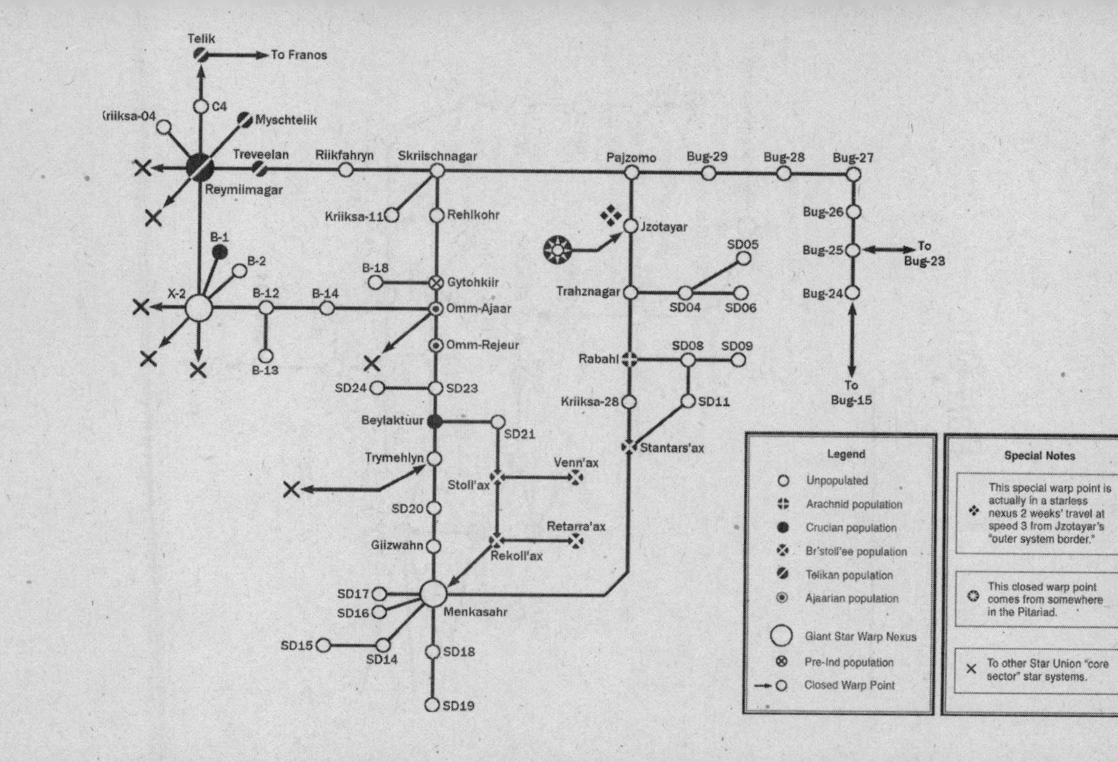
Telik
To Franos
C4
(riiksa-04
Myschtelik
Treveelan
Riikfahryn
Skriischnagar
Pajzomo
Bug-29
Bug-28
Bug-27
Reymiimagar
Kriiksa-11
Rehlkohr
Bug-26
Jzotayar
Bug-25
To Bug-23
B-1
B-2
B-18
Gytohkiir
SD05
X-2
B-12
B-14
Omm-Ajaar
Trahznagar
SD04
SD06
Bug-24
Omm-Rejeur
B-13
Rabahl
SD08
SD09
SD24
SD23
To Bug-15
Kriiksa-28
SD11
Beylaktuur
SD21
Stantars'ax
Trymehlyn
Venn'ax
Stoll'ax
SD20
Retarra'ax
Giizwahn
Rekoll'ax
SD17
SD16
Menkasahr
SD15
SD14
SD18
SD19
Legend
Unpopulated
Arachnid population
Crucian population
Br'stoll'ee population
Telikan population
Ajaarian population
Giant Star Warp Nexus
Pre-Ind population
Closed Warp Point
Special Notes
This special warp point is actually in a starless nexus 2 weeks' travel at speed 3 from Jzotayar's "outer system border."
This closed warp point comes from somewhere in the Pitariad.
To other Star Union "core sector" star systems.

Part One

The Eve of Destruction

CHAPTER ONE

Han Trevayne gazed up with large, dark, slightly almond-shaped eyes that held a perplexed look, and spoke with five-year-old gravitas.

"But teacher told us *nothing* made by people is more than two hundred and eighty standard years old," she stated firmly.

"She meant on Novaya Rodina where we live, dear," Li-Trevayne Magda explained to her daughter patiently. "That's how long ago people first arrived there—"

"Shortly after the Third Interstellar War ended in 2246," Ian Trevayne put in, unable as always to refrain from historical elucidation.

"—to found a colony," Magda finished, with a quick glare at her husband for confusing their child with unnecessary details. "But now we're on the world those people had come from."

"And where did people come *here* from?"

"Nowhere, Han."

The little girl's puzzlement deepened. "But they must have come from *somewhere*."

"That would be true on any planet but this one. But remember, this is where we all came from. This is Old Terra, where people—*human* people, anyway—originated, a very long time ago."

"It's even where *I* originated—a very long time ago," said Trevayne drily. Some might have found it an odd remark, coming from a man who appeared to be in his late twenties or early thirties.

"And," Magda continued, forestalling any further digressions, "it was only about five hundred years ago that people first left this planet. For thousands and thousands of years before that, this was the *only* planet with people on it. That's why it holds things like *this.*" She gestured at the half-ruined oval structure of ancient marble before them. "What did you say it's called, Ian?"

"The Colosseum. As I told you, Han, it's almost twenty-five hundred years old." Trevayne gazed up at the always-surprising height of the thing, and wished they had come incognito (as if that were possible) by the subway, the technology of which had of course changed many times but whose station was still in its original, twentieth-century location. That placement had been a bit of artistry, conscious or otherwise, for on emerging from the exit one found oneself, without warning, in the Piazza del Colosseo, staring up at this ancient architectural immensity. The impact was stunning and impossible to forget, especially at night when the Colosseum was floodlit.

But even approached along the Via dei Fori Imperiali, as they had done, it was impressive enough.

"What did they use it for?" Han asked reasonably.

"Games." Trevayne didn't go into the nature of those games. There'd be plenty of time later for her to learn the horrors of which humans were capable. "Anyway, there are things here in this city even older than this. Come this way."

He led the way through the fine afternoon, warm but not hot as Rome could often be in the spring. They passed the Arch of Constantine and proceeded along the Via Sacra, past the vast pit, a dozen feet beneath street level, which held the remains of the Roman Forum, the broken buildings and scattered columns and arches haunted by the psychic residue of all the history that had occurred there. To the left rose the green Palatine Hill where the foundations of the emperors' palaces still protruded from the earth like the masonry rib-cages of dead titans.

When they had landed at Western Europe's Galileo Spaceport, it had been Magda's (and, of course, Han's) first contact with the soil of Old Terra. Trevayne was determined to show them his native England, and as much else as could be squeezed into their schedule, but the official purpose of the visit had led them here first, and he wasn't really sorry as he looked around and then raised his eyes to the modern towers of today's Rome, even taller than he remembered but unobtrusively far away thanks to building restrictions.

"It's been a long time," he murmured. "Thank God they've preserved the central part of the city unchanged."

"When *was* the last time you were here, Ian?" asked Magda.

"Let's see . . . That would have been in 2412. I was eighteen at the time." He spoke casually, although the two statements taken together were enough to raise eyebrows even in these days of antigerone treatments.

"Or, strictly speaking, your *first* body was eighteen. So . . ." Magda did some quick mental arithmetic. "In terms of your elapsed consciousness, it was just under forty years ago."

Han listened to all this with a gravely puzzled frown. She knew there was something unusual about her father's background, but she had never entirely understood it.

Most people would have sympathized with her bewilderment.

Ian Trevayne had been the hero of the loyalist side in the Fringe Revolution of 2438 to 2444. Cut off from the bulk of the embattled Terran Federation, he had held the loyalist worlds of the Rim for the Federation and come close to fighting his way back along the warp lines through the rebelling systems of the Terran Republic. But in the climactic Battle of Zapata in 2443 he had been battered to a standstill, and had almost been among the all-too-numerous dead . . . almost, but not quite. Close enough, if one considered extensive radiation damage, spine severed below the fifth vertebra, extreme anoxia, concussion, and so forth. So close as to justify his flagship's chief surgeon's snap decision as to the only way to preserve his life: quick-freeze in a cryogenic bath without any of the usual elaborate workup. It had been a risky procedure at best . . . and the damage from the quick-freeze itself hadn't helped. But the workup for the brain tissue had *not* been omitted, for irreparable damage to that would have rendered the whole business pointless. The result: an undamaged brain in a body which was essentially unsalvageable because it could not be unthawed and survive, at least not without permanent impairment. And cloning had been ruled out as either impractical or illegal (not to say ethically repugnant); the sheer number of individual organs requiring replacement would have rendered it too hazardous, and cutting the brain out of a full-body clone to replace it with another was murder.

So he had spent eighty-one standard years getting "well and truly freezer-burned," as he himself had later put it. And while he had slumbered in cryogenic suspension, the war had been settled on the basis of the Terran Republic's independence while the Rim worlds formed the Rim Federation, somehow both in and out of the Terran Federation . . . which, strictly speaking, no longer existed as such because it had merged with the alien Khanate of Orion to form the somewhat exaggeratedly named Pan-Sentient Union. In short, all he had fought for had become more or less meaningless, washed away by the tides of history.

In due course, the boundaries and limits of medicine's restorative powers changed as well. It became possible to produce a full-body clone without a brain, hence dead—or, at least, unalive—by legal definition, and force-grown to a biological age of eighteen to twenty. Thus, with the legal objections overcome and the ethical ones rationalized away, Trevayne's forty-nine-year-old brain had awakened in a perfect replica of his own young-adult body.

Thus it was that, alone among all descendants of Adam, he had three ages. His legal age was a hundred and thirty, for he had been born in 2394. But the biological age of his current body was little over thirty, for an antigerone regimen counteracted the rapid aging of a clone produced from postembryonic cells. (Although, to his sternly unexpressed disgust, he was starting to see the early indicia of the male pattern baldness he'd already had to endure once. And his memory spanned a little over sixty years of consciousness, in two brutally interrupted segments.

It had been sheer coincidence that his second life had commenced, in the Rim Federation whose independent existence he had unintentionally made possible, shortly before that polity had faced a crisis unprecedented in the history of known space. For the first wave of the Arduan Diaspora had arrived . . . and nothing had been the same since.

The thought of the manner of the Arduans' arrival, and all its implications, brought with it the unwelcome recollection of why they were here: to participate in the celebration of something to which he was flatly opposed.

"Politicians!" he muttered to himself with a scowl, turning the word into something fit to be scrawled on the walls of public toilets.

Magda saw that scowl and heard that mutter, or perhaps she looked to the cloud-burdened west where the sun was setting into a perfect Roman late afternoon, for she spoke with the voice of female practicality. "We'd better be getting back to the hotel, Ian."

The hotel, which, among its other amenities, provided child care. "Yes," Trevayne sighed. "I suppose we *do* have to go to that bloody cocktail party, don't we?"

"Can't I come too?" Han piped up, having heard only the word *party*.

"You wouldn't enjoy it, dear," Magda assured her.

You might very possibly enjoy it more than I will, Trevayne mentally groused. But then he looked down at his daughter's face, which smiled back at him, working its usual magic on his mood.

Those huge dark eyes looked out of a face which

reflected its origins. Trevayne had once figured it out: half English (including a dash of African-descended Jamaican), one-quarter Japanese, three-eighths Chinese, and an eighth Tibetan. In short, a fairly typical modern human—but unique as far as Trevayne was concerned, even though he knew he was viewing her with the eyes of every father since time began. And, in fact, there was a uniqueness about her that everyone recognized, derived from her parentage and reflected in her name. There was normally nothing unusual about naming a girl after her grandmother, but in this case the combination of given name and surname never failed to raise eyebrows...

He sighed again. Magda was right about getting back to the hotel, of course, although there was much that he still wanted to show them while they were still in Rome: the Pantheon, the Campidoglio, the Trevi Fountain, and of course Vatican City, where the Swiss Guards still marched in their thousand-year-old uniforms and St. Peter's Basilica had never lost its power to inspire awe even as the beliefs behind it had frayed out. But for now... "Yes, let's start back." He took one last look around at the detritus of empire. To the left, the Palatine rose to its northern end, beyond the Via Nova, where a few centuries ago the archaeologists had finally gotten permission to dig up the Farnese Gardens and excavate the foundations of the Palace of Tiberius, confirming that it had been turned into office space for the bureaucracy while subsequent emperors had covered the hill with ever more grandiose residences. After those tumbled stones had yielded their last secrets, they had been left for the moss to cover.

So much for imperial grandeur, Trevayne philosophized as they walked back through the ruins of the Forum.

But he knew it was because of that very grandeur, rendered even more imposing by the mystique of ancientness, that the government of the Pan-Sentient Union had chosen this city for the ceremony to which he and Magda had been invited. The Orions were particularly impressed, for they had nothing like it, their own birthworld having been wrecked by internecine wars centuries ago. And the symbolism had been heavily stressed: this had been the capital of an empire based on transportation, held together by a network of roads such as this planet would not see again for two millennia. And now, the propaganda line ran, the PSU was following in that tradition, on a scale beyond the imagination of the Romans and using powers beyond the dreams of the Romans' gods.

You should have turned the invitation down, Trevayne told himself sourly, not for the first time. *But you just couldn't resist showing Magda and Han this world, could you?*

As they walked on, he tried to shake off the mood. *Remember what Cromwell said: "I beseech you in the bowels of Christ to think it possible you may be mistaken." What a hypocrite! He never for a second in his life considered* he *might be wrong. But the advice is still good. Hopefully, the Roman parallel isn't deceptive after all.*

But then he looked around again, and a chill went through him. *On second thought, maybe I should be hoping it* is *deceptive.*

For around him, the Roman Empire lay in ruins.

CHAPTER TWO

After many vicissitudes across the centuries, the Via Veneto was once again the fashionable street of Rome. Indeed, there had been attempts to recreate its glory days, of which the grandest was the reconstruction of the old Excelsior Hotel, on a larger scale and including amenities like environmentally correct accommodations for nonhuman guests (up to and including artificial gravity) but stylistically faithful to the original in its mid-twentieth-century heyday.

The Trevaynes arrived at dusk, with the gardens of the Villa Borghese still visible up ahead at the end of the curving, tree-shaded avenue. Entering the hotel's lobby, they descended a staircase to a barroom decorated in a style of plush retro luxury, its walls covered with deep red damask alternating with tall mirrors. It was already filling up with dignitaries who had rated an invitation to this party, preparatory to the beginning of the formal ceremonies tomorrow.

"You're not going to get into any arguments, are you?" Magda murmured as they entered the room.

"*Moi?*" inquired Trevayne, his eyebrows rising into arcs of bogus astonishment that such a question could be asked. He was reasonably confident that she wouldn't jab him in the ribs in this setting.

Passing one of the mirrors and catching sight of their reflection, he decided that the two of them were appropriate to the setting. They were both wearing the Terran Republic Navy's full dress uniform of deep blue and white with gold trim, in a traditional military style. Personally, he would have preferred civilian clothes, and Magda looked stunning in the current styles of evening dresses. (Chronologically she was in her seventies, but having had lifelong access to the best antigerone treatments, she was about the same physiological age as he.) However, they were here not just as admittedly very prominent individuals, but also as representatives of the Terran Republic, of which he had for the past six years been a naturalized citizen.

And as they began to move among the throng, he could see from people's expressions that those years had not sufficed to dull the irony of *that*.

Most of the throng were in civilian formal wear, aside from a small group of Orions off to the side drinking the bourbon for which their race had long since acquired a taste, their lean, furry, long-legged felinoid forms garbed only in jeweled harnesses. The few human uniforms in evidence were all the black and silver of the Terran component of the PSU Navy. With minor modifications, it was the uniform Trevayne had once worn...

He had just barely snagged a much-needed scotch when Magda pulled unobtrusively at his sleeve. As he turned, a man approached whom he recognized from his briefing, trailing a stream of hangers-on and extending his hand.

"Ah, Admiral Trevayne! *Both* Admirals Trevayne, I should say!" A politician's smile wreathed the dark African face. "It is a pleasure as well an honor to meet you."

"Likewise, Assemblyman Obasanjo," said Magda brightly. She had had the same briefing. Trevayne mumbled his concurrence and shook the hand of the man who, while relatively low-ranking in the labyrinthine governmental structure of the PSU, was very much the power-broker of the Terran component, using the automatic prestige that came with the homeworld as a fulcrum from which to manipulate the representatives of the Corporate Worlds, which after all these centuries were still the Union's economic powerhouse. He was, in the language of politicians, the man to come to.

A few more pleasantries were exchanged. "I trust, Admiral Li-Trevayne, that you are enjoying your first visit to Old Terra," said Obasanjo, who of course would have been equally well briefed.

"Very much. It is unique in my experience. Somewhat overwhelming, in fact. There's so much history to take in."

"I hope," Obasanjo said solicitously, "that it isn't too overwhelming for your little daughter."

Very well briefed indeed, thought Trevayne.

"Oh, not at all," Magda assured Obasanjo. "Han is having the time of her life."

"Ah, yes . . . Han." Obasanjo looked from one of them to the other.

Trevayne sighed silently . . . at least he hoped it was

silent and invisible. He was used to this by now, at the mention of the name "Han Trevayne." A friend of North American ancestry had once told him that it was rather like a man named "Hatfield McCoy"—a reference that had left Trevayne, history buff though he was, none the wiser. But he understood.

The Fringe Revolution had cost Ian Trevayne far more than his first body. His wife and daughter had died in the nuclear fires of a rebel attack that had unintentionally immolated a civilian residential area. And Trevayne himself had had to give the order that had sent his son, who had gone over to the rebels, to his death. Nothing had been left to him except his loyalty to the Terran Federation and his need for vengeance against the rebels. The two had dovetailed neatly, fueling a war that for him had become more and more personal . . . and increasingly focused on the person of Admiral Li Han, the new Terran Republic's most brilliant commander, at one point his prisoner, later his nemesis at the Battle of Zapata. Their enmity had become the stuff of legend.

Then he had awakened after eighty-one years to find himself inside a new body and the Terran Republic an accomplished fact—and, almost at once, an ally against the newly arrived Arduans, the latest in a series of alien threats that had emerged from the depths of space over the last several centuries . . . and in some ways the worst. For one thing, they believed in reincarnation with a kind of singlemindedness lost to humans ever since the "conflict of science and religion," for *their* religion and their science had confirmed each other. It made them contemptuous of death in a way flesh-crawlingly reminiscent of the Arachnids of the Fourth Interstellar War, with their unfeeling hive consciousness.

But still worse was the fact that the Arduans had arrived in the Rim Federation's Bellerophon Arm through *normal space* rather than along the warp lines that offered a way around the limitations of relativity.

Humans had blundered onto the warp network by accident. Certain others, such as the *Zheeerlikou'val-khannaieee* of the Khanate of Orion, had inferred its existence mathematically. But no one fully understood it . . . and no one had ever been known to attempt interstellar flight any other way. Why spend decades or centuries crawling along at speeds limited to that of light, when one could make instantaneous transit between warp points in different star systems? Admittedly, such transit was limited to systems (and, sometimes, starless locales in empty space) where warp points were to be found. And some warp points were "closed": undetectable and therefore unknown until one came through from *another* warp point. But these were small prices to pay for cheating Einstein. There was simply no incentive to make the staggering effort that traveling between the stars any other way required.

The Arduans, though, had had the incentive of species survival, for they knew nothing of warp lines but did know that a nearby supernova would shortly incinerate their home system, bringing the eternal cycle of reincarnation to an unthinkable end. So they had built the city-sized generation ships that had so inexplicably appeared in the Bellerophon system.

It was as though the entire sky had suddenly become one vast closed warp point, ready at any time to spew forth without warning hordes of enemies who had neither fear of their own deaths nor concern for anyone else's.

In its extremity, the Rim Federation had turned to its founding hero, whose seemingly miraculous return at this particular moment had echoed with mythic resonance. And so Ian Trevayne (physically barely postadolescent, but with all his memories) had found himself back on the active list... and allied with the Terran Republic whose existence he had almost successfully sought to prevent, and whose First Space Lord was none other than the hundred-and-twenty-three-year-old Li Han.

A certain adaptability on his part had borne cultivating.

But then he had met his old enemy's daughter Magda...

"Yes," he heard himself saying to Obasanjo. "When she was born, a year after the conclusion of the war with the Arduans, it was natural for us to name her after her grandmother."

"Her *illustrious* grandmother," Obasanjo nodded unctuously. "She is a living symbol of the reconciliation that has occurred since then, typified by your marriage." He nodded graciously to both of them. "I can still vividly remember the amazement that news caused."

"Understandably, I suppose, all things considered," conceded Trevayne. They had fallen in love in the course of the final campaign against the Arduans in the Bellerophon Arm. Li Han had lived just long enough to give her unspoken blessing before perishing in the desperate Battle of Charlotte. They had wedded after that, just before the final push by the Alliance fleet, even though fully expecting a bloodbath that either or both of them might not survive. But the unlooked-for resolution on Bellerophon had spared them that. Their daughter had been conceived shortly thereafter, and there had seemed only one possible name to give her, whatever everyone else thought.

"Typified also by his change of citizenship," Magda remarked mischievously. Trevayne had left practically everyone thunderstruck by moving to the Terran Republic.

"Ah, yes, that also raised a few eyebrows," Obasanjo nodded.

And caused a few ill feelings in the PSU and particularly the Rim Federation, Trevayne recalled. But that all seemed to have died down by now. Obasanjo's next words seemed to confirm it.

"And so what could be more appropriate than your presence here to represent our friends of the Terran Republic? All the more fitting because the two of you—and your revered mother, Admiral Li-Trevayne—were instrumental in the development that led directly to this great and glorious occasion we will celebrate tomorrow: the inauguration of the fifth Unity Warp Point!"

"That cannot be denied." Trevayne hoped he was keeping the sourness out of his voice.

From their first ventures through the warp points, all the starfaring races had accepted as a truism that they were as limited to the naturally occurring warp network as planetbound seafarers were to the configurations of oceans and continents. Or so it had seemed until the advent, in the midst of the Arduan war, of the Kasugawa Generator, which could create *artificial* warp lines, as well as enlarge natural ones ("dredging" was the common term) to accommodate greater ship tonnages. What made this a game-changer was the fact that the warp connections had nothing to do with the distribution of stars in normal space, which was why no one except professional astronomers had thought about the latter for centuries. (It was only by sheer coincidence that the Solar System's one warp point was paired with one in the Alpha Centauri system, next door as these things go.) By generating a new warp line between two systems close together in normal space previously unconnected by warp transit, the entire strategic picture had been changed and a deadlock broken. That plan had been Li Han's brainchild, and Trevayne had floored everyone by unreservedly supporting it, thus assuring its adoption.

Despite Trevayne's efforts, something in his tone must have betrayed his feelings, for Obasanjo gave him a sharp look. "I must also say, Admiral, that your presence here is particularly gratifying in light of the fact that in the past you have expressed certain . . . reservations about this great work. I gather that your concerns have been laid to rest."

"Not altogether, Assemblyman," said Trevayne, ignoring Magda's warning look.

"But, Admiral, you cannot deny the benefits that have accrued from this project." Obasanjo began to wax oratorical. "Truly we have beaten swords into ploughshares! The four Unity Points created so far have been a boon to humanity and its friends, greatly enhancing travel and commerce between important systems of the Pan-Sentient Union and its allied polities . . . including the Terran Republic. And now comes the long-awaited culmination of this great project: linkage of a system near Sol itself with one near

Khanae, thus allowing direct communication between the PSU's two capital systems!"

"No one denies the value of enhanced communications, Assemblyman. But that function is more and more performed by the *selnarmic* relay system." No nonmaterial signal could make warp transit. But courier drones could, and when the Arduan telempathic function of *selnarm* could be used to instantaneously transmit across a planetary system from one warp point to another...

"I yield to no one in my appreciation of the contribution our new friends the Arduans have made in this field. But the fact remains, Admiral, that *selnarmic* relay cannot transmit cargo or passengers. Our Unity Warp Points can!"

"That's not all they can bloody well transmit!" Trevayne drew a breath and forced himself to speak in level tones. "You can only create a linkage such as this if you assume that interspecies amity is a law like gravity, without exception operating ceaselessly and eternally. History is against such an assumption. I can personally testify that even amity among *human* groups and factions cannot be taken for granted."

This momentarily silenced Obasanjo, who knew he was looking at a man who personally remembered the Fringe Revolution. But he recovered quickly. "Surely, Admiral, you can see that we have put those bad old days behind us! Today, all is harmony between species and polities."

Trevayne wore a look of grim amusement. "Even in the most blissful of marriages"—he gave Magda a sideways glance, and smile wrinkles bunched at the corners of his eyes—"there is inevitably the occasional discord. And this Unity Warp Point offers the worst and most warlike among both species the most irresistible temptation, for it furnishes them with the most terrible capability: the ability to strike into the very core of the neighboring species' worlds!"

Obasanjo's professional *bonhomie* was growing somewhat frayed around the edges. "Well, Admiral, as you know, your reservations were accorded due weight. But the decision has been made, and the ceremony will go forward tomorrow. After which, I assume you and your wife will both be turning your attentions back to the matter of hunting down the remaining Tangri corsairs."

"Yes. We have been engaged in that for some time, but there is still much to be done." The predatory Tangri had decided to insert themselves into the Arduan war, seeking advantage from whichever side seemed ascendant. It had been a suicidally bad decision, for it had given Ian Trevayne a good reason to pursue the arguably long overdue extermination of their depraved polity. "Their remnants have fragmented into bands of marauders—ever smaller and, it seems, more elusive and wily."

"Well, I'm confident they will receive their just deserts at your hands in due course." Trevayne could have sworn that he could detect, underlying Obasanjo's heartiness, a certain relief that the Trevaynes would be gone. "But in the meantime . . ." Obasanjo took on a simpering bogus-conspiratorial look. "I shouldn't be telling you this, but the ceremonies tomorrow will be the occasion for announcing the *sixth* Unity Warp Point, connecting Sigma Draconis and Bellerophon!"

Is this his idea of mollifying me? wondered Trevayne, staring into Obasanjo's beaming countenance. "A great achievement, sir," was all he could manage.

"I was confident that you would think so. And now, Admiral, if you will excuse me . . ." And Obasanjo vanished into the swirl of networking.

"Nice going," Magda commented.

Trevayne was about to attempt an answer, but then he saw a small figure seated by himself on the far side of the room. "Excuse me. I want to talk to someone. Maybe you can smooth some feathers." Before Magda could remark on the need for precisely that, he walked away and approached the small, deceptively aged Eurasian man—deceptively, because he had qualified for antigerone treatments late and therefore had the look that humans still unconsciously associated with venerable wisdom even though he was barely into his second century. In his case, the impression happened to be true.

"Dr. Kasugawa?"

Dr. Isadore Kasugawa looked up from the cup of sake he had been nursing. "Ah, Admiral Trevayne! Please sit down. I was hoping to be able to exchange a few words with you."

"Likewise. I was sure you would be invited, as the inventor."

"So I was, as was Admiral Desai, without whom I doubt if I could have accomplished anything."

"Oh, yes. How is Sonja?"

"Well, as far as I know. I hardly ever hear from her any more. She declined the invitation."

Trevayne murmured something conventionally regretful. Sonja Desai, who had been one of his subordinates during the Fringe Revolution and who had negotiated the end of that war with Li Han after the Battle of Zapata, had avoided every opportunity to meet him after his resurrection. He wondered why.

"Well, if you do hear from her, give her my best. But at the moment, I wonder if I might pose a theoretical question to you."

"Of course."

Trevayne met the old eyes and held them. "Would it be possible to build a device that would *disrupt* a warp point?"

Kasugawa didn't seem as shocked by the question as Trevayne had anticipated. "Well, you must understand that naturally occurring phenomena are difficult to suppress, let alone destroy."

"You misunderstand. I mean: would it be possible to disrupt an *artificially created* warp point?"

"Ah." Kasugawa's eyes continued to meet Trevayne's, and much passed between them without needing to be said. "What a coincidence that you should ask! About nine months ago, I started giving a certain amount of thought to that very idea."

"I see." Trevayne and Kasugawa exchanged knowing smiles, and Trevayne stood up. "Thank you, Doctor. I believe I'll be able to get through tomorrow's ceremony somewhat more easily than I had feared."

CHAPTER THREE

A fast courier ship had brought them from Sol through the warp lines to this system whose erstwhile Tangri masters had named it Hulixon. Now, with the cloud-swirling blue curve of a life-bearing planet below, an interorbital shuttle carried them to the flagship of the Allied Joint Tangri Pacification Force. (Trevayne always chuckled inwardly at that name, although he conceded that "Pacification" sounded better than "Obliteration.") In the shuttle's forward viewscreen, TRNS *Li Han* grew. And grew. And grew.

And we're still not all that close, Trevayne reflected as that intricate immensity filled the viewscreen.

Some might have said that using a superdevastator in this particular campaign was an exercise in overkill—almost a matter of using a sledgehammer to swat flies. Admittedly, the "dredging" feature of the Kasugawa Generator had made this class of warship far more deployable by increasing the percentage of warp points that could accommodate its stupendous tonnage. And when billion-tonne Arduan "system defense ships"—barely mobile, but mounting staggering arrays of weaponry—had barred the way through the one warp point allowing ingress to the alien-occupied Bellerophon Arm, the raw fighting power of the devastator had been indispensable. It had been fortunate indeed that the Terran Republic had been developing this class, with two-thirds again the hull capacity of the supermonitor that had previously been the ultimate capital ship of space—and, subsequently, the *super*devastator, with twice the tonnage. As the largest ship that could pass through any warp point, it had been the final stage in the evolution of space warships, which had grown larger and larger for more than three centuries since the First Interstellar War, whose mightiest battlewagons would be too small to stand in the line of battle today. Not even the advent of the single- or twin-seat fighter had derailed the trend; and now, with new developments in space drive technology that cancelled out much of the fighter's traditional advantages in speed and maneuverability, it was increasingly marginalized. Once again, the capital ship reigned supreme.

The Tangri, however, had always tended toward smaller, faster ships, in keeping with their marauding style of warfare and their decentralized political system (by courtesy so called). And now, even that system was shattered. There was no possibility of encountering enemy units that would require a superdevastator to deal with them.

The symbolism, however, was important . . . and not just the symbolism of this ship's name. *Li Han* represented an earnest of the Terran Republic's commitment to putting an end to the Tangri Confederation once and for all.

Of course, Trevayne reflected, all the symbolism in the galaxy couldn't cancel out the deployability limitations of a superdevastator. Which was why this task force had a Kasugawa Generator with it.

The shuttle nosed through a cavernous opening's atmosphere screen and settled onto an extensive hangar deck. As the hatch wheezed open and the gangway extended itself, two honor guards came to attention. This was a joint Terran Republic/Rim Federation task force, predominantly the former. A second task force, partly PSU and partly Arduan in composition and under the command of Trevayne's old colleague Cyrus Waldeck, was operating a few warp transits away. Trevayne was in overall command; Magda commanded this task force. They descended the ramp, went through the ritual of requesting permission from *Li Han*'s captain to come aboard, then began accepting salutes.

"Welcome back, Admiral Trevayne, Admiral Li-Trevayne," Adrian M'Zangwe greeted. He had been chief of staff to her after whom this ship was named, and after her death Trevayne's flag captain. Now he was a rear admiral, commanding this task force's Terran Republic component. He had also worn a second hat as acting task-force commander in Magda's absence. "And how is your delightful little daughter?"

"She's back home on Novaya Rodina," said Magda, "where my godparents are doubtless spoiling her to within an inch of her life." Jason Windrider and Magda Petrovna Windrider, now in their 160s and 140s respectively but still spry, had served with Li Han in the Fringe Revolution and battled Trevayne at Zapata. *More irony*, thought the latter.

"How can they help themselves?" A smile split M'Zangwe's dark face. "If only *she* could have lived long enough to know..." He shook his head to clear it of painful memories, and spoke briskly. "Allow me to introduce Rear Admiral Rafaela Shang, who during your absence relieved Admiral McFarland as commander of the Rim Federation components."

"Ah, yes, Admiral Shang." Trevayne extended his hand. He was going to miss Alistair McFarland, whom he had known since the Fringe Revolution and whose accent, from the Rim world of Aotearoa, he had always found endearing. But Alistair had been pushing mandatory retirement age (calculated in terms of physiological rather than chronological age these days) even during the Arduan War. As he ran his eyes over Shang's staffers, he spotted the Intelligence officer. "Andreas! Congratulations on your recent promotion—especially given the number of career changes you've gone through."

Captain Andreas Hagen beamed. He had been a lieutenant commander, and doing a stint as an instructor at the Rim Federation's Prescott Academy, when he had been picked for a rather unique assignment: "technical liaison officer" to the freshly resurrected Ian Trevayne, who had had eight decades worth of catching up to do. The relationship had lasted longer than anticipated, for Trevayne had kept Hagen with him through the Arduan war. Afterwards, Hagen had transferred from his original BuShips billet to Intelligence.

"As senior spook in the task force," M'Zangwe explained, "Captain Hagen will be presenting part of the briefing we've prepared for you."

"Excellent. We're both in need of an update."

"Not just on the strategic picture," Magda added, "but on the situation here in this system."

"Yes, Admiral." Hagen nodded. "And in that connection, we're going to have a... special guest."

The being on the stage of the briefing room didn't really resemble anything from Old Terra's zoology or mythology. But humans, at first sight of the configuration of a large, bilaterally symmetrical hexapod which had liberated its front pair of limbs for manipulation in the course of evolving as a tool-user, automatically thought *centaur.* Actually, the upright torso was even less humanlike than the horizontal barrel was horselike, so the predominant (and totally misleading) impression was equine. Hence the traditional nickname "horse-heads," even though the face was, if anything, more suggestive of an ape than a horse (until one saw the teeth, at which time any resemblance to either vanished), and the cranium was protected by a bony ridge. That ridge was the only thing exoskeletal about the entire body, which was otherwise covered with short, thick fur in various reddish shades.

Anyone knowledgeable about extraterrestrial races would simply have identified the "special guest" as a Tangri. But Ian Trevayne had made an in-depth study of the species in the course of this campaign, and he discerned certain subtle indicia—flatter than average snout, duller than average rufosity of fur, and so forth—that spelled *Zemlixi*, the descendants of the agricultural societies long ago enslaved by the Horde culture he was here to extirpate.

Tangri history was a freak. In all other known advanced species, civilization had grown out of settled agriculture before beginning the climb of technological advancement. But the Tangri themselves were also freaks of a sort among tool-users, for they had evolved from purely carnivorous predator stock. For them, "agriculture" could only mean raising fodder for meat animals—and the plant life of their homeworld was nutrient-poor. The mobility that their physical form imparted—and the psychology that went with it—lent itself to nomadism. In the end, the nomads had triumphed over the farmers. Industrialization, when it finally occurred, had developed within the context of nomadism's values, and been employed to serve those values—the values of raid and plunder, now carried out to the stars.

It was as though Genghis Khan and Timur-i-leng had set the tone for all of subsequent human history. As though their descendants had never been assimilated by the civilized societies they had conquered, but rather had beaten and brutalized those societies down to a level of permanent subservience.

The *Zemlixi* were the descendants of those crushed proto-civilized societies that had been snuffed out—enslaved, and periodically thinned like any other herd. Their lot had improved somewhat over the centuries as the dominant Horde culture had required bureaucrats to administer the increasingly complex support structure that enabled it to sustain its depredations through ages of ever-increasing economic and technological complication.

This particular *Zemlixi*, Thertarz by name, had until recently been one such bureaucrat. He was now leader of the Hulixon Provisional Government.

Trevayne listened as Thertarz reviewed, with the aid

of translator software, the progress of events in this system. Hulixon had no indigenous inhabitants, only an imported *Zemlixi* population, which had eliminated one complicating factor. In accordance with what was now established procedure, the Allied fleet had cleared the system of the scattered Tangri spaceborne units, then landed Marines on the planet, distributing weapons to the *Zemlixi*, who were already in a state of insurrection. It had not been difficult to dispose of the remainders of the Daroga Horde, of whose domain this system had been a part. The problems arose afterwards.

"Nation-building" had involved enough headaches even for those who had coined the term in the late twentieth century. They had learned to their cost that you couldn't simply tell a population with no tradition of self-government that it was free and then walk away. It was far worse among the ruins of the Tangri Confederation. The *Zemlixi* were the deracinated descendants of peoples whose societies had been leveled and blighted even more thoroughly than the Mongols had once devastated the centers of higher Islamic culture. There was no foundation to build on; the building would have to be from the ground up.

The good news—at least in the short run—was that the *Zemlixi* were conditioned to obey the instructions of those placed above them. The difficulty was in finding someone to so place.

"Thank you, Thertarz," said Trevayne when the presentation was finished. "We are fortunate that you are here to take the lead among your people." This was not flattery. Thertarz really was one of their best finds among the liberated Tangri worlds.

"It is we who are fortunate, Admiral," came the synthetic voice, as Trevayne automatically edited out the sounds Thertarz was actually making. "What you have given us is beyond even the fulfillment of a dream, because we never dared dream it. For myself personally, I thank you for assigning Captain Gobinda as Resident Advisor."

"I'm glad the two of you work together well." There was a division of labor between the Provisional Government and the Resident Advisor's military administration, with the latter still in ultimate authority. Gobinda, as Trevayne already knew, was one of those with a knack for being tactful about it.

Hagen resumed the podium. "And now, Admiral, with your permission I will summarize the strategic situation." Trevayne nodded, and Hagen activated a display behind him. It was a flat screen, which was all that was needed to display the warp network. At lower center was the Hulixon system, with a green icon reading "TF 4.1," denoting the first task force of the Allied Fourth Fleet. At upper right, the icon "TF 4.2," denoting Cyrus Waldeck's task force, stood in a system with no close warp connections to Hulixon. However, the warp lines from both converged a few transits to the right on a system featuring a red icon.

"By now," Hagen began, "with the new intelligence sources that have become available to us, we have been able to confirm our original supposition as to the enemy situation. By the end of the Arduan War, their central fleet—the 'Confederation Fleet Command' is our best translation—was effectively broken. With our subsequent general offensive into their space, the individual Hordes were pretty much left to defend their own territories as best they could. In a sense, this wasn't all good; instead of a single monolithic enemy to strike at, we're facing decentralized opposition—the 'Free Raiders,' as they apparently call themselves—waging a kind of guerilla war."

"Also," speculated Magda, "it probably suits them better. To them, large political organizations are unnatural abstractions."

"True, Admiral. The primary loyalty of every Tangri of the Horde culture is to his own horde. But we can't place too much reliance on that. They're on the run now, and they're smart enough to put aside their feuds in the face of a common threat to their existence. Also, they have common goals: to get revenge against us, and to punish the *Zemlixi* who've 'betrayed' them."

Thertarz spoke, and his grimness came through the translator. "You have no conception of the things that would be done to us if they came back."

"Actually, I think I do," said Trevayne, who had seen worlds—human worlds—raided by the Tangri. "And that is not going to be permitted."

Hagen pointed to the screen. "As you know, we have been advancing into the domain of the Daroga Horde. Admiral Waldeck is in the territory of the Hurulix. Our advance has been facilitated by the sparse use of mine fields and orbital weapon platforms at the warp points."

"The Tangri have never emphasized fixed warp-point defenses," Trevayne nodded. "Not their mind-set. Their contempt for all other races is such that the whole concept of defense against those races seems as far-fetched as the idea of humans defending themselves against cattle. Except," he added with a cold smile, "cattle have been known to stampede."

"Which, of course, brings us to the next stage of our advance," M'Zangwe observed with a smile.

"Indeed, Admiral," said Hagen. He manipulated hand-held controls. A cursor ran along the warp lines from Hulixon to the system with the scarlet icon. A slightly longer series of warp connections led by another route from Cyrus Waldeck's current position to that same destination. Hagen let the white cursor flash beside the red icon. "Our plan for the two task forces to converge simultaneously at this system, which is believed to be the central stronghold of the Daroga, is going according to schedule—that is, it should culminate a little more than a standard year from now. As soon as we receive confirmation from Admiral Waldeck that he has secured the next system along his line of approach, we will be able to resume our advance." He moved the cursor to the warp nexus just beyond Hulixon. "This is a starless warp nexus, and our recon drones have established that it has only some hastily deployed minefields. Otherwise, it is held by a mobile force largely dependent on fighters, of which it has a very large number—its largest units are fleet carriers and a limited number of superdreadnoughts." He touched his control pad again, and an order of battle appeared at the upper left corner of the screen. "And the recon drones' findings suggest that these are not at the highest level of readiness."

"Why would that be?" Magda wondered aloud.

"The warp point of ingress is one of those which will accommodate no tonnage larger than that of a supermonitor," Hagen reminded her. "We surmise that the Tangri are waiting for us to dredge it to allow our devastators and superdevastators to pass through—a procedure which they can easily detect, thus giving them advance warning."

"Therefore," Trevayne said decisively, "we will make no attempt to dredge it until *after* we've secured the far side. I want the task force placed in readiness for a warp-point assault utilizing nothing larger than supermonitors. I don't believe we'll need the DTs and SDTs to deal with what I'm seeing here. And certainly any advantage of having them is outweighed by the element of surprise which we'll achieve by going in without them. Is everyone clear on this?" A chorus of affirmative noises answered him. "Excellent. Then as soon as we hear from Admiral Waldeck we will resume our . . . stampede."

There was no nearby star to give a sense of location, only the disorientingly infinite void of interstellar space. What distinguished this particular expanse of nothingness was invisible: the two warp points that lay eighteen light-minutes apart, one connecting with the Hulixon system and the other leading further on into the systems held by the Daroga Horde.

Squadron Leader Huraclycx was fleeing from the former to the latter in his fighter. Soon he would catch up to his carrier, in time to be recovered before the carrier transited the second warp point and made good its escape.

Huraclycx shifted his body on the framework that made it possible for a Tangri to assume the unnatural position necessary to pilot a fighter. The discomfort was such that most fighter pilots used the drug *sacaharrax* to mask it with euphoria. Huraclycx didn't and had only contempt for those who did. The stuff was addictive, and long-term use led to metabolic degeneration and an early death. It was one of the reasons for the mystique of fighter pilots as doomed, slightly mad swashbucklers. Huraclycx disdained that too.

So he flew on, stoically enduring without chemical buffering the physical discomfort. It wasn't quite bad enough to make him forget his rage and his hatred.

It had been anticipated that the human prey animals would use their mysterious technique for tampering with the physics of the warp network, enlarging the capacity of the Hulixon warp point to allow passage of their largest ships, the truly monstrous ones. Instead, they had done the unexpected. (But then their leader—*Trevayne* by name, as Intelligence had learned—was the master of the unexpected.) Without warning, a blizzard of AMBAMMs—anti-mine ballistic missiles—had come through the warp point, burning a path through the minefields. Hardly had the glare of antimatter annihilation died down when the first waves of ships had followed the AMBAMMs, led by the supermonitors whose hulls were the largest that could transit the warp point in its natural state—not devastators or superdevastators, but mighty enough.

The Tangri had not been caught napping. They had been able to launch clouds of fighters. But—and acid rose in Huraclycx's gut at the thought—for the past generation, fighters had lost more and more of their traditional advantage over large ships. It was galling for the Tangri, whose individualistic warrior ethos was so suited to fighter combat that they were willing to endure pain or risk dangerous drugs to indulge in it.

Partly it was a matter of the narrowing of the margin of superior maneuverability that enabled them to get into the behemoths' sternward "blind zones" created by their reactionless drives. But there was also the matter of steady improvement in shipboard defensive weaponry. Huraclycx had witnessed this as his squadron was decimated by long-range AFHAWK anti-fighter missiles before they could even close to the short ranges at which they were most effective. Those that did get into knife-range were ripped apart by the electromagnetically propelled flechettes of datalinked point-defense systems.

And now, along with all the other survivors, Huraclycx fled as still more human ships continued to emerge from the Hulixon warp point.

Hulixon! A fresh jag of fury shot through him at the thought, for it was one of the systems where the miserable, dirt-grubbing, shit-stinking *Zemlixi* had turned on their natural masters. The human word *treason* was too weak; this was an abomination . . . an outrage against the natural order of things. On certain other worlds, he had heard, the *Zemlixi* had taken obscenity to another level by allying with the indigenous inhabitants—mere sentient meat-animals.

They would pay. He, Huraclycx, would make them pay.

That was the real reason Huraclycx refused to use *sacaharrax.* It wasn't merely a matter of proving himself superior to his fellows in physical toughness, although that was never far from the mind of any male of the Horde culture. No, it ran deeper. He wanted nothing to do with anything that would ruin his health and shorten his life. He had to live, if he was to make real the visions that helped sustain him through the misery of fighter operations—the visions, in detail, of what he would do to the *Zemlixi.* And also what he would do to the humans and other species of prey animals who, using some process that substituted for intelligence (a uniquely Tangri attribute, by definition), had brought about the collapse of the Confederation and the unimaginable nightmare through which the Hordes were now living.

The blunders of the old leadership had made that possible. New leaders were needed. He would be one. He would be the instrument of the Hordes' resurgence.

But for now it was necessary to hold the central Daroga systems against Trevayne's fleet and the other enemy force now advancing through the systems of the Hurulix Horde. *Of course*, he mentally sneered. *They'll get little trouble from those cowardly, sniveling money-grubbers!*

But we Darogas aren't doing much better, are we?

He was thinking about it when he picked up the signal from his carrier and began maneuvering to a rendezvous.

CHAPTER FOUR

The light was extremely dim in the long, steel tunnel of Metifilli orbital station's freight marshaling section. Consequently, the three men walking down its center lane could not even see the curved walls a dozen meters to either side of them. Various leaks from the tankage baffles beyond those walls produced a discordant symphony of echoing drips. Well ahead, five figures seated at a card table glanced up in unison as the largest of the three approaching men stepped in a puddle. Two of the figures at the table rose; each one let a hand drift toward the small of their backs.

As the three newcomers approached, one of the three men who remained seated raised his chin. "Can I do sumthin' for you guys?"

"That depends," answered the newcomer who was walking point. "Are you the freight yard clerk?"

"One of 'em. Who wants to know?"

"Call me Ossian."

"Sure. And you can call me Ishmael."

"No, really," said Ossian as he approached the table

with an affable smile. "Ossian is my real name." He reflected that in this unsavory backwater establishment, using one's own name was probably unheard of.

"Suit yourself." The guy who had been doing the talking shrugged. "So what can we do for you, 'Ossian'?" The two figures who'd risen from the table—one a burly middle-aged man with an oft-broken nose and the other a thin young woman whose eyes were open just a bit too wide—drifted further to either flank. Ossian's two space-suited companions either didn't notice the maneuver or didn't care. Their closed helmet visors reflected the light panels that made this the brightest spot for over a hundred meters in either direction.

"Well," Ossian explained, "I'd like you to locate some cargo for me. It's somewhere in storage here."

Ishmael snickered; his companions affected broad, sardonic smiles. "Well, you've come to the right place, Ossian. See any containers that look familiar?" The smiles became derisive chortles. Stacked ranks of mostly uniform modular freight containers hemmed them in on both sides. The few that had started as something other than basic gray had long since surrendered their distinctive paint schemes to the fading of time and coatings of dust.

Ossian smiled sheepishly. "Well, I've never actually seen the container I'm looking for. Which is why I came to you. The stationmaster told me that you're the person to talk to when it comes to locating hard-to-find items, who keeps track of freight that goes astray. If you get my drift."

Ishmael's smile fell away, partly at the knowing tone with which Ossian had underscored his last sentence, partly because of Ossian's slightly widened stance.

"I'm not sure I do get your drift, Ossian." Ishmael glanced at his companions. The burly man and the thin woman each took a further flanking step. Another man rose from the table; the other retained his seat but hunched closer to the table: his arms were now concealed from the upper bicep on down.

Ossian, on the other hand, was smiling more widely. "I'm sorry about the confusion, Ishmael. I was pretty certain you *would* get my drift. The stationmaster expressly said you know how to take a hint, how to keep a secret, and how to make cargos disappear and then reappear later on. But since she seems to have been mistaken, why don't I just give you the container's locator code?" Ossian took out a bulky hand computer. "I can download it to your system, if you like."

Ishmael shook his head, rose. "I doubt I can help you. A lot of the containers we manage get inventoried the old-fashioned way." He patted a notepad in his breast pocket. "But if you give me a hardcopy of the bill of lading, I'll see what I can do." Ishmael stayed back far enough that he'd just be able to reach whatever Ossian held out toward him.

Ossian shook his head, but never took his eyes off Ishmael. "Sorry, no hardcopy. I've only got a locator code."

"Why? Did you lose the bill of lading?"

"No. The package I'm looking for never had one. It's not commercial freight. It's a government item."

Ishmael swallowed. "Then you *are* in the wrong place, no matter what the stationmaster said. We don't handle government shipments. Just commercial. Look around you. You see any government modulars in here?"

Ossian's two escorts took a step out to either side. "No," Ossian admitted. "I don't. But I didn't say the item I'm looking for arrived in a government container. In fact, I'm pretty sure it didn't arrive in a container at all. And the stationmaster agreed with my conjecture. After all, data cores for automated warp point courier drones are too valuable and too sensitive to be moved as freight anyway—even on official craft."

Ishmael took a step back, may have glanced at a nearby utility locker with its door slightly ajar. "Then like I told you already, you're in the wrong place. I can't help you."

"That's a shame, Ishmael. Because the stationmaster repeatedly assured me that you could. In fact, she was certain that you'd *want* to help me."

Ishmael's next half step brought him abreast of the locker. "Let's drop the charades. I don't help errand boys from Customs, Ossian." He didn't quite sneer when he added the name.

"Oh, I'm not from Customs, Ishmael. If I was, I doubt your stationmaster would have been so eager to make me happy."

"Eager to make you happy?" Now Ishmael did sneer. "Since when has Ramona ever been eager to make anyone happy but herself?"

"I can't tell you that, but Ramona did genuinely seem eager to help. Or maybe she just didn't want us to get angry."

"Oh, and why is that?"

"Because if we had gotten angry, we'd have thrown her in the deepest, darkest hole that Naval Intelligence has."

The words "Naval Intelligence" worked like a

starter's gun commencing a sprint. Ishmael and his fellow freight hands began dodging toward the cover of nearby containers, several producing small pistols from their pockets or waistbands.

But Ossian's two spacesuited companions were both much quicker and much smoother in their actions. With a surety of movement that marked them as seasoned professionals, the two drew handguns from the large, thigh-side utility pockets of their suits. As they dropped to their knees, the thugs' small handguns began popping fitfully—and inexpertly—in their direction. The two men both aimed the muzzles of their much more powerful (and expensive) coil pistols at the freight hand who was still seated at the table and seemed to be manipulating something beneath it.

A flurry of 4.5 mm lead-cored tungsten darts from the two special-issue naval sidearms tracked a pattern of red ruin across the seated man's chest just as his machine-pistol began stuttering underneath the tabletop. Its arc of fire rose as he fell backward in his chair, cutting a ragged perforation through the cheap pressboard slab beneath which he'd been hiding the weapon.

Several pistol bullets hit Ossian's space-suited escorts: the low-mass, low-velocity caseless rounds spatted harmlessly against the form-fitting ballistic armor they wore under their outsized suits.

Ishmael, reaching the open locker, pulled out a waiting shotgun—archaic but serviceable—and spun around to put a spread of single-aught buckshot into Ossian—

—who, dropping to one knee, had popped open the false frame of his apparent hand computer, revealing a large-bore caseless automatic. That snub-nosed weapon now blasted five times before Ishmael was able to even bring the shotgun around; two red divots jetted out of the black marketeer's left leg, one just above the knee. The shotgun fired wild—as much a pain-induced trigger reflex as an expression of lethal intent—and Ishmael went down, howling.

At roughly the same moment, his three standing lackeys were realizing that their gunfire was not having any discernable effect upon the two spacesuited figures. One kept shooting; the other two turned and fled into the darkness of the farther tunnel. Whether the one who kept firing was more brave, more dense, or both did not change his fate: he was hit multiply by the concentrated fire of the two kneeling men, his entire torso a pockmarked red ruin by the time he hit the deck.

The taller of the two spacesuited figures stood, pulled off his helmet, shook sweat out of a thick red shock of hair. "Clear," shouted Marine Captain Alessandro Magee.

The smaller slapped his faceplate up. "The hell you say," muttered Lieutenant Harry "Lighthorse" Li as he launched up out of his kneeling posture into a surprisingly swift pursuit of the two fleeing felons.

"Play nice," Ossian shouted after him.

"I always do," came the dwindling reply.

'Sandro McGee came to stand beside Ossian, looked down at Ishmael. "He's bleeding pretty badly, sir."

Ossian craned his neck to get a better look. "Why, you're right. He is. Would you like us to help you, Ishmael? Throw a stitch or two across that crater in your leg?"

Ishmael vociferously ordered Ossian to perform a

biologically impossible act. 'Sandro started to move forward.

Ossian put out a restraining hand. "Captain, no need to get irritated. I suspect Ishmael will begin to see the many errors of his ways when the blood loss and shock starts settling in, starts getting through that noradrenal combat rush. Tell me, Ishmael, are you starting to feel a little chilly? You're not looking too well—not unless you're usually gray-faced and covered in cold sweat."

Ishmael groaned. "You bastard, you damn near shot my leg off."

Ossian crouched down. "Well, if I hadn't, you'd have shot off *both* my legs—and possibly more, besides. But let's not quibble about almost-lost body parts, yeh? Let's talk about what I need from you before the doctors arrive. Well, *if* the doctors arrive. Seems like you've disabled the monitors in this old drop tank that some genius decided to convert into the system's orbital freight-holding facility. So who knows if this altercation even registered on the security screens in the stationmaster's office?" As Ishmael gritted his teeth and rolled his face into the deck to stifle his blinding agony, Ossian nodded sharply at 'Sandro. The big Marine captain touched a paging circuit on his collarcom: the combination medical and forensic team that had been waiting on the far side of the main freight doors was now cleared to enter the area.

"I didn't disable the sensors," Ishmael panted through his shivers. "They're just shitty sensors, is all. Everything is always breaking in this dump." He ended his assertion with another piteous groan and profound shudder.

"Hmm. I guess those sensors are *so* shitty that they

somehow severed their own wires. Because, you see, we checked them before we strolled down here to make your acquaintance, Ishmael. And if you keep lying to me, it might take longer for the doctors to get here. Longer than might be safe for you."

Ishmael's face was a ghostlike mask of quivering hatred, but he said, "What do you want to know?"

"I want to know how you and the others work it."

"Work what?"

"See? There you go again, Ishmael, wasting valuable time—"

"Okay, okay. Somebody further down the warp line toward Zephrain delivers the warp courier data cores to us here. They leave. We hold on to the cores: there's plenty of places for something as small as that to get . . . lost. Then, maybe a week later, someone from further up the warp line—up toward Orion space—pays us a visit and taps the data in the cores. They go away. Then a third group comes and takes the core back toward Zephrain. I think they return it to Sulzan, maybe. There's a courier repair base there, where technicians pull drones off-line for complete data-wipes and routine maintenance."

"Hmm. When the second bunch of visitors taps the core, are they just skimming the general data it's carrying, or are they digging down into its programming, where confidential files are embedded?"

"Confidential files? What do you mean?"

'Sandro pushed the toe of his boot into the black marketeer's uninjured thigh. "You know. Are they accessing any official data that was uploaded to the drone?"

"I don't know. But I think so. The group that came in to tap the core needed a government-issue crypto machine of some kind to get the data out and then record it. You wouldn't need that for regular commercial datafeed. Regular commo traffic might be coded, but you'd still be able to tap it. But if it's milspec or diplomatic signals, you can't even get the box to talk to your computer unless you—"

"Yes. We have a passing familiarity with the safeguards." Ossian stood. "I need identities of all these groups, of course."

"You can have them, but they're all bullshit anyhow. Which you've gotta know. We don't use real names in the small package trade . . . 'Ossian.'"

Ossian sighed. "You know, Ishmael, you're just not a quick learner. My real name *is* Ossian Wethermere, and every time you annoy me, things will just get worse for you. Now you're going to tell me where you keep the recordings you made of all your backroom transactions. And also, where you keep the duct tape that you appear to throw away after you've used it to secure each group of your visitors."

"Secure them?"

"Yes, secure them. As in, their hands are immobilized, and their eyes are covered so they can't guide anyone back to your initial meeting site. Where you arrange the time and protocols for how you're going to conduct your 'business' here."

Ishmael's brief unconcealed pulse of surprise was evident even through his rictus of pain. "What do you mean? I don't do anything like that—"

'Sandro leaned in. "Don't play dumb. You're not the only one who uses that little trick, Ishmael. You use duct tape to cover their eyes, bind their hands. Nice nasty rip when it comes off. Gets the other side bitching at you about your rough methods. You bitch back. But everyone settles down after getting the surliness out of their systems—and the idiots never stop and think how they've left hairs stuck to the tape. Usually with some follicles still attached. With which, should the need arise, you slimeballs can ID them for purposes of tracking, blackmail, insurance against your getting disappeared by their friends, or for just sheer, malicious fun."

Ishmael became even whiter than could be explained by the blood loss. "I'll show you where we keep 'em, all the—the follicle biosamples. Just . . . just fix me up."

"Oh, we will," Ossian said with a grin. "We will. We want you healthy and alert for the debriefings back on Bellerophon."

Ishmael started, more at the name of the planet than at the sudden appearance of the medtechs who came rushing around the near corner of the stacked cargo containers. "Bellerophon? Why there?"

Ossian's grin transmogrified into a grim line turned up at the corners. "Because that's where we handle intelligence matters that involve both humans and Arduans. And we insist, during your stay with us, that you remain well-fed and safe in our high-security facility. After all, any criminals who were willing to go to all this trouble to surreptitiously tap the contents of a *selnarmic* warp-point courier drone probably won't be too pleased if they learn that we are debriefing you in detail. They might decide they need to shoot you, too—except I suspect they'd aim a bit higher than I did."

Ishmael swallowed as a medtech slapped an auto-tourniquet on his savaged leg. "I'll tell you anything you want to know," he whispered.

Ossian nodded. "I know," he answered.

CHAPTER FIVE

Ossian Wethermere entered an unmarked and unmapped observation room 120 meters below one of Bellerophon's many wooded outbacks, where two interrogators were picking holes in yet another of Ishmael's increasingly lame prevarications. Alessandro Magee looked around, saluted. His wife, Jennifer Pietchkov, offered a small smile and equally small nod before gesturing through the one-way glass into the interview room. "He doesn't have the slightest idea of what he was actually involved in, does he?"

Ossian smiled back "No, ma'am, but we never expected that he did. We're just trying to get faces, names, leads."

"How's that coming?" asked Harry Li who, after receiving Wethermere's casual acknowledgment of his own salute, had turned back to look at the rather crestfallen detainee. Clearly, incarceration—even of the most comfortable kind—did not agree with Ishmael at all.

"Well," replied Ossian, "when it comes to getting

workable leads from our unwilling guest, there's good news and there's bad news."

"What's the good news?" asked Magee hopefully.

"Well, Ishmael hasn't maintained his tough-guy act. He's given us pretty much everything we've asked for when it comes to implicating others. Anything that might implicate him—that's a different story. And the genetic samples we pulled from his collection of hair follicles"—all of which the thug had cataloged and maintained with surprising precision—"pinged on a whole lot of promising identicodes. A good number of Ishmael's contacts and clients are black market middlemen: they deal in connections, not the contraband itself. A number of others were predominantly hands-on felons: fences, con artists, mules for really small packages, and petty frauds. Only a few hardcore criminals in the bunch. We figure they were probably peripheral players: muscle brought along just to make sure that the deals went down as advertised."

"And the bad news?" asked the habitually sour Harry Li.

"The bad news is that two-thirds of those suspects are missing or dead. About equal portions are in the morgue or at-large. And the last third of our suspects aren't even in the identicode master registry, so we have no way of knowing what their status is or how to track them."

"No identicodes?" Jennifer frowned. "How's that possible?"

Her husband shrugged his impressive shoulders. "There are plenty of backwater worlds in the Rim Federation, Jen. Even more in the Terran Republic."

"Yes, I know. But even if their birth didn't take place

in a hospital or wasn't otherwise officially recorded, the first time anyone leaves a planet, they're supposed to be gene-swiped. That's the law. Not only here in the Rim, but throughout the Republic as well. It's even become standard practice in Orion space."

Harry leaned against the one-way glass. Ossian decided not to point out that it was both against policy and a bad habit to acquire. "Jennifer, the key qualifier in your comment is the phrase 'supposed to be.' Like most laws and pronouncements, there are lots of places where the gene swiping protocols are not—or can't—be obeyed. To start with, lots of folks aren't born planetside or in big communities, so their first trip outsystem doesn't require that they pass through an identicode reader. It's easy to forget that, since there are so many shirt-sleeve planets at our disposal. But belters, moon-dwellers, folks who inhabit the older or out-of-the-way space stations have unrecorded babies every day. And when each of those little tykes grows up, each is likely to get a job offer from an interstellar black marketeer or con artist."

"Just because they were born off the grid?" Jennifer's tone was moderately surprised and profoundly disgusted.

Ossian shrugged. "It's an unfortunate but well-established fact that a person without an identicode finds it much easier to commit crimes that can't be definitively attributed. And so, if they are smart, they can avoid having a file accumulate on their activities and thereby dodge a lot of typical security checks, particularly if they restrict their activities to planets and communities that aren't fully tied into the database. Which is pretty easy to do in the Terran Republic, since a lot of worlds flatly refuse the 'intrusion' of submitting any personal information to a central database."

Jennifer looked perplexed. "I wonder why the Republic worlds are not overrun by crime, then."

"Oh, they breed plenty of criminals," Harry drawled sardonically, "but most of them leave home. Right away."

"Why's that?"

Magee spoke softly. "Jen, have you ever read about the average local penalties for crime in the Republic? And in the real backwaters, they are often carried out after a drumhead trial by an armed posse. Criminals there have pretty short life expectancies."

Jen stared. "And those posses never make mistakes?"

Harry Li's grin was feral. "Not much more than our beloved and overburdened court system does."

"Which errs to the side of *caution*, Harry—since real lives are involved. Proof beyond reasonable doubt, remember?"

"In determination of guilt, not sentencing," Harry countered.

"Yeah, and a 'try-and-hang' posse is a really great means of ensuring objective and measured 'determination of guilt,'" Jennifer retorted, color rising in her face.

Ossian had heard about scenes in which Harry and Jennifer debated social issues until the night threatened to become morning and the patience of both threatened to fray and split. He stepped in to prevent a midday command performance. "So, returning to the topic at hand..." Wethermere inserted a pause pregnant enough to signify triplets. The two social-issue combatants looked gratifyingly sheepish.

'Sandro Magee hid a grin behind a broad, red-furred

paw. "So, grilling Ishmael hasn't produced any useful leads, Captain Wethermere?"

"Not many. But the deaths and last known locations of his missing contacts are astrographically significant. They all fall along a line that stretches from the Rim's capitol in the Zephrain system, passes through Metifilli, and leads all the way to Skraozpfurr'n in Orion space. It's also significant that all the relevant homicides and missing person reports along that route were registered within the last five months."

Harry frowned. "But we only busted Ishmael a month ago. So how is it that the masterminds behind this scheme knew to start killing off their hirelings four months before we came on the scene? They had no reason to suspect that their operation was compromised."

Ossian shrugged. "Because it was not our grabbing Ishmael that prompted the killings and disappearings. The masterminds were clearly committed to using their hirelings only for a while, and then cutting them loose. And later, when no one who was clued-in to their operation was in a position to see or learn, their old bosses got rid of them. Permanently. In short, the intel braintrust running this operation has adopted an SOP of periodically burning dismissed assets to maintain a security firewall."

Jennifer shook her head. "In English, please."

"Sorry, Ms. Pietchkov—"

"Jennifer, please."

"Uh—okay; Jennifer. Apologies: I slipped into trade-speak. I'm pretty sure that the persons running this operation are such a ruthless bunch that they've decided to protect the secrecy of their pipeline by replacing the people who service it every so often. And then, when a little time has gone by and the people they've dismissed are no longer in contact with any of their current scam-artists, the bosses eliminate their former hirelings. That's called 'fire-walling' the operation: it leaves no external traces for us to find and follow."

"So we hit the nexus of their operations on Metifilli for nothing?" Harry's disappointment had evidently dissolved his sense of the tone and decorum that their difference in ranks required.

Up until eight years ago, Ossian had lived most of his life as a naval reservist. Consequently, he remained more accustomed to the casual exchanges of civilian life than the formal ones of the military. However, this time, he put a stern edge in his tone. "That is not correct, Lieutenant Li. If we hadn't grabbed Ishmael and his team of courier drone baby-sitters on Metifilli, we'd still be in the dark about the opposition's method of information transfer."

Li straightened up sharply. "Yes, sir. It's just frustrating not to have any leads to follow, now."

"I couldn't agree more—although we do have investigatory options, even though we don't have living leads. As I said, the deaths and disappearances follow the trail from Zephrain to Orion space with almost no variance. What little drift there is from that route probably occurs when the former henchmen put a little distance between the places they worked for these drone grabbers and the site of their next illicit activity."

"*Modus operandi* for most con artists and informers," put in 'Sandro.

Jennifer lightly punched her behemothic husband in the bicep. "You're starting to sound like a cop, now, Tank."

Alessandro Magee half-scowled at Jennifer's use of his size- and behavior-related nickname. Since becoming a father more than six years ago, during the late war with the Arduans, Alessandro Magee's customary problem-solving behavior had evolved from that of a bull in a china shop into that of a honeybear with a beehive. "Well, the professional slang kind of rubs off on you, Jen. Don't worry: underneath, I'm still just the big, dumb grunt you've come to love and domesticate."

Ossian smiled and silently reflected that while Alessandro Magee was big, he had never been dumb, and fatherhood had imparted a salutary sobering effect that made him both a better field agent and officer.

The door opened behind Ossian. Ankaht, Ossian's opposite number among their Arduan partners, glided into the now crowded room, surveying it with her largest, central eye while amiably fluttering the tendril-clusters that were her race's hand-analogs.

Harry Li stiffened slightly. Despite working regularly with Ankaht and her staff, his tense unease grew in direct proportion to an Arduan's proximity.

Jennifer smiled and her face went through a set of quick, subtle transformations, as if she were engaged in lively conversation—and she probably was, Ossian reflected. The telempathic link she was able to share with Arduans—but Ankaht in particular—facilitated extremely rapid communication. The best measurements by the forensic intel folks who'd surreptitiously monitored casual data transfer rates among Arduans indicated a tenfold speed advantage over human conversation.

Ankaht turned her three eyes upon the other humans in the room, gave a somewhat spasmodic nod: her attempts at adopting human physical gestures had improved but the results were still crude and rudimentary. Hardly surprising since, relying almost solely on the telempathy they called *selnarm*, Arduans had little physical speech and even less body language—beyond what they showed in the tendril clusters that served as their hands. It was that difference, along with the Arduans' reincarnative nature, which had made communication between their species and humans so difficult—tragically so. Those differences in communication had not only caused but perpetuated the horrifically costly two-year war that followed their first encounter with humanity.

And despite the armistice which ended that war, and the cautious cooperation which succeeded it, interactions between Arduans and humans were still challenging on both conceptual and physical levels. As if underscoring the latter, Ankaht adjusted a *selnarmic* headset on her earless and hairless cranium so that the new portable translator she carried—a "vocoder" which massed five kilos—would receive her telempathic sendings with maximum clarity. "Hello, colleagues," was the smooth alto greeting that emerged from the device. "I trust the human interview subject is not proving to be too uncooperative this day?"

Ossian gestured at the sound-proof glass. "Not intentionally, but as you've seen, he's difficult to debrief. He's relatively intelligent, but gets easily distracted and goes off on tangents that we don't initially know are, in fact, just tangents."

Ankaht's clusters—anemone-like bunches of ten prehensile tentacles—curled and flexed in frustration. "Yes. He has a disorderly mind. I suspect it is congenital, and may have led him into criminal behavior."

"Come again?" said Harry Li. His tone was flat, but Ossian heard a readiness for contention behind its careful neutrality. He wondered if the new vocoder was capable of detecting and alerting Ankaht to such nuances.

If it was, Ankaht maintained her typical equanimity. "I simply mean that his combination of traits—relatively high intelligence, impatience, undisciplined thought—will make him ultimately unsuitable for so many of the pursuits that you humans reward most richly. And since he would have discovered at an early age that, despite having greater perspicacity than the majority of his peers, he was not to be rewarded for it, that would logically lead to frustration and resentment with the system of education and labor that denied him suitable gratification."

"Whereas Arduan methods would have prevented him from evolving into a criminal at all?" Li's tone was now so provocatively flat that Wethermere was sure the vocoder had to be alerting Ankaht to it. He turned toward Harry—

But not before Jen had rounded on the diminutive lieutenant. "Ankaht didn't say, or imply, that, Harry."

Ankaht raised her left cluster. The smaller tentacles—tendrils, really—seemed to wave in a nonexistent wind: Ossian found the effect vaguely soothing. "I meant no offense, and have taken none from Lieutenant Li's question. Perhaps I can clarify. It is true that our Firstlings—our young—are provided with *selnarmic* intervention to help them recognize and manage any cognitive traits that obstructed forming adequate relationships with either their peers or our society in general. With proper resources, your species often does no less, and it demonstrates incredible inventiveness in doing so, since it does not have the shortcut of *selnarmic* contact. It is, after all, much harder to explain a difference than it is to show and share the feeling of that difference—which is what *selnarm* enables.

"But our Firstlings are no less susceptible to going astray when deprived of appropriate nurture. If we once were proud enough to think otherwise, we need merely look at the rift that divides our people today."

Magee nodded. "You're referring to your warrior caste's increasing rejection of *selnarm*."

"I am, Captain Magee. What you call our 'warrior caste'—and many of the *Destoshaz* have redefined themselves in just that way—became so demographically dominant during our long, slower-than-light exodus to this part of space that there were not enough of the *selnarm*-specializing castes, the *shaxzhu* and the *selnarshaz*, to provide that nurture. Our research, since arriving here, has identified this as a key variable in our collective loss of *narmata*—of the overarching social unity that we once enjoyed through our openly shared *selnarmic* connections. Indeed, the *Destoshaz* have become markedly more reliant upon vocalizing their thoughts and upon writings devoid of a *selnarmic* accompaniment. They are increasingly turning their back upon the rest of Illudor's children, upon the *narmata* that joins us as one."

"In short, the genocidal radicals among your *Destoshaz* warrior caste are becoming more individualistic and non-*selnarmic*—like us humans." Li sounded mostly mollified, but his tone was still sardonic.

"It would be misleading to believe the *Destoshaz* to be strictly a warrior caste, or that their changes make them more akin to humans," Ankaht demurred mildly. "After all, your species, lacking *selnarm*, has evolved a wide array of socializing customs, pedagogies, and rituals that transform your young into balanced members of your society. You have never relied upon *selnarm* as a socializing force. But the *Destoshaz* now increasingly assert that *selnarm* is merely emotional noise, and that past-life knowledge—*shaxzhutok*—is either useless or mostly illusory. However, like the rest of the Children of Illudor, the *Destoshaz* lack your many institutions that detect and correct antisocial development." Ankaht grew still. "It is not a revelation to anyone in this room that this troubles me more than any other development in either of our species, for I fear that this rift among my own people cannot help but increase hostilities with yours. And after all, that is what brings us here today, in our investigation of this unwitting human proxy you have captured: the certainty that he is but a cat's paw of a *Destoshaz* plot." Her cluster writhed briefly at Ishmael.

'Sandro leaned forward. "A *Destoshaz* plot?"

Ankaht looked at Ossian.

He shrugged. "I hadn't brought them up to speed on that yet," he explained. "But I think the time is right."

Harry Li looked from Ankaht to Ossian. "I know there are Arduan intelligence specialists working on this case, too, but I thought that was just, well, pro forma. You know, we each tend our own gardens and pull our own weeds."

Jen glanced at Harry—almost pityingly, Ossian thought—and said, "Harry, I think your—well, 'anxieties'—are blinding you to certain aspects of Arduan culture, and therefore why it would be essential that their personnel are partners in our investigation."

Harry folded his arms. "Enlighten me."

"Harry, tell me something: what do you know about Arduan economics?"

"Uh . . ." Li's reply trailed into annoyed silence.

"That's what I mean, Harry. Read a little about how they share resources, how their *narmata* makes them not only intellectually aware, but emotionally invested, in any distress within their own community. The motive we've officially conjectured to be the foundation of this conspiracy—profit—was always just a cover story, a blind to keep the real reason from generating a political firestorm. Culturally, the *Destoshaz*-as-*sulhaji* radicals would never carry out such a scheme for money."

Ossian studied her. "So you've known these crimes were politically motivated from the start, Jen?"

She shrugged. "Known? No. Guessed? Yeah. The mere fact that all the courier drones in question were modified to carry *selnarmic* messages made that a near-certainty."

"Yeah, that didn't slip my notice either, you know," Harry protested. "But it doesn't follow that *Destoshaz* are behind it. And for all we know, it could be humans trying to adjust or falsify data in the *selnarmic* data banks—you know, rile up tensions in *our* community with a false-flag operation. There are plenty of people still chanting the postwar slogan that 'the only good Baldie is a dead Baldie.'" Li darkened as he became conscious of having uttered the slur "Baldie" in the act of repeating the favorite slogan of human genocidalists. "Their words, not mine, Ankaht," he muttered contritely.

Her small tendrils rippled calm reassurance that no offense had been taken. "I am aware of that, Lieutenant. I have heard that epithet in the mouths of those who mean it. I can quite easily distinguish those expressions of genuine hatred from your simple recounting of their speech." Her eyes closed momentarily. "However, Jennifer is correct when she suggests that you are misunderstanding the *Destoshaz*-as-*sulhaji* radicals if you believe that they would stoop to criminality for profit—even to fund their activities. That is not their way. They are reminiscent of the truest exemplars of your ancient orders of knighthood, or holy warriors. Regardless of those sects' different origins and objectives, all shared certain traits: myopic worldview; intolerance for other opinions; fanatical conviction that their personal involvement was the direct will of deity; and utter depersonalization of their foes. In sum, these traits ensured that they could carry out genocidal massacres without believing them to be moral outrages.

"The *Destoshaz*-as-*sulhaji* evince all these traits, to the point where they consider those Arduans who do not share their beliefs to be heretical enemies of the true and pure will of Illudor, who lives through our reincarnated souls just as a body depends upon the cells which comprise it. So you may be certain that the *Destoshaz* radicals would consider any mutually profitable cooperation with humans to be an affront to the purity of their mission and the will of Illudor."

Magee nodded. "That's also perfectly consistent with the way the opposition has been burning all the criminals who've serviced their intel pipeline—all of whom are *human* criminals, I might add."

Ossian nodded. "It's not decisive evidence on its own, but if this is a *Destoshaz*-as-*sulhaji* plot, you can bet they'd consider that killing two birds with one stone. They keep their intelligence trail minimal while also killing off the humans who've been servicing it. There's a gruesome elegance to the strategy."

"It also reflects their moral disdain for your species," Ankaht said quietly. "They consider lying or race-treachery as repellent—even among non-Arduans. If you consider that the human criminals they have employed evince both those characteristics—"

Harry Li nodded. "Why, they're just doing the good Lord's work by putting down the very worst of us furry human scum."

Ankaht closed her eyes. "I am afraid that might be exactly how they would see their actions, yes."

Jen's brow had remained furrowed. "You know, there's one thing I don't get. If the data in the couriers is being copied, then whoever does the copying would have to have another *selnarmic* data core to transfer it to, correct?"

"Correct, Jennifer. *Selnarmic* data, as you call it, cannot be digitalized without a tremendous loss of fidelity. Consequently, the cores in our couriers are not digital, nor can they interface with such a format."

Magee folded his arms, leaned against the door jamb. "How is *selnarmic* data archived, then?"

Ankaht's clusters interlaced, wriggled a bit. "The data cannot be archived, not as you mean it, because it must remain dynamic." She fretted her smaller tendrils. "I cannot explain it well in your words, probably because I have not yet been tasked to do so. Perhaps, Ossian, you would be kind enough—?"

Ossian tried to keep from grimacing. "I'm no theoretical physicist, but I'll try. *Selnarmic* information is fundamentally quantum manipulation. That's why it's instantaneous."

"Which is what makes the *selnarmic* couriers so valuable," put in Magee. "One of them pops into a system, sends its *selnarmic* message to another one waiting to exit through a different warp point at the other end of the system, and bang—instantaneous message transmission. Beforehand, it took hours or even days waiting for radio or lascom relays to reach a conventional courier—if one happened to be standing by on the opposite side of the heliopause. Now, priority transmissions can travel from one end of known space to the other in a matter of one or two days, if there's an unbroken string of *selnarmic* couriers in place."

"Yeah, yeah," muttered Harry. "Shut up and let the captain get back to the nuts and bolts, will ya?"

Ossian smiled. "So, in order to keep *selnarmic* information truly intact, you can't convert it into ones and zeros. It medium is a real-time matrix of subparticulate patterns that cannot be turned into a sequence. You can't break it down, not even for the purposes of building it back up, because part of the information it carries is resident in the matrix of quantum uncertainty factors embedded in it." Seeing the look on Harry's face, he tried a different approach: "You pull one thread and the whole ball of yarn comes unraveled before you can make a map of it. So there's no way to look at it in parts; it's all or nothing. Observer effect creeps into the explanation somewhere, but that's where the connection between theory and application broke apart for me.

"Suffice it to say that you have to create a kind of sustained field-effect in which to store *selnarmic* data packages. That's what the *selnarmic* data core does. It creates and sustains a kind of extensive subatomic honeycomb of those fields. That's why it's got a self-contained long-duration power source and why tapping the core is a delicate business that can only be conducted by a person—or device—that can access it with an extension of their own *selnarm*." He turned to Ankaht, wondered if he was sweating from the effort of rendering a coherent explanation. "Is that relatively accurate?"

"Far better than I could have achieved." Her voice sounded as if she was "speaking" through a smile.

Li was still frowning. "So exchanging *selnarm* doesn't involve some kind of . . . eh, micro-telekinesis?" He wound up grinning at how improbable that explanation sounded, even in his own ears.

Ankaht's clusters rippled with mirth. "No. If Arduans were telekinetic, imagine what we could have accomplished in battle. When engaging your fleets, we could have thrown any switch, disconnected any wires, disrupted any magnetic bottle. Your early analysis of our systems misidentified *selnarm*-operated switches as telekinetically operated because they missed a key detail: the switches were connected to a *selnarmic* receiver. Our *selnarmic* orders went to that receiver, which then sent a standard electric current to activate the switch. Rather like one of your solenoids. *Selnarm* itself can only be used to exchange information, nothing else."

Jennifer rubbed her chin. "You know, I never thought about it before, but how did you ever discover how *selnarm* works, or that it's a dynamic matrix that exists at the quantum level?"

Ankaht nodded stiffly. "It was a relatively late discovery in the history of our people. Only after the theories of Myrtak—our equivalent of your Einstein—were accepted was there even a way to investigate the physics of the phenomenon. Which, I remind you, we still do not fully understand on the mechanistic level. We have complete control of its utilization, but exactly what occurs in those tiny field effects is still a matter of conjecture. Only two centuries before our exodus from Ardu began, scientists observed that the simplest forms of life that utilized what we call proto-*selnarm* experienced minute changes of energy when undertaking coordinated activities. Ultimately, our technologists learned how to create the fields similar to those they discovered in those microorganisms."

Magee straightened up, put his arm around Jennifer: the movement was subtly prefatory to leave-taking. "So what did you learn from the *selnarmic* core we found on Metifilli while we went hunting for more bad guys in the Surzan system? Were our opponents grabbing the *selnarmic* info, or were they after the human, digitalized data? Or was data-tapping just a play act, a stalking horse to steer us away from encrypted messages they've hidden within the data or even the programming itself?"

Ankaht became still. "We cannot say, Captain Magee."

"You haven't found anything yet?"

Jen put a hand on his arm. "I think—that's not what Ankaht means, 'Sandro." Magee looked genuinely perplexed.

But Harry Li frowned. "No, it's not what Ankaht

means. She saying that she *won't* tell us. Isn't that right, ma'am?"

Ankaht's clusters and limbs went through a slow, listless undulation: one of several Arduan versions of an uncomfortable human shrug. She raised one fitful cluster—

"More accurately, she *can't* tell you, Lieutenant," Ossian cut in. "And it's not her doing."

Li's eyes were wide. "It's yours—sir?"

"You vastly overestimate my place on the command food chain, Lieutenant. And you'd better remember to include a bare minimum of respect in your tone, as well, mister."

Li blinked in response to Wethermere's stare. "I'm—I'm sorry, sir."

"To answer your question, Lieutenant, we've entered a new phase of this operation, which triggers a number of predetermined security contingencies. One of which is a reshuffling of clearance levels. I'm sorry, but at this point, the confidentiality firewall shifts higher up the table of organization. That's as per orders cut jointly by the PSU, the Rim Federation, and our Arduan allies. So if you have any disagreements you'd like to air, I suggest you address a message to Admiral Ian Trevayne. He's the person at the top of this particular intel pyramid." *Although I suspect he confabbed with my great-cousin thrice removed Kevin Sanders before he signed off on the counterintelligence protocols.*

Harry Li had become noticeably pale. "I, uh, I won't be sending any messages to the admiral, sir."

"Excellent. He's a busy man. He rarely has time to consider unsolicited advice from Marine lieutenants barely a third his age."

"Yes, sir. Are we dismissed?"

"Nothing so formal as that, Lieutenant Li. I just wanted you all to drop by today so you get a look at what was happening as we wrap up this stage of the operation." Ossian sent a glance that he tried to invest with an apologetic quality toward 'Sandro and Jennifer. "I suspect ninety percent of the new security precautions are totally unnecessary, but we're entering a phase where we have to control information flow with absolute surety and precision." *Because now we get to the part where we have to start examining the possibility of moles and intel breaches within our own organizations, damn it.*

Magee straightened into a posture just one shade less formal than attention. "We understand, sir. Perfectly."

"I'm grateful for that, 'Sandro. And you all have two weeks leave. Enjoy it."

"And after that, sir?"

"More chasing down leads in startown dives and other open sewers, I'm afraid. I'll be a few weeks late joining you, though."

"Oo-rah, sir," smiled Magee, who saluted, put his arm back around the shoulder of his beaming wife, and left.

Harry Li followed, was half out the door, paused, turned to glance at Ankaht. "Ma'am, I'm sorry if I, well, if—"

Somehow the vocoder managed to impart the zenlike benignity of Ankaht's reply. "You have nothing to apologize for, Lieutenant. Enjoy your holiday. I will see you soon again, I am sure."

Harry "Lighthorse" Li's eyes drifted down toward the floor, then he nodded and closed the door behind him.

CHAPTER SIX

Ankaht stared at the closed door for a long moment, turned to face Ossian Wethermere. For a moment she wished she had some way to signal to him the sense of hope, and even personal security, she felt whenever he was around—and then she was immediately glad she couldn't do so. Other than those involving Jennifer, interactions with humans were so very fraught with uncertainty, so prone to misunderstanding and misinterpretation. And because Ankaht had exerted profound efforts to master their dominant language—the capricious and often contradictory polyglot tongue known as English—the humans tended to forget, or simply could not appreciate, just how alien and nerve-wracking it was for an Arduan—any Arduan—to communicate in words only.

Certainly, the vocoder did not *require* her to keep her communications free of *selnarmic* sendings: part of its job was to render those as speech acts. But actual *selnarm* meanings were wonderfully subtle, could be shifted in intensity or obliquity of angle, much like light. Words, on the other hand, were like brute hammers.

Even when whispered, words still meant just what they meant—that, and nothing more. You could always change the amplitude of your meaning by using one of the endless array of near-synonyms, or by affixing modifiers such as "very" or "slightly," but those were still crude adjustments when compared to the absolute precision of *selnarm*. And one never had to doubt that one's intended meaning had been imparted: equally precise *selnarmic* reception made that a surety.

Obversely, when the vocoder converted *selnarmic* expressions into speech, it was much like writing a delicate poem about love and cosmology using only single-syllable words rendered in capital letters. And so Ankaht had trained herself to think in words when communicating to humans. That way, the vocoder had few opportunities to attempt to approximate the nuances of *selnarm* by stringing together an infinitude of modifiers, which ultimately cluttered the underlying message beyond comprehension.

And so, had Ankaht succumbed to the urge to send even a simple pulse of appreciation for Ossian Wethermere—her opposite number in the bilateral effort to improve and protect relations between humans and Arduans—she could not have been certain of how the vocoder would have represented that *selnarmic* send. It could have emerged from the vocoder sounding like desperate relief, like a coy protestation of romantic love (unthinkable, revulsion), as if she was asserting that he was the more reliable and more authoritative of the pair of them, or something still more surreal than these alternatives. She had heard the vocoder produce some truly outré utterances in the past six years, many of them profoundly embarrassing.

Ankaht became aware that Ossian was returning her now-absentminded stare; she was fairly certain that the human word for his facial expression was "quizzical." "Is everything all right, Ankaht?"

She fluttered her left cluster. "Most assuredly. I was simply distracted by reflections upon the challenges our races face in achieving better communications." She glanced back at the door.

Ossian lacked Jennifer's pseudo-*selnarmic* gift, but sometimes he did seem to read her mind. "You're concerned about Harry Li?"

She dropped her cluster back to her side. "Somewhat. I must confess that even Jennifer's husband, Alessandro, worries me."

Wethermere folded his hands thoughtfully. "They've been on this detail for four years, Ankaht. Why are you concerned now?"

Ankaht lowered into a seat. "This investigation has now moved to that point where we have all but proven that the radical *Destoshaz*-as-*sulhaji* are behind the courier drone intercepts. Humans—particularly veterans of the war between our peoples—are likely to find their old suspicions reignited, and with them, their old antipathies. This is what I always feared: that, rather than deporting themselves to join the warlike Arduans in the Zarzuela system, *Destoshaz* zealots hidden within my community would attempt to undermine our partnership with humanity."

"They might not be the ones who are trying to stir up trouble. It could be that the commander of your Second Dispersate, Admiral Amunsit, and her forces in Zarzuela are behind the *selnarmic* courier intercepts."

Ankaht let air wheeze out through her vestigial

gills: an Arduan sigh. "There is much truth in what you say, but whatever the source of the problem, its consequences remain. Indeed, I have long feared that Amunsit and her agents have suborned many, even most, of the *Destoshaz* who have remained with us in the Rim Federation. In which case, the courier intercepts might be a coordinated activity between confidential agents here and the intelligence officers in Amunsit's own blockaded fleet."

Ossian frowned, leaned back. "Again, we always knew that was a possibility."

"A possibility, yes, but this newest information increases its likelihood."

Ossian nodded. "True enough. And that suggests that any *Destoshaz*-as-*sulhaji* who have remained behind here on Bellerophon and other Rim Federation worlds could all be part of a remote-controlled fifth column. And you know what that means."

Ankaht closed all three eyes slowly. "I do. But you must allow my people to handle any sequestrations. If Arduans see humans setting up internment camps for *Destoshaz*—even if the *Destoshaz* are openly warlike and xenophobic zealots—my race's speciate sympathies will trump common sense and necessity: they would fight you, even if they regretted doing so. No: we must sequester our brothers and sisters ourselves. It is the only way."

"No argument there." Ossian stared at the door through which Harry Li had exited. "And so this is why you're on edge about Harry and 'Sandro?"

"Yes, but no more so than I am about those of my own people who were involved in the war that followed our arrival."

"That would be just about every Arduan, then."

Ankaht waved one faltering, despairing tendril. "It is as you say. But Captain Magee and Lieutenant Li were so very intimately involved in that conflict. At its end, they were the leaders of the attack team that was poised to kill every member of our Council of Twenty. I fear that they could once again slip back into seeing my people as the enemy. With alarming ease."

Ossian sat slowly, nodded. "I understand your misgivings. But Ankaht, that was six years ago. And let's remember what those two Marines did right after they took your Council of Twenty hostage: to prove their genuine interest in negotiating, in achieving peace between our peoples, they and their whole attack group surrendered on the spot."

Ankaht looked at the door. "Yes, but would they have done so if Jennifer had not been with them, to ensure that they followed that peaceful path?"

Ossian opened his hands, widened them as if he were going to catch a ball: a gesture of appeal among humans. "I don't know how to answer that, Ankaht, since the only reason the whole assault group went in was to get Jennifer next to you, where you two could communicate and put an end to the conflict. If Jennifer hadn't been there, the entire operation would never have been approved. Or conceived. Since then, both 'Sandro and Harry have worked frequently with Arduans—almost on a daily basis, since we tapped them to lead this investigation's strike unit. You've seen that the two of them cooperate with your people, that they work hard not to judge, and to put aside the reflexes they learned during the war."

Ankaht sent a slow ripple of accord through her tendrils. "I do not dispute the genuineness of their efforts. But should some of my people prove to be oathbreakers, and incite war where we promised to live in peace, I am not convinced your men can resist the pull of their old reflexes, or of vengeful anger against all Arduans." Ankaht struggled with the decision to reveal the source of her deepest misgivings, regretfully concluded that the urgency of the matter trumped even the confidentiality she and Jennifer Pietchkov observed between themselves. "Ossian, you are aware that Jennifer cannot keep her feelings concealed during our exchanges; her pseudo-*selnarm* is not as precise or controllable as mine."

Wethermere frowned. "You've said something to that effect. But why do you mention it now?"

"Because my fears are intensified by detecting the lingering reservations Jennifer has regarding even her own husband's equanimity, should tensions arise between our peoples once again. I have not revealed this before because it is properly a private matter. But now, circumstances necessitate that I share it. And that she feels even more profound reservations concerning the behavior of Lieutenant Li."

Ossian remained silent for several seconds. "I wonder if Jennifer also shared this: that during that final attack, your security chief Temret killed the woman Harry loved."

Ankaht closed her central eye. "I sensed something like this, but, as in all these personal matters, I did not mention that I perceived it. Either way, I have never argued that Lieutenant Li has insufficient reasons for continuing to distrust and even dislike Arduans. I simply note that he has these lingering reservations—and that is a variable we must now consider more carefully. And not just in Lieutenant Li but in almost all the humans working with us on this investigation, because it is they who shall learn first if there is treachery amongst the *Destoshaz* whom you have permitted to live on your worlds."

Ossian nodded. "As always, Ankaht, your prudence is beyond reproach. But let's also remember that, at least in the case of 'Sandro and Harry, it is explicitly because of their restraint that we're all here today. Alive and working together."

Ankaht hoped the *selnarmic* translation capabilities of the vocoder would signal her wry smile. "One of Ardu's earliest and wisest *holodah'kri*, or high priests, observed that 'all paths are strange ones, if you follow them long enough.' So it is with our journey together, Arduans and humans."

Ossian smiled back. "Again, no argument from me, Ankaht."

"So. You will soon be returning to the systems where our opposition is intercepting the couriers?"

"Not right away. I'm overdue to put in my time to keep this." Wethermere tapped the captain's insignia on his shoulder. "I've missed the last two mandatory training deployments, and Admiral Yoshikuni has run out of patience. Word is she's a hard taskmaster and doesn't like taking 'next time' for an answer."

Ankaht was perplexed. "You speak of her as if you did not know her. I thought you served with her in the war."

"Well, yes, but that was six years ago. And we didn't have much contact. First time I saw her I was just a glorified letter-carrier. Then—well, let's just say that there were lots of emptied saddles higher up the chain of command, so I got pulled upward by that vacuum."

Ankaht did not mention that her own researches had confirmed what others said of Wethermere: that he had played a major, if often unadvertised and unrecognized, role in the outcome of the war against the Arduans. It had been at his prompting that one of the major naval innovations of the past decade, the improved energy torpedo battery, was deployed in a key assault flotilla that won several decisive engagements in the latter part of the conflict. "And so you are now directly under Admiral Yoshikuni's command?"

"Well, I'm going to rotate in as captain of one of the reserve ships participating in the wargames she's running in the Polo system." He grew quiet.

Ankaht sat. "Memories?" she asked.

Wethermere shrugged. "I lost a lot of friends thereabouts. Seems like a long time ago. Longer than six years, at any rate." He looked up again. His smile seemed strained. "It will be, er, interesting, to go back there and 'play' at war. And see if Admiral Yoshikuni is as tough a CO as they say. The wargames should be over in about a month, maybe six weeks. Then I return to the systems out beyond Zephrain. By that time, maybe the bad guys will be poking their heads up, again."

Ankaht reflected on the chain of worlds where the conspirators had been operating, and the other, nearby systems where so many others had gone missing or been found murdered. "So your consultations with other human intelligence services corroborated what Ishmael reported about the activities out there?"

"Yeah, pretty much. I've shared our analysis with intelligence liaisons from the Rim Federation, the Terran Republic, and even the Orion Khanate, and they all agree that we've got a pretty good model of what was occurring. They didn't see the big picture because they were all looking only at the pieces of the puzzle that happened to be within their own borders.

"We all agree that the opposition probably targeted that particular part of the *selnarm* courier route for two reasons. Firstly, it was close to Zarzuela and the Arduan enclaves here in the Rim, so it wouldn't look too unusual if a few *Destoshaz* were seen nearby. Conversely, on Earth itself, or in the Heart or Corporate Worlds, an Arduan would be both a unique and startling sight in any crowd. They'd attract way too much attention. And they probably chose Metifilli as the exchange point because it was only one warp point away from Sulzan."

Ankaht's lower eyelids tremored upwards in unison: an Arduan frown. "Sulzan is hardly an important system."

"No, it isn't, but that's one half of why it was perfect. It's an uninteresting system with low population and nothing of value except that it sits on the warp chain that links the capitol of the Rim—Zephrain—with Khanate space and ultimately, Zarzuela. The other half of Sulzan's value to our opposition is that, among the system's minor industries, there is a courier maintenance depot. Both the Navy and diplomatic services of the Rim, and then more recently, the general commercial carriers, set up a quality control and routine assessment station there. So after a set number of automated transits, when a courier pops into Sulzan, it sends a signal indicating it's reached its maintenance interval. The folks at Sulzan take it over by remote control, guide it to their repair facility, check out all its subsystems, fix or upgrade anything that doesn't hit spec, and send it on its way again."

"So that is how they got access to the couriers without arousing suspicion."

Wethermere nodded. "The opposition found someone at the depot to ensure that once the real couriers were put in storage awaiting their turn in the QC rota, they were replaced by a dud: a matching unit that took place of the actual courier, both in the holding yard and in the logistical database. At that point, another group picked up the real courier and carted it off to Metifilli. Then another group—the one we're really interested in—came along and tapped the courier's data core."

Ankaht's tendrils braided in frustration. "And then yet another group finished the process by picking up the genuine core and taking it back to Sulzan. Where it was swapped back into the QC rota and the false courier was removed." Ankaht suppressed annoyance. "And then, after a reasonable period of service, the leadership dismisses their old crop of hirelings, and—over time and at leisurely intervals—kills them."

"With probably one exception," added Ossian. "The group who actually taps the data cores probably doesn't get wiped out—or at least, rarely and not entirely. There are either some Arduans in that bunch, or humans who possess rare skills at tapping data cores. That's why getting a line on them is the next important step in our investigation. That's what I'll be doing when I get back to the field."

Ankaht reclined in her seat. "So what kind of data do your various intelligence experts think is being transmitted or tapped?"

Ossian shrugged. "They've pretty much come to the same dead end we have. If our opposition is tapping the standard digital data banks, the conventional intelligence target would be defense information, particularly regarding the forces blockading Zarzuela and their logistical support assets. But if that's the case, why grab only *selnarmic* couriers? I suppose it could be a ruse, an attempt to make us expect that the *selnarmic* cores are the real targets, but—"

"But," Ankaht continued for him, "our opponents will not presume us to be so stupid as to ignore the digital data banks, and we would thus still find whatever they have hidden there. Besides, why intercept the data once it has traveled so far down the warp line from Zarzuela, just to take it back up the line again? Unless, as Captain Magee speculated, the data itself is what you call a stalking horse: that the real messages being exchanged are encrypted within the programming and files of the core, which can be sifted out later. But once again, your codebreakers—or ours, if the secret messages are in the *selnarmic* core—will eventually discover and decode them. No matter which logical pathway we pursue, the outcome does not explain the enemy's method of operation: it is cumbersome, unnecessary, or both." Ankaht discovered she was looking at Ishmael. "It is most frustrating to be, fundamentally, as ignorant of what is going on as he is."

Ossian's grin was rueful. "You must find it pretty dull, listening to each day's incrementally more boring report about how much more Ishmael doesn't know."

Ankaht flexed her tendrils. "No, it has been quite a useful exercise for me. I have not encountered this kind of human much in my prior work with your species. Having Jennifer here to add her impressions to the data gathered by your interrogators was singularly helpful." *And it underscores that I cannot yet deal with most humans without the* selnarmic *perspectives she brings. It is only by working with—even* through—*her that I come to understand the nuances of their motivations, their foibles, their half-truths.* "Have any of your other intelligence experts given any credence to the possibility that this plot is somehow originating with the Orions of the Khanate?"

Ossian shook his head. "That was flat out dismissed. All the races of the Pan-Sentient Union have multilateral intel transparency. And, as the nominally majority members of the PSU, the Orions have unrestricted official access to every bit of coded data in the digital cores. So, while Zarzuela and Amunsit's fleet are within their boundaries, they have no strategic motivation to tap data that they either already have, or can't translate because they don't have the technical competence with *selnarmic* cores. The only conceivable connection between the operation we're investigating and the Orion Khanate is that some of the felons involved in the scheme may have some contacts among the Orion smugglers who ply their trade in and around the Zarzuela system."

Ankaht was surprised that she had not heard of these smugglers before. "These Orions operate in the Zarzuela system? Beneath the gaze of the blockade forces themselves?"

Ossian shrugged. "Orions have a different view of—well, highly independent traders. Reports indicate that the ones in Zarzuela are more of the gray-market variety, procuring unusual 'items of interest' for the diplomatic missions—theirs and ours—which move back and forth across the blockade lines."

Ankaht shook her head. "You should not be permitting those exchanges. Amunsit is *Destoshaz*-as-*sulhaji*.

She will only interact with other races in order to ensure her destruction of them."

"I agree with you, Ankaht, but when I send those memos up the intel chain of command I get nothing but silence. I copied a few to Admiral Trevayne: like us, he believes that Zarzuela should be completely quarantined. But the final decision rests with the politicians. And after all, if the diplomats and politicos aren't talking to someone on the other side of the fence, then they start to appear redundant."

Ankaht sent wry amusement through the vocoder. "If I remember his statements correctly, Admiral Trevayne is of the opinion that when it comes to the redundancy of politicians, appearances are *not* deceiving."

"Your memory is flawless. And I'm not always sure I disagree with him. But however you slice it, the diplomats want to look like essential players, so they meddle. Furthermore, a lot of the higher echelon intel folks are fond of pointing out that if we don't let Amunsit's envoys out for some controlled contact, we won't have the opportunity to send our embassies into Zarzuela. And so we'll lose the one peephole with which we can assess conditions and force concentrations in Amunsit's system."

Ankaht pulsed dismissive and slightly annoyed tendrils. "Useless. Amunsit is a bloodthirsty zealot by all reports, but she is also quite intelligent. She will only let visitors see what she wants them to see."

"Which I keep pointing out to the folks higher up the chain of command. And which they keep ignoring. Or, more likely, which keep getting ignored by the politicians to whom they must answer."

Ankaht realized that her eyes had drifted back to Ishmael once again, who was now slouched dejectedly in his chair. "It is a shame that he had to be brought in, at all."

Ossian, surprised, glanced at the criminal. "Why?"

"Because if there had been a way to leave him in his position, to secure his cooperation through leverage, we could have watched for the other groups who came to him in Metifilli. He was, as you say, their 'center person.'"

Ossian frowned, then smiled when he understood. "Yes, Ishmael was their 'middleman.' But we had no way of being certain of that before we took him down. And once we had him, and he was wounded, he was damaged goods. We couldn't leave him in the field. The best we could do was to make sure that our altercation with him and his disappearance appeared to be the result of a routine black market transaction gone bad."

Ankaht smiled. "So that the opposition remains unsure whether he was discovered by counterintelligence forces—us—or that he fell afoul of one of his occupation's many hazards."

"Exactly. Which is why this is actually a good point for us to lie low and watch for a while. That's almost certainly what the opposition is doing, and if they find no evidence that his disappearance was a result of the work he was doing for them, then they will almost certainly resume tapping data cores. Probably not at Metifilli, but it's not beyond the realm of possibility. Either way, we have to keep our eyes open in all those systems."

Ankaht nodded. "Yes. And in this system, too."

Ossian stared. "I don't understand."

Ankaht made sure her tone was apologetic. "Ossian, in order to ensure that their operation has not been detected, our opponents may do more—much more—than simply wait and watch for the signs of a counterintelligence operation out in the systems where they have been active. They may attempt to insinuate feelers here into our headquarters."

"Here? A mole?" Ossian frowned, rubbed his chin, shook his head. "Damn it, you're right. And damn me for not thinking of it already."

"It is understandable. Until recently, it was possible we were dealing with common criminals engaging in data theft. But now that it seems certain that my people are involved, we are probably dealing with professional opponents. And of course, I am sure it is not pleasant to accept that you must now commence a precautionary security investigation of your own personnel."

Ossian stared at her. "Well, yes. Although I doubt my security checks will elicit the greatest discomfort—or complaints."

"What do you mean?"

"Ankaht, if the enemy's focus on *selnarmic* couriers is neither chance nor a stalking horse, that points to Arduans as the highest tier of opposition leadership, does it not?"

Ankaht could hardly believe she had missed the reflexive implications of her warning to Ossian. "You mean—"

"Yes, I mean that you're going to have to conduct the same internal security check among your Arduan investigators, as well. And unless I'm much mistaken, some of those persons are not going to like having their loyalty questioned. Not one bit."

Ankaht closed all three eyes slowly. "You are quite right about that." *Quite right indeed.*

CHAPTER SEVEN

Mretlak, Ankaht's chief of intelligence, sent his summarizing statement like a slow, calm ocean swell. "And so, Lentsul, it is necessary that the entirety of our CounterIntelligence Cluster be subjected to a surreptitious security check. (Acceptance, ineluctability.) It shall be conducted by new members drawn from other Clusters, and overseen personally by me."

Lentsul's *selnarmic* reply was clipped, sharp. "All derived from typical human illogic and ingratitude." It was unlike Lentsul to ignore formal deference to his superior, but his *selnarm* roiled with resentment and anger. "I am baffled that you are not equally dismayed, Senior Cluster Commander Mretlak. As a *Destoshaz*, your caste is the one most subject to scrutiny and, therefore, most insulted. I would have expected you to refuse to carry out such a demeaning order."

Mretlak managed to suppress a quick pulse of exasperation. Lentsul, while extremely clever, fancied himself a more accomplished manipulator of *selnarmic* subtleties than he was. This attempt to insinuate, and thereby inculcate, a thread of pride-bruised rebelliousness in his superior was as amateurish as it was ineffective. "Lentsul, I am not insulted—because the order is not demeaning. It simply commands us to undertake an act that is as unpleasant as it is prudent. After all, the data theft we have been investigating cannot, in light of the most recent evidence, be an exclusively human conspiracy. The humans have no way to interface with *selnarmic* data cores or recorders, both of which are involved in the crimes. And logically, if our fellow Arduans are involved, we must presume them to be carrying out this operation with all the shrewdness and innovation that you invariably ascribe to our people. And such canny opponents might certainly attempt to infiltrate our CounterIntelligence Cluster as a means of watching for signs that we have detected their activities. Indeed, a double agent in our office might have been present from the start, since they would be an invaluable asset to help the conspirators acquire the *selnarmic* data cores and recorders that they need for their activities."

(Agreement, impatience) "Yes, I understand that. (Reluctance.) But why must I be included among those subject to suspicion? I am of the *Ixturshaz* caste and, six years ago, spared the humans who most threatened us—even when I was ready, with one squeeze of the trigger, to defeat their revolt on this world. If anyone had reason to hate them, it was me. But instead, I listened to Ankaht's appeals and laid down my weapon."

Mretlak felt the dull, aching misery behind Lentsul's send, so strong that the small, dark *Ixturshaz* could not suppress it, no matter how hard he tried. Lentsul had lost the object of his dreams and desire—one of the tall, slender, golden *Destoshaz*—in the early days of the war against the humans. Recalling that painful past brought those feelings of loss and bitterness back up from the depths into which they had subsided. Subsided, but not disappeared.

Mretlak's clusters rippled. (Sympathy, resignation.) "I made this same point to my human counterpart—Ossian Wethermere—but he and Ankaht asserted that only the two of them and myself could be held beyond suspicion—and only because someone must run the investigation." *And because if one of us were a double agent, it would be impossible to uncover. We each have too much authority, too many covert contacts, to be caught. Unless we were very, very stupid—and none of us are.*

But Lentsul was neither mollified nor diverted by Mretlak's explanation. "I appreciate that you wish to spare my feelings by reminding me that no one is exempt from investigation. (Suspicion.) But I wonder if it is also because I have never been as quick—or, in some cases, *eager*—to trust the humans as some of our fellow Arduans have been." *"Fellow Arduans" like Ankaht, no doubt—and possibly me, as well.* Mretlak was careful to increase the opacity of his *selnarm* very gradually before responding. "Lentsul, including you among the persons to be investigated in no way reflects specific suspicion of you. You have not been singled out in any way," was what Mretlak sent. But what he thought was: *On the other hand, by what reason would you, of all of us, expect to be excluded from this requirement? We have worked for almost five years now with the humans, monitoring activities from either race that might have threatened the accord between us. And you have always been markedly partial to your own side, and so reluctant to trust the humans in any way.*

For a moment, Mretlak feared that Lentsul had managed to perceive these thoughts through the neutral screen he had erected to keep his innermost ruminations from entering the flow of his *selnarm*. Then the little *Ixturshaz* settled himself more stolidly in his chair and pronounced: "That I make no secret of my unwillingness to trust humans too quickly should mark me as the Arduan who is *least* likely to be a double-agent. If I intended treachery, I would logically feign a congenial attitude toward humans, and thereby deflect any suspicions that I might harbor them ill-will."

As if you had sufficient selnarmic *skill to carry off such duplicity,* Mretlak added to himself. But instead, he projected (affinity, fellowship). "It may be as you say, but once the entirety of the investigatory team has been screened, we will not only be assured of operational security, but will possess a baseline against which we may compare any future checks. In actuality, Lentsul, such a procedure is long overdue."

Lentsul seemed to be sitting less rigidly than before. "I thought the humans already ran security checks on all their personnel. They were all drawn from standing intelligence services, were they not?"

Mretlak nodded. "Most of them. But their checks date back to the war. In the time since then, their situations—and attitudes—may have changed."

Lentsul sent (perplexity). "Changed in what way?"

Mretlak lifted a single tendril. "Changed in ways that would make them easier for our people to suborn. Some of the human intelligence personnel might have undertaken actions which compromised their integrity and which they must pay to conceal. Or they may have ailing family members whose care requires more funds than they possess. Or they may simply have become so disgruntled with their recompense that they were willing to entertain bribes."

Lentsul expelled a hoarse wheeze: an Arduan expression of sharp, baffled disdain. He sent (dismay, repugnance): "Since we have landed here, I have repeatedly witnessed the humans' perverse obsession with money, with material wealth. I still do not understand it."

Mretlak replied with (affirmation, concurrence). "It is not easy for us to understand, but ultimately, I believe it is rooted in their limited existence. They have but one life to live and so wish to fill it with all the things and experiences that we may accrue at our leisure over many reincarnations. In those of them that are morally weaker, they consider their honor and integrity a small price to pay for greater opulence."

Lentsul brooded in a cloud of (aversion, pity). "They are cursed beings, living beneath the certainty of final doom from their first hour of true awareness. It is a wonder that they are not all mad."

Mretlak suspected that Lentsul had long concealed a lingering suspicion that all humans were, in fact, just that mad. "I doubt a race of lunatics could have rebuilt their cities so quickly, or have reached an accord with us, or conferred autonomy and planetary systems upon us."

"Well, it is not as though we failed to perform deeds that commended us to their trust. Admiral Narrok liberated many of the humans' worlds from the Tangri, and Ankaht was ever their champion in the Council of Twenty's debates."

Mretlak (concurred), adding, "And she was, in part, fighting for the humans when she entered the *maatkah* ring with *holodah'kri* Urkhot, dueling our own high priest to the death because she would not recant her accusations, would not relent in unveiling his genocidal intentions toward the humans."

Lentsul physically squirmed in his seat. "That was perhaps a more, er, profound display of support for the humans than was seemly, Senior Cluster Commander. For one councilor to kill another . . . it disturbs me to this day."

"Ankaht simply responded to Urkhot's challenge, Lentsul. It was *he* who was willing to kill a fellow councilor—and it was he who died upon the *skeerba* of that dishonorable mania. That seems to be justice, in the end."

Lentsul radiated (grudging agreement, unease). "Yes, but even so, it remains . . . unsettling."

Mretlak let a companionable silence pass between them, gave no hint of how different his opinion was. Urkhot had started out a xenophobe and zealot and ultimately devolved into a megalomaniacal genocidalist who could not distinguish his own views from the will of Illudor. It had probably been a mercy—to both the community and to Urkhot himself—that he had been discarnated. Mretlak hoped the priest's soul would spend a long time in Illudor's care before it returned to the physical plane.

Lentsul broke the almost velvet waves of their shared *selnarm*. "Is there more for us to discuss, Cluster Commander?"

"There are a few final updates I should provide to you, Lentsul, and you may ask any questions you had hoped to bring up at the next coordinators' meeting. After that, you are to continue your current operations, but will not be included in the highest level of the operational strategy sessions until your own security review is complete."

Lentsul rippled a tendril. "I expected as much. I have a question that has been troubling me since this human 'Ishmael' was apprehended. Would it not be most prudent to simply shut down the *selnarmic* courier system?"

"If we were to interrupt local service, our opponents would certainly deduce that we had become aware of their operations and shift their methods of effecting the data theft."

Lentsul leaned forward. "Cluster-Commander, you misunderstand me. I do not mean a regional interruption of service. I mean the entire *selnarmic* courier service should be discontinued."

Despite his best attempts to suppress it, Mretlak's shock sent distempered ripples shivering across his *selnarm*. "Discontinue the entire service? Why?"

"It is the only way to establish absolute security, Senior Cluster-Commander. At this point, we have very few facts, but they are decisive. Firstly, we know that Arduans, with human assistance, have compromised the security of, and tapped data carried by, the *selnarmic* courier system. Secondly, we know they are willing to incur great costs and risks to keep this operation completely secret. From these two facts, we may safely deduce that the information they are accessing is sensitive, critical to our opponents' objectives, and not readily accessible via other means. By process of deduction, therefore, it is quite likely that their acquisition of it represents a strategic disaster for us. It stands to reason, then, that cutting off their access to that information is a top priority—so much so that we cannot wait to further delineate the nature of the information, its sources, or its recipients."

Mretlak reflected that Lentsul, like many of the quantitative- and logic-oriented individuals of the *Ixturshaz* caste, occasionally failed to adequately account for social and political nuances in his operational calculations. "There is merit in your suggestion, Lentsul, but it is not possible for us to take that path."

"And why not?"

"Because the humans and their allies have already become too dependent upon the *selnarmic* courier system. Before we arrived, they barely bothered with courier drones. The delay imposed by waiting for radio signals to cross a stellar system was not much greater than the inconvenience of waiting for the next crewed courier or other craft."

"So the humans and other aliens are unwilling to do without it."

"And our own leaders are unwilling to lose the leverage and profits we accrue from it. It is, by far, our single largest trade item with our neighboring races, Lentsul. Without it, we are just a cluster-full of small, scattered communities, insignificant within the scope and life of the PSU and its constituent polities. But the automated *selnarmic* courier system makes us a pivotal power—a status that the Council of Twenty has quite explicitly indicated it is not willing to jeopardize."

Lentsul detected the implication in Mretlak's phrasing. "You have already asked them if the system could be shut down, then."

"Not in its entirety, but rather, if certain segments of its service could be interrupted, ostensibly for purely tactical reasons. The change in courier availability might have forced our opponents to reveal themselves."

"And the Council rejected your request."

"Along with the human and Orion representatives that were briefed on it. And as I understand it, Admiral Trevayne is one of the most vocal opponents of shutting it down."

Lentsul's central eye blinked. "Trevayne is opposed to shutting it down? I would have thought his would be the first voice calling for it! It is a matter of grave security, and I cannot imagine, in the wake of the last war, that he supports the interests of the Arduan people."

Mretlak kept the air from hissing out his vestigial gills. "In the first place, Admiral Trevayne is motivated by other concerns. Namely, if the *selnarmic* courier drone routes were to shut down, that would play into the hands of his bitterest current opponents: those persons who wish to construct new, artificial warp points."

Now Lentsul saw the connection. "Of course. As long as information is moving just as quickly along our automated courier route, the pressure to create more warp points is modest. But if ready communication were lost indefinitely, then the combined popular outcry for a new relay option would be added to the current mercantile pressures for more direct cargo routes. And so more warp points would be created." Lentsul added (appreciation, acceptance), along with, "Trevayne is a practical human. Sane, at the very least."

"Lentsul, I think Admiral Trevayne's motives may start with practicality, but I doubt they end there. He understands that, in the times to come, more of our Dispersates shall arrive. And if there is to be peaceful integration rather than war, we must be a vital and willing part of this community of races, of polities. Our courier system has fostered ongoing cooperation between us Arduans and the PSU, has become the keystone to evolving a mutually beneficial relationship."

"Perhaps," Lentsul sent, "but the races of the PSU hardly seem to be our eager friends. Particularly the humans."

"And why should they be . . . yet? Who entered whose space, Lentsul? They did not come to our system: we came to theirs. Unthinkable amounts of blood were spilled on both sides. It is enough that, for most humans, their attitude toward Arduans is no longer one of hatred or even distrust. It is merely very guarded. Which is not so very different from their attitudes toward each other. Only since our arrival has the Terran Republic resumed truly amicable relations with the PSU and the Rim Federation. Lacking the *selnarm* to facilitate rapid accord and fellow-feeling, human social change does not come as quickly as we might like, but with patience and nurture, it does come. And that is good enough. Wouldn't you agree?"

Lentsul hesitated. "You make convincing arguments, Senior Cluster-Commander, and I find my mood improved and even hopeful. But perhaps I am like the humans in this one way: I, too, am slow to change."

Mretlak let (amity, wry accord) flow out with a warm *selnarmic* current. "You would not be who you are if you were to change quickly, Lentsul. And we would then not have the benefit of your discernment, because eager optimism is ever the enemy of sage, critical judgment."

Lentsul's own warm *selnarm* flowed back. "It is good to be appreciated for what one does best, Senior Cluster-Commander. Now, allow me to ask about one or two routine particulars before I must enter my security sequestration . . ."

CHAPTER EIGHT

Inzrep'fel, the *ha'selnarshazi* Intendant who was in direct thrall to *Destoshaz'at* Zum'ref of the Fourth Dispersate, clenched her lesser tentacles. "As always, the First Dispersate sends."

Zum'ref sent (equanimity, forbearance) at the announcement of this monthly occurrence. "And is it the same message?"

"No, *Destoshaz'at*: this time, the *shaxzhutok* depicted by the *shaxzhu* of the First Dispersate is the Peace-Feast at the end of the Kinstrife of Nunmarken. They seem to place particular emphasis upon Kef'trel's shock when he learns that he almost slew his masked sibling, Ya'fef'ah, in the final battle."

"And you are sure it is being sent by the First Dispersate?"

"Yes, *'at*."

"You are certain that the point of origin matches the last five years of monthly sendings?"

"Yes, *'at*. The sending began with the same *shaxzhutok* as always: the announcement of the First

Dispersate's destination, including a sustained image of the target star, in Ardu's main planetarium."

Zum'ref stood. "So. The Kinstrife of Nunmarken. The First Dispersate must be growing worried."

"Worried that we may have been destroyed by a mishap on our journey, *'at*?"

"No, of course not. You are *selnarshaz*; you should know the significance of the Kinstrife of Nunmarken."

Inzrep'fel lowered her eyes. "Alas, I do not. My mentor was a Sleeper, one who had walked upon the soil of homeworld, of Ardu. He had many such recollections of our collective past, of the deeper *shaxzhutok* that is our legacy. But he—"

Zum'ref felt his Intendant's *selnarm* tremor uncertainly, reeling itself in before it released a thought that she clearly feared was (impolitic, risky). And he understood. "There is no shame in uttering the truth, Inzrep'fel. Yes, your mentor had insufficient time to pass all his knowledge to you because, like the other First Sleepers, I returned him to his cryogenic slumbers. And judging from this latest *shaxzhutok* from the First Dispersate, it is well that I did so."

"Why do you say so, Admiral?"

(Surprise, disappointment.) "It is truly not evident? Then attend: the Kinstrife of Nunmarken is a warning against sins of pride, of intemperance, of arrogance. In this case, its sender evidently presumes we are still alive, out here in the most empty gulfs of interstellar space. Any other conclusion would, after all, be quite illogical. We know from the other Dispersates that the same sender has also sent them the same messages for five years, now. And none have answered. From the perspective of the sender, then, how likely is it that the collective, uniform silence of all the other Dispersates is because we all—*all*—met with fatal disasters during the course of our journeys?"

Inzrep'fel looked up, her eyes brightening with imminent comprehension. "It is most unlikely, Admiral. Indeed, it would be almost impossible."

"Exactly. So, since we know that such a powerful *solnarmic* pulse could not be sent by anything less than a Group of senior *shaxzhu* working in concert, it is clear that the postwar leadership of the First Dispersate not only presumes that we remain alive, but has recently come to fear that we shall not accept whatever new society they have founded."

"Then why not simply send us that message, as Admiral Amunsit has done with her updates from Zarzuela?"

"An excellent question, Intendant. I hypothesize that the leadership of the First Dispersate is now dominated by *shaxzhu*, possibly Sleepers. If so, they will follow the accustomed methods of their caste and their training: to communicate messages in the form of culturally iconic scenes from the vast repository of past-life events, of *shaxzhutok*, at their disposal. It is, of course, a most elegant means of communication—presuming that both sender and receiver have the same frame of reference, the same compendium of past-life memories at their disposal." He smoothed his *selnarm* as a fastidious predator might preen. "We are no longer in that situation, of course, having rid ourselves of such superstition-riddled inanities."

"And Admiral Amunsit?" asked Inzrep'fel.

"I suspect that because her *shaxzhutok* conversancy is now every bit as—restricted—as our own, that necessity compelled her to innovate and adopt the same signaling method that so many later Dispersates discovered: communicating through on-off *selnarmic* pulses. No content in the *selnarm* itself, but it was a natural means of transmitting one of our earliest telegraphic codes. A string of silences and signals of varying duration, each of which signified a different letter or speech-act. Slow, but far more precise and flexible than the traditional and largely symbolic *shaxzhutok* sendings that the First Dispersate clings to."

Inzrep'fel sent a careful, inquisitive tendril of *selnarm* out toward her commander: (unsurety, foreboding), "And what implications or meanings do you derive from the First Dispersate's iconic sending, Admiral?"

Zum'ref, irked, let his left cluster's tendrils spasm as he replied. "The conclusion is inescapable, even if it were not for the last four years of pulsed-binary *selnarm* updates from Amunsit at Zarzuela. In short, these patch-furred bipeds that she names 'humans' have thoroughly seduced and suborned the First Dispersate. And now they are trying to use our own sibling-*shaxzhu* to infect us with the same heretical soul-rot."

Inzrep'fel sent (regret, accord). "So it seems—but then, what must we do?"

Three years ago, Zum'ref's answering emotion would have been one of regret and mourning; now, all he could feel was brimming resentment, even bitterness. "We must learn from the mistakes of those siblings-in-Illudor who went before us. The war-leader of the First Dispersate—Torhok—reportedly foresaw this outcome: that the *shaxzhu* would attempt to undermine the proper, *Destoshaz* leadership of our fleets. Indeed, it was through just such internecine bickerings that Senior Admiral Amunsit in the Zarzuela system very nearly lost control of her own Dispersate on three occasions. She has been entirely too patient with her *shaxzhu*'s quaint but discordant *shaxzhutok* challenges to common-sense contemporary planning."

"But," Inzrep'fel pointed out, "she did propose that her *shaxzhu* be kept in cryogenic sleep until all the alien, tool-making *zheteksh* were eliminated."

"Yes, and that was her mistake: she *proposed* it. She was foolish enough to bring the matter before her own Council of Twenty before acting upon it. They forced her to rouse at least a few of the *shaxzhu* from cold sleep to share in the deliberations. And as if the *shaxzhu* weren't troublesome enough on their own, the majority of the Sleepers from other castes have many of the same soft-headed notions about 'communicating' with these alien animals. Even those of our own *Destoshaz* caste."

Inzrep'fel's *selnarm* was tense. "Then how are we to save ourselves from a similar fate, *Destoshaz'at*?"

Zum'ref managed to summon a modest pulse of (regret). "We have no choice: we must completely remove the danger posed by our own *shaxzhu*—and by our many thousands of Sleepers, besides."

"Very well, but how are we to render them harmless? They are, as you say, fairly numerous."

"Unfortunately, there is only one sure solution: we must kill those who threaten us."

"Kill *shaxzhu*?"

"Yes, and Sleepers."

Inzrep'fel blinked. "I foresee a problem, Admiral Zum'ref. The *shaxzhu* and the Sleepers are renowned for their subtlety, their cunning. They might work against us in secret until it is too late."

Zum'ref sent (approval, gratification) along with his concurrence. "This is most assuredly true."

"Then how shall we identify which ones must be killed?"

"That problem is easily solved, Intendant."

"It is?"

"Yes: we kill them all."

Part Two

The Deluge

CHAPTER NINE

The chestnut-haired little girl ran toward him along the beach in the dazzling Mediterranean sun, leaving her mother and sister behind. She waved to him and smiled . . .

A sickening foreknowledge took him. Courtenay! *he shouted desperately . . . or tried to shout, but no sound came, for he wasn't really there . . .*

And then the beach and the sea and the sky and the universe vanished, replaced by a glare and a roar so intense that the senses seemed to blend into each other—the roar blinded, and the glare deafened. The little girl was screaming as she burst into flames and began to melt.

And the buzzer wouldn't stop . . .

Buzzer . . . ?

The incongruity brought Ian Trevayne abruptly awake, drenched in sweat. Awkwardly, he jabbed the button on his bedside communicator, stopping the sound his sleeping mind had incorporated into the all-too-familiar nightmare. It was always more or less the same, and it had plagued him—although at increasingly long intervals, with the passage of years—ever since the early days of the Fringe Revolution, when he had learned of the death of his first wife and their two daughters, vaporized by the fusion bombs of the rebels of the Terran Republic.

The Terran Republic whose uniform I now wear. He always told himself that. It hadn't stopped the nightmares. And this time the dreary, leaden depression that followed was worse than usual, because that damned buzzer had awakened him in mid-dream, which always made the memory of the dream more vivid and slower to dissolve under the tide of waking-world sensations and thoughts.

"Yes," he mumbled in the direction of the communicator, unable to keep the irritation out of his voice.

"I'm sorry to awaken you, Admiral." The voice was, surprisingly, Rear Admiral M'Zangwe's. Even more surprisingly, the voice held repressed tension. "I wouldn't have done so, except that . . . well, we've gotten some peculiar sensor readings. Not an immediate threat," he added hastily. "Maybe no threat at all. But it's something I think you'll want to know about at once. Commodore Hagen is analyzing the readings now."

Both gloom and annoyance immediately fled from Trevayne's mind, as did the last vestiges of sleep. M'Zangwe was, to put it mildly, not one to jump at shadows. "All right, Adrian. I'll meet you and Commodore Hagen in the Intelligence Center in five minutes." As always, he couldn't help but smile at the ancient naval tradition that gave a "courtesy promotion" to anyone with the rank of captain who was aboard a ship in any capacity other than that of the ship's commander—the only person aboard who could be addressed by the sacrosanct title.

He became aware that Magda had also sat up in bed. "What is it, Ian?"

"Some kind of sensor returns that Adrian considers significant," said Trevayne as he reached for his clothes. "If he's concerned, I'm concerned. You'd better come too."

In the semi-gloom of TRNS *Li Han*'s Intelligence Center, Andreas Hagen stood silhouetted against the faint glow of the holographic display tank, facing an audience that included M'Zangwe, Rear Admiral Rafaela Shang, and Flag Captain Hugo Allende as well as Trevayne and Magda.

"All right, Andreas," said Trevayne as briskly as he could manage a few minutes after awakening. "What do we have?"

Hagen cleared his throat. "Well, Admiral, as you know the readings from the astronomical sensors, although not of immediate urgency, are periodically reviewed—"

Trevayne nodded. *Li Han*'s sensor suites—including the very long-range astronomical ones—were on the same scale as the rest of her. There were university observatories less well equipped for their function.

"—and the latest review turned up two new astronomical objects." Hagen drew a deep breath. "We have interpreted them as the flares of photon drives."

Trevayne, now fully alert, gave the Intelligence officer a hard look. "You realize the implications of what you're saying, don't you?"

"Yes, sir," said Hagen unflinchingly.

For a moment, Trevayne reviewed those implications himself.

The term "photon drive" was actually something of a misnomer for what was essentially an antimatter drive based on complete cancellation, exploiting the energies in the "quantum foam" of empty space by altering the parity rate of particle and antiparticle creation and annihilation. It emitted an incredibly focused source of energy and a very wide spectrum of radiation. Some preferred the term "pinhole drive" after the way it pinched a reaction aperture in the fabric of space-time. But the photons were at least partially the thrust agency, and the name had stuck.

At any rate, the principle of the thing had been known for a very long time. But nobody had used reaction drives—even this one—since the invention of inertia-cancelling drive fields. Admittedly, those drive fields were inherently limited to a velocity of 11.7 percent of lightspeed, later enhanced by the phased gravitic effect of the Desai Drive to about 50 percent, while photon drives could theoretically accelerate all the way up to Einstein's Wall, given enough time. But with the warp network allowing instantaneous transit between star systems, who needed that kind of capability?

The answer, it had turned out, was: the Arduans.

It had been by the photon drives' flares that the Bellerophon Arm's worlds' human inhabitants had known they were coming. And now, it seemed, such flares were in the sky again.

"Yes, sir," Hagen repeated. "It's got to be a subsequent Arduan diaspora."

Shang looked skeptical. "Does it have to be them? Couldn't it be some *other* race, unknown to us, that's decided to try slower-than-light interstellar colonization?"

"We thought of that, Admiral. But the sensors had been observing these flares long enough, before we reviewed them, for us to determine the ships' vectors and extrapolate them backwards. There's no doubt about it: their point of origin is the Arduan home system."

Magda spoke softly, partly to Trevayne and partly to herself. "In a way, it's too bad Cyrus didn't make this discovery."

Trevayne understood. Waldeck's Task Force 14.2, though predominantly PSU, also included Arduan elements. But this task force was a Terran Republic/Rim Federation affair, and therefore all-human. Trevayne had no Arduans whose brains he could pick.

"Well," he said to Hagen, "let's see this course you've projected for them."

They all gathered before the display tank. At the moment, the display was in the two-dimensional mode, showing the relevant portions of the warp network, with the green icon of their task force in the starless warp nexus just beyond Hulixon, still awaiting further advance by Cyrus Waldeck along the warp chain he was following. Tangri-held systems showed in red.

Hagen manipulated controls. For an instant, the tank's interior was chaos. Then it stabilized in three-dimensional form, with the string-lights of warp lines gone and the stars strewn about to reflect their actual placement relative to one another in normal space. The Tangri systems still glowed red, but their locations were seemingly random, as were those of the two green icons. Hagen did some more fiddling, and the scale expanded until two new icons appeared, yellow and trailing tiny tails.

"The tails represent their vectors," the Intelligence officer explained. "The sensor data is being automatically incorporated into the display. And at the same time, the computer is correcting it to account for the time lag in the observations. Remember, we're seeing these flares where they were years ago—about five years, in the case of the closer one. This shows where they are *now*. Incidentally, they are gradually decelerating."

"And where are they going?" Trevayne inquired.

For answer, Hagen turned to the controls again, but then paused. "Now, you must understand, Admiral, that there's an element of uncertainty in this. We have to make certain assumptions—notably, that they will not alter course, which presumably they have a limited capability to do."

"Why should they do that?" scoffed Allende. "I mean, they've been heading for a preplanned destination for who knows how many years. Why should they change their minds now?"

"Precisely, Captain. And on that basis, we can easily project their courses. But the results are somewhat puzzling." String-lights representing extrapolated courses appeared in the tank. For a moment, there was silence.

"Where is *that* one going?" M'Zangwe demanded irritably.

"Nowhere, Admiral. At least not in this region of space. The course doesn't intersect with any star system in normal space, or any such system with which we have any warp connections."

"Is it possible that it's out of control?" Shang

wondered. "Some sort of malfunction, or the crew succumbing to a plague, or—"

"That's not something we need speculate about at this time," said Trevayne firmly. "Evidently that one is just passing harmlessly through the spaces that are of no interest to us, and can therefore be ignored. This other one, on the other hand . . ." He pointed at the second string-light, which terminated at a scarlet dot.

"So they're headed for a Tangri system," said Magda. She turned to Hagen. "Which one?"

Hagen restored the warp-line display. With a light-pencil, he pointed at a red dot a few warp connections along the axis they were following. "Our intelligence assessments indicate it's a system held by the Daroga Horde. Incidentally, their rate of deceleration confirms that it is their destination."

"When are they going to get there?"

"Here again, the need to make certain assumptions makes a definite answer impossible. But with that proviso, we postulate an ETA of approximately fourteen and a half standard years from now."

Trevayne drew a deep breath and released it. "Thank you, Andreas. Captain Allende, please order a courier drone prepared. We need to pass along this information without delay . . . and I'd like very much to consult with our Arduan friends, who may be able to offer some insights about these later diasporas. But for the moment, I think that's all the action we need take." He turned to the others and smiled. "I will be very, very disappointed if we haven't wrapped up this campaign, and occupied that destination system, in *far* less than fourteen years! So when they arrive we should be able to have a reception committee waiting for them, including their fellow Arduans. Does everyone agree?"

There was no demur. It was agreed by all that the discovery was interesting but called for no urgent steps.

CHAPTER TEN

With the power plant dead and the grav generators off, the bodies in the forward section of the main corridor floated like drowned men in a stagnant pool. They turned slowly, globules of blood drifting behind and around each one in a widening pattern. 'Sandro Magee looked past the nearby corpses—each one in civilian coveralls rent by multiple, dark-rimmed holes—and moved his shoulders so that the neckless space-helmet was now aimed up the corridor and into the small bridge at the other end of the prospector ship. The hatch was open and another torso was just drifting out of sight beyond the rim of the coaming, trailing more dark droplets. "Are you seeing this, Doghouse?"

"We are, Bloodhound One," Ossian Wethermere's voice answered. "Recommend you proceed with extreme caution."

Harry Li, who was not on the command circuit, muttered. "Jeez, ya think?"

'Sandro cut a sharp glance at him and pushed off the deck with a grace that was almost incongruous in so large a man. As he did, his receiver crackled to life once again. "Say again, Bloodhound One. Negative read on that last transmission."

Evidently Magee's mic had picked up a fragment of Harry's insolent *sotto voce* comment. Or not so *sotto voce* after all, it seemed. "Nothing of importance, Doghouse. Just some housekeeping chatter on our end."

Harry waved to the two Marines with them and kicked himself more aggressively down the corridor. The trio arrived at the bridge with coil guns at the ready. Their suddenly relaxed posture told 'Sandro what they had found: more of the same. No survivors. And no attackers.

Magee shifted to the tactical channel as he continued to drift forward. "Any clues as to what happened here, Harry?"

"You mean other than a stem-to-stern massacre? No idea, 'Sandro. A few of the crew lived long enough to get to a weapons locker, another one managed to get a sidearm out of a holster. But beyond that, nothing. No sign of attacker casualties, no sign that the crew got a shot off. Whoever greased them was a known—and evidently trusted—group."

"Damn it, this just doesn't make sense."

"As if anything about this investigation does? The deeper we go, the wider and weirder the clues and connections become. I can't figure—"

Alessandro's radio crackled again, emitted a triple-tone which signified that its secure channel had been switched remotely. Wethermere's voice was calm and uninflected—which told Magee that the fecal matter had definitely hit the oscillating air circulator: Ossian typically communicated by emphasis and inflection almost as much as by words. So when his voice became flat—

"Bloodhound One, be advised: we've got a bogey inbound, emerging from the shadow of the debris-field at 87 by 18."

"A hostile, Doghouse?"

"Uncertain, Bloodhound."

"Do we call for the gig to auto dock with this ship and exfil at the double, sir?"

"Negative. Just gather your team on the bridge and observe radio silence."

"Acknowledged. And once we're on the bridge?"

"Check the ship's systems and await further orders."

"Received and understood. Bloodhound out."

Li was staring at 'Sandro from the other side of the bridge. "Did we find some trouble?"

"Do we ever find anything else? Call the other teams up here, Harry. Radios off once they've got the word."

"And then?"

"And then we wait."

Eighteen light-seconds away, snugged in the lee of a Brobdingnagian chunk of what had once been an Arachnid monitor, Ossian Wethermere leaned back in the well-worn captain's chair of the forty-year-old freighter-turned-Q-ship *Woolly Imposter*. He nodded at his commo officer. "Ensign Schendler, terminate all broadcasts. Confirm lascom array remains fixed on Bankshot One."

"Broadcast comms are now dark, Captain. Bankshot One telemetry test returns five by five."

"Very good, Dylan. Keep it that way. I don't want to lose contact with the rear."

"Aye, sir."

"Sensors, lascom inquiry to our remote sensor platform: update on the bogey."

"Forward deployed remote sensor platform Bankshot Two shows no change to the bogey, sir," replied Lieutenant Engan. "Of course, Bankshot Two's sensor suite is vastly inferior to our own. If we could just—"

"We don't need to read the lettering on the bogey's hull, Katharine. I'm just watching for them to light up some active arrays."

"Aye, Captain. As you ordered, I've been keeping my eye out for those."

"And you keep that eye well-peeled, Ms. Engan." Wethermere rubbed his chin. "Are they still running a drive field?"

"Affirmative, sir. And power output is steady."

And way too high for my comfort, Wethermere appended silently. *It's hard to believe a genuine belt-runner of any kind—freight, salvage, prospecting, mining—would need, or be willing to spend the fuel, to keep pumping out that kind of energy.* Belt folk were, by nature and necessity, a parsimonious lot.

But the bogey's steady, high-energy signature was only one of several mysteries. The first mystery, the one that had brought them to the system known simply as Home Hive Three, was news that one of the "persons of interest" who'd come to light during Ishmael's interrogation had made contact with a number of surveyors, prospectors, and salvage operators in the past four months. Nothing was known beyond that—except that three of the contacted groups were later reported journeying and tarrying in two backwater systems: Home Hive Three and Pesthouse. Scenes of gruesome battles in the Bug War of 263 years ago, the systems remained diffuse junkyards, and, in the case of Home Hive Three, no longer had habitable planets.

Home Hive Three had been the site of the first application of what was known as Directive Eighteen: the extirpation of a species. In one of the most famous, and one-sided, battles of the Bug War, the invading Grand Alliance fleet had rained a relentless hail of antimatter warheads down upon Planet One and Planet Two. An estimated twenty billion of the enigmatic and only partially individualized arachnids had been killed, many in the blasts themselves, but many more in the sequelae of tsunamis, firestorms, overlapping shockwaves, cyclones, and fallout. If any survived the attack, they did not do so for long. Ash-choked skies triggered a nuclear winter, turned the once blue oceans into lethal chemical stews, and destroyed all plant life.

Wethermore glanced at the external monitors: gutted ships' carcasses floated about them, ominous, gray, and silent. Even out here, in its furthest reaches, the entirety of Home Hive Three seemed to be repeating a ghostly word just beyond earshot: *graveyard graveyard graveyard.* Far beyond the inner planets, even this remote asteroid belt was marked by death-images of the battle that had killed the whole system. A blackened hetlaser turret—a museum piece anywhere else—drifted past, faint amber reflections of the distant primary picking out raw metal where it had been ripped and split away from a hull by titanic explosive forces. Other, smaller bits of detritus, indefinite given the range, trailed behind the scorched behemothic ribs of the wrecks, imparting gruesome momentary impressions that they might be the remains of the crews—arachnid, human, Orion, Ophiuchi. Collectively, it was as if a fantastical fleet of the dead—of slain ships and their crews—were making a lugubrious progress through a sparse valley of floating asteroid mesas, creeping toward final oblivion at the end of time.

And then the moment of reflection was past, and Wethermere turned his eyes back to the holoplot that showed the red bogey at the midrange twelve-o'clock position—which abruptly began moving toward the green icon that denoted the derelict prospector's ship at two o'clock.

"Sir—!"

"I see it, Lieutenant Engan. How fast is the bogey moving?"

"Twice as fast as our max, sir."

"Their tuners?"

"Gotta be redlining, sir. That crew is either impervious to rads or suicidal."

Or maybe both. Either way, they're cranking 0.10 cee out of that hull. Which leaves me two choices: sit on my hands and watch them do whatever they're going to do to Magee's team, or get moving. Which was no choice at all: "Mr. Lubell!"

"Sir?"

"Plot an intercept that will put us between the bogey and the prospector. Best speed. Execute."

"Executing. Sir, some evasive maneuvers—"

"—Will slow us down. We're already the tortoise compared to their hare. Make a beeline to get between them and Magee. Zhou?"

"Sir?"

"Bring up the auxiliary plant; I'm going to need a lot of energy for shields and weapons, I suspect."

"Sir, if I do that, they're going to know we're a Q-ship."

"All the better, at this point. We've got no time to

be coy, and just maybe, the prospect of a real fight will make the bogey pause." *But I seriously doubt it.*

The bogey's actions confirmed Wethermere's instincts. Active sensors reached out from it. The opposition force certainly knew two things already: that the prospector had been boarded by a team that could be carried by the gig that was docked with it, and that said boarding party had been in contact with a home vessel somewhere in the area. And in another moment, they would notice the energy bloom peeking out from around the leeside curve of the asteroid behind which the *Woolly Impostor* had been lurking. Time to get their attention focused on the immediate area of operations and keep it there—hopefully, myopically so. "Mr. Schendler, bounce our spectral-phased lascom alert off Bankshot One. Repeat three times: we need to be certain that the intended recipients get that message. Ms. Ross—"

Katharine Engan jumped in before Wethermere could issue orders to his weapons officer, J.T. Ross. "Captain, the bogey is attempting to get target lock on the prospector. And they're trying to get a bead on us, too, sir."

Wethermere paused. *Multiple targeting?* "Engan, spectrum and power analysis of their sensors: are they milspec?"

Engan's pause was not quite a second long. Her response was rapid but hushed, "Without a doubt, sir."

"Okay, time to match their bet and call. Light up our own active arrays. Task Bankshot Two to start piping us advanced targeting information."

"That's likely to get Bankshot Two pranged, sir," commented Lieutenant Ross.

"I'm hoping it will, Weapons. I want them to show us what kind of heat they're packing and the ranges at which they're comfortable using it." *Woolly Impostor*'s hull began to quiver as the engines reached maximum output and the drive tuners shuddered against the physical constraints of normal space-time. "Mr. Lubell, are we going to be able to get between the bogey and Magee in time?"

"With about a minute to spare, Captain. But that's going to put us very close to the OpFor. Very close."

"How close?"

"Inside two hundred kilometers, sir."

The bridge grew silent. At that range, conventional point-defense fire systems—active defenses that slapped away missiles—were all but useless. Also, the powers of both ships' respective weapons were at their most focused and destructive. "Ms. Engan, do you have a cross-section of that bogey yet?"

"Pieces of it, sir. Computer is interpolating—got it." She paused. "It's a gunboat, sir. *Moon*-class: Terran Republic manufacture of almost half a century ago. What's the Republic doing out here, and why are they attacking us?"

"They're not, Ensign. The Republic's last few *Moon*-class gunboats were decommissioned about ten years ago. Converted into outsize tugs or sold to security firms and planetary governments as convoy escorts, customs patrol ships, local defense."

"Which means they have the power plant and possibly the turrets to mount some serious weaponry, right—sir?" Ross sounded anxious.

Wethermere kept the smile off his face. "Well, when it comes to weaponry, 'serious' is a matter of perspective, Lieutenant." Just four months ago, Wethermere had been skipper of a devastator type warship: its secondary missile bays were large enough to swallow a gunboat whole. "But right now, yes, they've got the on-board systems to power and direct multiple milspec beam weapons." He paused, resisted his habitual impulse to rub a hand through his hair when puzzling out a problem. "Mr. Zhou," he said slowly as the green blip of the *Woolly Impostor* passed the halfway point to the line of intercept.

"Yes, sir?"

"No shields until I give the order."

"But sir—"

"Mr. Zhou, I understand the risks. But I'm betting that the OpFor has never even imagined a Q-ship like this one."

"But how do we know when they plan to—?"

"Ms. Engan, you watch your sensors like your life depends upon it—because it does. Along with all our lives, as well." *These bastards are playing poker, just like we are. Keeping some of their hand hidden, even though it* seems *as though they've put all their cards on the table. If that's a* Moon-*class, and she still has multiple mil-spec fangs that either haven't been pulled or were retrofitted by whoever bought her title, then she's got even more energy output that she hasn't touched yet. Her designers put in enough power plant capability to drive her at full speed while also powering her beam weapons. So when her commander pushes the power plant to those higher gigawatt levels—*

Damn it: the range and power of those weapons puts a spin on another *variable in the tactical equation.* "Schendler, raise Bloodhound One right now. Secure channel two."

"Sir, Magee is responding on secure two."

"Bloodhound One, this is Doghouse."

"Reading you five by five, sir."

"Good. I need a fast report on the ship's systems."

"Yes, sir. Inconsequential small arms damage throughout. Minor damage to control elements on the bridge; can't know functionality unless she was up and running. But the biggest problem is that someone took a sledgehammer to the containment rings."

"Alignment is shot?"

"Again, can't say without trying to start her up, sir. She's running off batteries, right now. And if the rings are messed up just enough to allow fusion to begin *before* finally losing containment—"

"That's sufficient, Captain." Wethermere looked at the respective position of the blips in the holotank. The bogey could start firing any moment now. "Bloodhound One, prepare to abandon ship."

"Sir?"

"Did I stutter, Magee? I said 'prepare to abandon ship.'"

"But the gig—"

"We'll get to the gig in a moment. Right now, I need to know about the condition of the prospector's escape pods."

"Grimy, but functional."

"Get your men in the pods. Then you and Lieutenant Li are to carry out the following orders..."

Wethermere did not allow himself to watch Ensign Engan closely. If he did, the rest of the crew would, and the pressure on her would be counterproductive. He, and they, just had to trust that, the moment that the enemy ship doubled its power output—

Engan's spine snapped straight. "Sir, energy spike—"

Wethermere turned to Zhou. "Bring our plants to full, and shields up."

"Aye, sir."

"Ross, launch a full spread of missiles. Soft-deploy a second wave of autonomous missiles from our bay under the cover of the launch, but keep that second wave inert. Lubell, bring us about and put us nose to nose with the intruder to protect the blind spot behind our engine decks. Schendler, activate the gig's remote helm and detach it from the prospector." Wethermere switched channels. "Bloodhound One?"

"Here, Doghouse."

"All hands abandon ship. Execute."

"Executing, sir." Magee's audio feed was rendered inaudible by a roar of background sound—the jettisoning rockets—and the Marine's sudden grunt under eight gees of acceleration.

The previously minimal activity in the holoplot—the red blip approaching the slower green blip—became a chaos of disparate motions. The smaller green blip that was the prospector spawned an even smaller one—the gig—which moved away in an arc that would ultimately carry it behind the intruder. A sprinkling of verdant snowflakes fluttered outward from the prospector at the same instant: Magee's Bloodhounds abandoning ship. Too small to be picked up by the ship's sensors, their individual locations were being established by each suits' transponder telemetry. Small actinic pinpricks launched from the *Woolly Impostor* towards the enemy, even as another cluster of dim, transponder-located icons—the autonomous missiles that had been ejected, powerless, from the main bay—emerged lazily from the rear of the big green icon.

The enemy's response was not surprising. A mix of force beams and hetlasers licked out at the *Woolly Impostor*'s missile spread and at the gig as well—which, if allowed to complete its sweep toward the enemy's rear, would be in an excellent position to mount a counterattack. One additional beam struck at Wethermere's ship itself.

Zhou waited to see the results. He almost preened when he reported, "Shields holding; capacitors running green."

"The gig?" Wethermere insisted.

"Badly hit, sir" reported Engan. "Venting atmosphere, damage to drives—"

Engan's report was interrupted by a sharp actinic bloom in the portside viewscreen.

"Gig destroyed," she amended.

No time for regret. "Magee and his men: their distance from the derelict?"

"Now passing out of danger range in the event of catastrophic power-plant failure."

"Excellent, but with the gig gone, we have less ability to distract the enemy, or compel him to divide his attacks. And it's essential that we keep the prospector ship intact. Range to bogey?"

"Four light-seconds, sir."

"Time to contact?"

"Approximately eighty seconds, at current rate of closure."

Not a lot of time left. At point-blank range, Wethermere doubted that even *Woolly Impostor's* outsized shields would save them from the attacker's military-grade weapons. "Schendler: time elapsed since we sent our engagement alert back through Bankshot One?"

"Just over five minutes, sir. It's going to be close."

Indeed it is, but then again, no one had expected that the adversaries who had hit the prospector a few hours ago had been operating from a rehabilitated warship. Or that it was captained by a suicidal maniac, given the rads the ship's tuners were pumping through its crew. "Then let's make every second count. Ross, do we have lock?"

"Have had one for a minute, sir. But they just pranged Bankshot Two."

"That's okay; we don't need a second set of eyes anymore." And that remote sensor platform had kept the bad guys a little bit more busy. Which was, ultimately, the name of the game.

"Sir," Ross appended cautiously, "is there any reason we're not using our own hetlaser?"

"Yes—because I want them to get close to us before they find out that we have one, Lieutenant. And be quick on the trigger when I call for it."

"Yes, sir!"

Engan's voice had risen a half-pitch. "Bogey firing missiles."

"Target?"

"Hard to tell, sir. We now lie along the same vector as the prospector. Could be either one of us."

But that's only half of the problem with keeping the prospector in one piece: if we leave the enemy's beam weapons unoccupied—"Ross, activate the sprint missiles we soft-deployed."

"Missiles now active and homing, sir."

And in the holoplot, those missiles began moving toward the bogey—which immediately committed its beam weapons to serve in the PDF role, thereby temporarily precluding their use as offensive weapons. Wethermere watched his missiles' icons disappear one after the other, checked the engagement clock: the missiles alone weren't going to buy enough time—

"Ross, our lasers are to target the bogey's—"

"Sir," Engan shouted. "The approaching enemy missiles are—are multiplying, sir!"

And so they were. A useless technology against warships because of insufficient killing power, multiple independent warhead missiles could be devastating against smaller, slower craft. And in the case of *Woolly Impostor*—

"Ross, belay that last order. Switch our lasers to PDF mode. Smartly, now! Engage!"

The Navy crew on Wethermere's bridge switched tasks in mid-execution with smooth, well-practiced precision. Ross' lasers began whittling away the first rank of enemy missiles. But that meant—

"Bogey firing beam weapons at prospector, sir. Minor hits. Now targeting us—"

Automated danger klaxons hooted throughout the cramped, converted freighter. "Shields held," reported Zhou, "but they won't next time. His beams won't be diffuse at all when he's spent another fifteen seconds closing the range."

Wethermere glanced at Ross. "And their missiles?"

"First wave eliminated, sir. Second wave is only four missiles—but they are not spawning more warheads."

Ossian glanced at Engan. "I confirm that, sir. But their lock is wavering—"

There was no time to hear any more. "Ross, reacquire the bogey with our lasers. Zhou, over-power our shields."

"Sir—?"

"Just do it. They'll have to take the last four missiles. Ross?"

"Sir, I have almost—lasers locked on target!"

"Fire and sustain. Burn the capacitors if you have to, just keep hammering him amidships."

"Aye, sir."

The *Woolly Impostor*'s weaker lasers faltered as they encountered the gunboat's shields, then again when they hit the relatively light armor. But the unremitting beams ultimately tore a widening gash along the side of the enemy gunboat. Charged plasma arced, and flames danced and flickered at the peripheries of that wound. *Damn it, that attack may have been too successful. If that ship blows up . . .*

But again, there was no time to think that far ahead. "Engan, what about their missiles—?"

She was staring at the holoplot. "They have shifted lock, sir." The four missiles that had been following the first wave had not hit the well-shielded *Woolly Impostor*, but had bypassed it. They were now heading for the smaller green blip farther along the vector: the prospector hull.

Damn it, they suckered me. "Ross, shift our lasers back to PDF mode. Acquire—"

"Sir, we've already lost fifty percent capacitors—"

"Then burn the other fifty percent. Shoot what you have, damnit."

Ross did. And vaporized two missiles.

But the last two struck the abandoned prospector in her engine decks. What began as a modest responding flare of flame burgeoned outwards into a blue-white sphere of annihilation.

"Bogey correcting her course, coming about," reported Engan.

"Our shields?" asked Wethermere.

"Solid," replied Zhou.

"Lasers?" he asked Ross.

She shook her head. "Burned out, sir."

"Then Lubell, back us away: open the range and cover our tail. And Schendler, send this encrypted but in the clear: 'the enemy ship is not to be—'"

At that moment, four green blips raced into the holoplot from where the intruder had originally emerged. And as they did, they were firing weapons.

"It's the cavalry from our carrier, sir. Delta flight—with plasma torpedoes inbound."

"No, damn it, no!" Wethermere snapped, standing up from the con. "Don't destroy—!"

The enemy ship was struck along the length of its already savaged portside hull by four of the torpedoes. The viewscreens suddenly whitened and then shut off.

Staring at the monitors, then the readouts on the sensor board, Wethermere resisted the urge to rub his brow in exasperation. *Well, there go both of the only clues we have—*

Schendler looked up. "Sir, message from the *Celmithyr'theaanouw*."

Wethermere sighed. "Is it Least Fang Kiiraathra'ostakjo, himself?" No doubt his friend, the Orion commander, was calling to find out if his fighters had rescued *Woolly Impostor* before any serious damage had been done to her, and to also do some oblique bragging on behalf of his fighter jocks.

Schendler shook his head. "No, sir. It is Councilor Ankaht on secure one."

Ankaht? Well, I might as well tell her the bad news: that we just destroyed every useful lead we had in this investigation. "Pipe her through, Mr. Schendler."

"Yes, sir."

Ankaht's soothing alto vocoder-voice seemed to swim up from a dark, still pool into his ears. "We are glad you are safe, Ossian. This was most unexpected."

"Yes. So unexpected that it caught us by complete surprise—and so we lost both ships. Almost lost our boarding team, too. Tell Jennifer that Tank is all right. But damn it, I think I just ruined our entire investigation beyond any hope of—"

"Ossian," Ankaht interrupted. Her voice was tense, as if she was constraining some news that both excited and horrified her. "Ossian," she repeated, "you have not destroyed the investigation: you have propelled it into its final stage."

Wethermere blinked in surprise. "I what? But how—?"

"The ship you fought was not guiding its missiles by lascom or radio, but by *selnarm* links." She paused. "Your opponents were Arduans."

CHAPTER ELEVEN

Raising his distinctly felinoid chin, Least Fang Kiiraathra'ostakjo waved away the datapad proffered by his human adjutant. "Ossian Wethermere, you may rest assured that the *selnarm* detected by Councilor Ankaht was *not* simply that of a lone Arduan operating with humans. Your caution and prudence in raising that possibility honors the name of your many-times cousin-uncle, Kevin Sanders, but your skepticism overreaches, this time. You know that Arduans do not operate as rogues; their actions are always aligned with the purposes of their community—whichever community that might happen to be.

"Secondly, *Celmithyr'theaanouw's* sensor suite was able to analyze the last spread of enemy laser fire. The signature—both its wavelength and intensity fluctuations—are unmistakable. They are distinctly those produced by the batteries of Amunsit's ships."

Jennifer, who was still hugging herself tightly even

though she'd spent a few reassuring moments chatting with Tank over the secure circuit, shook her head. "I don't understand: are Amunsit's weapons different from those of other Arduans?"

"They are slightly distinct, Jennifer," Ankaht confirmed. "Each subsequent Dispersate arrives with slightly altered technology. This model of hetlaser is somewhat more advanced than the ones which we brought with us from Ardu in the First Dispersate."

Jennifer looked from Ankaht to Kiiraathra'ostakjo and finally over to Wethermere. "So this laser didn't come from 'our' Arduans back in the Rim Federation, out near Bellerophon."

"No, Miss Pietchkov," said Kiiraathra'ostakjo with a slow smoothing of the whiskers on either side of his abbreviated and unusually flexible muzzle. "We encountered this more advanced Arduan hetlaser in the recent war. And since it is standard among the ships of the Second Dispersate, its only reasonable origin is from among the formations in the Zarzuela system."

"Meaning that, figuratively speaking, Amunsit's fingerprints—er, tendril-prints are all over it."

"I cannot think of another way to explain it, Jennifer," Ankaht offered in conclusion. "And with the *selnarmic* transmissions, that conjecture becomes nearly as certain as had we captured the gunboat itself."

Ossian, who was walking with his head tilted forward and hands behind his back, muttered, "All true. But we still have no explanation why Amunsit—or some of her lieutenants—are taking these actions. We know it's not something as simple as fostering a fifth column among the *Destoshaz* of the First Dispersate: they're more than a dozen warp points away from here. But that's almost all we know. Hell, why are they out in these old graveyard systems at all? And why are they killing almost all the specially-skilled humans they've recruited?"

Jennifer hugged herself closer, suppressed a shiver. "I just want to know how they got their tendrils on a warship. Yes, I know, it's a *small* warship—everyone's explained that to me enough times, now—but it's still a warship. How the hell does *that* happen?"

Kiiraathra'ostakjo made an apologetic rumble in his throat. "Ms. Pietchkov, as *Celmithyr'theaanouw* maneuvered to rendezvous with the *Woolly Impostor* after the engagement, my staff examined the PSU's integrated ship registry database. This includes supplements from the Rim Federation and the Terran Republic, which we exchange in the interest of coordinating security and law-enforcement activities. From the wreckage we have already been able to retrieve, we know that the ship which attacked Captain Wethermere and his crew was originally laid down as the *Shenboth* fifty-four years ago, was converted to a training vessel thirty-one years ago, was decommissioned twelve years ago and was remaindered into mothballs at that time. She was sold as a customs cutter to the planetary government of Overijssel four years ago. Only eighteen months later, all interest in the hull, including the outstanding bank lien, was bought out by what is clearly a legally fabricated holding company—what I believe your investigators call a 'shell company.' She was then transferred, along with other assets, as part of an exchange between that holding company and a sealed private trust."

"A sealed trust? What does that signify?" asked Ankaht.

"That the beneficiaries of the trust are not disclosed except to the administrators of the trust."

"Is that legal?" Jennifer asked with a sharp glance.

Ossian shrugged. "Well, if Kiiraathra'ostakjo's information is correct, Overijssel is a member of the Terran Republic. The Republic insists that all its member systems retain a great deal of local autonomy. That in turn means a lot of legal diversity within the Republic and, obversely, minimal universal codes." Ossian looked up as they passed the forward bulkhead. "Odds are if you need to make a shady deal legal, you'll find some planet in the Republic where it's permitted."

"And the crew of the prospector?" Jennifer asked. "Do you know anything about them, yet?"

Ossian shook his head. "No. Positive identification will take some time."

"But we should have those results before we get home to Bellerophon, right?"

Ossian glanced at Kiiraathra'ostakjo. "We would if the *Celmithyr'theaanouw*—and her labs—were traveling further with us. But she's not."

Ankaht looked from Ossian to the Orion. "Least Fang, I thought you would be working with us until we had concluded this phase of our investigation."

"Counsellor Ankaht, as much as I enjoy working with my old friend Captain Wethermere once again, I am unable to accompany you further. Your path back to Bellerophon would have me retracing the steps we have already taken. Regrettably, my path necessarily leads me onward."

"Where to?" Jennifer asked.

"Although it is atypical to share deployment information outside of the ranks, I believe your collective intelligence clearances allow me to inform you that *Celmithyr'theaanouw* is scheduled to put in a rotation at the Zarzuelan blockade before she is either upgraded or decommissioned. Her final disposal is yet to be determined."

Ankaht returned her three-eyed stare to Wethermere. "And you knew this?"

"Yes."

"And did not inform me?"

"You are not PSU naval, Ankaht. I couldn't: mandatory compartmentalization of strategic intelligence. But it won't make a great deal of difference. We'll pick up the smaller escorts waiting back in the inner system and take the evidence back to the labs and analytical teams on Bellerophon."

"Very well. Although I will confess that I have grown accustomed, and happy, to know that as we pushed forward, Least Fang Kiiraathra'ostakjo was our protector, waiting just out of sight but always ready."

Bowing was one of the human physical actions which had a close parallel in the Orions' impressive array of highly codified ritual gestures: Kiiraathra'ostakjo bent slowly at the waist as his haunches retracted, leaving him in a low jackknife profile, his tail inflected into a slight upward curve. "Councilor, your words do me much honor. It would be a pleasure to both continue the hunt with you, as well to continue instructing my friend in the finer points of my native language. Captain Wethermere is never quite so amusing as when he has been furnished with a few more phrases to mangle in the Tongue of Tongues." The Orion allowed himself a tooth-covered smile when he peripherally noticed Ossian's rolled eyes. "But Captain Wethermere is quite right. From the moment he invited me to travel with you, it was a surety that I must leave before your journeys were finished. Indeed, it was only possible for me to accompany you this far because your path of investigation closely followed the waypoints established for *Celmithyr'theaanouw's* passage to her new station. The captain was, according to explicit orders that originated far above either of us, not at liberty to share that information with anyone outside the command or field grade ranks. Nor was I."

Ossian noted that Ankaht, for whom other species' physical gestures were often more foreign than language, did not realize that the Least Fang would hold his posture of courtly compliment until she acknowledged his speech. "I'm sure Councilor Ankaht understands the constraints of your duty," Wethermere said, attempting to prompt an appropriate comment from his Arduan coinvestigator.

She may have even realized what Wethermere was trying to do: Ankaht seemed to start, and the voice from the vocoder seemed a bit rushed, "Yes, I do understand. Least Fang Kiiraathra'ostakjo, we shall miss both the might of *Celmithyr'theaanouw* and the wisdom of your counsel."

The Least Fang straightened, turned toward Ossian. "The repairs required by your ship are minor, my friend. We shall have them completed before the next watch."

Wethermere smiled crookedly. "I should have let the Arduans dent my hull a little more, force you to stay a few more days."

Kiiraathra'ostakjo brushed his whiskers slowly to hide a well-pleased grin. "You humans are entirely too—what is your word—maudlin? We lack such a word in the Tongue of Tongues, being warriors who possess no such defects of excessive sentimentality. Nontheless, I hope that our paths will cross again, Ossian Wethermere. Who else will see to—or could endure—teaching you the Tongue of Tongues?"

"I'll miss you, too," Wethermere said.

The Least Fang's felinoid eyes crinkled then widened. "And remain cautious in your journeys. This is strange prey you hunt. I think it is disposed to turn on its harriers, to ambush its ambushers. Since you do not know what you are pursuing, you cannot reliably predict its habits or its reactions. Be careful, Ossian Wethermere."

Who shrugged and grinned. "I'm always careful."

But Kiiraathra'ostakjo did not mirror the human's shift back to jocularity. "Yes, you are always careful. But now, be more so," he rumbled from deep in his throat. "I would see you again. Go now to put your ship in order. I am not, as you humans say, fond of good-byes."

The large-shouldered alien turned with swift, powerful grace and stalked aft, back through the forward bulkhead, already giving orders to his adjutants.

Ankaht ensured that her spine was erect but not tense as she and Wethermere resumed their progress into the bow of *Celmithyr'theaanouw* and passed through the final security hatches leading to the forward small craft bays. There, the pinnaces that had scooped up Alessandro Magee and the rest of his Bloodhound reconnaissance detachment were finally being secured into their fast-launch berths. The eyes of the human and Orion guards on the far side of the hatches prompted Ankaht to further groom her posture and demeanor to be as languid and nonthreatening as possible. All those eyes—whether the pupils were human and round or Orion and narrow—watched her with what their owners would no doubt have considered cool, businesslike attention. But to her Arduan sensibilities, so little accustomed to outward signification of inner emotions, those eyes seemed maniacally, ferociously intense. Had she not seen what such eyes looked like during actual combat, when Magee and Li and Jennifer and others had stormed into the very heart of the Arduan stronghold on Bellerophon, she would have found it hard to believe that there could be a greater physical expression of hostility than what she was seeing now. But having seen human eyes during close range combat, she knew to distinguish this lethally detached watchfulness from the barely controlled *beserkergang* of desperate soldiers.

It seemed improbable that Ossian Wethermere would notice the subtle changes she made to her posture, but then again, he was an uncommonly observant human. "This crew doesn't have a lot of contact with Arduans," he offered in a tone tinged by apology. "You're probably the first one that most of them have ever seen."

"I can appreciate the caution elicited by my strangeness—as well as by having their comrades attacked by members of my race, once again. And if Amunsit's direct reach has extended to these far systems, we may be on the cusp of events which will transform their suspicion into fear and ultimately, renewed hatred."

"Which is why we can't afford any mistakes. And

which is why, no matter what Kiiraathra says, it is damn near disastrous that I botched the encounter with that gunboat."

"Maybe not, Cap'n," added a new voice: Harry Li emerged from between the two blue-uniformed guards flanking the egress from the post-flight debriefing room. Jennifer, who had been moving steadily faster and further ahead, was already shouldering past Harry to get to Magee.

Wethermere smiled at the diminutive Li. "Good to see you, Lieutenant."

"Good to be seen. And to have some of our suits' biometric sensors see a known face among the crew of the prospector."

Ossian started. "You registered a tentative visual match?"

Lighthorse Harry Li nodded. "Several. Our suit-chips started flagging matches just a few minutes after we bailed out. Of course, we had no way to relay that intel to you: radio silence and insufficient range."

Ankaht let the lid of her central eye sink slightly, sluggishly. "It may not be wise to speak so openly of this, Lieutenant Li."

Harry looked from his Arduan superior to his human superior and back again. "Uh—why not? Ma'am?"

"Because, Lieutenant Li, the command staff aboard the *Celmithyr'theaanouw* is unaware of the advanced state of, and highly miniaturized biometric technologies available to, our investigation."

Li stared. "You mean—even the Least Fang himself isn't in the loop?"

It was Wethermere who answered, his eyes unblinking. "Yes. Even him."

"Damn," Harry muttered. "Why?"

"Compartmentalization: no one outside of our investigation may be informed of its particulars," Ankaht answered. Seeing the sour look that word elicited from Li, she added, "It is regrettable but necessary."

Wethermere smiled slightly. "Hmm. I seem to remember saying something similar to you about compartmentalization only five minutes ago."

Ankaht heard the vocoder infuse mild amusement into her reply. "Yes. Well. That is different."

"How so?"

"Because I was the one being excluded from the information within the compartment."

Wethermere's smile became broader. "Ah. I see."

"I suspect you do."

Li was almost scowling at the two of them. "Sir, ma'am, if you don't require anything further of me—" Li snapped one of his species' abrupt, almost startling salutes.

Wethermere returned a more relaxed version of the gesture. "Good job out there, Lieutenant. You are dismissed—right after you transfer the biometric data to my palmtop."

Li unclipped a data stick from the collar-liner of his duty coveralls and muttered a command at it. "Should be on your system, now, Captain." He snapped another fierce salute at Wethermere, nodded politely at Ankaht, and, turning on his heel, immediately started berating some of the Bloodhounds who had been slow to dress out and process to the debriefing rooms in the flight section.

As Wethermere produced his palm-sized computer and started bringing up the biometric data—visual records and a few genetic samples that had been gathered by Magee's Bloodhounds in the event that all other evidence was lost—Ankaht moved slightly behind him, peering around his arm to see what he did. At that close approach, she detected the characteristic, if faint, human musk. It was not an unpleasant odor: it evoked alien seas, but through that strangeness, it still carried the faint hint of common origins in briny waters. By comparison, the scent of Orions was thick and reminiscent of animal fats: their exclusively land-based evolution and predominantly carnivorous nature were clearly discernible even within the narrow range where Arduan olfactory sensitivity was greater than human. Humans had far better acuity detecting, and discriminating among, a far wider range of odors, but when it came to organics and esters, Arduans possessed a perversely sharp sense of smell.

Ankaht was almost surprised by Ossian's voice. "Does this data strike you as strange as it strikes me?"

She hurriedly scanned the information on the small screen. "The crew all had criminal records. Not typical prospectors or surveyors, then."

"Not typical at all. Not a single survey credential among them. But no true hardened criminals either—and not a single unidentifiable person among them: every one of the bodies that Li and his men actually got a sample from has a rock-solid identicode. None of the geneswap identicode forgeries we've found when investigating the black market types."

Ankaht felt the lids of her two smaller eyes drift upward slightly. "So this is a change in the operating profile of our adversaries. This group was recruited for a different purpose than the earlier ones. Which implies that we have touched upon a different branch of our opponents' operations."

"Yes, but what is this new branch up to? Look at this." Ossian poked one of his strangely segmented human fingers at the screen. "Half of these guys have records as accused or convicted claim jumpers or unlicensed salvage operators. They've all roved around a bit, but most are local to the border space between the PSU and the Rim Federation. Which is exactly where Amunsit has been putting this crew to work: look at the most recent places their identicodes have shown up."

Ankaht had already skimmed that information. "All systems on the chain of warp points that lead from Zephrain to Sol, but most of them here in Home Hive Three, Home Hive One, and Pesthouse. Which matches what we conjectured based on Ishmael's information. Yet there is nothing of value in any of these systems, except the naval base the PSU maintains at Pesthouse." She considered. "A base which sees very little traffic, and so is home to a number of secret testing and training facilities, if I am not mistaken. That might be of interest to Amunsit: the possibility of strategic intelligence to be derived from having a better idea of what is going on in that system."

Wethermere shrugged. "Yes, maybe. But of the three systems, it's the one in which they've spent the least time. It doesn't add up." The human frowned, called up the data on the "persons of interest" that had been gleaned from the extensive interrogations of Ishmael. Wethermere integrated the information they had on those persons' movements with the biometric trail that had been left by the various crewmembers of the ill-fated prospector ship. He and Ankaht saw the flashing green flags denoting significant overlaps at the same instant. "That's an awful lot of coincidence, don't you think?"

"As you say, coincidences such as these are a rare and endangered species. Too much to imagine that the *selnarmic* courier activities are not directly connected to the visits to these three systems." Ankaht studied the data more closely. "Interesting. The individual ships never comb these systems for very long. Although sometimes, the ships have exchanged crewmembers."

"And most of them are dead." Wethermere's finger ran down the column of red sigils attached to nearly all of the entries. "The rest are missing."

Ankaht counted the different ships that had been associated with these crews, noticed that they were all declared lost in transit, had been found abandoned and adrift, or confirmed as destroyed. "They employed eight different ships. And enough crew for half that many again. Visiting these three systems and a few others, always ostensibly en route to somewhere else, but always staying long enough to search for—what?"

Wethermere's frown had deepened. "The only two other systems they spend a long period of time in share something in common with the three worlds we've been focusing on."

"That they are systems in which you fought the Arachnids?"

"Yes, but a bit more than that, too. These weren't just worlds where we fought the Arachnids: these are worlds where the Arachnids lived, where they had hives and immense infrastructures." The human rubbed the bony protuberance that his species called a "chin." "Ankaht, is it possible that this is somehow connected with the original Arduan fascination with—and doubts about—our war with the Bugs? Could it be that Amunsit—or someone—is still trying to prove that the Bugs weren't real, trying to restimulate that as part of an anti-human propaganda campaign? That we aren't reliable allies or neighbors because we exaggerated the danger the Arachnids posed to ourselves, rationalized the extreme measures we took to ensure our survival? Might Amunsit be hoping to gather enough contrary evidence to drive a wedge between our peoples, to skew our growing relationship and cooperation?"

Ankaht made sure the vocoder emphasized her overwhelming sense of the dubiousness of such a scenario. "Perhaps, but given the evidence we had gathered even before our war with your race was concluded, it is an improbable errand. Amunsit is certainly aware that even a cursory examination of these systems bears out the essential accuracy of your accounts of that war. She would thus discourage such inquiries: zealots—Arduan or otherwise—do not go in search of contradictions to their own beliefs. Rather, they avoid potential contradictions and gravitate toward further confirmations of whatever it is they have decided is the truth. That is not what Amunsit's operatives would achieve by seeking for evidence in these places."

"Then what *is* she achieving?"

Ankaht turned toward her rather hideous but endearing human companion and mimicked—badly—a shrug. "I do not know, Ossian Wethermere. But I think we have enough information to make excellent use of the analytical devices and specialists back at Bellerophon—including my Arduan investigatory team." She reflected for a moment. "Indeed, particularly my team."

Wethermere turned off his palm-sized computer. "Why 'particularly' your team?"

"There is an additional piece of information, of data, that came out of this encounter, Ossian."

"You mean that the enemy missiles were *selnarm*-guided?"

"That is the piece of evidence most readily explainable to a human. What is more significant is the quality of the *selnarm* itself. It was—well, oddly withdrawn."

Wethermere's face contracted into what humans called a frown. "I'm not sure I know what you mean by that."

Ankaht rippled a consoling tendril in her colleague's direction. "Allow me to explain it this way: *selnarm* has many uses. We can use it for simple data transfer, for activating *selnarmic* control circuits, to merely signal our presence to each other. But we can also use it to impart our general emotional state, our shared *narmata* or speciate consciousness, our constant reflections upon how *shaxzhutok*—past lives—inform our present, and both our most superficial reactions and innermost thoughts. But the *selnarm* that was reaching out to those missiles"—she paused as she felt a pulse of fear, of having touched something monstrous, run through her before she could continue—"that *selnarm* was stunted. Almost like a slow-witted child's. Among us, a Firstling with little *selnarmic* ability is as close as our species comes to having what you call a mental retardate." She felt her tendrils coiling about each other and wrenching in worry and distress. "In our species, such deficiency in *selnarmic* connection is invariably connected with lower intellectual capacity—certainly too low to guide a missile and respond productively to both the routine and battle needs of a warship. But that was not the case here."

Wethermere's frown set more creases into his flexible face. "So, what does that mean, then?"

Ankaht shook the anxiety out of her tendrils. "It means that the Arduans controlling those missiles have fundamentally renounced the complexity—the richness and depth—of their *selnarmic* links, almost as if a human had removed their eyes so that they would develop more acute hearing. It is akin to an amputation. And that is a strange thing among my people."

"And it worries you."

"Yes, Ossian, it worries me. A great deal." *More than I can explain, just yet, my human friend.*

Because those are the requirements of the compartmentalization that I *must maintain, at the behest of my own Council of Twenty . . .*

CHAPTER TWELVE

It was the first time the investigatory team's alpha-clearance staff had all been together in one room since returning to Bellerophon. Ossian Wethermere stood, surveyed the faces, felt that the moment had a fateful quality to it.

The three Arduans—Ankaht, Mretlak, Lentsul—were as comparatively still as ever. Most humans would have probably characterized their demeanor as inscrutable, even vaguely threatening, but Ossian had long ago learned to watch for the subtle gestures and changes in skin tone that marked their emotional transitions. Ankaht and Lentsul were of the small and dark physiotype, Mretlak of the tall and golden variety. Of the three, only Lentsul's skin possessed the dull, lusterless quality that was the Arduan equivalent of sitting with one's arms folded.

The humans—Alessandro Magee, Harry Li, and Jennifer Pietchkov—were not remarkably animated, either. Hardly surprising. Although none of the senior command staff knew exactly what was coming, they all had a pretty good idea—and mixed feelings—about the expected announcement. *Well,* Ossian reasoned, *no reason to drag it out.*

Wethermere glanced at Ankaht beside him, then gestured at the hardcopy—hence, un-hackable—reports in front of each person. "We have finished the investigatory summaries. Most of which you're familiar with. All the results have been subjected to double-blind data cross-checks, meta-analyses, heuristic algorithm testing, and the result is the same every time. All the data we've gathered is one hundred percent consistent. And it is one hundred percent inconclusive in regards to indicating which one—if any—of the various enemy objectives we have extrapolated is the most likely cause of the covert activities we have discovered."

Harry Li, who had learned not be insouciant around Wethermere, raised a hand. "Sir, are you saying that the information we've been chasing is, in the final analysis, worthless?"

"Not at all, Harry. What I'm saying is that we're pretty sure we haven't misread any data, gotten fooled by disinformation, or generated any analytical artifacts of our own. The facts stand up to all the tests and crosschecks. But when we try to make them conform to some hypothetical operational outline, they don't line up. It's like having a bunch of points in a connect-the-dots picture—but so far, we're not seeing any shape. Just a cloud of random dots."

Ankaht's confirming nod was as stiff and unnatural as ever. "We have explored and expanded almost every scenario that you—and our analytical staffs—have proposed to us, every clandestine plot that would explain why the opposition force has conducted these operations, what their final objective might be. And, to use the particularly human phrase, we have come up empty-handed. The opposition's actions are interrelated—both in terms of operations and personnel—and demonstrate a number of strategic and paradigmatic similarities which all but prove that the same mind, or collection of minds, is behind all of them. But we do not know what information they have been passing, nor do we understand why they have been surveying and scouring old battlefields from the Bug War, or how the two might be connected."

Lentsul's skin seemed to become a bit more reflective. "Could it be an immense, and elaborate, counter-counterintelligence ploy?"

Jennifer goggled. "A what?"

Lentsul glanced at her. "An attempt to get us to reveal how our counterintelligence works, who drives it, its strengths and weaknesses."

Harry frowned, leaned forward. "And to what end would they pursue such information?"

Mretlak shrugged. "It would enable our adversaries to either avoid or eliminate our counterintelligence assets as a prelude to mounting an overt military operation. However, I doubt this is the motivation behind the activity we have seen."

Lentsul grew less reflective. "With respect, Senior Cluster Leader, I did not say I thought this alternative to be the likely answer, merely that it might possibly explain why we cannot identify an operational objective."

"I understand," returned Mretlak, "but that is the very reason I doubt this as the motivation for Amunsit's covert activities within our borders. The mere fact that we cannot match the enemy's actions to a clear underlying motivation would ultimately drive us to consider just what you have proposed, Lentsul: that it was all a goad to get us to reveal how we operate, and so, how to preemptively eliminate us. And so their actions would have been counterproductive, having alerted us to such an attempt. No, it would be much wiser for them to have set us an investigatory challenge connected to an actual, but minor, covert activity, one that we would have ultimately solved and thus paid no further heed. That would have been the most likely ploy they would have used to mount a serious counter-counterintelligence operation."

"And we considered that possibility at length, Lentsul," added Wethermere. "And we are indebted that you pointed it out. Frankly, it was the most plausible scenario suggested to us."

Lentsul straightened slightly but his skin seemed to grow more lustrous: he had clearly not been expecting such a compliment from a human, was both surprised and gratified—and trying to reveal neither.

"So," continued Wethermere, "we have only two choices: to abandon the investigation or to follow the only remaining leads we have."

Ankaht stood alongside him. "And clearly, we cannot abandon the investigation. Although the opposition's objectives become ever more mysterious, their fixity of purpose, their dedication to these operations, becomes correspondingly more obvious. Anything of such importance to them cannot be ignored. So we have no choice but to follow all the evidentiary paths back to the one thing they have in common: their point of origin."

Jennifer saw what was coming now: her eyes closed as if she had just witnessed a friend die.

"We must journey to Zarzuela itself," Ankaht finished, "or as close to its peripheries as we may venture."

Harry leaned far back in his chair. "Councilor Ankaht, isn't that rather—well, suicidal? And as I understand the situation, even more suicidal for you than it is for us?"

Ankaht's vocoder alto was unperturbed. "While I would not call it suicidal, Lieutenant Li, it is indeed an action with considerable risks. And yes, while Amunsit has agreed to a limited and careful exchange of envoys and affiliated personnel with the PSU, her attitude toward the survivors of the First Dispersate—and me in particular—is that we must be discarnated as traitors."

"So then just how do we—?"

"We're not sure of that ourselves, yet, Lieutenant," Wethermere broke in. "In large part because we are not cleared for receiving detailed information regarding the blockade protocols and contingents around Zarzuela. We have requested authorization for that access from Admiral Trevayne and expect that his approval will meet us at Zarzuela. At that time, we'll be able to learn what we need about how access to the Zarzuela system is granted, how we might be able to get in, which of us are permitted, and which are least at risk if we do so. Or maybe we'll determine that our primary task is to watch and assess who exits the system, who they talk to, where they go."

"Either way, we must discern and observe who or what Amunsit is using to orchestrate her operations outside of the Zarzuela system," supplied Ankaht. "I suspect we will need to conduct both investigations—inside the Zarzuela system and without—simultaneously."

"Agreed," said Wethermere. "We'll have a few more assets this time, but for the most part, it's going to be the same team, with all of us running the operation."

"Thereby minimizing the possibility of new internal security risks," appended Mretlak.

"Exactly," Wethermere agreed with a fast smile. He not only found Mretlak a skilled intelligence analyst but something of a kindred spirit: a person whom the war between humans and Arduans had thrust into unexpected and, in some regards, unwelcome prominence. "Our cover will be as new team of diplomatic and trade liaisons."

"Won't they have access to our actual identities already?" asked Jennifer glumly.

"Some of us, yes. It's a near certainty that Ankaht will not be able to enter Zarzuela or be openly associated with us in any way. Given the migration of the First Dispersate's *Destoshaz*-as-*sulhaji* from Bellerophon to Amunsit's camp, we must presume that Ankaht is well known to our opponents. As to the rest of us—well, that's one of the first things we're going to need to determine: what Amunsit's counterintelligence people know versus what they don't. They've only been free to send a few envoys out, so they've had to conduct most of their intelligence gathering through human or Orion proxies."

"Who have access to reams of data. Which will certainly mention you somewhere, Captain. Or even Tank, here." Harry Li's frown was one of genuine worry.

Wethermere nodded. "Yes, that might very well be the case. But then again, they can hardly be relaying *all* that data, Harry. And besides, having data is only half the problem: knowing the right questions to ask, the right people to research—that's the tricky part. Fortunately, the internal security review we completed last quarter is paying some pretty big dividends as we enter this new operational phase. We found no leaks, and no evidence that our off-the-books investigation has been detected. With any luck, my name has not been heavily associated with Ankaht's. Mretlak's association with her is more likely to have been known by *Destoshaz* émigrés —but then again, if the émigrés aren't thoroughly debriefed when they arrive in Zarzuela, it may be that the right information hasn't been gathered. So they might never have tweaked to the wartime cooperation between Ankaht and Mretlak."

'Sandro shifted, caught Wethermere's eye.

"You have a question, 'Sandro?"

"You mentioned an increase in assets?" the big man inquired with a slow smile.

Wethermere returned the smile: the career Marine's focus on nuts-and-bolts practicalities was always a refreshing break from the wheels-within-wheels intricacies of dueling counterintelligence gambits. "Yes. The *Woolly Impostor*'s weapons and sensor suite have been upgraded to full milspec. The cargo bay has been converted for fast deployment and recovery of two integral fighters. And we're adding to our running crew—mostly professional Navy, but a few folks with survey and prospecting credentials."

"Why them?" asked Tank.

"Well, first of all, the opposition force obviously perceives a need for those specialists in their own roster of operatives. Given that we're going to follow their path, I think we should have a few of our own, if for no other reason than to have an insider view of what they might be trying to achieve with those personnel. Secondly, we're potentially heading into *terra incognita*. The PSU has a lot of systems under its collective flags, and it's done a much better job charting warp-points than it has with space-normal astrophysical objects that are essentially low-value real-estate. There are lots of underutilized belts, rarely visited gas giants and moons. If our quarry—whoever that turns out to be—is habituating those out-of-the-way places, then it will be helpful to have some folks who are used to operating in precisely those environments."

"I think there's one other asset we could use, sir. And in as much quantity as available," commented Harry glumly.

"And what's that, Lieutenant?"

"Luck, sir—lots and lots of luck."

Wethermere couldn't help smiling, just as he couldn't help that smile from being rueful. "I concur, Lieutenant. Emphatically. But I'm afraid 'luck' isn't on any of my requisition lists. On the other hand, if you could initiate an effectual request based on your relationship with some deity—"

Harry shook his head profoundly. "My relationship with deity wouldn't get me off the hook for littering, sir."

Wethermere felt his smile widen. "Then I guess we're just going to have to make do with the luck we've got." Ossian looked at the gathered faces. "Any more questions, comments? No? Then we're done here. We ship out in seventy-two hours. And as we say in the Navy, make 'em count. Don't know when we'll be back this way again."

If ever, he added silently.

✧ ✧ ✧

Lentsul stared down into his bowl of poached Richthoffen Fish. It had started as an acquired taste, but it had grown on him over the past six years, as had many of Bellerophon's features. Having been born on one of the First Dispersate's immense generation ships, Lentsul had groused considerably about the many inconveniences and oddities of life on a planet. But over time, he had come to enjoy the feeling of sunlight on his still-wet skin after a long, gliding swim through the rolling whitecaps of Salamisene Bay, the smell of the plants that sent their pollen into the dew-wet dawn air, the change of seasons, and much of the local food. Many of his compatriots and birth-cluster-mates had expected him to be one of the many who could not (or would not) adapt to life on a planet: many of Illudor's Children were now, first and foremost, creatures of deep space, of the immense habitats that had held dozens of generations before them.

Much to his own and his peers' surprise, Lentsul was not of this number, but, instead, was one of the Arduans who heard and responded to the call of a natural biosphere. And who was now, therefore, loath to leave it. "I fail to see why I am needed on this journey," he sent as he half-hid behind the rim of his food bowl.

Mretlak did not look up, replied with a calm that implied that he had been expecting just such a question. "You must travel with us because you have invaluable knowledge about the details of our investigation, are intimately familiar with the many accountability checks each datum has received, and, above all, because you have the most skeptical mind among us. Where the rest of our group might relent in their suspicion, you will cling to it, and by that tenacity may well prevent us from racing over a precipice. You are coming because we need you, Lentsul, and because you are without peer."

"You are kind in your opinion of me," Lentsul sent back with, he hoped, a convincing overlay of modesty. "And given your profound gift for foresight, Senior Cluster Leader, you will thus anticipate my greatest skepticism in regards to this entire enterprise."

"The humans. Again." Mretlak let the air escape slowly from his vestigial gills.

"Yes. But not 'again'; *always*. And not all humans. Wethermere is different. He is--less savage."

"I think you mean he does not make his living preparing for close combat. And yet I hear he is not fearful of it. At all. And what of Jennifer Pietchkov? Is she, too, 'savage'?"

Lentsul rolled his sloping shoulders, let his arms and clusters roil slowly through the Arduan equivalent of a profound shrug. "She may not be savage, but she is subversive. Her words were what swayed the Council—and stayed my hand."

"And here we sit, in our new home, at peace. How were her words anything but a boon to us?"

"I certainly cannot debate that," Lentsul replied, while making sure to suppress his deepest, truest response: *I cannot debate it because she is* zheteksh*—a soulless, unreincarnative creature that makes intelligent noises. She may even be* intelligent, *I suppose—but still, she is not of Illudor, despite this strange pseudo*sel-narm *which she possesses. Her comparative mildness may have helped stop the war, but it is difficult to remember if that was because her words were wise, or because they inveigled us into rationalizing our* *acceptance of a surrender which allowed us to avoid certain annihilation. Did she save us Arduans—or did she calm us so that we may be contained in separate communities on far-flung worlds, divided so that we may not merely be conquered but, ultimately, exterminated?*

Mretlak looked up from his own meal. "And even though you cannot debate the value of Jennifer's intercession, you retain your doubts about humans?"

"Senior Cluster Leader, there shall only be a dozen or so of the children of Illudor traveling with the many humans of this expedition. And several of these humans are the same ones who killed so many of my security team six years ago. And have since investigated matters concerning our people. How is it just or wise to give them such power and autonomy over our people and our affairs without us securing a corresponding measure of authority over them?"

"Justice was not the determinative criterion in either the matter of staffing our investigation or in the matter of crewing and commanding the coming expedition. Indeed, it was not even a consideration. Rather, it was sheer pragmatism that guided our arrangement with the humans. Consider the investigational realities alone: at Metifilli and elsewhere, the humans were able to pass freely among their own kind, asking questions and observing conditions without attracting special notice. We Arduans could not have done so. We are still so rare outside our own enclaves as to immediately attract a great deal of attention."

Lentsul tried to ensure that his logical critique of Mretlak's assertions was not tinctured by his reluctance to lose an argument. "Even if that extremely one-sided investigational protocol was necessary, should it continue now? How can we know that the humans will not twist these incidents to their own political purposes? Indeed, by allowing the humans to dominate the planning and control of the investigation, is that not equivalent to—what is their own expression?—putting the fox in charge of the hen house?" Lentsul was dimly aware that foxes were cunning terrestrial predators and that chickens were among their favorite prey.

Mretlak had resumed eating, sent a wave of (calm) along with his response. "The humans could say the same of us, of course. When we commenced our investigation into the possibility of a fifth column of *Destoshaz*-as-*sulhaji* terrorists here in the Rim Federation, there were no humans involved in either the planning or the field work. We were given complete autonomy."

"Yes, so long as we reported all our findings to them."

"Just as they are bound to report all their findings to us."

Lentsul switched a tendril in annoyance. "As if we have any means to determine whether they conceal information from us."

Mretlak radiated (mild amusement, amity). "True. But again the truth runs both ways: humans have no way of knowing if we are hiding something from them within our *selnarmic* discourses—discourses which they cannot even detect." Mretlak finished his meal. "The imbalances between the human and Arduan components of this investigation have been nowhere near so extreme—or one-sided—as you seem to perceive, Lentsul. And in all cases, the necessary objective of building trust has intruded political considerations upon our investigational protocols." Mretlak set aside his bowl and utensils. "From the first, preference has had very little to do with the choices we have made; they have been driven by pragmatism, by the drive to achieve desired results."

"Well, whatever balance may have existed is gone now," Lentsul averred. "We three, along with the running crew and security staff of one ship, will be operating among dozens of humans. Some of whom were sworn to kill us only six years ago."

Mretlak wiped his mouth with the aid of his many tendrils, an action that humans reportedly saw as akin to pushing one's face into a writhing mass of striking asps. As he wiped those tendrils off, he sent. "Lentsul, with all our clues and leads now pointing directly to Zarzuela, who do you suspect stands more to lose from whatever ploy Amunsit has set in motion: us, or the humans?"

"Well . . . she will surely discarnate us as traitors to her vision of the will of Illudor."

"True. However, there are but a few million of us at risk and all blessed with the surety of reincarnation. Conversely, the human innocents number in the billions, none of whom have the hope of awakening into some later life if they are expunged from this one. So does it not make sense that the humans desperately need our help? I, for one, suspect we shall be among the safest persons aboard the *Woolly Impostor* and its new escorts, for we are the only irreplaceable crewmembers."

Lentsul poked at his soup again. "I suppose that is logical," he allowed. *But humans are not so much creatures of logic as they are creatures of passion,* he added well beneath the surface of his *selnarm*. *And no creature of passion becomes so unpredictable as when it becomes desperate. As the humans may become, if things go awry . . .*

Moments after swearing to herself that she would not do so, Jennifer waved goodbye one last time as the command car lifted on half fans. It swung away from the outskirts of Melantho's suburbs, aimed its nose toward the rolling green slopes among which they were nestled. "It's not right," she said through a knotty swallow that kept the tears to a minimum. She watched six-year old Zander dwindle beneath them, his godparents Roon Kelakos and Marina Cheung flanking him. "One of us should stay behind."

She heard Tank shift in the seat beside her, wondered why the hell she was poking at this oft-poked sore spot. Thankfully, his voice was gentle, almost a murmur, as he replied. "Orders, Jen. Nothing to be done about it."

It was wrong to push, she knew, but it was also wrong to maximize the chance that Zander would wind up an orphan. "You could have appealed the orders."

"No, Jen, I couldn't."

"Tank, that's crap. Ossian would have understood, he would have—"

"Jen, the orders didn't come from Ossian. He was just relaying them."

Jen started, turned to face her husband. He was staring ahead into the growing dusk cloudbank between them and the rest of their long flightpath from Melantho to Van Felsen Marine Aviation Base. His jaw was a stark line, the cheek muscles bunched up behind it in some muscular parody of mumps.

"So who cut your orders?"

"Admiral Yoshikuni. And Arduan Admiral Narrok, at the urging of Tefnut ha sheri."

"The *holodah-kri*? Since when do high priests start making military staffing requests?"

Tank sighed. "Since the high priest in question also serves as the oldest member of the Arduans' Council of Twenty. Who probably requested me personally since I didn't kill him when we cut through to the Council's sanctuary six years ago. I suspect Ankaht has been sending positive reports to the Council, too. No way to dodge this assignment, Jen. I'm not a civilian."

"Okay, Tank. Tie . . . and truce. You know I have to go."

"I know that Ankaht thinks you have to."

"And do you doubt her?"

Tank's jawline was obscured by a rippling play among the tense muscles there. "No," he admitted. "None of the other human sensitives even come close to your abilities, Jen."

Which had, until now, been a source of quiet pride for Jennifer Pietchkov. And which had now transmogrified into a parent's nightmare. Ankaht had anticipated Jennifer's reluctance to accompany the expanded investigatory detachment. That's why her Arduan friend had taken the step of showing her the latest results from the ongoing efforts to pair other humans who possessed *pseudoselnarm* with *shaxzhu*-caste Arduans. After years of work in some cases, they had barely made progress equal to that which Ankaht and Jennifer had made in their first four months of contact. It was simply not enough to help an Arduan navigate the interspecies communication barriers and understand human behavioral subtleties, as would become increasingly necessary when the investigation moved further and further into regions of space where Arduans were known only by reputation and report. And as had been proven in the extensive debriefing of Ishmael, the process of gaining information from an unwilling human subject and making all its nuances clear to an Arduan investigator would be hopelessly crippled if the translator was anyone other than Jennifer. Of course, the reverse was also true: if the investigation came into direct contact with Amunsit's Arduans, then Ankaht needed Jennifer as her translational conduit back to the other humans, whether to help them interrogate or anticipate the actions of the *Destoshaz*-as-*sulhaji* of the Second Dispersate.

"Don't worry, Jen." Tank's voice was a murmur again. "Roon and Marina are the best; they'll take care of Zander like one of their own."

"I know," she murmured back. "He'll be fine with them. Just like one long vacation."

They glanced at each other, smiled, stared back at the darkening horizon.

Jen felt the smile slide swiftly off her face, peripherally saw the same happen to 'Sandro's equally forced expression. Yes, Roon and Marina were the best. And that just didn't matter a damn, not to her, and probably not to Tank. Zander was their only child, their beaming bright-eyed boy, and nothing would or could undo the wrongness of their leaving him behind, for whatever reason. Or make it feel any less miserable.

Silent, they swept onward toward the approaching thunderheads on the horizon.

✧ ✧ ✧

At Ankaht's faintest *selnarmic* gesture, Temret, her guard captain and sometimes-confidante, drifted away as she walked through the arbor that was the entrance into the inner garden. As Temret's young, vigorous, but somewhat monotone *selnarmic* echoes died away, a new pulse grew from in front of her. It was ancient, filled with the whorls and knots and textures that came from both a long personal lifetime and much journeying along others via the recollective pathways of *shaxzhutok*.

As Ankaht emerged into the center of the concentrically arranged hedges and beds of the garden, the source of that wondrously complex *selnarm* turned to greet her: Tefnut ha sheri.

"Eldest Councilor," she sent, along with (warmth, joy).

"My colleague and race-daughter," he replied with (pride, delight). They brushed tendrils lightly and then, without any communication other than the shared habits of movement that allowed each to anticipate the intents of the other, they commenced a slow circumnavigation of the innermost hedge.

They had almost completed their first half circuit before Tefnut ha sheri sent (wry, mischievous), "You have not taken such melodramatic precautions to ensure our privacy since the last days of the war, Ankaht. Has my request made such waves among the human commanders that you must report the results in secret?"

Ankaht reached out a *selnarmic* tendril that asked (patience, absolution): "Revered *holodah-kri* and model of my best behaviors, I must tell you that, after much reflection, I elected not to pass your request on to Captain Wethermere and the higher human command staff."

Ankaht felt a brief pulse of genuine disappointment

emanate from the old Arduan, but then Tefnut's waggish ebullience returned. "Ah. So you didn't want to be carrying a weathered tough-hide like myself along on your adventures. Well, I'm sure there's wisdom in that, too. Youth does not want to be slowed by the infirm—no, let us call it 'measured'—gait of its elders."

"Tefnut, I am of middle age, myself."

"Which to *me* is still callow youth," retorted the member of the First Dispersate who had lived the most years—but who had not been born on Ardu itself, as Sleepers such as Ankaht had. "But the seriousness of your *selnarm* tells me that this was a difficult decision for you, one fraught with many contending considerations. Come, my near-Firstling; what troubled you in reaching this decision?"

Ankaht struggled for a moment: *where to begin?* "Revered Tefnut, the situation among our people is too sensitive for them to be without you at this juncture."

"You mean without *both* of us, Ankaht. But proceed."

"You flatter me outrageously, *holodah'kri*. But if it is true that our people look to us first for leadership, then it is true enough that both of us should not be risked on any single venture. And there is no doubting who, in a choice between us, must stay and who must go. Your *selnarm* is closest to Illudor's own, your voice most informed by the very *shotan* of our harmony, our *narmata*. And so, in this time of both political and theological turmoil, you must be our peoples' strong spine and anchor."

Air escaped from Tefnut's vestigial gills like air wheezing out of a wine-skin. "Six years ago I was ready to discarnate. And still you are not done with me. You are a cruel taskmaster, Ankaht."

She gently set aside the jocular tone. "I am not done with you because fate is not done with you, revered *holodah'kri*. We have no choice but to contend with profound challenges in every sphere of our existence. And upon the matter of your continuing presence among us: have the new antigerone treatments proved efficacious yet?"

Tefnut swept a few impatient tendrils at the sky. "Bah. Who can tell? When you creak and wheeze as much as I do, it is hard to discern any small reductions in those sounds of decrepitude. And who knows if the humans have deciphered our genetics as accurately as they claim they have? But they try. They do try. Alas, they do not understand—or rather, they seem unable to remember—that in extending my life, they prolong the misery of living in this old, desiccated husk of a body."

"Dear Tefnut, we must trouble you to do so a while longer, yet."

"I know, Ankaht. I am simply complaining. Grousing, as the humans say. I am old, so it is my right."

"Of which none shall deprive you, Tefnut. Now tell me, what word from Megarea?"

Tefnut ha sheri paused in his slow pacing. "Ah. Now I see why we are walking in the garden again after all these years. Secrets to tell and be told."

"Yes, Tefnut. I had to be sure our conversation could not be overheard, and no enclosed space is safe. Nor any too close to a city."

"Yes, of course. Now, then: Megarea. The artificial fertilization projects have decanted their first Quickened Firstlings. It is as we hoped, and dared to expect: there is a demographic shift in the characteristics that predict later Casteing. There has been an aggregate eight percent increase in those likely to become *selnarshaz*, a four percent increase in probable *shaxzhu*. But I repeat, this is only probability. It will be at least two years before these Firstlings will be Casted. However, this, too, is promising: there has been a marked shift to the *ibzhur* physiotype."

Ankaht sent a pulse of (relief, affinity), the latter since both she and Tefnut were of that small dark Arduan variety known as the *ibzhur*. "So, that almost certainly predicts an increase in *Ixturshaz*, *selnarshaz* and *shaxzhu*." For the *ibzhur* physiotype was far more associated with those castes than was the *yedvree*, or tall-golden, physiotype.

"Yes, and so we may hope for a corresponding decrease in *Destoshaz*. But I am concerned."

"That the trend will not continue?"

"No. I am concerned that the humans will discover what we are doing and fear that we are breeding an army of fast-grown clones for war against them, rather than forcing a demographic shift among our own people."

"Yes, although our own people would be more distressed by the latter."

Tefnut's gait became slower and his send was (tired, melancholy, worried). "Too many secrets. The lesson of this one life, and all before, is that secrets are treacherous creations. It is as though they keep trying to make themselves more discoverable."

"It is true, but we have little choice. If our conjectures are correct, we must return our caste proportions to what they were before the Dispersates commenced. We must have fewer *Destoshaz* and more castes whose *selnarm* is more focused on the maintenance of *narmata* and the edification of *shaxzhutok*."

Tefnut sent (waggish amusement). "Of course, the priest in me cannot help but wonder: is the current demography of our race not an expression of Illudor's will? But if it is, then why would He allow us to effect these demographic shifts? Would not Illudor's present manifestation not frustrate or preclude our attempts to alter what he presently is?"

"Alter Illudor by changing our demographics? How could this be?"

"How could it not, near-Firstling? Let us think through the theological ramifications. If we can influence the proportions among the castes, then are we not shaping the consciousness of Illudor Himself—or at least the lenses through which he experiences the universe and then communicates that back to us through the *narmata* which is the medium that joins us, and the *shaxzhutok* that connects us to the collective archive of our experience?"

Now it was Ankaht's turn to slow her walking pace. "This is a keen, but troubling, insight, *holodah'kri*. Because as you say, the constituent parts of our species, and the mix of their respective aptitudes, should directly reflect Illudor's Will and all the particulars of his manifestation at this time. So are we then the agents of His Will? Or—" She paused before the alternative, stunned that it was the high priest, the *holodah'kri*—who had brought her to the edge of what loomed like a cosmological precipice.

Tefnut's *selnarm* was oddly tranquil. "Or is the entity we call Illudor not divine in the sense we have maintained He was? Yes, Ankaht, we must look at this possibility with all three eyes if we are to see it clearly and fairly. If our present actions are not explicitly the Will of Illudor, then it might be rightly said that we possess the power to recast the nature of Illudor, at least in some small measure. And that, in turn, is potentially yet another argument in support of the growing proposal that Illudor is not divine, but rather, a macroentity."

Ankaht felt suddenly cold on this summer's day. "I have read that there is new research on this, arising from discoveries made while genetically altering the proto-*selnarmic* entities that we have used in triggering devices."

Tefnut signaled (confirmation). "Yes. It is humbling, if not terrifying, to consider the possible parallels between ourselves and the simplest organisms that possess *selnarm* only so that they may work collectively without any direct physical connection. It seems to invite us to ask: are we like that ourselves, only more sophisticated? Are we a huge entity that is neither physically nor spiritually unitary, but rather, is comprised of an overarching subconscious whose processes are carried out by us, much as a computer network can share tasks by distributed processing?"

"You mean, our many minds function like a myriad of networked, but ultimately separate and otherwise unintegrated, computers? Then how is it that we remember the past, that we—?"

Tefnut's tendrils waved soothingly. "Ankaht, we may not answer all the questions at once. In the case of questions so esoteric and tenebrous as these, we may not ever have answers at all. These speculations cannot be called 'information,' yet, for they are only theory—and for now, and perhaps forever, may not be amenable to substantiation. Moreover, as a *holodah'kri*, one must ponder one's duties to such a theologically provocative concept, which naturally leads me to contemplate 'what is to be done with it?'"

Ankaht rolled out a *selnarmic* flow of (protection, negation). "For now, we do nothing with it, revered *holodah'kri*. The distress within our people is great enough over the split with so many of the *Destoshaz*. Will they weather this, too? In the past, the reassurance to them—and to ourselves—would have been, 'with Illudor's help.' But now—"

Tefnut's answering *selnarm* was of (rue, melancholy). "Yes: now, the very topic is whether or not that help exists. It is difficult to know how to proceed, when to ask the very question gives rise to the problem we fear."

Ankaht signaled assent, but, beneath it added, *it is but one of the problems we should fear, old friend. And I am not sure it is the worst.*

Not sure at all.

CHAPTER THIRTEEN

Ossian Wethermere resisted the urge to lean forward and rest his chin in his cupped palm: not the proper command image. A captain had to be—and appear—ready to act at a moment's notice. The ennui that affected mere enlisted mortals was, presumably, alien to officers, and so, had to be utterly absent from their demeanor. Even when they were bored beyond human endurance.

For almost two weeks, his small expedition had been parked in a distant, deep-space holding zone of the Amadeus system, well off the beaten trail to (and half of the heliopause away from) the warp point that connected it with Zarzuela. They were equally far away from any planetary orbits. So, the highlight of their week had become the arrival of the provisions shuttle from the 92nd Reserve fleet, a blended force of smaller, older Orion and human craft that had been tasked with rear area security and logistical support for the other three line fleets in system and any craft in transit to or from Zarzuela itself.

And, as reportedly happened frequently, permission for those transits had been stalled for weeks now, immobilizing the *Woolly Impostor* and its two new companion craft. The larger of the two was the *Fet'merah*, an Arduan bulk-hauler of nearly ancient registry, now converted into a carrier for up to a dozen fighters or small craft and furnished with sizable missile bays. The other was the *Viggen*, a PSU-built customs patrol corvette that was considerably smaller than Ossian's Q-ship (even in terms of its armament), but had been built to be one of the fastest ships in space. Capable of a blistering 0.135 cee, it was, to Wethermere's mind, the equivalent of an old-fashioned getaway car.

But he and his small flotilla were going nowhere fast. Immediately after arriving in system from the modestly trafficked warp point to M'vaarmv't, the glum prospect of an interminable delay grew from "likely" to "assured." Rather than the perfunctory transponder and identity check which was the typical arrival ritual, *Woolly Impostor* and its companions had been shunted into a processing box in deep space. That zone was already populated by enough ships to make designated anchorages necessary. Sam Lubell, Wethermere's go-to helmsman for six years now, voiced the opinion that he couldn't recall seeing such crowded space outside of a planetary orbit. "What about you, Captain?" he asked.

Wethermere's reply ran athwart that of the Q-ship's other captain: its new skipper, Commander O. A. Knight. Ossian's curt "No" vied with Knight's drawled, "Maybe."

The two men glanced at each other, Knight nodding deference to Wethermere, who was the ship's master and the mission's de facto commander. Ossian smiled. "I don't have anything to add to my 'no,' Skipper. But it sounds like you might have a story to tell."

O. A. Knight, a typically laconic man, could be coaxed out of his extended silences by the possibility of recounting one of his spaceman's tales. As were the best of such narratives, they were typically amalgams of outrageous but verifiable fact and tall tales that made the life of Paul Bunyan sound like a dry, academic biography.

Knight rubbed his chin, nodded his appreciation to Wethermere. *Probably more for my calling him "Skipper" than anything else.* Except for those bridge crew who had served on board an admiral's flagship, the notion of not having the senior officer manning the con and giving the orders was not merely strange but contradictory. It was certainly unusual at the level of a three-ship detachment, where the burdens of commanding the unit were not so onerous that they materially interfered with commanding one's own ship.

But Knight's dossier, which had come across Wethermere's desk when he was selecting crew for this unusual mission, had called dramatic and immediate attention to itself. A commander, Knight was ten years older than Wethermere and overdue for promotion. He'd seen action in the war against the Arduans, but it was mostly the kind of small, peripheral engagements that just didn't grab the attention of the top brass or the imagination of the politicos who consistently exerted downward pressure on the size of the field officer corps (but seemed to conceive of a limitless need for staff officers). Ironically, Knight had been in some very tight spots, far away from the reassuring proximity of a fleet. Commerce raiding in Ajax, working as a decoy to flush out Arduan lurkers in Aphrodite, scouting for orbital defenses in numerous systems on the final drive to Bellerophon: O. A. Knight had steered three hulls (two were shot out from under him) through some harrowing engagements, but never in a big fleet-to-fleet clash.

Furthermore, the commander was an inherently unassuming and terse man, so the politicking that career officers often used to overcome a lack of fleet-level combat ribbons was not among his assets. But that same demeanor was the source of his rocklike solidity and natural authority on the bridge. He was the Old Man (the monklike tonsure that remained of his hair was prematurely gray) who spoke little, missed nothing, and never flinched. And you could tell that about him the first ten minutes you sat on his bridge.

Wethermere had been able to tell it just by glancing at his service record, and knew, with the lack of ego that came from not really seeing himself as career Navy, that here was a man who was infinitely more qualified than he was to be at the helm of a Q-ship on an unpredictable snoop and poop. Wethermere's crew would have opined otherwise—and they'd been with Ossian long enough to hold firm opinions on the matter—but Wethermere conceived that it would be very handy indeed to have one command-brain running the ship, while another one remained focused upon the whole detachment and how its actions impacted the Bigger Picture of their mission. And so he had taken the unusual step of making Knight the ship's captain, which caused a further "courtesy brevet" confusion: whereas Wethermere was a genuine or "post" captain,

Knight held that title merely by virtue of being the ship's commanding officer. For those crewpersons who had served aboard a fleet flagship, this was only slightly disorienting; for the others, it took more than a little getting used to.

Lubell was staring at Knight. "So, Captain Knight, you've been someplace where the traffic was this heavy?"

Knight squinted at the monitors, then at the dense cloud of green motes in the holoplot. "Six years ago, I was commanding a flank security detachment at Polo."

Wethermere, remembering the details of Knight's dossier, had wondered if this might have been what he was going to recount. Lubell blanched, Zhou's usually expressive face set in lines.

"I watched those ships—ships several of you were in—line up to transit the warp point. What you were probably too busy to notice were the clouds of ships behind you. Literally clouds of them. Looked like a nebula of steel filings, from the flank. And the support craft stretched all the way out to us." He nodded at Zhou and Lubell. "We all wanted to be in the van of the attack that day. We all knew that was the battle in which we might finally break the Baldies'—er, the Arduans' backs. But then we learned what had happened to all of you." He shook his head slightly. "Those of us who were not in the first wave still don't have the gall to say that we were at the Battle of BR-02."

"That would mean there are damned few of us left who can make that claim, Skipper."

"That's true, Mr. Zhou. And that's just as it should be: no one has the right to speak for, or take the place of, fallen heroes."

In the faint nods that passed between Knight and his veteran bridge crew, Wethermere saw an acknowledgment that was also the beginning of a bond founded not merely upon rank and duty, but shared experience—even if Knight had only been there to see the aftermath of the horror, rather than live it himself. Wethermere felt a great sense of relief, of gratitude, of certainty that the new skipper and Ossian's hand-picked crew were going to fit together just fine—

"Skipper, fleet elements are starting to shift to—I don't get it, sir."

Ossian, from a chair just behind Knight's right shoulder, looked into the holoplot. The larger triangles that denoted stable formations of ships or whole flights of fighters started fragmenting into individual blips. "Anything on the comms?"

Communications Officer Schendler shrugged. "Maybe, Captain. There sure is a lot of activity all over the bandwidth. But we're not in that command loop, so we can't hear what they're saying."

Wethermere glanced sideways at Knight. "Looks like they're scattering."

"It does indeed," was the commander's reply. "No pattern to it, though."

"Yes, almost as if—"

"Sirs," interrupted Engan from her post at the sensor controls, "take a look at this." She put an expanded, system-wide plot on one of the main 2-D screens. It was not only the ships of the 92nd Reserve that were simultaneously bomb-shelling in every direction and undertaking evasive maneuvers. Even the three standing line fleets in the system—the 9th, the 23rd, and the 3rd Auxiliary—were breaking out of the various defensive postures from which they not only guarded the warp-point into Zarzuela, but patrolled Amadeus' other two warp points, those that led back to the logistical bases and reinforcements in Barricade and M'vaarmv't. Only the immense forts arrayed in a rough hemisphere around the access path to the Zarzuela warp point were not moving—because they couldn't. Those immense constructs of composites, steel, and advanced armors were too massive to move except over weeks or months of constant, low-level thrust.

"Any change in the Zarzuela warp point?" Knight asked.

"All normal, sir," confirmed Engan. "No fluctuations indicative of either egress or ingress in progress."

Wethermere leaned back in his chair. "Then why the hell are our fleets swarming like a bunch of bees from a kicked hive? Schendler, raise Admiral Maoud of the 9th. And don't take any guff from his commo staff. I need to find out—"

"Sirs," Schendler interrupted tensely, "OpComm of the 92nd Reserve has just broadcast a general navigational warning to all ships in the system, along with evasion directives."

Knight's diction was suddenly clipped, hard-edged. "Lubell, patch those recommendations through to the plot. Lay in a course that will center us between the warp points back to Barricade and M'vaarmv't."

"Skipper," Schendler said cautiously, "that's not what the current directives indi—"

"Mr. Schendler, those directives are for civvies who won't know what to do if a hammer comes down. I do. Mr. Lubell, lay in that course; I want to have as many withdrawal options as possible, so I want to be able to reach either warp point." He turned to Wethermere. "Anything to add, sir?"

Wethermere thought, then nodded. "Mr. Lubell, come alongside the *Fet'merah* as we go. We're going to tuck inside her."

Sam Lubell blinked. "Sir, there isn't enough room."

"There will be. Mr. Schendler, raise the *Fet'merah*. I need her to release three of her fighters. They are to enter our bay, then we enter hers."

"Yes, sir."

Knight's brow was furrowed, more in perplexity than concern. "Captain, so I can know what you're planning—what gives?"

"Commander, right now, the *Fet'merah* is running a Rim Federation transponder. But what if the source of all the commotion is an Arduan threat, and we are overrun? In that scenario, if we turned the transponder off—"

Knight nodded, came as close as he ever did to smiling. "Sure. Then the OpFor's scans will just read it as an Arduan hull. At longer range, that gives us a chance to blend in or scoot later on. Of course, the *Viggen* is still out of luck."

"True, but she's got the best legs of any of us. If one of our ships is going to be able to run fast and far enough to elude pursuit, then get beyond detection range, and ultimately make herself small enough to hide on a splinter of cometary junk or asteroid, *Viggen*'s the one."

"Got it."

Schendler turned to the dual con. "Captain Wethermere, *Fet'merah* has acknowledged and is deploying fighters as instructed."

"Very good. Ready our bay to receive them—smartly, now."

"Yes, sir. And sir, Councilor Ankaht wishes to speak to you."

"Patch her through."

"Aye, sir. Link is active."

Ankaht's usually smooth alto was thready with an edge of excitement. "Ossian, I believe we have just now had a breakthrough in discovering the concealed data that the *selnarmic* couriers were carrying."

Now? "Ankaht, that is excellent news, but I think we're going to have to wait to—"

"Captains, bogeys—a wave of them!"

Wethermere stared and saw that Engan had not exaggerated. Coming up from "beneath" the ecliptic and between the placement of the Zarzuela and Barricade warp points on the clock-face of the larger plot were a blizzard of small but incredibly swift bogeys.

"Any comm chatter on whose ships those are? Or how they appeared so suddenly?" demanded Knight. Then he paused, his eyes narrowing. "How the hell are we getting those sensor returns, anyhow? The far edge of that plot is better than fifteen light-minutes from here."

Wethermere muttered. "Arduans."

"What?" chorused several crewpersons, most of whom added, "Sir?" after the first stunned moment.

"As part of a broader test program, the Rim Federation recruited a number of Arduans to man key sensor and comm relay positions within its line fleets, particularly in potentially hot salients. Using their *selnarm* as a transfer medium, we can now get an almost instantaneous snapshot of sensor readings in any part of a system where they are operating."

Knight nodded—a bit sourly, Wethermere thought. "And that, too, is probably need-to-know info. More compartmentalization."

Wethermere only shrugged. "I'm afraid so. Commander, see if you can confirm whether those are ships or not."

Knight's left eyebrow elevated slightly, but he half turned to call over his shoulder, "Lieutenant Engan, you heard the captain: whistle up a confirmation that those bogeys are ships. Get type and class, if you can." He turned back to Wethermere, his voice lowered. "What are you thinking, Captain?"

Wethermere gestured toward the holoplot with his nose. "Look at their vectors. All straight as a ruler, no sign of velocity change in any of them. And nothing but deep space behind them."

"Well, it's possible that there's a warp point somewhere in the outer system that no one's charted."

Wethermere shook his head. "Not in Amadeus. Or any of the other systems that maintain the blockade on Zarzuela. There aren't many systems which have been as extensively surveyed as these have been, over the last six years. Fleet HQ was insistent on eliminating any possibility that some undiscovered warp point might open up, let a horde of hostiles into our blockade formations through a surprise backdoor."

"Then what—?"

"Captains," Engan said in a puzzled tone, "even though we're reading sensor feeds through the *selnarm* link being tapped by the Arduans on the *Fet'merah*, I cannot get confirmation on type or class or whether the bogeys are even ships. Only velocity confirmation: all bogeys are moving between 0.65 and 0.66 cee."

"Are you getting mass estimates?"

"Not from the fleets, Captain Wethermere, but there's been some open broadcast chatter from the holding tank of nonmilitary hulls over near the Barricade warp point. Some of the auxiliaries there are reporting objects massing less than ten metric tons. There's speculation of objects smaller than that."

Wethermere nodded. "Meaning that a lot of these bogeys are much smaller than any ship capable of mounting a Desai drive."

Knight's eyes opened wide. "So, they can't be using a space-warping engine to achieve that speed. That's their space-normal velocity. And the last people who demonstrated that kind of real-space velocity were the Arduans. Which means that this is an attack."

"Yes," muttered Wethermere, "but not the kind you mean. Those bogeys aren't ships; they're chunks of debris. That's why they're not maneuvering. That's why no one is detecting any drive fields in operation."

"But how—?"

"Commander, the 'how'—and more importantly, the 'why'—of this situation is something we can wonder about later. Assuming we survive."

Knight looked at the rapidly approaching wave of bogeys: there was now a dim yellowish cloud moving with them. "There's the confirmation of your scenario, Captain: a navigational hazard field moving right along with the main debris. The flotsam and jetsam. All of which, no matter how small, is still absolutely lethal at those velocities." He squinted at the approaching cloud, then at the readouts. "I'd say we have about eight minutes before it grazes past us. But it's going to pass very close to the Zarzuela warp point first."

"Of course it is," Wethermere said quietly. "That's its aimpoint, more or less."

"It's aimpoint? You mean—the forts?"

"Exactly." Wethermere looked up. "Schendler, have we got those fighters on board from the *Fet'merah*, yet?"

"Just now, sir."

"Then make best speed for her, and tell Cluster Leader Temret we're coming into his main bay pretty hot." He turned to Knight. "No reason to waste time out here, eh?"

Knight agreed. "As you say, sir. Are we heading back into M'vaarmv't, then?"

Wethermere looked at the holoplot, at the approaching yellow haze and the uncountable red signatures of larger debris within it. "Yes, Skipper. M'vaarmv't. If we make it in time."

By the time they reached the warp point into M'vaarmv't several minutes later, the confusion in the Amadeus system had spun up into outright chaos. Attempts to coordinate action among the civilian craft that supplied and supported the blockade had utterly broken down: the plot was filled with neutral bogeys fleeing out of the path of the approaching debris cloud the way starlings fly before a storm. The 9th Fleet was moving up out of the ecliptic to avoid the onslaught of the sub-relativistic junk, but not without apparent protests and hot debates: the coded channels used by that fleet were punctuated by swift back-and-forth exchanges that were completely unlike the sharp, curt transmissions that were characteristic of orders being given, confirmed as received, or clarified.

And the cause of the implicit rolling debate was obvious: left to their own devices, the forts blocking the egress from the Zarzuela warp point were expending their considerable firepower to blast lanes through the oncoming debris. With help, they might have been able to clear an even wider cone. But even as the individual red bogeys—objects large enough for the sensors to tentatively identify as ship-sized objects—were ground away by the relentless firepower housed in those titanic composites of armor and weaponry, the yellow haze kept approaching. Following tactics that Wethermere himself had innovated at the Battle of BR-02, the forts next unleashed a steady stream of antimatter missiles in an attempt to vaporize the smaller detritus, which had been unavoidably increased by the destruction of the larger objects which had been on collision courses. The strategy was to sweep a pristine lane through the debris, so that the oncoming cloud would pass around the various forts, there being nothing left along the actual vectors approaching them.

But the strategy which had worked so well at BR-02 was far less optimal here at the gateway to Zarzuela. The debris was not only more dense, and was being constantly and unavoidably repropagated by the fragments resulting from the destruction of the larger chunks, but its speed was so great that targeting was severely degraded. Furthermore, even when hits were scored, the amount of time that the destructive energies from the forts were actually in contact with their targets was an infinitesimally small fraction of a second. The overall effect—the "maximum thermal coupling" imparted by each fort's batteries—was so brief that the destructive energies often failed to finish the job, reducing the oncoming debris rather than vaporizing it.

"Trouble up ahead, sirs." Engan's voice was tense. "Congestion at the M'vaarmv't warp point."

"Civvies on the run?" Knight inquired.

"No, sir. The 92nd Reserve is pulling out in echelon. Civvie craft are starting to collect around the edges."

Knight's voice was almost as much of a growl as Kiiraathra'ostakjo's. "And it's going to get a lot worse. Look at the plot, sir." In the wake of the two blips that marked the *Fet'merah* and the *Viggen*, a constellation of similar-sized purple pinpricks were coalescing into a dense cluster, moving at various speeds and approaching from various vectors but all collapsing on the same point in space: the M'vaarmv't warp point. "They got the idea a little after we did, but they're making up for lost time."

"I don't know if that's going to matter much," Schendler reported from his station. "I'm getting a general broadcast again, this time warning off all civilian craft. It doesn't look like the fleet is going to let any civvies through until they've finished pulling out."

Knight nodded, looking at the long van of the 92nd Reserve. "They don't have the time to share the warp point. Passage is one ship at a time, with a minimum safe transit interval of about three seconds, given possible velocity changes and last minute nav corrections."

Lubell squinted at his readouts. "They're well off that performance standard, sir. Average interval is almost seven seconds."

"That's pretty typical, Lieutenant. It's a reserve fleet. Partly, they're out here to keep their edge, to run the drills which will improve their performance.

According to deployment reports, they've been on station less than a month. Too early to expect much better of crews that haven't trained and fought together recently—if at all."

In the plot, one of the icons denoting a fort flared yellow and turned into an omega symbol: lost, probably with all hands. The bridge was suddenly silent.

"Any indication or report of what hit it?" Wethermere asked.

"No, sir," Schendler answered quietly. "There's a lot of panicked chatter in the clear about it. Nothing big, that's for sure. Probably something less than a kilogram in mass."

"They don't have the right sensor arrays to see or target this junk," Knight muttered. "With barely enough motive power for long-term repositioning and station-keeping, forts don't need sensors for detecting bottle-sized navigational hazards at long range."

"Or it could have been a handful of nuts and bolts, all hitting within a five-second interval," commented Wethermere. "Same effect, and they'd never see it coming."

Another fort flared yellow, seemed to list in the holoplot.

"I have live-feed," Engan almost whispered.

Wethermere considered: should he show the crew scenes of irresistible doom, or keep it hidden—and thereby double their fear by allowing their imaginations to run wild? That choice was no choice. "On secondary screen, please, Ms. Engan."

The screen brightened, showed what appeared to be a flattened octahedron, bristling with sensor masts, turrets, launch tubes. Or rather, it showed what was left of that fort: one of the octahedron's tips had been sheared off, the rough edges of that amputation site sparking and flaring. At two points on the adjoining face of the octahedron there were deep, flame-gouting divots. A glittering ghost-trail emerged from the opposite face: whatever had gouged those holes in the fort there had, at least in part, breached the far side. Wethermere had seen forts subjected to thirty minutes of bombardment from enemy capital ships that looked better than this one—which had been hit only five seconds ago by objects so small that they failed to register on anyone's sensors.

Small specks started emerging from the other faces of the octahedron, like a cloud of fleas scattering off the hide of a stricken elephant: escape pods, hundreds of them. With any luck, they'd get clear before another—

A fast pattern of ferocious explosions rippled along equatorial line of the fort before a titanic blue-white blast obliterated it—and blanked the screen by exceeding its safe luminosity limit.

Wethermere saw the omega symbol appear in the holoplot, followed quickly by another two.

Knight looked back at him, murmured. "Sir, I know this is a covert op, but if we wait around with the rest of the civvies—"

"I appreciate your concern, Commander. I share it. But that debris field isn't going to hit us here. It's going to finish sweeping across the face of the Zarzuela warp point, come reasonably close to the one into Barricade, and pass out the other side of the system."

"So you're suggesting that we stay here . . . sir?"

"Our *orders* are that we stay in the exit queue like everyone else, right now. We're pretty much at the head of the pack. Doing anything else calls attention to us. We'll take stock of the broader situation when we get to M'vaarmv't."

"The broader situation?"

Wethermere shrugged. "This changes the situation in Zarzuela entirely. And I suspect that this is not an isolated attack. If Amunsit and her allies are somehow behind this, then I doubt this is the only surprise they're springing on us. We need to stay in one place long enough to gather some big-picture intel and figure out our next move. Because I think it's pretty clear that we're not going to be paying a visit to Zarzuela anytime soon, wouldn't you agree?"

Knight nodded. "One problem, Captain. I've been watching the plot and listening to the chatter. The 92nd Reserve has become so discombobulated trying to get itself through the M'vaarmv't warp point that they're not really running traffic control. I don't think there's going to be an orderly queue, Captain. More likely to be a free-for-all."

Wethermere looked at the way the blips in their wake were racing to outpace the two denoting his mission force, or to work around the sides and get ahead in a desperate bid to reach the warp point first. He sighed. "Ensign Schendler, you are to raise the 92nd Reserve's auxiliary liaison and find out what they're doing to establish and enforce an egress rota for the system. Looks like we need to doublecheck that there's even going to be a policeman at this intersection."

Two minutes passed before Schendler could get anyone with the 92nd to respond. Another two minutes passed before he had bounced down to the craft which had been assigned to act as the new navigation control hull: the actual one had transited the warp point ten minutes earlier. Audible over the background noise in the new ship were impatient orders and sharp countermands. Schendler made his inquiry about the exit rota and was told to wait.

That had been three minutes ago. Over the course of the delay, forts had been dying, one after the other, until the approaches to the Zarzuela warp point looked like a graveyard where omega symbols stood in for headstones. The debris cloud had almost moved fully past it, a long and now somewhat ragged oblong coursing swiftly toward the Barricade warp point. Several small ships which had been farther out into deep space—"behind" the Zarzuela warp point, as it were—seemed to hang there pensively, although in one case, there seemed to be a rescue operation underway, one ship moving to the assistance of another.

Schendler listened intently to his headset, spoke into its pickup, paused, listened intently, looked up, shook his head.

"Report, Ensign," ordered Knight.

Schendler sighed. "I wish there was something to report, sir. First I was told they had no orders or authorization to impose a rota, particularly since they would not be around to enforce it. Then someone else came on the channel and contradicted that, claiming they were in the process of cutting the orders and drafting the announcement. And then a third voice told me to get off the line: they'd received orders to move to the transit point themselves and were transferring the auxiliary navigation authority to another hull. And then the line went dead."

Knight glanced over at Wethermere. "I don't think we're going to be able to fly under the radar on this one, Captain. If we're going to get through that warp point in time, I think we're going to have to tell them who we really are."

Wethermere suppressed a sigh—and saw, in the plot, that the small ship that had been in need of assistance well in the lee of the warp-point's approach envelope came to life with a startling burst of speed. It maneuvered sharply toward the warp point's approach envelope as the tail of the debris field finished passing by.

Knight nodded at the fleeing ship. "And there's Amunsit's covert watchdog, running home to report that the gate is standing wide open."

The small ship arrowed toward the warp point and disappeared.

Wethermere ground his molars for a moment before ordering, "Schendler, raise the acting flagship of the 92nd, using my clearance code. Lubell, coordinate with the Arduan pilot aboard the *Fet'merah* about entering the fleet's formation. He won't be familiar with our protocols for approaching and maneuvering in the van of one of our fleets. Let's get the hell out of here."

CHAPTER FOURTEEN

David Nanmin liked being in charge, probably because he had always stood on the sidelines while being passed over for leadership positions. Even during the resistance on Bellerophon, where he and his fellow graduate student Toshi Springer had provided crucial observation of Arduan orbital elements during the war, he was always the guy who was a "valued member of the team." Never the superstar; just another player. That this, in part, might have reflected his own deeply denied self-image, was another possible truth that he had been successful at suppressing.

But the war was over, and his doctorate—with honors for his service during the war—was well behind him, as was his brief, abortive attempt to strike up a relationship with Toshi. (When relating the story to others, he called his embarrassing attempt to turn an ill-advised New Year's tryst into a relationship a "break-up." Any external observer over the age of seven would have more correctly labeled it a mortified rejection. Toshi had extricated herself as rapidly as possible, since either David had been unwilling or unable to discern certain subtle signs that she was distancing herself from him—such as her relocation to another city.)

But there had been consolation in the many well-funded assignments that had followed, and, since his involvement in the Bellerophon resistance garnished his basic competence with a faint nimbus of fame, he was never without important and lucrative work to do—or without some easily impressed graduate student to share his bed. At least for a while.

His current assignment in the New India system, two warp points beyond Zephrain in the direction of Bellerophon, had an unfortunate dearth of such graduate students. But that lack was adequately compensated by both the money and the prestige of the job: he had been retained by Rim Federation Joint Services Intelligence to plan and deploy a phased array to study the earlier astrophysical phenomena that many suspected of being the drive flares of subsequent Arduan Dispersates. This had necessitated a two-year commitment overseeing a professional staff that all had high clearance levels and considerable experience. Even with David Nanmin at the head of the room, the only stars that were going to be in any of his coworkers' eyes were the real ones they had come to study. But two years of saving a generous salary (because there was no way to spend it out at a secure facility orbiting the gas giant in the system's sixth orbit) meant he would emerge from this post with a prime assignment on his résumé and enough money to make up for the lost time he had spent in this recreational wasteland.

Which was proving more frustrating all the time. "Do you have the sifted observation data for track 17b?" he asked the phased array's scheduling guru, Alessa Leming.

She sighed. "Yes. More nothing."

David wasn't surprised—147 telemetry projection searches had come up empty-handed already—but he was not immune to another pulse of frustration. He shook his head, put his hands on his hips. "Well, damn it, where the hell is the source of that signature?"

Alessa threw her bird-thin fingers up in dismay. "There is no logic to these negative results. The first observers traced this particular flare for weeks before it faded. We had reasonable parallax plottings, which should have given us the source's trajectory to within two degrees of error. We saw no further flares, so there should not have been any acceleration or course changes possible. And we have scoured every segment of the sky which it might logically be located in now, given that information. Yet, nothing. Something is wrong. Perhaps there is an error in the original observational data."

David frowned. Alessa was both correct and incorrect. She was correct in asserting that something was wrong: the New India phased array was so powerful that it should have been able to detect not only marginal reflections from the surfaces of one of the immense Arduan colony ships, but, just as certainly, should have detected the way its passing occluded the stars behind it, rather like a torpedo of shadow moving through the otherwise illuminated heavens.

But Alessa was incorrect in suggesting that the error might lie in the original observation data. Unknown to all but four of the other top specialists on the New India detection project, the confirmatory database was several times larger than advertised. This particular flare had been seen not only by half a dozen official and academic observatories, but by almost five dozen naval and covert assets whose contributions could not be acknowledged in the generally shared data set. Dreadnoughts on long-range patrol, deep-space cachement sites, stealthed listening and warp-point monitoring posts inside Tangri space: these and many more facilities had observed and recorded the flare, which only deepened the mystery for David. Because whatever was, in fact, wrong, it wasn't the observational data. There were simply too many completely independent and yet corroborative sightings that had been reported with professional-grade precision.

So what *was* wrong? The trajectory of whatever had emitted the flare sign had been estimated to approach within 0.1 light-years of the New India system. That was why Joint Services Intelligence had chosen it as the site for the phased array: it would get the closest possible look at whatever was approaching. "Too close for comfort," one of the admirals in the planning sessions had quipped.

Wait: too *close for comfort . . . ?*

No. It's not possible. No.

David ignored the chill on his palms as he aimed a none-too-steady index finger at Alessa's forehead. "Dr. Leming, I need you to bring all available array components to bear on grid-field coordinates m17 by q12."

"Dr. Nanmin, granted that you have the authority to—"

"Dr. Leming, this one time, just do as you're asked. No debates. If I'm wrong, you can tell me—over lunch, if you like—just how much this unplanned retasking of the array has set back our observational agenda. But if I'm right—well, if I'm right, we'll have bigger concerns."

Leming might have heard something she had never heard before in David's tone: unambiguous resolve, not undermined by even the faintest tone of social insecurity. Or she may have begun to realize what that section of the star-field—the grid comprised of quadrants m17 by q12—meant in terms of searching for the source of the flare. "Attitude alteration under way in all relevant array elements, Dr. Nanmin. System is recalibrating—"

David looked outward along the new search parameters, which essentially followed a corridor that led straight into the New India system itself. *If the telemetry at the time of the flare was correct, then the only possibility is that the source changed trajectory* after *it was observed, that it has new telemetry—*

He heard Alessa Leming gasp. "Dr. Nanmin—there are—look!" She patched her readouts into the control-room's main display. A bright array of contacts were virtually on top of them, the stream of bogeys stretching halfway back to the heliopause. "Why didn't anyone see them before? What about the Navy—?"

"The Navy didn't see them because they are at the other end of the system, with a minimum presence, minding the warp points. As to why no one saw them—this system has almost no population, and we're as far away from those small settlements as we can get. That's pretty much standard operating procedure for a secret project: to put it where nothing, and no one, is present to observe you."

"Those objects—they are moving so fast."

"No faster than we estimated the source of the flare was moving, I'll bet. Send a coded warning to the naval station near the warp point, and put another one in the clear over the civilian channel. Rig each relay along the line to record and repeat as long as possible."

"You mean—?"

"I mean we can't be sure we're still going to be here to transmit, Dr. Leming. But until then—"

Leming stared at the screen, rigid. "But how—how did the source—?"

"We didn't think through all the variables, Alessa," he murmured through a sad smile. David Nanmin had a momentary sense of his life since Bellerophon coming full circle. His rise to modest fame had started by detecting the approach of Arduan artifacts, and it was likely to peak and end with him doing exactly the same thing. "Yes, the flare telemetry data was perfect, but it was a ruse. It set us looking along that trajectory. Because the moment the thrust—the flare—was over, they began changing course. To trick us."

"It is the Arduans again, after all?"

David did not say what he wanted to—*isn't that obvious?*—but simply nodded. "Of course. And we neglected to consider this: they already had inertialess drive when we first encountered them. Then they found and adopted the Desai drive very quickly during the early phases of the war. If they had any way of transmitting that discovery to a later Dispersate . . ."

"Yes, I understand." Leming looked as though she

might vomit. "If they built a large enough Desai drive, they could have pushed their space arks into a new vector without our ever seeing it, since those drives have no exhaust signature."

David nodded, noted that the approaching haze of contacts was now overlapping the icon denoting their array control station and the gas giant it orbited. "With forty percent cee at their command, they were able to shift to their real target: this system."

"But why here—why us?" Leming choked out.

David shrugged. "I don't have the faintest idea. I'm a scientist, not a military—"

The datafeed from the most "trailing" sub array in the network went dark the same instant that a small sphere of white light bloomed in its approximate position, almost a full light-second "behind" their control station.

"But nothing hit it," Leming protested in the direction of her sensors.

"Nothing our sensors could detect," David corrected. "At 0.66 cee, a single screw would be devastating. A chair would be catastrophic. A chunk the size of this station might very well—"

The gas giant that no one had ever bothered to give a name of its own—New India Six—sported a sudden, core-probing glare, like an acetylene torch burning its way down into a fog bank. For a fraction of a moment, the striations of its upper reaches of hydrogen spun into a fractal ruin of whorls cascading away from a widening hole left in the torch's glowing wake: a slow-motion view of cyclones traveling at many thousands of kilometers per hour. Then, as if striking the bottom of a blue-black well—which David glimpsed as a ball of frozen methane and water and solids that were New India Six's core—the subrelativistic chunk that had cut through the gas giant's soupy atmosphere emitted a blinding flash, part of which emerged from the opposite side of the immense planet.

David had an impression of the upper reaches of the atmosphere destructuring into gaseous arms of glowing plasma, of lightning racing out from the equatorial belt like an actinic spiderweb, and of immense fragments blasting up out of the tube the impactor had carved to the core of the planet. He had just enough time to turn to a white-faced Alessa Leming and observe, "We have seen an event—and a planetary core—that no humans have seen before us. Are you relaying this live?"

She nodded, eyes riveted to the images of outrushing debris, some pieces the size of moonlets, but had nothing to say in reply.

David was glad the images were being sent to the Navy picket units as a long stream of uninterrupted video, glad that posterity would remember him for being the name most associated with relaying this truly unique data before he—

An eight-kilometer long chunk of tumbling planetary core struck the New India phased array control station with such force that it effectively vaporized upon impact.

Lieutenant Commander William Chong stared at the main view screen. It was cycling again and again through an accelerated replay of the last two minutes of the existence of the New India phased array. The bridge of his ship, the fast attack carrier *Tibor Peters*, was silent.

Lt. Bonnie Pinero, at the sensor station, murmured, "Sir, you knew the chief researcher out at New India Six—Dr. Nanmin—didn't you?"

Chong shrugged. "I knew him in passing. More by reputation than personally. He watched the sky over Bellerophon when we had no satellites left. He did his job. And he's died doing it again, giving us not just the sensor data, but the crucial information that reveals its significance."

"With respect, sir," asked his adjutant, Ensign Guy Bock, who was still staring at the data, "what information is that?"

Chong was disappointed that Bock hadn't interpolated the obvious significances of the data, hadn't realized Nanmin's deepest purpose in sending his sensor readings as long as he could. "First, Mr. Bock, Dr. Nanmin's sensor sweeps tell us that we are in fact under attack by the Arduans, that this system was one of their targets all along, and that the newly arriving Dispersates must have the Desai drive, since it would otherwise have been impossible to redirect them from their trajectory so late in their flight path."

Bock swallowed. "I see, sir."

Chong believed that he might—now. "Furthermore, it tells us that the Baldie, er, the Arduan *selnarm* can now be used to communicate over interstellar ranges—they would be unlikely to have the Desai drive, otherwise—and that they are now here to fight a very different kind of war."

Lt. Steve Adler at Weapons drew more erect. "In what way, sir?"

Chong nodded at the mustard-colored navigational haze traveling across the system at two-thirds the speed of light. "The Arduans could only have generated that density of material traveling at those speeds in one way: they destroyed their colony ships to create a cloud of subrelativistic kinetic kill vehicles. Because that's exactly what every button, bunk, and bulkhead on those behemoths has become: megaton-level impactors. In some cases, a lot more than megaton-level. Lieutenant Pinero, any sign of gravimetric destabilization following in behind Dr. Nanmin's communiqué?"

"Yes, sir. I'm getting a strange reading from the general region of New India Six."

"More precision, Ms. Pinero. Strange in what way?"

"The readings are—well, diffuse, sir. And a little weak. As though the gas giant's effect on the system's entire gravitic plane has spread over a wider area and is beginning to diminish in its cumulative force."

"That's because it has, Lieutenant Pinero. I think we can safely presume that New India Six has undergone core destabilization."

"Which means—what?" Pinero wondered aloud at the sensor playback that showed the last moments of the research station's existence.

Chong exhaled slowly. "I'm not an astrophysicist, but if the gas giant's core was hit with sufficient energy to break it apart, the planetary atmosphere is probably diffusing into an elongated ellipsoid of charged plasma. Even if the planet reconsolidates, the time scale of that process will likely be measured in hundreds of millennia. Meaning that the gravitic equilibrium in this system is compromised. Keep recording all data, including astrophysical, Lieutenant Pinero: the experts back home are going to want to run simulations of the navigational sequelae."

Bock sounded embarrassed, but determined to learn—which Chong could respect. "What kind of navigational sequelae are you anticipating, Commander?"

"In the most general of terms, Ensign, I am anticipating that this system is about to become a nonstop train wreck. The largest gas giant has been destabilized—possibly shattering in the process. The rest of that hailstorm of impactors is approaching along the ecliptic, meaning that its next contact point is with the asteroid belt just starward of New India Six."

"Sir, there's a lot of open space between asteroids. A lot."

"Mr. Bock, I am familiar with the density of common asteroid belts. However, look at the density estimate of that cloud of debris and the almost incalculable number of discrete contacts within it. It would be freakish if there weren't at least—*at least*—a thousand asteroid impacts. Each of which is going to generate thousands of more highly energetic stone fragments, while barely affecting the course of the impactor which destroyed it. And then those fragments will start feeling the pull of New India Prime, getting drawn in toward the inner planets." Chong leaned back, repressed a sigh. "Within two months, this entire system will be a navigational nightmare. Any ship coming through either of its warp points will have only one piece of reliable data: that they are taking their lives in their hands. Which is why we can be sure that this is part of a larger strategy."

Adler's speculation was almost *sotto voce*. "You mean, that the Arduans wanted to interdict this system. To cut the only pathway connecting Zephrain and the Bellerophon Arm."

Chong nodded. "Precisely. Which is why we have to get back, in good order, with as much data as possible. Mr. Bock, you are to oversee the evacuation of the warp point monitoring station. I do not want to try to tow it back through the warp point: this is not the moment to engage in time-costly operations, and it does not look like that death-cloud is going to come close enough to harm it. But inform the skipper of the frigate *R. J. Hassala*—Lieutenant Pio Canlas—that he's drawn the short straw: he'll run sensors and record until best estimates show he has thirty minutes left before any stray subrelativistic impactors might reach this point."

"Aye, aye, sir. Any message for New India Two, sir? Send them details, warn them?"

Chong wanted to hang his head—more because of the fate of the civilians than Bock's lack of perspicacity. "Ensign Bock, how far off is India Six?"

Bock glanced at the plot. "Approximately fourteen light-hours sir, on the other side of the system."

"Exactly. How far is India Two?"

"Six light-hours, sir." Then: "Oh."

"Yes. It took the results we're seeing now fourteen hours to reach us at the speed of light from India Six. The debris that savaged everything there was traveling at two-thirds the speed of light. Which means, over the same fourteen hours, it has traveled about 9.4 light-hours. Which means it reached New India Two about an hour and a half ago."

Chong looked up at Bock, whose unusually pinkish face was now quite red. He no doubt anticipated a mention of his singular failure to track time properly when his next performance review came round. Chong would regret including it in his file, but would not flinch from doing so: a naval officer had to be able to keep constant and unerring track of various mission and event timelines. This might have been Bock's only serious gaffe in this regard, but it was singular enough to freeze his progress for years. "Dismissed, Mr. Bock. Helm, commence evolution into withdrawal formation Mike Delta Seven. Time to head home with news that no one will want to hear."

CHAPTER FIFTEEN

The conversation with the senior intel officer on the acting flagship of the 92nd Reserve Fleet was neither so swift nor easy as Wethermere had hoped. After overcoming the officer's intrinsic (and inherently self-important) assumption that fleet intel would have been apprised of any and all covert operations undertaken in or near their strategic theater, there followed the unavoidably convoluted explanation of how it was that a Federation spec ops transponder code was being emitted by an Arduan bulk carrier named the *Fet'merah*. The concept that there was a human Q-ship in the belly of the comparatively whalelike Arduan hull required no small number of proofs. It also required several tedious rehashings of how and why Wethermere had elected to hide his craft inside the alien ship.

But at last, the necessary explanations had been tendered, received, and (mostly) understood, and

Wethermere's small flotilla was allowed to form up with the 92nd Reserve. As part of its rearguard.

Ossian protested this, citing the criticality of his mission. He was asked to explain why it was so critical. Naturally, he could not provide that explanation without violating a dozen secrecy protocols. So ultimately, Wethermere was not allowed to depart the system sooner than the rearguard itself.

Which did not seem so worrisome a delay until Engan looked up in alarm from her sensors, announcing: "The Zarzuela warp point is active, sirs."

"Do we have any visuals?" asked Knight.

Engan glanced sidelong at Ossian. "We do, if Captain Wethermere allows us to send our covert code to get an automatic tap into the microsensors lying doggo near the warp point."

Wethermere nodded. "You have authorization. Show us what's going on."

After a few moments delay, the bridge's primary screen showed a veritable cascade of Arduan super-heavy dreadnoughts gushing out of the Zarzuela warp-point with less than two-second intervals between them. Thirty were already in system and there was no intimation of a break in the pace. And as they formed up, they began heading for the M'vaarmv't warp point at best speed. Smaller, faster craft fanned out from their flanks, leaping ahead toward the same destination.

"Well, damn," breathed J.T. Ross at the weapons console.

"Indeed," agreed Commander Knight. "ETA of their fastest ships?"

"Assuming constant course and speed, thirty-eight minutes. About fifty minutes for their battlewagons."

"Time to our transit, given current intervals?"

"About twenty minutes, sir."

Knight nodded, glanced at Wethermere. "Doesn't get much closer than that."

"No, it doesn't. And it doesn't get much more worrisome."

"You mean because this Arduan plan is running like a well-oiled machine?"

"That and—"

"Captain Wethermere, Councilor Ankaht on secure two."

"Put her through to the con, Ensign Schendler."

In the small screen nestled between Wethermere's and Knight's chairs, Ankaht's face was very still, her voice very calm. "You have, of course, seen Amunsit's fleet emerging."

Wethermere couldn't help smiling. "It's kind of hard to miss."

"Yes." She paused. "You do not seem surprised by these attacks."

"Well, I wasn't expecting them, but in retrospect, there were some warnings."

Knight frowned. "Oh? Like what—sir?"

"Like that recent series of flare anomalies that astronomers speculated might be new Dispersates decelerating prior to arrive in certain of our systems. I always wondered if the lack of more intensive news investigation into those phenomena was the result of official suppression. I'm not wondering about that anymore."

"But wouldn't your superiors tell you if they had strategic concerns? I thought you have sufficient clearance for that sort of intelligence, Ossian."

"Well, yes and no, Ankaht. I have the clearance level, but any classified military analysis investigating a connection between those flares and new Dispersates would not be in my pipeline, so to speak. This sort of intel is 'need to know,' and I didn't need to know. It's purely strategic intelligence: big picture stuff. Admiral Trevayne would have full briefings on it, maybe Admiral Yoshikuni."

Knight frowned. "And what about the Arduan Admiral, Narrok? He'd almost certainly have some info—or might have been consulted, even."

Ankaht was the one to answer. "No, not Narrok."

Knight did a good job suppressing his surprise. "You seem very certain of that, Councilor."

Ankaht paused. "Our fleet is not part of the PSU or Rim Federation command structures, although its existence and operations are subject to the approval of both. Neither admiralty has reason to share such intelligence with us."

Wethermere looked at Ankaht; her two smaller eyes blinked once, rapidly. "But that's not why you're so sure."

"No. It's not. But I may not say why."

"You don't have to say: I think I know why."

Ankaht's voice was wry. "I suspect you do."

Knight's eyes flicked sideways at Wethermere. "But I don't. How does Councilor Ankaht know who's in the intel loop and we don't? Particularly if the Arduans are supposedly further outside that 'need-to-know' network you were talking about?"

Ossian shook his head. "Sorry, Skipper, but if my guess about that is correct, then openly speculating on how Ankaht knows about Admiral Narrok's exclusion from the intel on the flares would be a practical violation of the compartmentalization of that information." *And an indicator of just how many secrets stand between Ankaht and me,* he added silently. *Of course she'd be aware of who was in the know and who wasn't, because if fleet intel thought, for one second, that the drive flares we saw earlier were from subsequent Arduan Dispersates, who would they have tapped to be their primary subject matter expert? Ankaht, of course. Even more than Narrok, she had access to the big picture, was already keeping various human secrets as part of her cooperative intelligence work with me, and was one of the few Arduans who had a long personal perspective on her race's scientific advances as well as its social evolution during its long exodus.*

And Wethermere would not have been informed of any of that because he had no need to know that such a debrief had even occurred, much less be apprised of its contents. His rank was far beneath the higher echelon command grade, so—other clearances notwithstanding—he had nothing to do with the top brass that set strategy for the entirety of the PSU. And now it was time to change the topic. "Ankaht, you said you had a breakthrough regarding the intelligence that Amunsit's agents were exchanging through the *selnarmic* drones?"

"Yes, although the breakthrough is in the structure of the messages, not their content."

Knight, who was still catching up on the details of the earlier phases of the investigation, asked, "I'm sorry, what exactly does that mean, Councilor?"

"It means we have found the signals they were

swapping secretly, and have been able to record them. As we suspected, they were embedded as part of the *selnarmic* data."

Wethermere nodded. "Logical. That ensures that we humans couldn't make sense of it, or so much as detect it. So, what kind of data is it, do you think? Numerical, lexical, visual?"

Ankaht closed her eyes slowly, opened them again. "It is difficult to explain. The data is related to sensory reproduction streams within the broader *selnarmic* message."

Wethermere nodded but said nothing.

Ankaht studied him carefully. "You don't have the faintest idea of what I meant by that, do you?"

"Nope, not a clue."

"Ah. So, I will try an analogy. You are familiar with your own species' imagistic poems, are you not?"

"Yes: poems where the form was an implicit part of the content, was supposed to be more evocative of sensory experience than mental experience."

"Yes." Ankaht seemed surprised. "I was not aware you had much familiarity with poetry."

Wethermere's smile was faint. "I am a man of many surprises. So, go on: these *selnarmic* data packages are like an imagistic poem?"

"There is a crude similarity in that they are sensory, but these, I think, are not audial or visual. Unless I am much mistaken, they resemble the structure of our taste, olfactory, and tactile *selnarmic* impressions. But their content is—garbled."

"Garbled in what way?"

"Again, I propose an analogy. Consider a poem. Your more formal traditions arrange them into stanzas which, within the same poem, all follow identical or near-identical formats of meter, rhyme, line length. Now imagine if you saw that same structure but there were no recognizable words in it. Not merely nonsense verse, but characters of all sorts—including numerals and punctuation marks—arranged in stanzas, and with some characteristic line-ending repetitions. But you saw no words: just random characters arrayed in the pattern of words. You would know you were looking at the form of a poem, but would perceive none of its content. That is analogous to the mystery this data presents."

"Captains," Lubell announced, "looks like we've just been moved up in the transit rota. Estimating five minutes."

"Thank you, Mr. Lubell," Knight said.

Wethermere, smiled, nodded, looked back down at Ankaht. "We'll be heading back to M'vaarmv't soon, I'm told."

"This is good. I would ask you to consider one recommendation from me, Ossian."

"Certainly. What is it?"

"When we get through the warp point, do not stop to converse further with the officers of the 92nd Reserve Fleet, do not stop to consider the alternatives or the next step we should take. Run. Run as far and as fast as you can, back to Zephrain, maybe back to Bellerophon. It is a formidable strongpoint, particularly if all the fleets of the Rim Federation are behind it."

Wethermere stared. "Ankaht, that is—interesting advice. I don't know how to ask this except directly: are you making this recommendation based on confidential information to which I am not privy?"

"No, Ossian. I am making this recommendation because I am fairly sure that the significance of our investigation is now past. Whatever events were to be effected by the data exchanged on the *selnarmic* couriers has, in fact, been effected. We are living in the midst of its consequences. I suggest, therefore, that we have a new mission."

"And what is that?"

"To survive."

After Wethermere's detachment passed through the warp point and started angling sharply away from the 92nd Reserve, the hails started coming in thick and fast. After five minutes, the comms finally became still—but only for a moment.

Schendler turned to Wethermere, slightly pale. "Captain, Rear Admiral Kolenski of the 92nd Reserve is on the line himself. He is not merely asking that you reply. He wants you on the carpet in his ready room within the hour."

So much the worse, then. "Schendler, you are not to acknowledge that communiqué."

"But sir, the admiral expressly ordered that you—"

"You have my orders already, Ensign. If you feel you cannot carry them out, I will place you in hack, albeit without prejudice."

"Yes sir," answered Schendler, who turned to readdress his comm console with considerable rigidity.

Knight muttered out of the corner of his mouth. "Captain, you know regulations. I don't have to tell you that you are cooking your own goose, but good."

"Commander, you are right: I do know regulations. But I've also worked with Ankaht for six years. You know the way a master statesperson can read the mood of the people, almost foresee the general trend of coming events? She's like that with her own species. And she told us to run. Run like hell. And that's what we're going to do. So right now, the choice is between blind regulations, or Ankaht's instincts—which match what my gut is telling me, too. This whole op is bust and we've now got less than thirty minutes before those Arduan super-heavy dreadnoughts come through that warp point from Amadeus." He leaned forward. "You didn't survive your posts by not developing some gut-feelings of your own, Commander, probably better ones than either Ankaht or I have. So: what's your gut telling you?"

Knight frowned, then turned to Lubell. "Lieutenant, when we get clear of the *Fet'merah*, I'm going to need best speed away from this warp point and the van of the 92nd. I presume that Captain Wethermere is going to order the skippers of *Fet'merah* and *Viggen* to do the same."

Wethermere nodded. "Just did it." He turned to the force's lead helmsman. "Make sure the others put our backs to the gale and crowd as much canvas as they can, Mr. Lubell."

Kolenski of the 92nd was clearly in the process of organizing a pursuit—fighters were launching, pinnaces forming up on them—when literally and figuratively, all hell broke loose.

Advanced mark Arduan SBMHAWKs—self-guided missiles capable of traversing warp points independently—came through the warp point into M'vaarmv't in waves, many of them destroying each other as they materialized in the system, their atoms rushing headlong into the same impossibly small volume of space and canceling each other out in violent, actinic spasms.

But for every one that was lost, nine or ten more made it—and there were hundreds upon hundreds of the hunter-killer devices swarming among the only partially reorganized echelons of the 92nd Reserve Fleet. Rusty crews and old ships dotted the blackness with the brief flashes of their passing. The heavies of the mixed-species fleet—super-monitors, mostly—managed to patch their data-links together and deliver a withering counterfire that burned down the torrent of missiles like flamethrowers clearing a field of wheat.

Commander Knight watched without comment as Kolenski's pursuing fighters swept back around to arrow toward the desperate fight for the warp point. The two rather outdated forts that were the sentinels against this unthinkable eventuality were already sitting in debris fields of what had been their own armor, weapons, power plants, crews. They fought on, but their outgoing fire diminished in inverse proportion to the mounting incoming fire that was gradually turning them to junk. Knight's jaw muscles bunched.

"We can't go back, can't help." Wethermere said quietly.

Knight nodded. "We'd get crisped just by coming too close to the secondary explosions from the real heavies."

"That, too," assented Wethermere. "But the fact of the matter is that our job is to report what we saw. With our Arduan contingent, and having bigger and better sensors than we ought to, we might have picked up some useful intel for a debrief."

Knight nodded. "Speaking of Arduans, should we *really* remain inside the *Fet'merah*, given what's going on out there? We don't exactly look like we're playing for the home team, if you know what I mea—"

Schendler looked up. "Captains, Cluster Leader Temret on secure two. He says it's urgent."

Wethermere nodded, spoke as soon as he heard the different hiss of the new channel's static. "Report, Temret."

"Captain, a number of the other ships that are already converging upon the next warp point, the one to Ahaggar, are focusing active scanners on us."

"Getting a cross-section of our hulls?"

"It would seem so. They are using ladar sweeps."

Wethermere saw Knight about to give orders to Zhou, who was also in charge of flight ops. Ossian shook his head. "No time to cut *Woolly Impostor* loose from *Fet'merah*'s belly, anymore, Skipper. If you saw an Arduan vessel start to deploy some kind of surprise package, what would you do?"

"Vaporize them. Posthaste."

"Me, too. So we're going to have to stay inside the *Fet'merah* and talk our way out of this one."

Temret's vocoder voice was both rueful and wry. "You may need to commence talking soon, Captain. Look at the relay from our holoplot."

He and Knight glanced at their own holoplot, which hazed for a moment as it was updated by the one on the *Fet'merah*'s bridge. At the farthest range of detection, and along their current line of advance, three large blips were moving in their direction now. Away from the warp point into Ahaggar—and on an intercept course.

"Temret, do you have any type and class data on those newcomers? And where did they come from?"

"I may answer your second question while my sensor operator completes the scans necessary to reply to your first. These ships are several of a small detachment of what seem to be warships, all of which were apparently already under way to Ahaggar when we entered the system. These three turned about shortly after the other fleeing ships started their detailed scans of us. They are all Orion hulls: a destroyer, a light cruiser, and a cruiser, respectively. Specific class identification within those types remain uncertain at this range, but their drive emissions and maneuver characteristics all point toward older marks. In the case of the destroyer, a very old craft indeed."

Wethermere forgot and rubbed his hair for a moment. Snatching his hand away, he observed, "This could be tricky."

Knight just stared at the understatement, then nodded slowly. "Considering that the smallest of the three could still reduce every one of our ships to atoms without committing more than a third of her batteries to a single salvo, well, yes, sir. This could be tricky."

Wethermere shook his head. "I'm not talking about the danger from their guns, Knight: I'm talking about the specific situation. As you point out, we're in an Arduan hull. Twelve hours ago, that would have been, at most, a curiosity: Arduan ships aren't seen this far away from Bellerophon very often. But now, this hull is—understandably—suspect. Extremely suspect. Now let's add this to the equation: we'll be talking to Orions. They don't know the Arduans as well as we do, having only had contact—to put it tactfully—with Amunsit and her fanatics. Now, if those three approaching vessels were Rim Federation warships, the cruisers are big enough that one of them might even have an Arduan on board as a *selnarm* communicator. But not the Orions."

"And it doesn't help that no one seems to know we're running a covert snoop and poop out here," concluded Knight. "So yes, I suppose you're going to have to do some pretty fast and friendly talking, Captain Wethermere."

Somehow, Ossian found the good grace to smile. "Commander, if I didn't know better, I would say, judging from the tone of your voice, that you are actually enjoying my predicament."

"No, sir. I'm simply glad it's you, not me, who has to try to sweet talk a bunch of combat-provoked Orions."

"Can't say I blame you—or would feel any different if our roles were reversed." He shifted the direction of his speech. "Very well, Temret. I need to reach those ships now, using your commo mast. We're going to need all the clarity and range we can get. Which means we can't use the hardware here aboard the *Woolly Imposter*: we'll degrade the signal too much by trying to send any communications through your hull."

"Acknowledged and agreed. We are ready to attempt to contact the oncoming ships."

Wethermere watched the three larger blips creep closer as Temret tried—repeatedly—to raise the ships. The only response was dead air.

"Temret," he asked, "any acknowledgment at all?"

"No, sir."

"Have you tried sending a distress signal?"

"As soon as they failed to respond to our second resend."

Wethermere measured the rate of approach: three

minutes until they entered the outer range band of the Orion ships' probable largest batteries. Operational security notwithstanding, he had no choice left but to violate his mission's secrecy protocols. Again. "Temret, I say three times: transmit our secure ops code to them using my full PSU naval prefix."

"Yes, sir. Transmitting now."

More seconds ticked by. More of the light-seconds separating Wethermere's humble detachment from the Orion heavies evaporated. As the other civvie ships in the plot began drifting further away, Engan turned toward the con. "Sirs, even through *Fet'merah*'s hull, I am detecting power spikes in the Orion ships. Seems like they are powering up their main batteries."

Well, of course they are. "Temret, any response?"

"Just came through now, sir. They are evidently processing our, and then their, messages through a translation program. But the gist of their communiqué is that they have no record of the code we sent."

"But they at least recognize the PSU command prefix as authentic and current?"

"Sir, they did not mention that either way. My impression is that they are both extremely suspicious and not well-acquainted with English."

Which made sense, unfortunately. Orion rear-area units were very likely to have little if any contact with humans, and were very far down their own forces' intel food chain. Well, there was only one thing left to try. "Temret, patch me into the channel you're sending on."

"Yes, sir. You intend to make a personal appeal?"

"No, I doubt that would do any good. If they don't believe you, there is no reason they're going to believe me."

"Then, if I may ask, what are you planning to do?"

Wethermere could not repress a resigned sigh. "I am going to try communicating to them in their own language." *With my fingers crossed.*

"You are live on the channel on my mark, Captain. And . . . mark."

Wethermere breathed deep, mentally reviewed the relevant grammar, and said in the Tongue of Tongues, "This is Captain Ossian Wethermere, PSU serial number R213740-421, currently in command of covert operations detachment Imminent Vapor, code Capstone Papa Niner. Please confirm and respond."

The rate of the Orions' approach decreased slightly. Wethermere waited a few moments, then followed up with, "Please confirm that you have received our transmission."

After several moments, a flurry of snarls, caterwauls, and purring coughs replied.

Knight glanced at Wethermere. "What did he say?"

"It was 'she,' and I believe she said that they are relaying my message to the commander of their honor guard. Or maybe that they are awaiting permission to have the honor of being the first to open fire upon us,"

Knight was not amused. "Sir, don't we have a translation program for Orion on board?"

"Only a very basic one: the capability wasn't deemed mission critical. And it won't help us with translating this. This Orion is speaking in a very strange dialect: a lot of colloquial idioms. Our translator would have as much success with it as we would have understanding Chaucer in the original."

"Understanding who?"

"Never mind, Skipper."

The channel's thin thread of static changed slightly. The Orion speaking now did so haltingly. "Acknowledge is given. Making approval is completed."

Wethermere released his held breath, saw that Knight was doing the same. "We are grateful. Have you located and checked our clearance codes, then?"

"No."

Wethermere started. "Then why have you accepted our credentials?"

"Reason is given from our Least Fang flotilla lord, Kiiraathra'ostakjo. He says that the Tongue of Tongues can only be so butchered by the human Ossian Wethermere. You are to formate into our space-pride and travel with us through the warping point."

CHAPTER SIXTEEN

Lieutenant (j.g.) Victor Menocal of the PSU Fortress Command knew he couldn't hear the inexplicable objects hurtling through the Orphicon system at upwards of two-thirds the speed of light. But he fancied they made a weird, malevolent whistling sound as they flew like demons escaped from Hell and loosed on the universe.

A few minutes earlier, one of them had struck a gas giant in the outer system, and an astronomical research station orbiting that planet had transmitted the image of a vast, spreading, leprous red blotch on its yellow-orange surface. Now Menocal, like everyone else in the control center of Orphicon's orbital fortress—a small one, for no one had menaced the peaceful Heart Worlds for generations—waited in stunned silence, telling himself over and over again that the world of Orphicon, which their fortress orbited, was a much smaller target.

There was a lull in the reports, and his attention strayed to the viewscreen, and his homeworld of

Orphicon below. The terminator was creeping over the Naiad Ocean; it would be early morning on the subtropical coast where the ancestral home of the Sanchez family, his maternal bloodline, crowned the cliffs and looked out over the ocean to the east.

His mind strayed to the story his late grandmother Lydia Sanchez-Menocal had once told him. She, then twelve standard years old, had been standing on that cliff when her mother Irma Sanchez had returned from the Arachnid War, wearing the Wounded Lion of Terra, the highest decoration for valor that the old Terran Federation had been able to bestow on its sons and daughters. He, Victor, had always known their story. Irma had brought the infant Lydia—then Lydia Sergeyevna Borisova—to safety from a world about to be consumed by the seemingly unstoppable Bug hordes, and subsequently adopted her. They had been reunited on that cliff, and Irma, after trying to explain to her barely comprehending adopted daughter why the years of cataclysmic violence through which she had waded had been necessary, had answered Lydia's timid question with, "That's right, Lydochka. The Bugs are never going to come."

Thank God Lydia didn't live to see this, thought Menocal. *The Bugs may not have come, but it may be that something even worse has.*

"Commander!" came the quavering young voice of the comm tech, shattering Menocal's thoughts. "Urgent, from the astronomical station. They say . . . they say . . ."

"Calm down, son," said Commander Hannity in a steadying voice. "Report."

The tech gulped, and obeyed. "Sir, they've tracked one of the things and . . . it's due to impact the planet."

The silence that fell on the command center was more than the mere absence of sound.

"Any data on it?" Hannity demanded. The Old Man was only in his late thirties, but as he sat in his command chair and stared straight into the viewscreen his face seemed that of an old man indeed. Yet his voice remained under tight control.

"Uh . . . they say it's one of the smaller ones, sir—maybe the size of a fist. It's traveling at about 0.67 ccc "

"So, given that speed, it doesn't really matter if it isn't very massive," said Hannity. He took a deep, unsteady breath. "Time of impact?"

"The time they estimate is . . . less than a minute from now, sir."

And there was nothing else to be said. No one even suggested the possibility of targeting such a thing with the fortress's weapons. Nor was there any point in alerting the planet. Everyone gazed at the serene world in the viewscreen, as though seeking to fill their eyes and memories with it before—

Out of the corner of his eye, Menocal fancied he could glimpse the briefest possible flash—an almost invisibly swift streak of reflected sunlight.

Against the darkness just on the shadowed side of the terminator, a red point of light appeared. In less than a second it turned orange and then yellow and then dazzling white. Then it dimmed and expanded and reddened.

"An ocean impact, and near the equator," Commander Hannity said tonelessly. "So there will be tsunamis, and hurricanes, and salt rain all over the planet."

Where the pinpoint of light had first appeared, there was now a spreading blob of bright orange.

"It must have smashed right through the ocean floor—probably halfway to the core at that velocity. And now the magma is welling up," Hannity continued, speaking to no one in particular. "More heat, more boiling . . . more salt rains . . ."

The red flare had now swelled into a monstrous fireball, reaching up to the top of the planet's atmospheric envelope and flattening out there. Around it, rings of cloud rushed outward, rippling as the shock wave through the ocean water distorted the cloud cover. For a time there was clear air around the fireball. As the leading edge of the tsunami entered the day side at hundreds of miles an hour, that mountainous wall of water could be perceived as a ripple that, as Menocal watched, swept over and far beyond the shore.

Menocal didn't listen to the reports that began to come in—of coastal areas washed clean of life, of a world shuddering to cataclysmic earthquakes as though in the throes of a planetary ague, and all the rest. He stared fixedly at the ruined coast where the old house was gone, as was so much else.

"Do something!" yelped Assemblyman Obasanjo, not for the first time.

He had, of course, no business on the bridge of the luxurious VIP transport that had brought him and a gaggle of staffers to the Christophon system to confer with his allies of the Waldeck family that essentially owned the planet. But then, just after they had departed for the return voyage to Old Terra, had come the word of the inexplicable objects whipping through the system at more than half the velocity of light. And when the chief power broker of the PSU

Legislative Assembly had blustered his way onto the bridge, no one had been disposed to say no.

They had just departed from the planet when the unbelievable message had arrived, quavering with the tones of panic, followed by an addendum that one of the larger chunks of matter was headed for Christophon's sun at almost four-fifths of lightspeed, its several tons of mass enhanced by relativistic effects. Before the implications had even had a chance to sink in, they had witnessed the incredible in the view-aft.

The local sun, about ten light-minutes behind them, glowed in automatically stepped-down intensity so they could look at it. They therefore saw the surface of the photosphere, to one side, seem to acquire a dimple. Then, at appreciably the same moment, the other side of the sun erupted in a shower of flaming matter... and the entire great sphere seemed to *waver*... and then, almost before the receptors could compensate, it ballooned out in a fireball before whose dimensions imagination reeled. And as that star-hot wave front came closer, the light from it took less and less time to reach them, so they were no longer seeing the events of ten minutes earlier, and to their eyes the fireball seemed to be growing even faster than it was.

"It must have passed straight through the convective and radiative zones, and maybe even the core, and out the other side," the captain said calmly. "Of course we had no way of knowing what the result of such a thing would be—it's never happened before."

"Do something!" Obasanjo's voice had now risen to a near-scream. "Get us to the warp point and out of this system! Go faster!"

The captain sighed, and didn't bother trying to

explain the reactionless drive to Obasanjo, whose scientific ignorance was profound. "We're going as fast as we can, Mr. Assemblyman . . . and this ship isn't exactly built for speed. That wave-front is moving a lot faster than we are. We won't be able to reach the warp point before it catches up with us."

Obasanjo's mouth hung open. "But . . . but . . . we'll *die!*"

"Probably. Our only hope is that by then, this . . . stellar event will have grown so attenuated that the ship will be able to survive it."

They watched the titanic fireball grow with soul-shaking rapidity. Silhouetted against it was a black circle: the planet of Christophon . . .

And all at once that circle seemed to catch fire, and fray away around its circumference, as the wave-front reached it. They watched a world die.

"It won't be completely vaporized," said the captain, eerily calm. "The planetary core will survive as a small, dense object orbiting . . . whatever is left of this sun. We just don't know what that will be. This is outside the normal course of stellar evolution."

"But what about *us?*" Obasanjo's voice was now a full scream.

The captain turned and looked at him somberly. "This ship is far less massive than that planet, Mr. Assemblyman," he said, as though that was all the answer required. As, indeed it was.

The entire viewscreen grew sun-colored as the expanding star seemed to fill the universe. Then the receptors went out and the screen went black. It grew very hot . . .

CHAPTER SEVENTEEN

"I tell you, Ian, the Tangri have some new leadership!" growled Cyrus Waldeck.

"We know that, Cyrus," Trevayne assured him. "In fact, we've been able to acquire some intelligence information about one of their rising stars."

Waldeck gave him a sharp look from under his shaggy eyebrows. He was, Trevayne thought, visibly aging. The face, with its features so typical of his clan of Corporate World magnates—thin-lipped mouth seemingly discordant with the massive jaw and large hooked nose—was beginning to sink in a little, and become a mesh of wrinkles. But then, even for someone who had for all his life had access to the best antigerone treatments money could buy, a century and a half plus *was* getting along.

Trevayne could never look at that face without recalling the history behind it. Humanity's interstellar colonization had followed a pattern of three waves, with wars in the "troughs." First, after the discovery of warp points in 2053, the worlds most accessible via the warp network—the Heart Worlds, as they were known today—had been settled under governmental auspices. Then, in 2206, had come first contact with the Khanate of Orion, and the era of interstellar wars had begun. The next group of colonies, with corporate funding behind them, had occupied "choke-point" systems astride the warp access to the systems beyond. That had become important after the Third Interstellar War, when the virgin systems—the "Fringe Worlds"—had seen a great surge of colonization by ethnic and cultural groups seeking to preserve their identity from submergence in Earth's cosmopolitan-ism. The Corporate Worlds had been in a position to control the flow of goods and even information to and from the burgeoning new colonies . . . and robber baron capitalism had returned, with the Waldecks of Christophon among its most prominent and successful players. Generations of exploitation had eventuated in the Fringe Revolution and the sundering of the old Terran Federation that Trevayne, in his first body, had fought to save. The younger Cyrus Waldeck had fought beside him, with a fury fueled by class vindic-tiveness. But he had exhibited a capacity for growth unfortunately rare among his kin, and now he fought for wider loyalties.

His task force and Trevayne's had converged as planned on the central Daroga system, and fought their way through two of its warp points in the teeth of heavier fixed defenses than the Tangri were wont to emplace, not to mention fanatical resistance by the Daroga Horde's mobile forces. In the end, though, the system had been secured, and the brutalized remnants of its *Zemlixi* population liberated.

But then the campaign had slowed down. Probing outward through the system's other warp points deeper into Tangri space, they had encountered the closest thing to guerilla warfare that was possible in space. Swift carrier forces, very difficult to catch, operating from no fixed bases, skulking among asteroid belts and gas-giant Trojan points, avoiding hopeless toe-to-toe battles but carrying out annoying mosquito-bite raids with swarms of fighters, doing no great damage but generating tension and frustration in the occupiers.

And now the asymmetric warfare had been taken to a new level . . .

"Intelligence information?" Waldeck echoed. "How?"

Trevayne and Magda exchanged a look, and she took up the narrative. "As we know by now, there's obviously a closed warp point somewhere in the outer reaches of this system, the existence of which they managed to wipe from all their nav databases we captured, through which they've been mounting their raids. But they've gotten bolder." She paused, then resumed as though unwillingly. "You've been off with your task force, Cyrus, and don't know about this yet. You see, we've been keeping a *very* tight lid on it." She gestured to indicate the flag quarters' outside viewscreen; the planet *Li Han* was orbiting showed as a cloud-marbled blue curve. (Not as blue as Earth, for this was a drier world, with steppes as its predominant landscape, not unlike the Tangri homeworld. The Darogas must have considered it quite a prize.) "They mounted a raid on the surface of this planet."

"*What?*" Waldeck surged halfway to his feet before subsiding. "How . . . ?"

"It was a very small raid, Cyrus, on a remote outlying area in the opposite hemisphere to this one," Trevayne explained. "It only got in because of its complete unexpectedness. And the raiders fled before we could react. So at least they didn't have time to wreak widespread horror on the local *Zemlixi* population. Although," he added grimly, "any time would have been too much." His eyes were still haunted by the things he had seen, for which obscenity was too weak a word.

Magda looked at least equally grim. "It was nothing but sheer terrorism, designed to make the *Zemlixis* think we can't protect them from punishment for collaborating with us."

Waldeck shook his head slowly. "I can see why you've been trying to keep this under extremely tight security. But how successful . . . ?"

"More than you might think. Their choice of an out-of-the-way target enabled them to get in undetected and delayed our reaction, but it also makes it easier for us to clamp a security blackout over the area."

Waldeck scowled. "Also, our wonderful free press isn't here yet, to play their traditional role of publicity agents for terrorists, who in turn provide them with great copy." He dismissed the subject with an impatient gesture. "But do I gather that this information came from *Zemlixi* survivors?"

"Right. The leader of the raid apparently wants to establish himself as the scourge of disloyal *Zemlixis* and the instrument of the Hordes' vengeance. So he announced his name, apparently hoping to make it a word of terror. It's Huraclycx. We cross-checked it against our intelligence databases. We believe he's a

Daroga fighter pilot—or at least used to be one, as recently as a year ago. Now he's evidently risen in the ranks. We have no way of knowing how high he's risen." Trevayne looked thoughtful. "Only paranoids deny the existence of coincidence, but it shouldn't be overused as an explanation. I can't rid myself of the feeling that he may be behind some of the tactical innovations that have been making our lives miserable lately."

"That's just intuition, Ian," Magda began. But before she could continue, the communicator buzzed. When the screen came to life, it showed Adrian M'Zangwe's face . . . but some fraction of a second passed before Trevayne recognized him, for his normally ebon face was a dark ash-gray, filmed with sweat, and he was clearly exerting every ounce of his immense self-discipline to hold his features steady.

"Adrian—?" Trevayne began, alarmed.

Unthinkably, M'Zangwe interrupted him—and not with the conventional regret for having to disturb him. "Admiral, please come to the flag bridge at once!"

"What is this about, Adrian?"

"Admiral, I . . ." M'Zangwe seemed to pull himself at least partially together. "Admiral, I'd rather not talk about it over the comm network. We're trying to keep it under wraps. In fact, for now we're not letting anyone off the flag bridge, and . . . Admiral, *please* come!"

Trevayne and Magda looked at each other, unable to imagine what had brought a man like M'Zangwe to this pass, but obliged to take it seriously. "Very well, Adrian. Admiral Li-Trevayne and I will be there directly."

"Thank you, sir. And..." M'Zangwe swallowed hard. "You'd better bring Admiral Waldeck as well."

The psychic stench on the flag bridge couldn't have been any more palpable if Trevayne had possessed *selnarm.* It hit him as soon as he entered. All the personnel at their various consoles were staring fixedly ahead in almost a caricature of strained self-control.

"All right, Adrian," he demanded as soon as he and his two companions reached the comm station, where M'Zangwe and Andreas Hagen stood over a junior communications officer who was trying to be as inconspicuous as possible. "What *is* this?"

M'Zangwe had by now recovered enough of his poise to speak normally. "Admiral, we've received a coded top secret report via *selnarmic* relay from the nearest PSU base. At first we rejected it out of hand as some kind of insane hoax, despite the code. But there's no possible doubt..." His voice was starting to fray again. He drew himself up into a position of attention, as though to physically stiffen his resolve. "Admiral, the PSU's human worlds are under attack."

For a heartbeat, his three listeners simply stared, as though what he had said made no sense. Then Trevayne and Magda and Waldeck all spoke almost simultaneously:

"Who...?"

"How...?"

"Where...?"

M'Zangwe gestured to Hagen, who wore a haunted look. The Intelligence officer shook his head to clear it of ghosts and tried to answer the queries in order.

"As regards 'who,' Admiral Trevayne, we have no

idea, although some notion may begin to emerge from the pattern of the strikes. As for 'how,' Admiral Li-Trevayne, the report gives us some data. The attack has taken the form of kinetic strikes on planets and, in some cases, stars."

"Did the report include damage assessments?"

Hagen looked even more miserable. "You must understand that, while the projectiles varied greatly in size, some were fairly massive—tons, in fact. Surviving observers were able to transmit sufficient data to calculate their rest masses, and—"

"Did you say *rest* masses?" Trevayne snapped with a perplexed scowl.

"Yes, Admiral. You see, the objects' observed velocities ranged from 0.66 cee to 0.81 cee. Relativistic effects therefore . . ." Hagen trailed off, for the horror-stricken looks on his listeners' faces reflected their dawning realization of the monstrous implications of what he was saying. Magda, in particular, clearly saw that "damage assessments" would be a practically meaningless term.

Waldeck was the first to find his voice. "Where?" he repeated in a voice under iron control.

Hagen could not meet the old admiral's eyes. "The data from the report has been fed into the computer, sir. If you'll come this way . . ." He led the way to the holo tank and summoned up a display of the warp network covering the human portions of the PSU. It was a familiar sight for all of them . . . except for one thing. Certain systems blinked red, while others shone a steady scarlet.

"The systems with blinking red lights are known to have been hit, but the extent of the strikes' effect isn't known. The steady red lights indicate that... that the destruction of the planet in question was... well, total." Hagen swallowed, mastered his voice, and resumed speaking into the silence. "As you can see, the Heart Worlds were badly hit, the Corporate worlds even worse."

They stared into the tank, locked in something beyond horror, for they were now in an unimaginable nightmare from which there would be no waking up.

"Christophon...?" Waldeck croaked, staring at one unblinking red light.

Hagen continued to avert his eyes. "We know what occurred there because a few ships that happened to be in the outer system at the time were able to observe it and make warp transit before the effects caught up with them. You see, a particularly large, fast-moving projectile slammed into the local sun—literally right through the core and out the other side. The energy release evidently destabilized the self-perpetuating stellar equilibrium, and..." Hagen stopped talking, for Waldeck wasn't listening. He was gazing fixedly at the little red light that was the funeral pyre of his family, his tradition, his society. For a moment, his mouth worked, but no words came. Then he clamped his face into a mask of iron.

In a very quiet voice, Trevayne spoke succinctly. "Real-space display." Wordlessly, Hagen obeyed, and the stars in the tank rearranged themselves into their true spatial configuration. The red lights now assumed more of a pattern. And they all knew that pattern was oriented in the direction of the long-doomed sun of Ardu.

"I think we can stop wondering about 'who,'" said Trevayne in the same quiet voice. "Ankaht has warned us about the *Destoshaz*-as-*sulhaji,* and what may have happened to the later Dispersates, hasn't she?"

"How could they have aimed these rocks, or whatever they are, with such precision from across interstellar distances?" Magda wondered aloud, because she needed to banish the silence but could not bring herself to speak of what they all knew to be billions of dead. "I mean, planets are so infinitesimally tiny on the astronomical scale, and they're moving in their orbits."

"I don't think these things were precisely aimed. Remember the size of the generation ships? And remember also the Arduans' indifference to death, or 'discarnation.' If they decided they could dispense with one of those monsters, they could guide it up to a certain point, without decelerating, and then blow it up into a multitude of fragments that would continue on the same course—a titanic shotgun blast. The vast majority of them wouldn't hit anything . . . but they wouldn't need to. Only a few would suffice to . . ." He couldn't continue. The leaden silence descended again. This time M'Zangwe broke it.

"Admiral, what are we going to do? We've got to go back—"

"We've received no such orders, Adrian," Trevayne reminded him. "Of course, I think I have a certain latitude to act on my own initiative, under . . . these circumstances. But you're forgetting one thing."

"Sir?"

"In the course of this campaign, we've liberated a number of Tangri worlds, most recently this one, and started the *Zemlixis* on the road to self-government. What's going to happen to them if we go away and leave them to the tender mercies of the Hordes? If there was ever any doubt about that, there can't be any longer—not after what just happened on this planet."

"But Ian," said Magda, "we've got to do *something!*"

"And we assuredly will. Cyrus . . . *Cyrus!*"

"What?" Waldeck, who hadn't heard his name at first, straightened up abruptly. "Uh . . . yes, sir?"

"I want you to take your task force back at once. You will proceed to the base at Pesthouse and, on my authority, assume command of the reserve we've been keeping there in case any trouble comes out of Zarzuela. There you will take whatever action seems indicated against the incursions that I'm quite certain are following hard on the heels of . . . what has occurred." Like all of them, Trevayne found himself taking refuge behind circumlocutions.

"Yes, sir," Waldeck repeated in a mechanical voice.

"And Cyrus . . . I want you to remember something." Trevayne held Waldeck's eyes until he was fairly sure he had the man's full attention. "If there's any truth to what Ankaht has told us, the *Destoshaz-as-sulhaji* have become horribly alien to the Arduans we know—including the Arduans in your task force. Do not confuse the two."

"I won't, Admiral." Waldeck was clearly operating as a machine, but at least the machine seemed functional. "And you . . . ?"

"TF 14.1 will remain here. We won't advance any further into Tangri space. Instead, we will concentrate on securing this system and, by extension the liberated warp chains behind it. In particular, I want that closed warp point in this system found! I want screens of fast light units thrown around the inner system, to locate and follow any raiders who escape through it.

When we depart, I want us to be in a position where it will suffice to leave only some of our lighter units here. I've given the *Zemlixis* my word that I won't permit them to be slaughtered and brutalized. And I keep my promises."

Waldeck drew himself up. "With your permission, Admiral, I'll return to my flagship and set in motion preparations for departure."

"Right, Cyrus. And for now, don't reveal what has happened to anyone who doesn't need to know. I—or, rather, we," Trevayne amended, glancing at Magda, "will compose a message to the entire fleet. Our personnel will have to be told, before Rumor Central makes it even worse than it is." *If possible*, he silently added.

"Of course, Admiral." And Waldeck was gone.

Trevayne turned a brooding look at the tank, where the malevolent red lights still shone. "Andreas, this isn't necessarily complete, is it?"

"No, Admiral. It's just the systems we know about from the report. But," Hagen added hurriedly, "the report assured us that Earth is all right."

"Good." But Trevayne continued to contemplate the display. "I wonder what the situation is in the Orion parts of the PSU?"

CHAPTER EIGHTEEN

Least Claw Showaath'sekakhu-jahr (or Showaath as she was known to her littermates and a few select friends) quickly scanned the five pickups that comprised the portable holostudio she had installed upon the rented shuttle. Her lead technician followed her gaze pensively: while Showaath was not a prima donna when it came to interviews, she *was* particular and exacting.

But then again, if she hadn't been, she would not have been able to retain the undisputed position as top Orion interviewer and investigative journalist throughout the Khanate—and beyond. She had been the apex predator of her chosen field ever since, six years ago, she had been trapped on Bellerophon and compiled a documentary series of its occupation and liberation that was as comprehensive as it was gripping and defining. Orions at the top of their respective fields certainly exhibited *noblesse oblige*, but never the (often false) humility evinced by their human colleagues. If you were going to dominate your litter, you had to act the part, which meant, among other things, not suffering fools gladly and not suffering incompetence at all. And you couldn't do that from behind a desk. *Theernowlus*—the Orion concept of accruing honor through risk-taking—was not just a martial concept: it applied to all professions to whatever measure it could. And Showaath had discovered that, with the Zarzuela blockade always generating incidents, and the Tangri perpetually launching raids, she was never at a lack for a combat zone to cover.

Today's combat zone was very different in one regard: there were no guns involved—yet. But in terms of savagery, desperation, and the possibility to expand into a nation-destroying conflagration, it rivaled the most ferocious battlefield she had ever seen. The debate over approving a second set of Unity Warp Points had become a flashpoint that further polarized unionists and isolationists, Great Families and labor collectives, traditionalists and reformers. The cohesion of her species—and so, its future—hung in the balance.

Walking forward into the small lounge nestled atop the bridge, Showaath peered through the reinforced gallery windows that looked out over the craft's bow: beyond it, and far, far below, the blue oceans of Khanae III seemed to rise toward them slowly.

"The angle of descent will soon become steeper, Least Claw," the pilot announced. "I recommend you take a seat."

"Give us a good ride," was her only reply. She leaned a hand upon a nearby bulkhead, turned to send a question back at her production manager, "We'll have less than an hour with the four Kimhakaa'Khan'a'khanaaeee. I want to have our recorders ready and the *hercheqha* luncheon served the moment he comes on board."

"It is as we have discussed and prepared, Least Claw. We shall make full use of every second that the Khan's Councilors deign to spend with us."

"Excellent. I trust it to your claws, then."

The shuttle banked slowly, but the inertial compensation system kept Showaath from feeling any change in momentum. It was, however, unexpected. "Pilot, were we not in a direct glidepath, as you informed me earlier?"

"We were, Least Claw, but we have been redirected."

"Redirected? How? Why?"

"I am unsure Least Claw, but there seems to be—"

Far ahead, and up in the midnight-blue reaches where the planet's atmosphere verged upon space itself, there was a brief, blinding white streak—as though Showaath had inadvertently glanced at an active arc-welder. As she raised a hand that was far too slow to shield her eyes—which now showed her a fading green after-image of the beamlike phenomenon—she asked, "Was that a—a plasma bolt of some kind, pilot?"

"I do not—do not know," he replied as, visible even from where Showaath stood on the low gallery that peered down into the rear half of the bridge, his communications panel suddenly began flickering wildly. "Mixed reports, Least Claw. From ships in orbit as well as ground stations. It may have been some freak cluster of cosmic rays impacting the—"

Then, the nature of the phenomenon no longer mattered: its effects commanded everyone's full attention. To the front and to the sides, similar beamlike strikes streaked planetside. Except, they did not really streak, Showaath amended: they were there—fully realized—all at once. "Pilot, get us back up—"

But the shuttle performed a steep nosedive—so steep that it imparted a lurch that even its inertial compensators could not fully counteract. "Debris—or near-relativistic kinectic kill devices—Least Claw. Scores of them. More coming from—"

The cockpit and passenger windows strobed with a blue-white light so absolute and intense that it seemed to be attempting to gouge out their eyes. In the next instant, the shuttle bucked, veered under the sharp, savage buffeting of a sudden cyclone, then it righted. Still pitched downward at a forty-five-degree angle of attack, that angle revealed a scene so surreal that Showaath—who had seen many, many planetary attacks both from above and below—could not immediately make sense of it.

Fuming tracks of flame led from the highest reaches of the atmosphere all the way to the ground, widening as they went. Blue-white explosions, bright as white dwarf stars, dotted the intervening space to the ground, shock waves shredding clouds, lower ones generating tidal waves from the downward atmospheric compression of the airbursts. But the ground, the green expanses of New Valkha, the capitol and adopted homeworld of all Orions, seemed to be in motion, rippling like the surface of some stiff, chunky, resistant liquid under the impact of the bright attacking shafts that had somehow burned all the way through the atmosphere to reach it.

Many exploded on the surface—and Showaath's practiced eye told her that she had never seen detonations so large, many easily measuring in the gigaton range. But many more apparently bore into the planet itself before unleashing their titanic forces, throwing up gouts of earth in which each discernible chunk had dimensions best measured in dozens of kilometers. Coronae of bright white energy came up through the great rents in the planet's surface, shading into yellow and orange as mundane matter was vaporized or sent soaring upward—

A shard of bedrock the size of a small mountain shot past the shuttle, higher up into the atmosphere. Showaath was the first to recover her voice. "There's no time to evade. Luck is our only hope. Straight up, pilot; we have to—"

The hinge of an EVA manipulator arm, once affixed to an Arduan colony ship over ten kilometers long, struck the shuttle amidships at a velocity of 0.66 cee. To an outside observer, the craft would have appeared to, perversely, both fly apart and fold in upon itself. The wings and further components of the airframe spun spastically away from the explosive force of the impact, whereas the center of the fuselage disintegrated. However, some of the debris was actually sucked downward by the powerful vacuum the hinge left in its blinding wake—and was then vaporized a microsecond later as the ferocious energy of its passage caused that down-reaching column of air to spontaneously combust.

Destoshaz'at Zum'ref looked upon his work and saw that it was good.

"This wasn't their original homeworld, was it, Admiral?" asked Inzrep'fel deferentially, gesturing at the viewscreen.

"No," Zum'ref answered his Intendant. From the vast volume of information supplied by Amunsit, he had gleaned some knowledge of the histories of the aliens they must extirpate, including the furry ones the humans called the *Orions.* "No, they originated on a planet called Valkha, Khanae III. Then, about five hundred years ago, they moved the capital of their interstellar empire here, to Valkha'zeeranda or 'New Valkha.'"

(Mild curiosity.) "Why did they do that? Was the homeworld threatened with destruction by a supernova, as ours was?"

"No—they did it themselves. It seems that about eighty years before that, they had wrecked Old Valkha in a series of internecine wars. Whatever wasn't obliterated by nuclear weapons was contaminated by chemical and biological agents. The survivors naturally wanted to find worlds that weren't ruined, so they made space flight an urgent priority. Luckily for them, they soon discovered warp points."

(Revulsion.) "Animals! *We* would never have . . . But then, what did it matter if they jeopardized the existence of their species, given the fundamental meaninglessness of their lives?"

Zum'ref said nothing. He continued to gaze into the viewscreen, at the day side of a planet that no longer had the distinctive look of a life-bearing world. *They may have thought Old Valka was devastated,* he thought. *They had* no *idea.*

He had commanded that special attention be given to the targeting of this system, and there had been no trouble finding volunteers to guide the mammoth generation ships to the point where the hit ratio was optimum before setting off the explosives that would discarnate them and reduce the ships to clouds of debris. He had also ordained a higher than usual quantity of relativistic rubble for this system, maximizing the chance of planetary strikes by large fragments. He had not been disappointed. Multiple such impacts had blown much of the atmosphere out into space, and choked what was left with dust. And even through those dense dust-clouds, great rents could be glimpsed, like obscene fissures in the world, still glowing with the magma that had welled up when the planetary crust had been smashed open, glowing a shade somewhere between orange and *murn*.

Now the auxiliary craft, such as the superdreadnought-sized one he rode, had arrived and were sweeping through the system, hunting down and annihilating the demoralized surviving Orion mobile forces. Not all of them, of course. Some had escaped through the system's warp points.

But that was all right. In fact, it was highly desirable that the news of what had happened here should spread. Essential, in fact . . .

On some subliminal level of the *selnarm* that they used less and less in ordinary intercourse, he detected a certain uneasiness in Inzep'fel. "What is it?" he demanded.

"Ah . . . *Destoshaz'at*, forgive me, but I cannot help wondering if this level of destruction is altogether wise. After all, life-bearing planets are not particularly common, and our race can make good use of them—unlike . . ." The Intendant gestured at the viewscreen.

"Yes," ventured one of the staff officers near them on the balcony that overlooked the control center. "And we could reap even more economic benefit from such worlds with the aid of a slave labor force of the indigenous—" He halted abruptly as Zum'ref rounded on him and sent (AUTHORITY).

In his study of the in-depth intelligence information Amunsit had provided on the humans, Zum'ref had read that those patchy-furred mistakes of Illudor had always been at a loss to explain the quality they called *charisma.* None of them seemed to doubt its existence—there were too many historical examples for that—but they had never really succeeded in defining or explaining it. And it had proven equally elusive for Arduans, for no direct linkage to any manifestation of *selnarm* had ever been proven . . . and its existence among humans seemed to clinch the case for the nonexistence of such a linkage. But whenever an Arduan did possess it, *selnarm* amplified it.

And he, Zum'ref, had it. He had always known he had it, and it had enabled him to emerge as the unquestioned leader of a dozen Dispersates. And now he exercised it to the full.

"Do not speak to me of 'economic benefit'! We cannot let such crass considerations deflect us from our great mission. Remember what we are! We are the purified form of our race, cleansed of all the false civilization of the *shaxzhu* that had weakened and corrupted it. We are the true Children of Illudor. And we are not merely Arduans, or even merely *Destoshaz.*" He drew a breath, and let the thunder of his voice ride outward on a wave of *selnarm.* "We are the *KAITUNI!*"

It had the effect it always did, igniting the fires of fanaticism in his listeners' central eyes, and even in the smaller and normally less expressive flanking ones.

The coining of that term had been his master-stroke, marking the culmination of his rise to absolute power. It could not have been precisely translated into any human language, but to their race it conveyed "promised/sworn to the quest." Any race, he had declared, could simply name itself after its homeworld, as the inhabitants of Ardu had done. But they themselves had risen above that. Their identity was no longer linked to a single ball of dirt—least of all a ball of dirt they had left behind them, and which probably no longer existed, having been consumed by the fires of the Sekahmant supernova. No, they had transcended that. Now they belonged to all of Illudor's creation. And they were destined to rid that creation of defective life-forms that failed to measure up to the ideal toward which Illudor's plan strove—and of the weak-willed First Dispersate, who had allowed themselves to be seduced into acceptance of, and even alliance with, aliens that were as misshapen spiritually as they were physically. And Zum'ref had fashioned a new name to consecrate themselves in—and become one with—their new quest; they had put aside the label of Arduans and became the Kaituni.

"But Admiral," the staffer asked timidly after a moment, "I still do not understand why we targeted the Orions with the heaviest kinetic strikes. Why not the humans? Surely they are the greatest danger. After all, it was they who dealt the First Diaspora its worst defeats. And their industrial capacity is unrivaled, even after the devastation our strikes have dealt them."

"You forget," Zum'ref reminded him, "that in the long run the Orions may well be the greater threat because they favor smaller craft."

(Understanding.) "Ah, yes, of course, Admiral. Forgive my stupidity."

(Indulgence.) "No, it is easy to forget that, unknown

to our enemies, the day of the smaller warship is about to return. After all, the weapon that shall impel its return is such a recent, and radical, development."

Some would have said that it was only natural that they of the Dispersates would have been the first to discover that weapon, for it had been ongoing research into the "pin-hole" basis of their generation ships' photon drives, that had led them into the more esoteric regions of quantum physics—including the "teleportation" effect that was inherent to quantum entanglement. He, Zum'ref, knew better. It had been the will of Illudor.

"In the meantime, however," he continued, "we must not lose sight of our strategy of luring our enemies' heaviest units to us."

"But Admiral," Inzrep'fel demurred, "remember the humans' industrial power. Even after being defeated, they will rebuild more quickly than the Orions."

"We will not give them the time. With the Orions eliminated as useful allies for now, the human response is going to be predictable: defend the Heart Worlds, and especially Terra. And this impulse will not be limited to the human elements of the PSU. Amunsit has made it clear: the Rim Federation has a strong emotional attachment to the homeworld—'More Terran than the Terrans' is a phrase of theirs she quoted. And even the breakaway Terran Republic won't be able to stand by and watch the birthworld of their race go into the flames. Thus we will draw their most powerful ships—the devastators and superdevastators—to us." (Serene self-satisfaction.) "And when we do, those ships will be no more."

CHAPTER NINETEEN

"It is strange to think that lacking aptitude for a foreign tongue would save, rather than forfeit, one's life," Least Fang Kiiraathra'ostakjo observed, his lips carefully concealing his formidable teeth as he smiled. "Yet, that is just what saved you."

"And I'll bet you've been just dying to be in the same room to share that quip with me and others," Captain Ossian Wethermere replied through a small grin of his own.

Ankaht stared at the two of them, marveling at the jocularity with which the two alien commanders touched on the topic of how close that moment had brought them all to death—but particularly for the non-Arduans in their ramshackle flotilla. Because for the humans and Orions, death was *zhet*—complete annihilation, no hope of reincarnation. And yet both those alien races had evolved strangely analogous rituals of joking about death's proximity. Perhaps it was the only way they could endure the stress of such a horrific fate. Ankaht had wondered that before, but had not been in so terribly opportune a vantage point to observe how it operated day in and day out when all their lives were in constant jeopardy.

The flight from M'vaarmv't had been harrowing. None of Kiiraathra'ostakjo's Honor Guard flotilla had any Arduans aboard—indeed, they had even been relieved of their human crew components—so communication had been restricted to line of sight compressed lascom messages. All other active arrays were left dark to minimize the possibility of Amunsit's forces detecting them at range. Which was indeed a crucial precaution, since two of the Least Fang's ships had never been retrofitted with Desai drives. Consequently, the flotilla was traveling at half the speed of their potential pursuers, leading the Orion Least Fang and the human captain to agree that they would be unlikely to make it to the Ahaggar warp point if they were discovered.

And so they traveled with minimum communication, using stealth and maintaining maximum distance from the immense Arduan fleet that simply swept the 92nd Reserve out of the way in less than half a day. Ankaht had monitored the attackers' distant *selnarm* carefully, noting that there was a discernible measure of circumspection in their sends. She suspected that reports had reached Amunsit that the humans had integrated Arduans into their fleet communication structures and so, she had taken appropriate precautions.

The Orion ships of Kiiraathra'ostakjo's Honor Guard were, as it turned out, storied craft from one conflict or another. Of all of them, only the heavy cruiser *Hsar'sheao* and the *Celmithyr'theaanouw* itself could be called modern ships in any meaningful sense of that term. The majority were pushing half a century of service; no small number had been in vacuum for twice that duration. There was one battleship, one battlecruiser, three light cruisers, two destroyers, and one frigate, mostly running with skeleton crews. There was also a destroyer-sized "raiding carrier" that had apparently been laid down in response to the need for a class of ship capable of carrying out commerce raiding while also being small, fast, and easily hidden. And there were a good number of auxiliaries and civvies who had stuck with them during the long, slow journey to the Ahaggar warp point.

Ankaht had noticed that, among the civilians on board *Woolly Imposter* and *Fet'merah*, this impressive-sounding roster of military ships boosted confidence and a sense of hope that they might all survive to escape to some port of safety. However, given her involvement with military matters in the war with the humans, and her access to the military assessments that were swapped by brief lascom bursts between the Least Fang and the captain, she was painfully aware that, confronted by two of Amunsit's super-heavy dreadnoughts, the entire flotilla would have been reduced to plasma and junk within fifteen minutes time—less, if the old ships were actually foolish enough to try to stand and fight.

Now in the Sreaor system, near the border of Rim Federation space, they had managed to find what amounted to a largely ignored trace of less-traveled systems that allowed them to veer out of the evident path of Amunsit's fleet while still remaining roughly parallel to it. In Sreaor, a backwater system where human and Orion populations were both present and increasingly mixed, they found enough time and space to refit, give the overtaxed crews adequate rest, and to compile a roster of the various ships they'd picked up along the way.

That ragged array of vessels was the still-functional remains of both the commercial and official local traffic that had been shattered and scattered by the onrushing leviathan that was the Zarzuelan fleet. One or two were modern warships. A PSU light cruiser of recent mark and mixed crew had been scooped up after fleeing from a head-on encounter with Amunsit's forces: it had been journeying to replace a now-vaporized ship in the 9th Fleet. The others were smaller hulls, mostly frigates and a few destroyers that had been decommissioned from fleet rosters and transferred to local defense forces. Custom cutters were among the most common of the other official craft, although navigational survey ships, buoy tenders, missile tenders, repair and recovery ships, and minesweeper/-layer dual function hulls were also present in the group. The civilian craft were, in terms of both size and role, as polyglot a mix as could be imagined.

But as Kiiraathra'ostakjo and Wethermere labored, in their first face-to-face meeting, to both compile a comprehensive roster and assign duties and formation slots for all their new charges, the Orion seemed somewhat evasive about reconsidering the placement for the unusually large cargo ship with which his Honor Guard flotilla had been traveling. Or rather, Ankaht and Wethermere had speculated, which he had been escorting.

When Kiiraathra'ostakjo additionally waved off a routine inquiry into the manifest of that large ship,

Wethermere dropped his datapad on the table, leaned back, laced his fingers behind his head and asked, "Okay, Kiiraathra, so what are you hiding in the freighter?"

The Orion feigned uncertainty. "We have several freighters . . ."

"You know which one I mean. The one that you keep trying to avoid talking about. The one that is a massive unipiece cargo hull, not a modular bulk hauler. Not a lot of call for vessels that have such a huge, contiguous volume of space available." He smiled faintly. "So tell me, Kiiraathra'ostakjo: what's in the box?" His smile became a wide grin, his lips stretched taut over his teeth so as not to give offense. "Or are you under orders not to let that cat out of the bag—to coin a phrase."

"Ha and ha. Very amusing, my mostly furless friend. But I am not at liberty to answer your question."

"No? Not even if I *guess* what's in the box? Using just *one* guess?"

"This is not a game, Captain."

Wethermere shook his head. "No, you're right, Least Fang, which is why the special orders you were given when you started escorting that ship cannot be allowed to remain as impediments to our planning now. That, too, would just be playing a game: following orders that have ceased to have any relevance to our current situation. And worse, doing so might put a dangerous strategic asset right in our enemies' hands—er, tendrils—if we're not careful."

Kiiraathra'ostakjo had reared back. "You know what it is. Already. How?"

Ankaht started at Wethermere. "Yes: how?"

Wethermere waved away her surprise and possibly incipient indignation. "No, I didn't have any back-channel access to classified information. But all the pieces fit," he concluded, glancing at the Orion. "That's why you were able to agree so quickly to our request that you accompany us during the closing phase of our investigation in the old Bug systems. Who would guess that you were helping one covert operation to conduct another: making sure there weren't any undetected pirate collectives that could have ruined your journey to Bellerophon. Because it was imperative that the freighter's cargo remain absolutely safe—since it's one of the most expensive and important payloads in all of known space."

Ankaht found herself growing impatient. "Which is—what?"

Wethermere shrugged. "A warp-point generator. More specifically, one half of a matched pair. This one was bound for Bellerophon, where it would have been activated later this year, at the same instant its twin would have been triggered in Sigma Draconis."

"Yes," Kiiraathra'ostakjo confirmed with a slow sweep at his whiskers. "The formation of the warp point required that all checkpoints and waypoints were reached on schedule. Any variation activated an abort contingency. The PSU administrators in charge of establishing what was to be the Unity Warp Point Six would not go forward under any circumstances, at this point. They have no way of confirming the fate and whereabouts of my half of the warp-point generator. Indeed, they will now logically fear that it may have fallen into Amunsit's hands, and may ultimately be reverse-engineered by her technicians so that she may change the strategic pathways of the current conflict, possibly outflanking us. Which is why it must be returned to Rim Federation space as soon as possible."

"Not Orion space, Least Fang?" Ankaht asked.

The Orion admiral's gaze faltered. "No. Orion space is—in turmoil. We have had news from the most recent ships that we have integrated into our flotilla. It is news that we kept quiet, at least until we could ascertain its veracity. But it is now confirmed by the crew of the emergency courier we picked up two days ago, the one that had been bound for the Zephrain system, but had to hide here when she ran afoul of Amunsit's rearguard patrols. And the news the courier has confirmed is—troubling."

Wethermere seemed as surprised as Ankaht. "How bad?"

"Our capitol, the world you humans call New Valkha, is destroyed. The Arduans' relativistic kinetic kill vehicles struck there as well, reduced it to a mantle-shattered ruin. And their ships were there within hours of that bombardment—a massive fleet of them."

"But how could Amunsit's ships get there so quickly?" Ankaht wondered.

"They didn't." Wethermere, still looking at Kiiraathra'ostakjo, nodded, understanding. "It's a different fleet. Damn it. Those flares *were* new inbound Arduan Dispersates, weren't they?"

The Least Fang worked his jaw fretfully. "It seems so. My people are facing many more ships than Amunsit could have created—many, many more. And there are some reports that the same torrents of kinetic kill vehicles that cleared away the forts in the Amadeus system have been used to shatter many other worlds, even whole systems, in the PSU and beyond. It is difficult to distinguish the genuine news from the terror-spawned rumors, but we may be sure of this: the Khanate is crippled. Its leadership is scattered and in flight, but probably heading back to gather at Old Valkha."

"I thought your true homeworld had been rendered . . . uninhabitable." Ankaht kept her phrasing carefully oblique. The fate of the Orions' planet of origin was a source of some embarrassment to them, as it had long been a prime argumentational "proof of Orion aggression and instability" by the race's most bigoted detractors.

Kiiraathra'ostakjo's reply was preceded by a low-chested rumble. "We have attempted to restore Old Valkha. There has been considerable progress, but it is still an—an unpleasant world. But that matters little, now, because its history alone makes it the single most important planet left in the Khanate. It is the heart of our honor and the womb of us all. Our leaders will go there to rally the families and clans and plan a war such as we have never fought before. I would go there, as well"—the muscles along his long jaw rippled spasmodically—"but I may not. My duty is to see this half of the warp-point generator to safety. And there is no safety to be found in the Khanate now."

Ankaht sat slightly more erect; she was certain her next observation would not be cheering to the Orion admiral. "Least Fang, I fear that there may be no safety traveling further along our present path, either. Once we leave this system, we have but one choice other than returning to the heart of the Khanate: to follow your planned path forward to Zephrain. There are many branching paths by which we may come there, of course, but all eventually gather at that system like the many courses of a sprawling watershed collect into a single river. And I do not see how you plan to get through Amunsit's fleet."

"You are, of course, correct," Kiiraathra'ostakjo agreed. "That is why I do not plan to get through her fleet, but rather, around it. Once word of these events reaches the Bellerophon Arm, I am sure that Admiral Yoshikuni will move swiftly to bring her main elements up to join the home fleet under Admiral Watanabe in Zephrain itself. Together, I am fairly sure they will be able to defeat Amunsit. Admiral Yoshikuni has one of the most impressive lists of capital ships on record. Her devastators and superdevastators will make short work of Amunsit's formations, no matter how great their numbers. And so, if we shadow Amunsit's formations at a respectable distance, then, when we see them shift forward to join battle with the full Rim Federation fleet, we shall know to watch for any moment of chaos and uncertainty in the Arduan ranks. We shall use that moment to move around them, slip back to our own fleet, and continue onward toward Bellerophon, bringing the warp-point generator out of the range of the front lines."

Ankaht acknowledged the wisdom of the strategy. "Most prudent, Least Fang. But I am unsure you have fully realized the significance of a troubling piece of data that was gathered as we watched Amunsit's fleet overwhelm our own."

"And what data is that?" he asked. Wethermere leaned forward.

"It might seem strange to think in terms of the smallest of warcraft, rather than the largest, but did you note Amunsit's immense waves of fighters?"

"I certainly did. And it puzzled me: fighters are almost incapable of damaging the first-rate of capital ships, these days. It seemed a profound waste of so much industrial effort and raw resources to produce so many fighters."

"So it might seem, but consider this, Least Fang: in losing a fighter, Amunsit loses nothing of value."

The Orion started. "Granted that you believe your people reincarnate when they are killed, but a fleet cannot be stripped of its trained combat pilots. If that occurred, it would be—"

"Please attend, Least Fang. Your logic is impeccable, but you miss a key datum. At the end of the last war, our Admiral Narrok introduced an innovation: fighters that were remote-controlled through *selnarmic* link. The pilots remained safely behind in their carriers. Word of that concept would assuredly have reached Amunsit through the *Destoshaz*-as-*sulhaji* who fled to Zarzuela. This means that in every performance metric, their fighters will now match yours, if for no other reason that there is no need to accommodate living beings on board each craft. They will be more efficient, capable of far more wrenching maneuvers, and most importantly, can be expended lavishly without any decrease in the ranks of trained fighter pilots."

Wethermere rubbed the fur on top of his head backward. "Which is why we saw Amunsit's fighters overwhelming the 92nd Reserve Fleet like a non-stop blizzard of gnats. No amount of losses stopped them—and if they got close enough to a capital ship, they simply rammed it. I didn't believe those reports at first; I thought we were misreading accidental collisions by damaged ships as intentional suicide runs, but now—"

"Rest assured: your first instincts and perceptions were correct. And if Amunsit has been producing a stockpile of such fighters, it is almost a surety that your own equivalent fighter wings will never achieve parity. Even if your pilots are more seasoned and better trained, they would be crippled by the unrelenting attrition they would experience fighting outnumbered against a foe who risks nothing in the combat."

"They 'would be' crippled?" repeated the Least Fang grimly. "You foresee a reasonable alternative to engaging the enemy's fighters?"

"I do not," replied Ankaht, who then looked directly at Wethermere. Who was, as she suspected he'd be, still rubbing his hair, but with a familiar, intense, almost dazed look on his face. She had learned it meant he was not only thinking hard, but had embarked upon ideational pathways that were, to say the least, unconventional.

Kiiraathra'ostakjo followed Ankaht's gaze to the human and then grumble-growled. He shook his neck as if being pestered by a hornet. "Oh, no—not more of the captain's outlandish schemes. I had my fill of those in the last war."

"We won those engagements, didn't we?" Ossian asked with a grin.

"Yes, and we were very nearly killed each time we did so. It is still a matter of amazement to me that I am alive, and I pay for that past folly by occasionally recollecting how you convinced me to follow such bizarre schemes. And now you would have me do so again?" Despite Ankaht's rudimentary understanding of Orion body-language, she could tell that the Least Fang was struggling mightily to suppress one of his race's closed-mouth grins.

"Oh well," Ossian replied with a raised hand, "if you'd rather I didn't contribute to our strategy—"

"Cease being—what do you humans say?—coy, Ossian Wethermere. I suppose habit alone requires that I listen to yet another one of your wild plans. First, tell me how you propose to match Amunsit's waves of fighters in open combat."

"By not engaging them at all."

Kiiraathra'ostakjo's eyes closed. "And so the madness begins again. Explain this to me, human: how do we defeat craft without engaging them?"

Ossian shrugged. "Let me start with an analogy: if I shatter a dam to flood a valley so my enemies may not march across it to reach my forces, have I not, practically speaking, defeated them?"

The Orion opened one eye—grudgingly. "I suppose we may allow this conclusion—for sake of argument. But when the waters recede, your enemies will still be there."

"Yes—but I won't be."

The Least Fang reclosed his eye, his brow lowering as if he was attempting to suppress an imminent headache. "And so you mean to simply flee? Again?"

"We would not be fleeing, Least Fang, but moving toward a new objective."

"Which is?"

"Which we don't know. Yet."

The Orion's brow had lowered to the point where

his shut eyes were almost lost in folds of his flexible, furred hide. "I forgot how unpleasant this part of your scheming was, Ossian Wethermere. In the past, I think I ultimately agreed with you simply to stop the pain. I will be stronger, this time. Explain yourself fully." Kiiraathra'ostakjo muttered the last sentence in a tone as fatalistic as that commonly used by condemned men to utter their last words.

"There's really not a lot to explain," Wethermere assured the Orion. Ankaht secretly doubted the human's claim, but did not interrupt. "It's a matter of deduction, given what you just told us about the relativistic kinetic kill vehicles striking throughout the PSU, Kiiraathra. Those multiple attacks, all happening at the same time, are not chance. Which means that Amunsit knows—or has a pretty damned good idea—of where these new strikes are landing, and where the new Arduan fleets are going to show up. And if that's true, they might not be worried about what we wrongly perceive as their 'rear area'—because it might not *be* a rear area. Amunsit may be counting on whatever fleet hit New Valkha to watch her back as she moves toward Zephrain."

"Yes, but Amunsit cannot be sure that we do not have units—whole fleets even—in between those two forces."

"Maybe . . . but maybe not. What if Amunsit's agents plotted out all our strategic concentrations over the past six years, tracked them through redeployments? If she did, then it's a surety she passed that info on to the new Dispersates."

Kiiraathra'ostakjo shook his head. "How would Amunsit have such ability, though? I mean no offense," he said, turning deferentially in Ankaht's direction, "but not even the Councilor or the other most accomplished *shaxzhu* of the First Dispersate possess such ability."

"I can't tell you how. But, in considering if there's an alternative explanation, let me ask you this: if Amunsit doesn't have that ability, then how did she manage to ensure that those kinetic kill vehicles took out the forts keeping her fleet out of the Amadeus system? And if that tells us that she was able to send targeting data to the inbound Dispersates, it also tells us that she could send any other strategic data she might have, as well. Naval depots, transport hubs, command and control nexi, industrial centers: they would have targeted all that, and more. However, it seems unlikely that the new Dispersates would have had the resources to hit them all."

"Which is the only reason that this is still a war, not a slaughter."

"Yes," Wethermere concurred, "but it's also an opportunity."

"What kind of opportunity? To strike back?"

"Yes, eventually. At a time and a place of our choosing. Fighters and all. Because the actions and placement of Amunsit and the new Dispersates gives us an opportunity to glimpse their strategy."

Ankaht saw it. "Of course. Since the new Dispersates cannot target everything, what they struck must point toward what they need to achieve, their larger strategic plan."

Ossian nodded. "Exactly. But to gather that information, we need to stay almost totally hidden. Happily, this system is an excellent choice for that. However, we will still have to gather more news on what was struck, and where other Dispersates have arrived, so we must send out a recon unit. We have to both keep tabs on the progress and position of the Zarzuela fleet and also learn more about other strikes. Once we have enough intelligence, and have sorted the truth out from the rumors, we'll be ready to know where to go."

Kiiraathra'ostakjo seemed to have forgotten his headache. "Let us presume that your conjecture about there being other Arduan fleets in other directions is accurate. Let us also accept your conjecture that their commanders are not concerned with rear security. In that event, Amunsit might not attempt to press into the Bellerophon Arm but, rather, hold the narrow approaches from it to keep Admiral Yoshikuni's immense fleet bottled up there."

"That's true."

"In which case, following the logic of your plan, we might end up fleeing to safety back along the route we have just come. Into whatever sprawl of chaos the Khanate has become in the invaders' wake."

"That, too, is true," Wethermere conceded with a nod.

Kiiraathra'ostakjo shook his ruff. "In the years that have passed, Wethermere, you have changed in only one way."

"And what is that?"

"Your plans have ceased to be outrageous; now, they are utterly insane. So, quickly: detail our reconnaissance unit's intelligence-gathering protocols before I change my mind. Or put one of us out an airlock."

"*Which* one of us?"

"I haven't made up my mind about that either. Yet."

Part Three

The Flood

CHAPTER TWENTY

After knocking on the tall doors, Admiral Yoshi Watanabe waited until a smoky contralto voice thready with age bade him enter the office of the Rim Federation's Consular Liaison for Arduan Affairs.

The room he entered reminded him of a small cathedral: walls that shrank inward and upward into a high ceiling comprised of a tessellated array of groined vaults. Tall, narrow windows—four meters high, at least—gave the impression of vertical murals depicting the Old Town of some quaint city on distant Earth's European continent. At the far end, behind a very large mahogany desk, sat an impeccably groomed silver-haired woman whose body still had enough curves to suggest the vital physique that she had possessed many decades ago.

"Madam Consul," said Watanabe as he saluted.

"Oh, let's not be so formal, Yoshi," Miriam Ortega remonstrated with a smile. "And don't stand all the way at the door. I can hardly see whether you're smiling or scowling, from this distance."

"Neither, Ms. Ortega."

Miriam sighed, rose, came around her desk: it was not a short trip. "Yoshi, for now, in private, you will call me Miriam or I will spread vicious rumors about your love of fluffy toy poodles."

"I don't even have a dog."

"That doesn't matter. I have a way of convincing people on pretty much every planet in the Zephrain system—but particularly here in Prescott. Who's that lurking behind you?"

"I'm Hilda Silverman," offered the young blond woman behind Watanabe. "But everyone calls me Hildy."

"Well, will *you* call me Miriam?"

"Well, sure I will—Miriam."

"See, now, Yoshi? How hard can it be if your adjutant can do it?"

Watanabe stifled a sigh, walked into the room, hand outstretched toward Consul Ortega. Hildy trailed behind with a gait that he could only characterize as "chipper." "Ms. Silverman is not my adjutant: she's my flagship's 'sensitive.' The best we've got, since Jennifer Pietchkov is—otherwise occupied."

"I . . . see. I do not mean to offend you, Ms. Silverman—you are most welcome, here—but exactly why have you brought your sensitive with you, Yoshi?"

"Because it is my intent to furnish you with her services, should the coming situation unfold in such a way that you shall need them."

Miriam's smile became slightly more angular, slightly more a matter of self-control than simple affability. "Exactly what are you expecting, Yoshi?"

Was she really going to make him spell out the obvious? Well, yes, she probably was. That was consistent with what rumor said of her. Miriam Ortega was a formidable figure in Xanadu's politics. In the Federation government for decades, and its chief justice for almost two decades after that, she had finally stepped down three years ago, citing advanced age and a desire to "freshen" the court by removing her familiar and well-established voice from its deliberations. However, no sooner had she stepped down than Kevin Sanders—the spymaster who, like Miriam, was also ostensibly "retired"—had immediately initiated the suggestion that she be tapped as the Rim Federation's Consular Liaison to the Arduans of the Bellerophon Arm. His suggestion had not been overt, of course, but when it arrived, it had the hallmarks of his methods and reasoning as clearly as if it had come on his own letterhead.

Suggested in a cordial diplomatic memo submitted jointly by Terran Republic admirals Li-Trevayne Magda and Ian Trevayne (Miriam's past lover, in what could only be described as Ian's first life), the recommendation called out and lauded Miriam Ortega's many singular qualifications for the post. It cited her proximity to the war with the Arduans and subsequent exchanges with them, her demonstrated ability as an excellent interspecies liaison, and her qualifications as the Federation's consummate and elder stateswoman. Who was now, unexpectedly, free of her judiciary responsibilities. No other candidate existed with either her credentials or her sudden availability. And so Miriam's retirement had, instead, become the start of a new career.

Of course, it had been anticipated that this would be a fairly leisurely post. Human-Adruan relations were good, Amunsit's Zarzuelan fleet was fenced in beyond any chance of escape, and the primary purpose of the presence of the Consulate on Xanadu was to ensure that the increasing *modus vivendi* between Arduans and humans (much of which was being brokered unseen by Ankaht and Captain Ossian Wethermere of PSU Naval Intelligence) existed and proceeded under an official aegis. And so it had been a perfect career-end occupation for Miriam Ortega: low stress, flexible hours, self-crafted agenda, occasional strategizing, and state dinners.

That had changed abruptly and dramatically in the last two weeks as Admiral Amunsit's Zarzuelan fleet had come charging out of the Orion border systems, even as news was pouring in from every corner of PSU space about the relativistic kinetic kill vehicles that were devastating installations, worlds, even whole systems. The old day-to-day routines were beyond recollection, given the horrors that now surrounded them.

But all this seemed not to have perturbed Miriam Ortega in the least. So far. But Watanabe suspected even her composure would be sorely tried by the news he came bearing. "I'm afraid I do not have good news, Madame Consul—er, Miriam."

"I expected that, Admiral. You have come to tell me in person. That's a great deal more inconvenient than simply sending me a message. So I am presuming that this is news that needs to be kept out of any electronic transmission system—since, ultimately, all such systems can be compromised. And that usually means bad news."

"I'm afraid that's correct, ma'am. And that explains why I've brought Ms. Silverman with me."

"Indeed? I already have the Council of Twenty's

First Councilor, Amunherh'peshef, here on-planet, should I need to communicate with any of the new Arduan—intruders."

"True, Madam Consul—but who shall help you communicate with Amunherh'peshef? The vocoder is a fine device, but trust me: it is crude and obliterates nuance. And you will need a skilled sensitive like Ms. Silverman to be sure you are able to detect—and impart—the kinds of subtleties that might be crucial during negotiations for our possible—" Watanabe could not bring himself to speak the word "surrender."

"For the possible cessation of hostilities?" Ortega furnished.

Yoshi felt his face grow suddenly hot: somehow, it felt worse that Ortega had had to save him by finding a palatable euphemism. "Yes, Madam Consul." He hadn't meant to become more formal, but instinct—and the somber direction of the conversation—made it feel unavoidably appropriate.

Miriam seemed to concur. "Do you mean to imply that all hope is lost, Admiral? Already?"

Watanabe looked up sharply. "Absolutely not, Madam Consul. But the news, as you surmised, is not good, and we had best provide for all eventualities." *And I will be damned if I get Hildy Silverman killed. But I can't be sure how this battle will turn out, and she has a daughter and a husband back on Bellerophon*—"So it seemed best to handle your introductions to Ms. Silverman first, which more or less reflects preparations for a worst case-scenario. Be assured, I am not here because I expect to be defeated, but because my staff and I do have doubts regarding a decisive victory against the approaching fleet from Zarzuela."

"Very well. I am ready to hear your news, Admiral."

"Yes, Madam Consul. The most important item is our report from the pickets monitoring conditions in the New India systems, which is too sensitive to put even on coded lascom: the morale implications are too profound to risk it being intercepted or discovered in comm records later on."

For the first time, Miriam Ortega's face fell into lines that suggested her true age. "So the conditions there are as bad as suspected."

"Worse, ma'am. Due to the high-velocity collisions and the generation of extremely energetic secondary and tertiary impact debris showers, the system is currently impassable for a fleet, and will be for some time."

"Really? Even if a fleet avoided maneuvering directly across the system, but followed the edge of the heliopause from the ingress warp point to the egress warp point?"

Watanabe shook his head. "Madam Consul, we can only track the *large* debris with any precision. We know where there are other, smaller objects, but we can't keep a fix on all of them. Worst of all, they are spreading throughout the system, generating more collisions and debris all the time. And as I'm sure you're aware, the variations in vector and velocity of every piece of that secondary impact debris makes any general navigation plots almost useless."

"Admiral, I am no military or space expert, but I was under the impression that your ships, in order to operate at subrelativistic pseudovelocities, must still be able to detect—and either destroy or deflect—navigational hazards smaller than a marble. If that is true, then why are they not functioning in New India?"

"Oh, they are functioning, ma'am, but their tracking capacities are completely overwhelmed. What you are referring to—collision mitigation systems—are designed with very occasional debris encounters in mind. One object per minute at most, and those are isolated in deep space: tracking and destruction is fairly straightforward under those conditions. But in New India—Ma'am, the number of contacts are hundreds of times that amount, and they can be closing on us at high speed from almost every facing. Most are coming from starward, and along the plane of the ecliptic, but even that trend is diminishing. As a result of the very first impacts, some debris shot outward and struck bodies in the local limit—or Kuiper—belt and Oort cloud. And now, some fragments from those secondary collisions are coming back in-system.

"The Bellerophon couriers which were trying to reach us last week sent in some of their fastest, nimblest scout ships. Three made it into the inner system. One was hit—and vaporized—by extremely high-velocity junk. The other two had to turn back when they detected several new relativistic kinetic kill vehicles inbound at a range of four light-minutes."

"A second set of attacks?" Ortega's voice was admirably calm and collected.

"No, ma'am: just a few purposeful stragglers."

"I'm sorry, Admiral: could you explain how 'stragglers' would also be 'purposeful'?"

"My apologies for that confusing turn of phrase, Madam Consul. We project that after the inbound Dispersates were done redirecting the paths of their colony arks, but before they broke them up into immense clouds of lethally fast junk, they probably detached some parts and decelerated them, slowing each subsequent package a little bit more than the one before it. That way, the wreckage of those objects would arrive in dribs and drabs after the big deluge smacked the system."

Ortega nodded. "So that, in addition to the increasing amounts of post-impact debris flinging itself around the New India system, there will be periodic arrivals of new relativistic kinetic kill vehicles, adding an additional level of unpredictability to an already chaotic navigational environment."

"Precisely so, Madam Consul. Consequently, all we were able to get from the scouts by lascom was that, even without the conditions in New India, there would have been quite a delay back at Bellerophon, anyhow. Much of the fleet was still returning from the just-concluded wargames. Many of the further detachments are still in transit back to their primary duty stations. That means the fleet will not be gathered for many weeks. Their estimates are that it would take at least a month for even seventy percent of the total capital ship tonnage to be ready in Bellerophon itself."

"Which means it will be at least three weeks too late to help us here."

"Yes, ma'am. I would say that, between what the barrage by the approaching Dispersates did to New India and the bad luck of having our main fleet still recollecting itself in the Bellerophon Arm, we are entirely on our own."

Ortega nodded. "I take it you have other news."

Yoshi straightened his shoulders. "I must update my estimate on how outnumbered we are likely to be. My analysts are now running estimates from three-to-one to five-to-one."

Ortega studied him for a moment. "And you think those estimates are still low, don't you, Admiral?"

Watanabe did not want to, but he nodded. "I do not fault my analysts: they were working with the best numbers we had available when we started running the inferential data algorithms, twelve days ago. But we started the exercise with significant handicaps. Our sources—both military recon units and civilian witnesses—invariably had to flee before they could get complete data on the numbers and types of ships they saw. And the reports we've had since then, of apparent enemy actions deep in Orion space, suggest that the Dispersates have sent their fleets to systems other than those they bombarded. Consequently, there might be a second, larger fleet following on behind Amunsit's. And even if there isn't, the reports from Orion space suggest that Amunsit's fleet may not have any need to cover its rear or flanks."

"Because she may have recently-arrived friends back there, destroying any of our units which could have moved in behind her."

Watanabe considered Ortega narrowly. "Madam Consul, for a woman who professes ignorance of military matters, you seem a surprisingly quick study."

She smiled slightly. "Yes, Admiral Trevayne often made the same observation. So, Amunsit needs hold nothing back for rear-area security: she can put everything up front in attacking us."

"Precisely. And there's another variable that problematizes our estimates. From the reports we have of the fleet that emerged from Zarzuela, we do know the Arduans have abandoned their former decision to field a very limited number of ship classes. They have now shown us an equivalent of almost every combat class we have in our own formations: monitors, dreadnoughts, cruisers, frigates—but none of our three largest classes, the super-monitors, devastators, and superdevastators. And no large carriers, although they have produced an immense number of special light carriers that don't seem to so much support flight operations as they simply dump their combat wings as soon as they arrive in-system. And the collective size of those wings is—enormous."

"Again, no precise numbers, just that they are enormous?"

Watanabe tried to keep his face from becoming grim. "Collectively, the Arduans have been deploying thousands of fighters in every engagement. How many thousands remains unclear. Any ship that stays around long enough to perform a nose-count gets swarmed by them. Their weapons are not as advanced as ours: they apparently did not get enough technical intelligence to copy our sustained-fire energy torpedo systems for either their main hulls or their fighters. But with their numbers, that hardly matters. Whether they use hetlasers, force beams, or missiles, they are like army ants attacking an elephant: the elephant can destroy hordes of its attackers, but that doesn't even begin to touch the vast numbers arrayed against it. Or change the inevitable outcome."

"I see." Miriam leaned back against her desk: a young woman's posture that still seemed to suit her and did not detract one bit from the gravitas of her advanced age. "So tell me, Admiral: do you have any *good* news?"

"Well, ma'am, if we stay in deep space, where the

Desai drive operates, the fighters of both sides lose most of their advantages. They can't keep up with the larger ships because they're too small to mount Desai drives, which virtually double their speed once they are outside the Desai limit of any given planet or star. That will force the Arduans to come at us with their capital ships alone. They'll try to bring up their fighters, but if we give ground at the right pace, the fighters will fall behind the line of battle while the comparatively smaller Arduan capital ships get hammered to pieces by our devastators and super-devastators. We'll take a lot of damage, but we're big enough to handle it. Their ships, even the monitors, will get pounded into rubbish pretty quickly if they stand toe to toe with us."

"But they have an immense numerical advantage in capital ships as well."

"Which is why they'll actually hurt us. Otherwise, we'd blow them to dust before they could score any significant hits against us. This way, Madam Consul, we'll know we've been in a fight, but I believe we'll win it. However, if they show up with another fleet equal to the size of the one we expect that Amunsit is bringing..."

"Understood, Admiral. I only ask that you perform miracles, not the impossible."

"Thanks, ma'am. That will certainly help morale, I'm sure."

Miriam laughed at Watanabe's deadpan quip. "I do not wish to keep you from your duties, Admiral. Indeed, it sounds like you have a fleet to put in order."

"It's already in order; it's just awaiting the word. And today, the word must be given."

"Then I wish you Godspeed, Admiral. And be assured that I shall certainly see that Ms. Silverman is given the opportunity to help us, should the necessity arise." And Watanabe saw the look in her eyes which added, almost as clearly as if she had whispered it in his ear, *And I shall see to her safety.*

Watanabe nodded his professional respects and personal thanks, saluted, stepped back, and shut the old-style manual doors in his own face.

They closed with an echo that sounded like the first footstep of approaching fate.

CHAPTER TWENTY-ONE

Yoshi Watanabe stared at the holoplot. For the fourth time in the last hour, he studied the dense clusters of green specks denoting the ships of his fleet and tried to take comfort in that impressive array.

And it was an impressive array. Not up to the gargantuan standards of the three main battle fleets of the PSU, the two of the Terran Republic, or the Federation's Bellerophon Arm Fleet, but a vast array of firepower nonetheless. No fewer than three superdevastators and seven devastators formed the core of a vast swarm of smaller capital ships, although no one seeing those accompanying monitors, superdreadnoughts, and battleships of both regular and heavy marks would have ever thought to apply the adjective "small" to any of them.

Arrayed in support positions behind the thirty-eight forts which enclosed the warp point to Rehfrak like a great bowl of high-tech weaponry, armor, and shields, the capital ships of Watanabe's Home Fleet waited in several groups that would be able to converge firepower upon entering forces from a number of angles, and yet make good time carrying out an orderly withdrawal that was also an evolution into a single van. Behind these mammoth ships, carriers lurked like prowling pumas, ready to deploy fighters if and when it became feasible to provide close support or add to the anti-missile counterfire possessed by the ships of the line. Supporting both categories of ship were the smaller cruisers and destroyers, rarities in this epoch of the titanic hulls which had dwarfed them into both strategic and tactical obsolescence. Now, they largely existed as converted special-function craft, which either provided additional bases of defensive fire against both missiles and smaller enemy ships, or as redundant relays, in the event that the fire-coordinating data-links were jeopardized by losses among the capital ships. The cruisers and destroyers were large enough to house computer suites capable of maintaining net integrity until direct links between the remaining heavyweights could be rerouted.

It all looked quite impressive, Watanabe allowed, but would it be impressive enough? Judging from the intermittent trickle of enemy recon drones now coming through the warp point from the other side, the Arduans were certainly not the tactically simplistic foes they'd been six years ago. Having spent years fighting against inventive human defenders and monomaniacally reembracing their military roots, Amunsit's *Destoshaz*-as-*sulhaji*-driven war machine had clearly adopted a number of defensive protocols from their recent antagonists. They had also innovated a number of their own new systems that capitalized upon their greatest single advantage: *selnarmic* control and communication links.

In the last war, the Arduans typically initiated a barrage of recon drones that ultimately saturated the defenders so badly that one of the drones was sure to survive the punishment long enough to return with a snapshot of what existed on the other side of the warp point. This time, however, the Arduans sent in waves of pinnaces sowing bottle-sized microsensors, closely followed by a mix of both automated and crewed survey escorts that gathered the readings from the sensors. Since the data was harvested instantaneously by *selnarm*, the escorts had only one task: after entering the system, they immediately performed a 180-degree tumble and then accelerated to get back out as quickly as possible. Perhaps four out of five did not make the transition fast enough: Watanabe's hundreds of energy-torpedo banks—the new standard weapon throughout all the modern formations of the Federation, as well as the Republic and the PSU—kept the warp point drenched in a steady stream of withering fire. But the overlapping plasma discharges and exploding ships often interfered with targeting sensors just long enough for an occasional enemy escort to escape once again. Which meant that Amunsit would have a pretty fair idea of what she was facing when she finally brought her formations through.

It also meant that she had seen the absence of point-blank defenses near the warp point. Whereas, at the start of the last war, Watanabe would have seeded the area with virtual thickets of laser buoys and sleeper missiles, the Arduans of the First Dispersate had demonstrated an ingenious way to quickly annihilate those defenses. Their specially designed *Urret-fah'ah* minesweepers (called "stick-hives" by their human adversaries until their proper name was learned after the war) were fundamentally a cluster of clearing charges that swept clean immense swathes of space around the warp point less than a second after entering it. This had the net effect of eliminating the great majority of area denial ordnance the humans used to block ingress from a contested warp point. Consequently, Yoshi had placed his mines and buoys further back, distributing them as a smaller bowl arrayed around the warp point. Their firepower was now an impediment to any enemy ships attempting to rush the forts, particularly those which tried to close and launch their fighters—for suicide runs, if nothing else.

As if that thought summoned the inevitable into existence, a wash of red pinpricks started flooding out of the purple hoop that designated the warp-point in the holoplot. "Transit," shouted Sensor Ops.

"Readings?"

"Mixed, sir. Various classes of ships, highest concentration of arrivals supportable by this warp point. And apparently some hulls are immediately undergoing modular separation, Admiral—and the modules are putting out a heavy density of defensive fire against the forts' missile barrages."

"Then save the forts' missiles, and task our energy torpedoes to kill those modular ships." Amunsit's Arduans had evidently saved another surprise to spring on him. It rapidly became clear that the modular ships were conjoined hulls that were detaching from each other, each part serving as what might be called a defensive fire dreadnought. They were immense hulls with nothing but armaments designed to burn down the missile salvos that the Arduans had rightly come to expect from the forts defending a warp point.

Watanabe frowned. But surely the Arduans would therefore be *expecting* his shift to energy torpedoes. It was the best way to kill these defensive ships, which came through linked so as to maximize the number which transited the warp point without increasing the risk of having multiple hulls catastrophically rematerializing in the same volume of space. But if that were true—

"Comm ops, immediate message to fleet: shift energy torpedoes back out of the offensive fire net immediately."

"Sir? Do you intend—?"

"Immediately! They are suckering us, damn it. Send that order!"

"At once, Admiral—"

No sooner had the countermanding order to detask the energy torpedoes been sent and obeyed than enemy SBMHAWKs began flooding out of the warp point. Watanabe leaned forward to issue the order he had foreseen giving. "Energy torpedoes are to commence anti-missile defensive fire. Immediately."

"Yes, sir! But now, how do we engage those defensive dreadnoughts?"

"Instruct the forts to use their missiles. They are to employ launch protocol Zulu Hotel Five. That won't get all of the defensive dreadnoughts, but it will attrit them significantly. And at their current range, the armaments on those dreadnoughts can't hurt us."

In the next half minute, it became obvious that the Arduans' attempt to catch Watanabe off guard—with his batteries dedicated to killing the dreadnoughts, not guarding against a torrent of missiles—had mostly failed. The unprecedented number of SBMHAWKs that came through the warp point in one long rush did manage to score a few hits upon the forts, but none suffered any disabling damage.

But in the meantime, Amunsit had fed in even more of the modular defensive dreadnoughts during brief lapses in the SBMHAWK barrage, so that the net effect was that she had slightly increased the number of them on the Zephrain side of the warp point by the time five minutes had elapsed.

At which point, Arduan monitors started rushing in and Watanabe realized how wrong his analysts had been, and how limited the reports they'd been working from.

Firstly, the transits of these new Arduan ships were so closely spaced that they were arriving faster than they were being reduced to junk, even by the combined missile fire from the forts and, now, Watanabe's own capital ships. But it wasn't just that the numbers of Arduan monitors were increasing too quickly; they were also dying a little too slowly. "Sensor Ops, get me data on those Arduan monitors. Do they conform to the class stats reported in prior engagements?"

"Sir," replied Sensor Ops with a slight quaver in his young voice, "our technical intelligence on their monitors is still incomplete. But these seem to have more armor and shields than were reported to us. Of course, it's possible we just didn't get complete data on—"

"No," Watanabe cut him off. "It's a new sub-class. Look at the drive field characteristics, the power spike, the tuners. These ships are heavy assault hulls, designed to secure a foothold by being able to absorb more damage for a short amount of time. They're not meant to last for years but months, at most. They exist solely to function as the edge of the wedge when the Arduan fleet has to crack its way through warp-point defenses."

Which is just what they were doing. Now that a frail ring of what Watanabe already thought of as heavy assault monitors had established a thin perimeter beyond the warp point, conventional capital ships started flooding through. Along with them came immense framework hulls that were nothing but engines propelling a huge grid of flimsy, single-shot missile bays. Once these bays were cut loose from their tugs, *selnarmic* fire-control directors on other ships sent launch commands almost immediately. Each framework annihilated itself by unleashing a single wave of heavy missiles equal to the combined broadsides of any two of Watanabe's devastators. Watanabe's defensive assets labored to keep up with this flood—which allowed yet another wave of conventional ships to pour in through the warp point.

"Sir," Commo Ops obtruded cautiously. "I've had a contingency warning alert from our lead minisensor. Enemy hull density near the warp point has now reached Stage II."

Which meant that, although it would take hours yet, the mathematics of the engagement were already inevitable: the thirty-eight forts guarding the warp point from Rehfrak were ineluctably doomed. The enemy weight of metal was already too great to retake and effectively "shut" the warp point again. The rate at which incoming tonnage was now accumulating would be able to absorb all the damage the forts and

Watanabe's fleet could throw at it, and still increase sufficiently to be able to reduce the forts to junk. And once that happened...

"We hold here for the planned duration," Watanabe ordered through a long, faint sigh. "We will commence withdrawal evolution Romeo Baker One when that time has elapsed, or until I either move up or countermand that evolution. At that time, the forts' commanders are to switch over to automated control and their crews are to abandon their facilities by individual escape pod. Until then"—Yoshi leaned back in his chair—"we stand our ground and kill them."

While they—increasingly—kill us in return.

Amunsit recovered readily from the shock of warp-point transit—she was always among the first to do so—and noted that the command system recovery subroutines initiated by proto-*selnarmic* biots already had her ship ready for orders, even before her crew had recovered enough to carry them out personally.

"Evasive protocol Sefnur-two," she sent at the *selnarm* pickups. "PDF batteries are to preferentially sort enemy missiles by proximity and time to impact." Her flagship, the monitor *Rakhu'umt*, cut sharply to starboard and pitched down, but thanks to the inertial compensators, Amunsit felt only the faintest hint of that motion. Even that marginal sensation was probably imagined, suggested by the rapid change of perspective relayed by the primary viewscreen.

Her crew now recovered, Amunsit allowed herself to relax into her command couch once again. "Report," she ordered, glancing at the holopod.

"The human—apologies: the *griarfeksh*—capital

ships are finally withdrawing from the forts, as per the most recent report—"

—After twelve hours instead of the estimated eight, Amunsit fretted behind the high *selnarmic* wall she maintained as part of her command image—

"—and their deployment is not structured so as to suggest the presence of cloaked formations."

"Confidence of that projection?"

"Results differ when considering enemy elements employing tactical cloaking versus strategic cloaking."

"I require tactical assessments only. I know there is no way for us to infer distant reserves that might be cloaked. I seek only gaps or misleading weaknesses in the present battlesphere."

"Yes, Admiral. Confidence regarding the absence of tactically cloaked adversaries stands at eighty-five percent."

Amunsit allowed herself the luxury of savoring that estimate for a long moment. "Excellent. Commence phase two."

"Sending courier back to alert the echelons in Rehfrak now, Admiral."

Amunsit sent (acknowledgment, approval), considered calling for a casualty report, but simply glanced over at the holopod again. Most of the *murn*-colored human forts were now ringed with a *vrel*-hued sheath: they were heavily damaged, probably in imminent danger of becoming inoperative or of being wholly destroyed. Most of the enemy's largest ships had pulled well back from them, although one devastator had lagged behind. Still near the forts, it seemed to be covering the withdrawal of a slightly smaller ship—a monitor—that had apparently suffered some species of drive failure. Several of

Amunsit's heavy superdreadnoughts, the backbone of her fleet, veered out of echelon to engage: perfectly acceptable, since they were part of the reserve kept to exploit unforeseen opportunities. At almost the same instant, the human ship adjusted heading to better face these new threats—despite the fact that the range was three light-seconds. Amunsit was suffused with (caution, watchfulness, anticipation): such an immediate response should have been impossible at a range of three light-seconds, since the information could not travel faster than light. Unless . . .

The extent of the First Dispersate's betrayal is as reported, then. It is most fortunate that we have confirmed this so inexpensively—

An urgent probe from her Tactical Prime lashed at the edge of her *selnarm*. "The *griarfeksh* are communicating faster than they should, Admiral. I can't explain it—wait. No! It is—they are using *selnarm*, Admiral! *Selnarm* links! But I thought the humans were incapable of *selnarmic*—?"

"No," Amunsit interrupted, uncoiling from her semi-repose, "it is not the humans." Her bridge staff turned, puzzled, in her direction.

Amunsit savored the moment. The time had come to share the outrage of which her intelligence operatives had heard whispers, and about which defectors had speculated. And she would be able to reveal it as having been finally confirmed here, in the very teeth of the battle, as the great mass of her fleet came flooding through the secured warp point to sweep the last of the forts aside as so much irradiated junk. Revealing this horror now would double the implicit outrage at the underlying treachery, since the vast majority of her

Destoshaz warriors would be learning it at the same moment that they arrived in the Zephrain system, witnessing how many thousands of their cherished comrades had been discarnated. All because the humans had been aided by an even worse enemy of Illudor.

Amunsit rose. "The humans are not responsible for what you are detecting," she repeated for emphasis. "The *griarfeksh* hide no greatness. They are just what we have determined them to be: soulless *zheteksh*, without reincarnation or *selnarm*. What you are detecting are the traitors of the First Dispersate who refused to join us in Zarzuela. Instead, they have joined the enemies of our race—the enemies of Illudor—in an attempt to ensure our destruction." She paused, and to amplify the effect of that caesura, stared around at her rigid crew before she finished. "You see now the depth of our peril and the urgency of our quest. These humans were able to turn our own kind—our own brothers and sisters—against us. And in so doing, they have split the heart of Illudor in two. We must make Him whole again, must purge the traitors of the First Dispersate from the Holy All that is His Mind and His Will. Then, and only then, may we be one people, will our *narmata* be serene and unified once again."

Among the *Destoshaz* of the Second Dispersate, *selnarm* had only been used for basic communication since its contingent of *shaxzhu* were purged. Consequently, the bridge crew not only sent a wild maelstrom of (rage, vengeance, hatred, horror) but emitted a vocal chorus of sibilant barking coughs that were the Arduan equivalent of roars of incoherent fury.

Amunsit rode the surge of their emotions, used the dominance of her *selnarm* to bind it into a wave, a unified collective will. "Now, we sweep them before us. All of them."

Her crew, released from the mesmerizing shock of the moment that she had bound into her charisma, returned to their tasks with a vengeance.

The human devastator was already catching up with its fellows, the monitor having recovered from its brief engine failure. Tactics Prime stared into the holopod, estimating distance, and sent, along with (eagerness, vengeful rage, precision), "If we accelerate quickly, we can catch the *griarfeksh* devastators. Our ships are smaller, faster, and they will not perceive the special threat that we bear within the hulls of some of our monitors. We could destroy many, maybe most, of them if you would allow—"

Amunsit soothed his (eagerness) with (sagacity, patience, savoring a kill). "Never spring a big trap to catch small game, Tactics. You will show little promise as an aspirant to command if you cannot innately understand that. And there is no game in this system that is large enough to be worth revealing the weapon to which you allude. We must come up with another stratagem to overwhelm the humans, today."

Tactics Prime thought. Then sent (canniness) and "That means we must resist any impulse to strike or chase them hard, now. We must wear them down."

"And then?" She wondered if his tactical thought would be a recapitulation of her own.

"And then, when we have chased them far enough, we will use our fighters to destroy them. And by using our fighters to cripple their largest ships, we will, in turn prompt them to misconceive the doctrine we have developed for the greater engagements to come. They will see us use our fighters decisively here and project that this is the diadem in the crown of our campaign strategy. They can hardly have reason to believe otherwise: since the Traitor Narrok offers his counsel to them now, and was the one to develop the *selnarm*-controlled fighter concept, our enemies will thus know that we are not losing pilots, only easily replaceable equipment. They will therefore presume that this use of fighters is our trump card. Which will ensure that they are wholly unprepared for the greater surprise we hold in reserve, at such time as we spring it."

Amunsit felt an unuttered nuance in his plan. "I sense that, when referring to our use of fighters here, you do not simply refer to the wave attacks we have used elsewhere."

Tactics Prime answered, "No, Admiral—or to put it more accurately, what I envision *is* a wave attack, but they will not see this one coming. Not in time."

Amunsit felt the images and outlines of his nascent tactical innovation, sent (approval, congratulations) as she reassured him, "Yes, Tactics, I suspect you may indeed have a future in command."

After all, his plan *did* closely match her own.

Yoshi Watanabe accepted the cup of green tea proffered by the limping ensign—well, the CPO who had been brevetted to ensign—but waved away the accompanying cup of noodles. He knew the Arduans were up to something. He'd learned to sense it in the last war. However, the last five days—during which he had mounted the most desperate fighting retreat of his career—had sharpened that sense to razor's-edge acuity.

Over the course of those days, Watanabe had been the one springing the surprises. That is largely why his fleet was still in existence, although it had now been chased halfway back to Xanadu. He'd fought a sharp engagement just within the heliopause of the main system, then seemed to run—only to unleash his cloaked reserve of devastators and supermonitors when the Arduans pressed their pursuit within ten light-seconds of the system's outermost planet. Using *selnarm* to communicate through the field effect that concealed his force in the shadow of the planet, Watanabe had sprung his hulls out of stealth at the optimal moment and then watched them spend two hours sending an unrelenting torrent into the enemy's trailing flank. Whereas eight years ago, the impact of the attack would ultimately have been limited by the number of missiles available, this time it was able to continue nonstop, carried out by the immense array of energy torpedo batteries on all the humans' capital ships. The Arduans were so badly hit, with so many ships flaring and tattering into mobile debris fields even as their drives gave out, that Amunsit eventually had to retract that flank and withdraw to dress her ranks. By which time Watanabe had scooped his units back together and quit the battlesphere just far enough to reform into a refreshed and strengthened line.

But ultimately, that had only bought him half a day. The Arduans of the Second Dispersate came on harder than ever. And while they could be slowed, they could not be stopped. It did not matter how many times Yoshi was able to tempt them to overextend into a gap in his lines that was actually a prepared kill zone, or how often they fell for his trick of dressing his ranks for the final showdown—which compelled them to do the same—only to scoot off and leave them with nothing to show for their efforts but three wasted hours. No matter how many skirmishes he won, the Arduans' numerical advantage was always decisive, always washed over whatever tactical innovation he had employed and set him back on his heels yet again. And he was running out of both time and space.

Watanabe had been able to spring one last trap—set up weeks in advance—when the Arduans, of necessity, chased his fleet past the main system's largest gas giant. There Watanabe once again stood his ground, a bit starside of the huge planet's orbital path. Seeing their prey inside the gas giant's large Desai radius, the Arduans deployed their fighters—and as they did, came under extremely high-velocity railgun fire from several of the sizable nearby moons. The Arduan fleet hitched to a stop while their fighters turned and hunted down their mostly automated bushwhackers, taking some significant losses in the process. And in that interval, Yoshi once again slipped away.

That had only been yesterday, but it felt like a year ago. The Home Fleet was now operating in comparatively constrained space, having less running room as it fell back closer and closer to the Federation's capitol, Xanadu. And this morning, the Arduans' foremost echelons had begun an evolution into a new formation, akin to an elongated wedge.

"What are they doing?" Sensor Ops wondered aloud.

"I don't know," Watanabe commented, "but they didn't want to show us this trick until now." *Not until they had chased us right up against Xanadu itself.*

In the plot, enemy ships began clustering into a

dense cone at the head of the wedge, but even as they did, their contact-icons became erratic, intermittent.

"Sensor Ops, what's happening with our arrays? Why are we losing clear location on the bogeys?"

"Our arrays are fine, Admiral. They're, uh, cloaking, sir."

Watanabe felt momentarily disoriented. "At this range? They've got to know their cloaking won't work when they're this close. Hell, we'll have lock again before—"

A red gush of tiny enemy icons came jetting out the nozzlelike end of the approaching cone of Arduan ships.

"Admiral, missile launch—hundreds! Thousands! No—"

"Understood, Sensor. Tactical—"

"All batteries engaged for PDF and firing, sir."

Nice to have my mind read, Watanabe observed silently, but also conceded that on this bridge, over the past five days, they had come to know each other's in-combat habits extraordinarily well. Indeed, the first crew had become quite adept at finishing each others' sentences.

On the screen, and in space, it appeared as though a wide, thin disk of supernovas had flared into existence between the receding and approaching fleets like an immense plate of white fire, creeping closer to Watanabe's fleet as the mean range of intercept diminished. A few enemy missiles were even getting through, but mostly, the problem seemed to be—

"Mean range at intercept is dropping too sharply, Tactics. I want more distance from those warheads, Mister."

"Trying, sir. Their volume is higher than our intercept capacity, ever since we lost another of the devastators two days ago. We're still getting all the missiles, but with less time to spare."

"So their warheads are going to inch closer until they get right on top of us."

"Looks like it, sir—unless we give ground faster."

Damn, that's just what I can't do anymore. And Amunsit knows it. "Tell me, can you get a lock on any of the enemy ships?"

"No, sir. I can't see anything through that rolling blast pattern. And sir—"

Watanabe saw it before Tactics or Sensor Ops could call out the alert. The missile detonations, while somewhat less intense, became individually expansive, almost whiting out the whole screen. The enemy was firing Anti-Mine Ballistic AntiMatter Missiles—AMBAMMs. Immense warheads for clearing minefields—and a weapon system that the Arduans had never used until now. And, with a sudden plummet of his stomach, Yoshi was fairly sure he knew why they had waited until today to unveil it . . .

"Sensor, fix targeting arrays on the near edge of the detonations."

"Wha—what, sir?"

"The near edge of the line of detonations: target arrays are to be preranged to that limit. Expect bogeys. Just do it, damn it. Tactics, prepare to launch fighters and to shift to—"

With the AMBAMMs having approached to within one half of a light-second, there was a sudden drop in the resulting free-energy spike—

Sensor Ops' shout was not panicked, but loud as she

tried to keep up with all the slightly larger contacts that were suddenly appearing—on the viewscreen and in the holoplot—from where the concentrated high-energy interference had been creeping closer just a moment before. "Bogeys, small ones, bearing 05 by 344, 10 by 271, 358 by 02 . . . !"

"Tactics," shouted Watanabe, "dedicate all energy-torpedo batteries to close-range fighter intercept. All missile tubes are to fire on the enemy capital ships that will be right behind them. Salvo until we're out of danger or dry."

"Yes, sir. Salvoing missiles and firing batteries. Carriers report double-time launch ops underway."

In the viewscreen, Arduan fighters approached like a glittering cloud of glinting needle-tips. In retrospect, Amunsit's tactic was plain: she had moved her carriers forward, first counting on the interference thrown up by the cloaked heavies to obscure that positional change. And then, once the sensor disruption from the massive wave of missile detonations had both reached its peak and made its closest approach to Watanabe's fleet, she had launched her fighters. With almost every encountered Arduan ship carrying at least one flight wing, the numbers of inbound bogeys went beyond hundreds, or even thousands. It was in the tens of thousands. And there was no way to shoot them all down before they got close enough to—

Watanabe did not miss the irony of his ethnic origins as he gave the order: "Tactics, reserve five percent of energy torpedo batteries for counteracting kamikaze attacks."

That was the moment that the first of the small, fast Arduan fighters angled straight for his bridge.

CHAPTER TWENTY-TWO

Miriam Ortega removed the ear bud that she used for secure communications and put it down slowly, was conscious that her head was bowed. At the upper edge of her vision, she could still see Hildy Silverman's sandaled feet. Usually perpetually in motion, those almost dainty feet were now utterly still. "Our fleet?" Hildy's voice asked after a long moment.

"Yes, it's been defeated." Miriam was mindful that she had about an hour of normal existence remaining. Then, there would be invaders landing on the planet she had inhabited for—well, no use counting years at this stage of the game.

"And Admiral Watanabe? Is he—?"

Miriam sighed. "He is dead."

When Hildy began her next question, there was the hint of a quaver in her voice. "And the other sensitives and officers that I—?"

"Hildy." Miriam looked up. "They are dead. All of them."

Hildy's voice was suddenly very small. "*All* of them?"

"All," repeated Miriam. "Every ship, every escape pod, every drifting spacesuited survivor: all killed." She looked up, stared out the window at the quaint architecture of Prescott City. "It's a miracle they agreed to a parley under a flag of truce, in Government House." She jerked her head at the window behind her, where the capitol dome was located.

"I guess they were only interested in killing combatants. That's how they were during most of the first war."

"Hmm. Yes," Miriam responded, allowing her genuine distraction mask the subtler tone of dubiety. Nothing with these Arduans—who referred to themselves as "Kaituni," in their terse communiqués—was similar to the last war. Not their equipment, not their tactics, not their apparent demographics: nothing. So was it good news—a reprise of their prior disinterest in noncombatants—that they were willing to parley in about an hour's time? Or did they have other, unfathomable motivations?

"And maybe we hurt them badly enough that they need to try to establish a truce."

Miriam nodded, but considered the situation from additional angles. Yes, Yoshi had certainly fought as hard, as well, and as long as anyone could have expected or hoped. He had been outnumbered by more than six-to-one in tonnage, and far more than that in the sheer number of hulls. Even so, he had used his *selnarm* communications specialists to ensure that his fleet had reaction times almost as quick as those of Amunsit's armada. Using that communication speed in conjunction with his own tactical innovations, Watanabe had managed to kill almost thirty percent of the invader's tonnage—which was to say, for every ton he had lost, he had destroyed two.

But ultimately, his tonnage had been reduced to zero, every ship a victim to the incessant pounding of Arduan fighters, missiles, hetlasers, and force beams. In exchange, hidden sensor arrays indicated that while the Zarzuela fleet was operationally intact, it was very badly attrited. With only seventy percent of its hulls surviving, and almost a quarter of the survivors inoperative until receiving extensive repairs, it was clear that Amunsit now had little choice but to settle into a defensive war. With disproportionate losses in its heavy assault monitors and fighter wings, her fleet would have been unable to break through Bellerophon's imposing defenses, many of which were Arduan-built and in place from the last war. Six years ago, Bellerophon and its home defense fleet had not, ultimately, been attacked from without, leaving its vast structure of forts and immense system defense ships intact. Bellerophon was, as Ian Trevayne had once commented, "the Gibraltar of the Federation." Miriam smiled to remember how his staffers had nodded approvingly, vigorously—and then gone bobbing off to consult their history books to find out just what "Gibraltar" was.

Still, all that did not mean that the Kaituni had, in any way, experienced any change of heart since entering the Zephrain system. Meaning that the parley was probably not an opportunity for the government of Xanadu to dicker, but simply to get a measure of their new, and infamously intolerant, masters. And to hope for their benign disinterest.

The door chimes, favorites of Miriam's, sounded

altogether too cheery and banal today. "Come in," she said.

The doors parted slightly, revealing Senior Councilor Amunherh'peshef. Alone. Wearing his vocoder. "I have come, as you asked. Unattended and unannounced."

"Excellent, and thank you. Allow me to introduce Hildy Silverman, one of the best sensitives we have. I suspect we may be working together today."

Amunherh'peshef fluttered congenial tendrils at Hildy. "A pleasure, Ms. Silverman. Tell me, Madam Consul, are we going to the meeting with the Kaituni delegation?"

"Very possibly," Miriam answered. *Although I think it's equally possible that we're just a small enough group that we could make it out of here on the lam, if we have to.* "I'm just waiting for a call from—"

The computer's communication software activated and toned twice. Miriam spoke aloud. "Answer call." Then: "Hello?"

"Miriam?"

"Yes, Darrell. It's me."

"Good. Are you alone?"

Miriam looked meaningfully at Hildy and then Amunherh'peshef before she answered, "Yes, I'm alone."

"So why no video link, Miriam?"

"Something I learned from Ian Trevayne about situations like this: minimize anything you narrowcast or broadcast. We should presume security is compromised. The enemy may, after all, have agents among us presently. Or much earlier, giving them the opportunity to emplace sleeper bugs that the invaders are just now awakening with coded broadcasts."

Darrell Schweitzer, vice-president of the Federation

High Council, paused. He was a capable man, and charming, but had no wartime experience, like most inhabitants of Xanadu. The last war with the Arduans had been bottled up beyond the warp point that led from the Astria system into Bellerophon. But if given the chance, he was sure to adapt quickly. "Okay, Miriam. You're the seasoned pro here, so you call the shots on communication protocols. Look: the leader of these fleets, Amunsit, has agreed to come to Government House in forty minutes to discuss the terms of the occupation."

"Did she say that, *specifically* that?"

Schweitzer paused. "No, but words to that effect."

Yeah, I'll bet. "I'll get over there right away, but first, I think we should— "

"No," Darrell interrupted. "No, Miriam. Don't come here."

"Why not?"

"Because"—Darrell sounded uncomfortable and embarrassed—"because the Kaituni specifically asked that you not be at the meeting."

For the first time in a very long time, Miriam Ortega was completely taken off guard. "They excluded me from the gathering? Me, specifically?"

"Yes, Miriam. I'm sorry."

"Don't be. I'm not. But I'm puzzled: did they say why?"

Darrell sighed. "They explained that this is not going to be a negotiation and they do not want to contend with requests or questions from traitors."

"How am I a traitor? I'm not one of them,"

"No, they don't mean *you* are the traitor, but they do point out that, as our Liaison to the Arduan Consulate, you are likely to be an advocate for their interests. And they are dead set against having any such disputation at their meeting with us. Amunsit is bringing her own representatives who have experience communicating with humans, and assure us that a standard vocoder will be good enough for both sides. Although we'll need more than one vocoder."

"Why's that?"

"Well, with the government's full complement gathering here, we can hardly—"

"What? *All* the members of government?"

"Yes. You were told about that an hour ago, weren't you?"

"Well, I was told that it would be a 'full house' . . . but I didn't know that was literally going to be the case."

"Yep, everyone who's in town right now. So just sit tight, Miriam. We'll want you watching and commenting on the proceedings from where you are, with the Arduan Consul. Look, I've got to go. We're going to have to come to order soon, get consensus on a few issues."

"Is consensus going to matter, if Amunsit has said there's not going to be any negotiation?"

"Damned if I know, but legislators need to feel like they're, well, legislating. My attitude is, if it calms them down enough to sit through what is likely to be a pretty grim list of occupation ultimatums, then the honored representatives can all frolic in Government House's fountain and have a sing-along, for all I care."

Miriam smiled. Irreverent comments like that were exactly why she had always liked Schweitzer. "I see your point." She lowered her voice. "Are you going to be sending live feed of the meeting with Amunsit to me here, in my office?"

"Yes."

"To our secure surveillance facility, also?"

"No, that would disrupt the standard overwatch protocols on your own office, Miriam. We've got no good reason to distract the personnel keeping an eye on you. We'll have enough recorders and live feeds on the meeting with Amunsit, as it is. I've got to sign off now."

"Go herd legislators, Darrell—and be careful."

"Ahh, legislators might growl a lot, but they're not really dangerous."

No, Darrell, but Amunsit might be. "Let me know if you need anything from my end."

"Will do, Miriam. See you."

Miriam murmured her own farewell and closed the comm application. She thought for a moment, looked up at Amunherh'peshef. "Senior Councilor, I haven't wanted to bring this up because, officially, I'm not supposed to know about it, but I believe your people have been conducting research into the likelihood that your long journey across space not only shifted the bulk of your race's demographic into being members of the *Destoshaz* caste, but that they have been trending towards a recidivistic form. Evolutionarily reverting to a more primitive, less—well, let us say less 'civilized'—genotype." Miriam stopped, stared at Amunherh'peshef.

Who blinked all three eyes. Rapidly. Three times. "That . . . that is somewhat accurate," he reported through the vocoder.

"Senior Councilor, please. We don't have time to pick our way through the delicate minefield of secrets we know about each other but shouldn't. We are confronted by an unprecedented situation which threatens both of us and we need to be frank and forthcoming."

Amunherh'peshef's eyelids closed and opened slowly: in Arduans, it signified considered, yet profound, consent. "It is as you say. How may I help?"

Miriam crossed her arms. "I need a ten-minute review of what you've found out regarding the fundamental reasons, and ways in which, these later-Dispersate *Destoshaz* might think and act differently than those of the First Dispersate. And why. 'Why' is a very important piece of the puzzle, for me."

"Very well—but in ten minutes?"

"Maybe fifteen, Senior Councilor—but that gives us just about enough time to turn on the live feed from the capitol, pull up our chairs, wish we had some popcorn, and watch the opening ceremonies of the conquest and oppression of Xanadu."

"I see." Amunherh'peshef's voice became more firm, then. "Perhaps we had best get started, then."

"Perhaps so."

The ten-minute presentation took almost twenty minutes. But the results were fairly clear—and worrisome. "I can see why you did not want to share these statistics," Miriam commented as the last graphs and pie-charts vanished from the far wall's half-holo display.

Amunherh'peshef's tendrils wilted slightly and recovered: the Arduan equivalent of a mild shrug. "Who would wish to advertise that their race was becoming monstrous? The trend we discovered in our own—the First Dispersate's—*Destoshaz* was onerous enough. But what little we have learned of Amunsit's Second Dispersate suggests that the recidivistic trend increases asymptotically. I now wonder if the last Dispersate departed just before the day when Sekahmant finally novaed and destroyed Ardu, or rather, much earlier."

"Why earlier?"

"Because it may well have been that the changed population of Ardu had so regressed into violence and discord that, long before the final doom was upon them, it ceased to be capable of the coordinated work necessary to launch another Dispersate. Unlike you, we had no Dark Ages in any of our cultures, and now we may see why we were so different from you in that regard. Among humans, it is society that devolves, but, being uncasted, your demography remains unchanged by that decline. Your potential for learning, for higher achievements, may lie dormant, but it remains, awaiting the hints of organization and growth that will nurture its return.

"But with us, the evidence is pointing to a more sweeping and profound downward spiral, just as our upward course was uninterrupted. For centuries before the Dispersate, we had known no war. The synergies of thought and belief and common interest that united our world were not arduous achievements; they were natural consequences of our increasingly inclusive and broadly attuned *narmata*. In retrospect, it would have been strange if our need for national distinctions had *not* withered and eventually fell away, the way your butterfly rises up and leaves behind its cocoon. For us, dissolving the boundaries between states was not a battle, nor an abandonment: it was the shedding of a redundant feature."

As presented by the vocoder, Amunherh'peshef's voice became lower, darker. "We never had a reason to contemplate that there might be an equal but inverse course of devolution, if our unitary culture suffered a debilitating crisis or sustained threat. But now we see that there is an inverse phenomenon. Just as there was little obstruction to our achievement of greater unity and peace while our society was intact and growing, the surety of our planet's impending death triggered a reciprocal decline toward those primitive traits that recall the dispute and discord of our early societies. I fear that began happening from the moment we learned of Sekahmant's imminent self-destruction and our need to flee Ardu however we might—and in so doing, break away from the environment and rhythms that had nurtured and maintained our best traits and social accomplishments." His tendrils fluttered in what even Miriam could read as a gesture of shame and despair. "As we rose, so did we fall."

Before she could arrest the impulse, she reached out and touched the Arduan's smooth, sloping gold-yellow shoulder. The texture was akin to that of a muscular seal: strange, but not at all unpleasant. Amunherh'peshef flinched—whether from surprise or revulsion, she could not tell—but she also didn't care, at least not for the duration of this one moment, this one statement she felt had to be made. "Your race has stumbled, but has not fallen. You and your Dispersate are proof of that, and your people shall rise to their former heights once again. I am sure of it."

Amunherh'peshef's three eyes blinked sharply, and though his skin seemed eager to twitch away from the alien contact, he remained where he was. "Your faith in us restores my own. If it is even evident to an alie—to a human, then perhaps we foresee a truth when we embrace the same vision, rather than a forlorn hope for a self-image that we cannot bear to surrender."

The moment was past: Miriam removed her hand. "We of the Rim Federation are the better for having you here among us, no matter how unfortunate the consequences of our first meeting were." She looked out her windows toward the distant dome of Government House. "Or how unfortunate the current circumstances seem to be." Miriam checked her delicately wrought antique watch—an anachronistic affectation, but a beautiful grace note that she felt added just the right panache to her appearance—and moved quickly to her computer. "It's just about time for the show to start, I think." She turned on the communications application, searched for an incoming link—the live feed from Government House—and was surprised to see no pending comm channel flags blinking. There was no signal at all.

"Miriam," Hildy said softly, "I believe our visitors are already here. Look out the window."

Miriam glanced up; dark, slightly bulbous delta shapes were circling down out of the clouds: Kaituni transports. Between and around them, flitting like so many anxious hornets, were their transatmospheric fighter escorts.

Miriam frowned, pressed the virtual button that would recall Darrell Schweitzer at his personal comm number. There was no response—and then, the carrier tone dropped out abruptly. The line had gone completely dead.

Miriam felt a pulse of dread, and her earlier reservations returned: *All the government in one place?*

She tried various comm links to reach her colleagues in any one of a dozen different offices, scattered throughout the city—and discovered that none of them were in service.

Miriam resisted the urge to look out the window. "Hildy," she said, keeping her tone of voice casual, even a bit cheery.

Hildy had proven to be an eager, skilled, and very perceptive aide in matters pertaining to liaison work with the Arduans. Luckily, she hadn't been with Miriam long enough for her perceptivity to become so refined that she could discern that the older woman's current calm was pure theater. "Yes, Miriam?" was all she said.

"Are you familiar with the remote surveillance facility we use to monitor events here and in the Arduan embassy?"

"Yes, ma'am."

"I need you to go there at once. Use the tunnels. Oh, and given all of today's overdramatic nonsense, you might as well seal them behind you. Use protocol one: it's the easiest." *And also the most absolute.* "I need someone to keep an eye on what's going on in this building and the Arduan embassy."

"But Miriam, what about the facility's routine security staff? Surely they will be watching the—"

"The surveillance facility's regular staff have just been reassigned to overwatch the security of Government House from a remote site, Hildy," Miriam lied. A lie which Hildy would discover as soon as she opened the door to the surveillance control room and found the customary team there. But with the tunnels sealed using protocol one, it meant that she would also be safe and unreachable from any conventional surface entry in the city. She'd have a long trek out of that bolthole, but it also meant that she would be able to report what she saw in the monitors of the surveillance center—whatever that turned out to be.

Hildy was frowning as she gathered up her folders, her palmtop computer, and began moving for the tunnel entrance which was concealed in a reading alcove at the back of the study adjacent to Miriam's office. "Madam Consul," she said quietly, using Miriam's formal title for the first time since the late Yoshi Watanabe had introduced them, "I'm not sure I should be—"

"Hildy, my dear, you've picked a very awkward time to be voicing reservations about my requests. Trust me; I need your eyes in the surveillance room—and I need them there now. We can discuss your present concerns when this silliness is resolved—but not before." Miriam smiled. "Now, scoot."

Hildy's mouth smiled in response, but her brow retained the frown. "Yes, Madam Consul." She walked into the adjoining study with an uncharacteristically measured gait.

Miriam stared out the window at the descending Kaituni ships—including several types she'd never seen in any intelligence briefings—until she heard a dull clump in the study: the tunnel entrance had not only been closed, but was now hermetically sealed behind the full course of stone that had slid into place behind it. To anything less than a deep densitometer scan, the wall of the alcove was now as solid and thick as all the others.

Amunherh'peshef's voice emerged from his vocoder. "A question, Madam Consul."

"I'll try to provide an answer worthy of it, Senior Councilor."

"Your dismissal of Ms. Silverman. Most peculiar. She might have been quite useful to us—to me—in relaying any nuances of Amunsit's interactions with your government. The vocoder is—a crude medium of translation, at best."

Miriam nodded. "Yes, Senior Councilor. I'm aware of that. Keenly, painfully aware of that. But I had other considerations."

"And they were—what?"

Shadows flitted across her window like haunts, just before Miriam saw the two sleek delta aircraft which had cast them appear from behind the roof of the neighboring Health and Medical Bureau Building. The vehicles began to stoop, like accelerating hawks, down toward Government House's dome.

"*Those*, Senior Councilor. Those are my considerations."

She knew the safety protocols: during the Fringe Revolution, she had drilled along with everyone else, living in fear of possible rebel bombardment. But this day, she was slow to follow the reflexes she felt pushing her down beneath the lower edge of the window frame. It was not age which slowed her, but a split-second, and wholly unprecedented, state of mind: morbid curiosity. That she should have lived so long, and done so much, to have been standing here to see this—

Missiles and plasma bolts shot from the transatmospheric Kaituni fighters toward Government House and the capitol complex surrounding it, but they were not the largest hammers being wielded against the seat of Xanadu's government. Their launch must have also confirmed and fixed general targeting coordinates for batteries on orbiting ships. A moment after the smaller weapons of the fighters peppered the capitol complex with gouts of orange flame and gray-brown dust, a brace of HVMs—high-velocity missiles that traveled at almost five percent the speed of light—shot downward in a blazing white ring that bracketed the cupola atop the dome of Government House.

The entire building complex disappeared in the flash, and amidst the cyclonic outrush of the blast wave, beams from orbiting ships played back and forth within the furious holocaust.

"Madam Consul!" Amunherh'peshef's vocoder screamed.

Miriam dropped, suddenly terrified and panting, a moment before the windows all along that wall of her office blew inward, the air momentarily filled with a glittering sleet of ostensibly blast-proof glassteel. The pieces chewed into her desk, shredded the woodwork and shelves lining the far wall, riddled her computer, sent a tattoo of shards through the back of her empty chair. Then the air seemed to rush back out a bit, then huff back inward, and she had the brief, surreal impression that she was living in a giant, respirating lung.

But then, the expansion-backdraft pressure cycle equalized and the room was still.

Only for a moment. As Amunherh'peshef rose unsteadily to his feet—several superficial torso wounds leaking his species' dark maroon blood—sounds of gunfire erupted both overhead and below.

Miriam looked to the Arduan Councilor, who

clutched his vocoder, which said: "Troop landers, on the roof—and in the street. They must know that this is where—"

"Yes. They know we"—*or at least* I—"will be here." Miriam had a brief recollection of Hildy's face, glad that least one thing had been saved from the inferno of this day, and started violently when a firefight broke out abruptly on the other side of the doors to her office.

She heard automatic weapons of several types. She heard a deep hissing boom—a human plasma gun—drowned out by the rushing roar of Arduan rocket launchers. Explosions rocked the room, knocked over the bookshelves on the far wall, blew holes in the wall, through which she could see flames, smoke, arms and legs and falling silhouettes. And could hear more weapons, and screams throughout. Screams that grew more shrill—

The redoubtable Miriam Ortega dropped behind the ruins of her desk, trembling, hands over her ears and felt, for the first time, like an old woman. Not a gracefully aging woman, but old and weak and very vulnerable in the middle of weapons that were all capable of turning her into just so much ground meat and bones in a fraction of a second.

And, although she had been married, had children, loved and lived a rich life—all because Ian Trevayne's mortal wounds and medical cold sleep had taken him from her—it was nonetheless his face, his gentle smile, that she now saw. And clung to, in the impregnable realm of memories that were far away from this intolerable present.

But the present cacophony of death found a way

to echo even in that inner sanctum of recollections: Ian had been—first, foremost, and always—a soldier, a man whose profession was war. So, this had been his world: navigating this horrible chaos of sights and sounds, each of which was, in fact, a split-second warning of approaching death, jumbled in with a dozen other equally dire but different threats. *Ian, I always imagined I knew what you had experienced, knew the horrors of the duty you found respite from when you returned and came back into my arms, but this—*

The deafening reports ended abruptly. Two voices continued screaming—until two additional machine gun stutters ended them, as well. When Miriam heard the now-savaged doors creak open on their mauled hinges, she could not resist the impulse to stand, regardless of the danger. She was not going to meet enemies while crouched and trembling like a snared rabbit behind her desk. *Besides, it's not as if they're going to overlook me.*

The group of Kaituni entering were visibly different from the Arduans that Miriam had come to know and respect. Even their warriors and security personnel effected a profoundly different appearance. This group was wreathed in body armor that seemed to shift and contract as if it were comprised of interleaved laminate sheathes made of slick, thin rubber: the suits whispered like voices from the grave as the Kaituni troopers entered the room. Their weapons—unlike the multipurpose paramilitary models still carried by the First Dispersate—were large-bore, cassette-fed battle rifles of some kind, each with a different underslung heavy weapons system, the types of which eluded Miriam's limited knowledge of such hardware.

But more arresting still were the sweeps of color that adorned each of the suits; all similar, but with variations that probably denoted differences in role, rank, or both. And at the center of this flying wedge of guards was a medium-sized golden-variety Kaitun whose movements immediately reminded Miriam of a Siamese cat she had once owned—or who had owned her. That matter had neither been very clear, nor ever resolved. And that sinuous cat's disdain-tinged autonomy was somehow reflected in this Kaitun's movement as well: this was a creature that tolerated no master and admitted to few, if any, peers.

Miriam waited to see if there was a selnarmic exchange between the central Kaitun (whom she presumed was Amunsit) and Amunherh'peshef. Once you knew Arduans well enough, there were sudden flurries of slight movements—tendril gestures and almost ticlike head motions—that indicated that one of their high-speed telempathic exchanges was in progress. But from what Miriam could tell, Amunsit simply stared at Amunherh'peshef, and he stared back. Then the admiral's eyes turned towards Miriam. "You are the Consular Liaison, Miriam Ortega."

It was a statement, not a question.

CHAPTER TWENTY-THREE

"Yes, I am Miriam Ortega." Miriam kept her tone and volume level as she continued. "And I protest your cold-blooded massacre of the government of both this planet and much of the Rim Federation. Any civilized rules of conflict—"

"Do not apply here," Amunsit's vocoder announced. "Rules imply contracts. A person cannot make a contract with an animal, with a *zhettek* such as yourself, such as your species. *Zheteksh* are not capable of higher functions, or the higher understandings necessary to be party to agreements with actual persons. Which this *flixit*-brained traitor"—she indicated Amunherh'peshef—"has either forgotten or misrepresented in his exchanges with you. I suspect the former, since I cannot see any reasonable course by which the First Dispersate's surrender would serve as a means to ultimately lure you *griarfeksh* into either subjugation or extermination. Rather, he and his followers have actually come to believe the heresy they spout: that you humans are in fact persons."

"They are," insisted Amunherh'peshef. "And they have sensitives among them who—"

"Yes, sensitives who were able to infect your weak minds with the infantile rot that a species which has any evidence of telempathic capability—no matter how limited and outré—is somehow a brother race, a species of persons. Idiocy and heresy, both. The *gri-arfeksh* and other aliens are not of Illudor: they do not reincarnate, they are bound by no common sharing of *narmata*, and have no access to *shaxzhutok*—although in that regard, they may have an advantage over us."

Amunherh'peshef's mouth sagged into an almost perfectly round hole. "You reject—you contemn—the visions of past lives, of *shaxzhutok*?"

"I do not reject them, but I do not consider them a basis for authority. The *shaxzhu*, and their *selnarshaz* servitors, have ruled us long enough with their inarticulate babble about past lessons and the archived lives of exemplars. Whom, you will note, were overwhelmingly representatives of their own castes." Her tendrils threshed restively. "But this is pointless and tiresome, to say nothing of irritating. You"—her left cluster rose up in Amunherh'peshef's direction and the hooklike claws clacked together for emphasis—"let down the wall of your *selnarm* and reveal your identity."

"I shall not let down my *selnarm* but I shall identify myself. I am Amunherh'peshef, Senior Councilor of the Council of Twenty. And I—"

Amunsit's golden skin became almost incandescent. "The arch-traitor himself. Well, second after the Eldest Sleeper Ankaht, that is. You figured prominently in Torhok's reports, before he died."

For a moment, Amunherh'peshef seemed too stunned

to speak. "Torhok's . . . reports? But Torhok has been dead almost seven years, and he hadn't the power of *shaxzhutok*, certainly not enough to send the iconic invocations of our commonly held tales, of the parables—"

"Prating fool." The vocoder infused Amunsit's voice with a rich measure of contempt. "Still trapped in your worship of lives and deeds of the past. Still consulting the long dead for answers to the urgent present. Idiot. Torhok and the rest of the Dispersates needed no complex *shaxzhutok*. We only needed *selnarm* itself to signal across the distances, to flash on and off just as all binary codes do."

Miriam understood. "Morse code."

"What?" asked Amunsit.

"Morse code was a way of communicating, a code that was simply comprised of long signals, short signals, and extended silences between them."

Amunsit's teeth snapped—a gesture and sound that Miriam had never heard from an Arduan before, and found aversive and fearful. Amunherh'peshef flinched as if he had been poked by a hungry cannibal.

Amunsit gestured toward Miriam. "The human sees it. Torhok was the one in the First Diaspora who stumbled across the simplicity of the method which was already in use among the later Diaspora."

"And by this," murmured Amunherh'peshef, "you knew when and where the other Dispersates were coming, coordinated the recent deluge of attacks against this part of space."

Amunsit's response was slow, as if she were savoring every word of it. "Targeting our arrivals and bombardments optimally was the simple part of the task, since all our ships had been sent forth into the same thirty-light-year footprint of space, as seen from Ardu. This meant that changing destinations was not so arduous, given that we had as much as eight years at 0.5 cee to effect it. That gave every Dispersate a four-light-year radius of potential destination change within the footprint. Given that we had Dispersates Three to Sixteen at our disposal, we were able to assign a sufficient force to almost every target in the region of space toward which we were headed."

Amunherh'peshef's vocoder voice was small, stunned. "You have—fourteen Dispersates arriving near here?"

"Near each other in real space does not equate to near each other on the trail of warp points. Since there is no strong relationship between warp-point links and the physical proximity of the two stars so linked, this provided us with the opportunity to deliver strategic, system-killing strikes throughout the polities that the humans call the PSU and the Rim Federation. And since my agents—and your defectors—were able to build an encyclopedic database of industrial centers, transit hubs, fleet stations, refitting depots, and a host of other strategic targets, we were able to both cut the pathways whereby your fleets might reinforce each other, as well as inflict maximum destabilizing damage. By the time your military units and key planets have recovered, the outcome of this war will be a foregone conclusion.

"It was that same collection of data which allowed us to expand both our competencies in science—notably, genetics and advanced computers—and reform our fleets so as to be truly wartime tools of destruction. As you have experienced, we are no longer shackled to a few classes of warship, supported by vehicles and systems designed largely for explorers and planetary pioneers. Our equipment is now proper for warriors, arriving to conquer, not settle like so many neutered *bilbuxhati*. And, again unlike the First Dispersate and even my own when it arrived, the later Dispersates have spent the last five years doing nothing but training in the personal operation and tactical doctrine of using this vastly expanded armory of weapons. Which includes some with which you are not yet acquainted, and one which you taught us how to make and to use: a warp-point generator."

Miriam hoped she had been able to keep the brief flash of panic from registering on her face. Perhaps she had; perhaps Amunsit was too poorly versed in reading the facial nuances of humans.

Or perhaps she was simply too absorbed in her own preening: she had turned toward Amunherh'peshef once again. "Where is your sensitive, traitor? I would—study—such a human."

"I do not have a sensitive assigned to me," the Senior Consul replied truthfully.

"The sensitives were all assigned to the fleet," Miriam half-lied. "So you'll have to consult your own genocidal captains as to where you might find their remains—if any are left." She suppressed, but did not eliminate, the fury from her tone of voice.

Amunsit stared at her. "You speak boldly for a *zhettek*, aged creature. It is the one puzzlement I have not resolved in my contemplation of your species. Logically, having no hope of incarnation, you should be more eager than we are to retain your life, but—at moments such as this—you seem willing to risk it for no gain. I do not understand this."

"There's a lot about us you don't understand," Miriam said through half-clenched teeth. "As you'll learn soon enough."

"A threat. How quaint and pointless." Amunsit's vocoder voice was more bored than dismissive. Then she turned back to Amunherh'peshef and, in one smooth motion, raised her right tentacle cluster. The wrist-surrounding machine pistol she had ready in it stuttered briefly. Amunherh'peshef staggered backward, the slugs evidently exploding within him. He fell to the marble floor, and a dark maroon pool of blood spread out to cover the spattering that had been left by the impacts, as if guiltily trying to paint over its own mess.

Amunsit turned back to Miriam, paused, and then approached her. With the Kaitun showing no signs of stopping even as she drew within five feet, Miriam backed up before the alien's casual but implacable advance. Hating her age, her powerlessness, she felt her buttocks push up against the wall behind her.

Amunsit stopped, less than half a meter in front of Miriam. In a tone as calm as she might have used to ask a mess-mate to pass the soup, the Kaituni admiral said, "I shall ask one more time: where are the sensitives? You would not have sent all of them to the fleet; you knew we were coming. You would have retained some, in the event that the battle for this system did not go as you hoped."

"Oh, we retained one," Miriam admitted, being sure to allow the conviction of that truth to surge in her voice for the sake of the vocoder. "But when we heard you were coming, where do you think we sent her?" Miriam turned and pointed a blue-veined finger out the ruined window behind her—straight at the seared expanse of rubble where the capitol complex had once been.

Amunsit stared at the distant patch of blasted ground, then at Miriam. Perhaps it was the tones of conviction relayed by the vocoder, or perhaps it was the almost inevitable logic of the human's explanation that induced Amunsit to glance away. But Miriam was fairly sure that her lie had succeeded, and that Hildy was now—and only now—truly safe. But to be sure, it was best to change the conversation, to redirect this monomaniacal ravager in Arduan form. "You look like an Arduan," Miriam muttered, "but you certainly don't act like one. What the hell happened to you—to your people?"

It was the ego-hooking lure that Miriam had hoped it would be: Amunsit turned, stared again, but even a human could see that the look in her eyes was different. The burning topic of the moment had changed. Questions that might inadvertently point to Hildy's continued existence were now far out of Amunsit's mind.

"You are right, human: we are different. And what happened to us was a deliverance from our own laxity, our own decline. We are the Kaituni, and had it not been for the practical and disciplined society which evolved on Ardu as its day of destruction approached, we would have succumbed to the same seductions with which you misled and corrupted the First Dispersate. But I do not blame you *zheteksh*. All organisms fight to survive, and will do so using whatever means are at their disposal. No, it was the moral decay and insipid, heretical optimism of the *shaxzhu* that nearly undid us.

"We took the measures necessary to ensure our survival and that of Illudor. For if you know even the most simple realities of our relationship with the One God of All, you know that just as we depend upon him for unity and life, so he depends upon us to be the agency whereby His Will is expressed in the physical universe. Without us as his faithful children, Illudor would be silent. So our duty is not just to ourselves, but to our god: we are indissoluble, linked, different parts of the same continuum of existence. And our current *Destoshaz'at*, he named Zum'ref, understood the quest that Torhok's reports necessitated we undertake.

"That quest has redefined us, made us something more than mere 'Arduans'—for why should we keep a name from a dead world any more than we should be subject to its equally dead histories through the *shaxzhu*? Rather, Torhok's messages revealed to us that our new identity had to be, as Zum'ref proclaimed, the Kaituni: those sworn to the Quest. Just as the circumstances of our planet's demise had compelled us to flee into space, so the circumstances of our journey's end called us to battle, and revealed that resurgence of the *Destoshaz* caste was a sign from Illudor himself that our survival—and his—depended upon our readiness to win a great war against a massive tide of *zheteksh* foes." Her machine pistol rose to point at Miriam. "Which is to say, against you."

"I am not your enemy. None of us are."

"You are right—at least insofar as even the most ferocious predators are not truly enemies. They are dangerous forces which must be destroyed so that thinking creatures—the Kaituni—may safely survive, and in so doing, carry on the presence and will of Illudor in the physical world."

Miriam smiled. "You almost sound as though you believe that. But I have seen your type before, Amunsit: you exist in every species I know. You have draped yourself in pious words to validate the ravenous personal ambition that is your true motivation."

Amunsit started back, then seemed to pause. When her voice came from the vocoder, it was amused, and possibly pleased. "I see why the First Dispersate was so easily fooled by your species. Some of you have remarkable insight, for *zheteksh*. But no matter: I am not here to debate, but to gather information. You will tell me where the Bellerophon fleet is, its strength, and its current orders."

"Actually, I would if I could," Miriam lied. "But you may notice that I am not a military officer. I am not even a legislator, who might ostensibly hear such things. I am a Liaison to the Consulate of a people—not even a member-state—located within our borders. I had no access to military information. None of any significance." Miriam congratulated herself on that final qualification: lies were often detected because they tended to be absolute statements, simple contradictions of a fact. In contrast, reality was shot through with shades of gray and qualifying statements. Such as she had ended with.

Amunsit stared at her. Miriam watched as the Kaituni admiral holstered her machine-pistol and her vocoder announced, through a sigh, "That is logical. I believe you."

Miriam nodded—and in that moment, felt her chest split open, cold rushing into the interior of her body.

She looked down in time to see Amunsit's cluster rip free of her lower left chest, hooked claws carrying two ribs out of her sliced and bleeding torso.

As Miriam Ortega fell, Amunsit's other cluster came up from the holster and swept across the aging woman's neck. Miriam saw her own blood fly up at the periphery of suddenly narrowing vision, had the vague sense she was falling, hit the wall, rolled off, saw Amunsit towering over her, gore dripping from both claws.

As Miriam's field of vision began contracting from a tunnel to a pinprick, she heard Amunsit's vocoder-voice casually say to her entourage, "We are done here. Commence the bombardment. Leave nothing standing. Or alive."

CHAPTER TWENTY-FOUR

The type B blue giant star known as Pesthouse had no planets, of course. Such a massive protostar, condensing from the interstellar medium, developed a gravitational field so powerful that it sucked all the available matter into itself without allowing any secondary condensation processes to occur around it.

But, Cyrus Waldeck thought, it might as well have a planetary system, given the sheer tonnage that now orbited it.

He stood gazing out the wide viewport of his quarters in the massive space station that was only one element of the immense base that PSU maintained here against the possibility—now so abundantly realized—of trouble from the Arduans of Zarzuela, as well as the never-openly-discussed possibility of a change of heart among the friendly Arduans of the Bellerophon Arm. Of necessity, the base orbited at a great distance from that raging blue-hot inferno beside which the smaller main-sequence suns that warmed habitable planets were like tallow candles. Further out, in fact, than the system's three warp points, whose distances from that hellish primary ranged from nineteen to twenty-eight light-minutes. Few could transit those warp points without an uneasy awareness they were skirting the edges of that monster star's radius of total destruction.

Out here, however, that star was reduced by distance to little more than a point-source of bluish light. But that light was eye-wateringly intense—in fact, the total luminosity was more than equal to that of Sol as viewed from Earth—and it was reflected off the flanks of the secondary weapon platforms, space docks, manufacturing and repair facilities, and other orbital constructs that made up the base. Further away, it also revealed superdevastators whose size made them seem deceptively close.

Not even all the unimaginable horror that had filled every incoming report for the past four months could keep Waldeck from feeling grim satisfaction at the sight of those magnificent, invincible ships.

The communicator on the desk behind him beeped for attention. "Speak!" he rapped.

"They're ready now, Admiral," said the voice of his orderly.

"Very good." Waldeck turned and walked to the adjoining flag briefing room. The task force commanders of Second Fleet rose to their feet as he entered. There were more of them than might have been expected, for "Second Fleet" hardly described the concentration of naval power that had managed to assemble here. Several were Orions, and Waldeck hoped the pills he took against his unfortunate allergy to their fur would be no more ineffective than usual.

"As you were," Waldeck rumbled, and they all sat

down around the long conference table. A bulkhead overlooking them consisted mainly of a large flat viewscreen. A two-dimensional display was all that was needed to represent the warp network, which somewhat resembled a circuit diagram from the early days of electronics. At the time this station had been constructed, that had been all that was needed.

And it's still *all that's needed,* Waldeck told himself savagely. *These later Dispersates may be coming at us out of three-dimensional space, but they can't do us any harm until they light somewhere among our systems. And then they have to advance along the warp lines like anyone else. Which they foresaw, which is why they used up all their generation ships, turning them into rubble for use as projectiles.* His mind flinched away from that thought, as it always did, and as always he clamped the lid of almost a century and a half of habitual self-discipline on it. "I'm going to begin by asking Captain Chuan to give us an updated recapitulation of the strategic picture," he began, referring to his staff Intelligence officer.

"Yes, sir." Aline Chuan stood up and activated the screen. The relevant portions of the warp network appeared, seemingly diseased with irruptions of red. A cursor flickered over one of those leprous intruders. "We know about the fall of Zephrain, of course—"

"Of course," Waldeck echoed. His memory leaped the span of almost a century to the days of the Fringe Revolution. He had been there when Ian Trevayne had held Zephrain and the Rim systems beyond for the Terran Federation from which they had been sundered save a tenuous clandestine warp linkage through the officially neutral Khanate of Orion. Miriam Ortega had been Trevayne's partner . . . and lover. The last part had been the worst-kept secret in the Zephrain system. Waldeck wondered how generally known it was now. And he tried to imagine how the news of Zephrain's fall was going to affect Trevayne.

"—and so we know that the Bellerophon Arm is now sealed off—which is clearly the invaders' intention, as they seem to be fortifying the Zephrain system. We know this because of the abundance of *selnarmic* courier drones in the Arm, coupled with the link that Admirals Trevayne and Li Han created between the Terran Republic and the Borden system during the late war."

"Understood," Waldeck nodded. The link to Borden had been the first use of the Kasugawa warp-point generator, and it had been instrumental in bringing the war with the first Arduan Dispersate to an end. And now it provided a *very* long communications route all the way back to Sol. "But however we got the news, it's bad. We have no realistic expectation of linking up anytime soon with forces from the Bellerophon Arm, which as we all know has become an industrial powerhouse since the last war." He looked around the table, meeting each pair of eyes, human or otherwise, in turn. "And that is especially bad news in light of a report which has now reached us, and which I would like Captain Chuan to summarize."

"Yes, sir. The information came to us fairly promptly, as it went through Orion space and reached Sol within a week, via *selnarmic* courier and Unity Point Five." Chuan drew a deep breath and moved the cursor. "A new hostile fleet has occupied the Alowan system."

All of the faces registered shock, followed by

muttered exchanges. But Least Fang of the Khan Tirnyareeo'zhelak, commanding TF 2.5, was silent and immobile, save that his whiskers quivered with the effort he was exerting not to emit a howl. Waldeck understood. Alowan was the primary sun of the populous Orion world Pairsag. *Or at least* formerly *populous,* Waldeck mentally amended.

"Fleeing survivors were able to provide a surprising amount of information, from which the Intelligence analysts on Terra were able to draw certain inferences," Chuan continued, speaking above the low hubbub, armored in expressionless formality. "For one thing, this is an armada of immense—indeed, unprecedented—size. From the survivors' impression of its numbers, coupled with our knowledge of how many parasite ships a given diaspora is likely to carry, the analysts calculate that this force represents the combined resources of no less than *seven* Dispersates."

The shock in the room was now complete, and a dead silence fell. Tirnyareeo broke it.

"Do we have any knowledge of what these *chofaki* have subsequently done?" he demanded. "Have they entered the Sak system?" He pointed a clawed finger at the screen, indicating the system at the other end of one of Alowan's warp connections—an uninhabited system, but one possessing three other warp points, all leading into the Orion heartlands.

"No, Least Fang. They advanced through Alowan's other warp point, into the Telmasa system, which as you know is lifeless, and continued up the warp chain." Chuan moved the cursor along the warp lines indicated, and Tirnyareeo stiffened anew when it touched the system just beyond Telmasa: Kilean, with two Orion-inhabited planets. The cursor proceeded through the icons of system after system until it reached Home Hive Two.

Vice Admiral Chandra Konievitsky, commanding TF 2.7, leaned forward and studied the screen intently. "It's pretty obvious where they're headed."

"Yes," Waldeck nodded. "Orpheus-2, just two transits beyond Home Hive Two. It's the choke point they've got to secure in order to get to the warp chain linking Sol to Zephrain. Which just proves what we already knew: they've picked their targets very well, using intelligence information that is very good indeed. These incoming diasporas know infinitely more about us than we do about them." *Thanks to the Arduans in Zarzuela*, he didn't need to add. He turned back to Chuan. "How far along this warp chain have they gotten?"

"It's impossible to say exactly, Admiral, as out information is somewhat out of date, despite the best efforts of the recon probes we've been sending along the warp lines. But I can tell you they're advancing slowly."

"Yes," said Tirnyareeo, russet pelt bristling. "I am certain the defenders of Telmasa and Kilean have taken a heavy toll of the *chofaki*!"

"No doubt, Least Fang; from all indications the local forces have been maintaining a determined delaying action. However," Chuan continued carefully, "the principal reason for their slow progress has been congestion due to their sheer number of ships. Since only one can safely transit a warp point at once, it is taking them a lot of time to . . ." She let the depressing thought trail off.

Waldeck wasn't nearly the history buff that, say, Ian Trevayne was. But from somewhere he recalled that in World War II, when Marshal Zhukov had closed in on Berlin, his greatest problem had been "artillery traffic jam": he'd had so many guns that there hadn't been room to emplace them all within range of the Nazi capital. This, he reflected bleakly, was evidently another such military *embarrass de richesses.*

He shook loose from the thought and rapped on the table's edge for attention. "All right, everyone. We all know why the PSU's fleets haven't been able to get in motion and concentrate. They've been maneuvering for a third of a year to try and counter scattered incursions, in the midst of all the chaos that followed the Deluge." Like everyone else, he used the now-universal term for the waves of kinetic strikes that had wreaked such unthinkable devastation. "After all, with so many systems—and their courier services—totally disrupted..."

"Yes, Ahhdmiraaaal Waaldehkh," said Tirnyareeo. "We all know this. And we all know how futile and possibly counterproductive movement without a definite objective can be. Nevertheless, I must tell you..." He paused, then spoke on as though with an effort. "I am forced to admit that patience has never been among the more conspicuous virtues of my race. There are those among the *Zheeerlikou'valkhannaieee* who will mutter that the human members of the Union are less than prompt in responding to incursions which have fallen, and continue to fall, most heavily on our worlds." He quickly raised a hand, palm outward and with claws retracted. "Be assured, Cyrrhusss, I would never suspect *you* of dilatoriness, and neither would anyone who knows how much you have to avenge. I only tell you how some members of my race will feel."

"I understand, Tirnyareeo, and I appreciate your words," said Waldeck. "And I'm gratified that you understand the difficulties that have faced us in the absence of a clear appreciation of what the primary threat is." His voice hardened, and his gray eyes narrowed into slits of resolve. "But now there'll be no more random motion—no more chasing our tails. Now we *do* know where that threat is, and what its target is." He gestured at the screen. "And *this* time we're finally in a position to respond, because we've got the single biggest fleet of the PSU right here! I therefore intend to take the following actions.

"First, I'm going to advance our main body to Orpheus-2, as I expect to meet them either there or Home Hive Two or both, depending on how rapid their progress is.

"Second, I'll dispatch couriers to the patrols in the nearby systems—which are mostly lifeless former Bug systems, anyway—ordering them forward to join us in Orpheus-2. Speaking of reinforcements, we will of course request them from the bases at Alpha Centauri via *selnarmic* relay.

"Third, once we're in Orpheus-2, I'm going to send an advance force further along the warp chain to harass and delay the hostiles as much as possible, for I'd prefer to meet them with our main force in Home Hive Two.

"Fourth, I intend to move as many orbital forts as I have time to, given their slowness, into the systems in warp proximity to what I anticipate will be the main battlefield—that is, into Home Hive One, Orpheus-1 and Orpheus-2." Seeing a few puzzled expressions, he explained. "This is to contain any possible hostile breakthroughs from the decisive battles I expect to fight. *However,*" he added with a tight smile, "I don't really expect any such breakthroughs." He swung on Chuan with an abruptness that made her jump. "Am I correct in supposing that these ships are their usual parasite warships?"

"Yes, Admiral, that appears to be the case for the most part. They have a certain number of vessels of monitor size, some of them apparently for specialized purposes in connection with warp-point assaults—an innovation since the last war. But as a general rule we're looking at ships of heavy superdreadnought size or less."

"Just so." All at once, that which Waldeck had been holding sternly in check ever since he had learned the fate of his homeworld came boiling to the surface, and he no longer tried to contain it. His face took on the choleric red that was a family characteristic, and his voice rose steadily. "At Zephrain, Admiral Watanabe had only a very few devastators and even fewer superdevastators. We have the bulk of the PSU's entire inventory of those ship classes here. If Alpha Centauri responds as I anticipate, we should have *two thirds* of that inventory in time for the decisive battle. I don't give a good goddamn how many monitor-sized or smaller ships they've got. Our devastators and superdevastators, with their heavy gee-beam armament, will *eat* them!"

Heads nodded around the table. The gravitic disruptor, or "gee-beam," developed during the last war, inflicted damage in direct proportion to the mounting vessel's engine power. This, plus the massive projector it required, made it unsuitable for lighter ship classes. But it was one of the things—besides their sustained-barrage-capable batteries of launchers for heavy bombardment missiles and SBMHAWKS—that made devastators and superdevastators so, well, devastating.

"But Admiral," said Konievitsky hesitantly, "at Zephrain, even Admiral Watanabe's heaviest ships seem to have had their defenses overloaded by enormous numbers of fighters, employed without regard for losses."

"I'm not overly worried about getting swarmed with kamikaze fighters, Chandra. To repeat, Yoshi Watanabe had only a very limited number of devastators and superdevastators. The volume of defensive fire *our* big ships are going to be able to put out is something else again. And I believe we have enough carriers to provide adequate fighter cover—some of which," he added, inclining his head to Vice Admiral Sheeraiee, commanding TF 2.11, "are crewed by our Ophiuchi allies." He didn't need to add that the avian-descended Ophiuchi were the best fighter pilots in the known galaxy. "Furthermore, many of our heavy fighters have been retrofitted with rapid-firing energy torpedo systems. Unfortunately, that program hasn't been as far advanced in the PSU as it has in the Rim Federation. But it's enough to restore some of the old punch to our squadrons."

This time the nods were more emphatic. The energy torpedo—a plasma weapon fired as a ballistic projectile at near-light speeds that gave it hit probabilities close to that of a beam but out to standard-missile ranges—had been greatly refined since the last war and was now the primary armament of all ships smaller than devastators. Most recently, further refinement had produced a smaller variant that was practical as an integral fighter weapon. It had given the fighter, once believed to be on the way to obsolescence since the Desai Drive for ships had robbed it of so many of its old advantages, a new lease on life.

"But remember, the main thing to keep in mind is this," Waldeck concluded, "In a stand-up fight, any ship of theirs that comes within range of our battle line is dead. The Kaituni don't know what they're up against, but they're going to find out."

He saw he had them, for the faces around the table lit up with an animation whose absence lately had worried him. The oppressive sense of doom that had held them for four months had almost caused them to lose sight of the fact that they possessed by far the mightiest warships ever built—the ultimate killing machines ever conceived by any of their races. And here at Pesthouse they possessed an unprecedented concentration of those ships, with all their unimaginable firepower.

"Yes!" exclaimed Tirnyareeo, speaking for them all. "And may our claws strike deep!"

CHAPTER TWENTY-FIVE

It was a cool, blustery winter day in the Riverside district of Prescott City. (The Xandies still called it that, not simply "Prescott," as they would later shorten it.) He walked slowly toward the seawall, along the street between the small but character-rich old houses shaded by native trees. He came to the address he had dreaded, opened a gate in a low stone wall, and proceeded reluctantly to the front door. It swung open to reveal the woman who had opened it—an obscenely butchered woman who nonetheless moved in a ghastly undead fashion even as blood flowed from her.

Her mouth opened slightly to form the well-remembered smile... and blood spurted from it.

There was blood everywhere...

Ian Trevayne awoke, shivering and drenched with sweat. He reached across the bed, then belatedly remembered that Magda was still aboard her own flagship. He arose unsteadily, fumbled for his robe, and stumbled through the door into the main sitting room of his quarters, still in the darkness of night-watch but bathed in the illumination that flooded in through the wide viewport. He collapsed into a recliner and stared out at the Alpha Centauri system where he had only just arrived.

By the time the allied governments of the PSU and the Terran Republic had finally shaken loose from the state of shock that had held them paralyzed after the incomprehensible series of catastrophes that had overtaken them, no one had been in any mood to quibble about the fact that Trevayne had, on his own initiative, sent Cyrus Waldeck and his task force to Pesthouse to organize the PSU's strategic reserve there. In fact they had been inclined, in a way almost unprecedented in the annals of governments, to commend him for doing the sensible thing.

They had also belatedly ordered him home from Tangri space with his large fleets, to the defense of the home worlds. (*The recall of the legions*, he had thought, summoning up a parallel from British history as naturally as he breathed in and out.) Under the circumstances, he had seen no constructive purpose to be served by pointing out to anyone that at the time he'd received that order he had already been under way toward that destination for a month.

He had known that order would be coming, so the main thing holding him back had been the moral dilemma he had put himself in by his promise to protect the liberated *zemlixis* against a vengeful come-back by the Hordes. But he had left a substantial task group built around carriers and their escorting battlecruisers to deal with any incursions through the troublesome closed warp point in the system that had previously been the central stronghold of the

Daroga Horde, reasoning that his limited number of devastators and superdevastators were what would be called for in combatting that which was ravening through the home systems. He had also deployed dense minefields and medium-weight battleline units around all the known hostile-interface warp points. Then, reasonably confident that he had honored his commitment to those who had trusted him, he had ordered the massive core of his fleet to commence the voyage home, confident that he would encounter the expected order somewhere along the way—and that no one would begrudge his jumping of the gun. Rather the opposite, in fact.

The route, though long, hadn't been as circuitous as it had once been, thanks to some newly created warp links. Thus it was that he was now here in the great warp nexus of Alpha Centauri, one transit away from the "dead end" system of Sol. It was this system's seven warp points that had enabled humanity to explode outward in many directions in the first great colonizing surge of the late twenty-first century. Because of its unique strategic position, it was very strongly defended. But two standard weeks before Trevayne's arrival, the heavy elements of that defense force had departed in response to Cyrus Waldeck's summons. Trevayne had learned of the reason for that summons: the immense Kaituni armada advancing from Alowan toward Orpheus-1, where Cyrus would need every available ship to meet them.

But then, on the heels of that, had come other news.

TRNS *Li Han* and the rest of the fleet were in orbit around the center of mass of the double planet system of Nova Terra and Eden, at an orbital radius that rendered visible both of the twin life-bearing water planets which would have made this system a pearl beyond price even if it hadn't been a warp hub. The Sol-like light of their primary, Alpha Centauri A, was reflected off their oceans as they revolved around each other in stately sixty-one-hour epicycles. At this point in its eccentric eighty-year orbit, the smaller companion star Alpha Centauri B was approaching periastron, already closer than Uranus is to Sol, an orange-tinted mini-sun or super-star that was visible in the skies of the twin planets even by day.

All in all, quite a spectacle. But Trevayne stared at it without seeing it.

He was seeing another, not too dissimilar binary star system—the one called Zephrain. And remembering it as it had been nearly a century ago.

When the vicissitudes of the Fringe Revolution had stranded him and his battlegroup in the isolated Zephrain system, fresh from learning of the death of his wife and daughter at the hands of the rebels, he had placed himself under the command of Admiral Sergei Ortega, the local commander—who had been killed when the rebels had attacked, leaving Trevayne to batter them back . . . and, in the process, kill his own son, who had joined the rebellion. Afterwards, with a dead void where his soul should have been, he had landed on Xanadu, Zephrain A's colony planet, to give pro forma condolences to Sergei's daughter.

Who had given him back his soul.

Miriam Ortega, in her thirties, had been no conventional beauty. But hers had been the kind to which conventional canons of beauty were irrelevant—an intensely alive, vividly expressive face. And then he had seen her smile . . . and had shortly begun to smile again himself.

More importantly, her dynamism had been at least the equal of his. Together they had formed the Rim provisional government. And they had been lovers as well as partners.

Because of her, he had ceased to think of Zephrain merely as an abstraction to be held for the legitimate Terran Federation government, along with the Rim systems beyond it. He had come to love Xanadu and its melting-pot people—"Xandies," they'd called themselves—almost as much as she did.

And then, as he'd attempted to fight his way back to the Federation, had come his near-death in the hell known as the Battle of Zapata, followed—immediately, as far as his consciousness had been concerned—by his strange resurrection inside a youthful copy of his own body. And there to greet him had been a hundred-and-sixteen-year-old woman—seemingly in her late sixties by grace of antigerone treatments—with a face that, however wrinkled, was still unmistakable in its high-cheeked curve-nosed uniqueness, with its extraordinarily expressive smile. . . .

It hadn't been an easy adjustment—her a mother by another man, and a multiple grandmother, and he holding more than five decades of memories within a new twenty-year-old body. But he had adjusted, and settled into an autumnal affection that had never died—for her, and also for Xanadu and its people—even after he had married Magda and moved to the Terran Republic. It was an imperishable part of his life. Or it had *seemed* imperishable . . .

He closed his eyes, shutting out the binary stars that

were so like Zephrain, and tried to summon up the memory at the heart of the nightmare from which he had awakened: the first time he had met Miriam. He recalled the street, the raw salt wind off the Alph estuary beyond the seawall, the gate in the wall, the door . . .

But he dared not let his mind venture any further. The nightmare had overwhelmed and superseded the real memories. He squeezed his eyes even more tightly shut, and a strong shudder ran through him.

He felt a slim hand on his shoulder. Magda had entered unheard. Under that firm but gentle pressure, his shuddering subsided.

"I just came aboard," she said after a moment. "I . . . heard the news."

She knew about him and Miriam Ortega, of course. He had told her long ago, and jealousy or resentment would have been preposterous after so much time and under the present circumstances. Now she stood above him in silence, until she finally sensed that he needed for her to say something besides condolences.

"Ironic, isn't it? We were only able to get the news from Zephrain—which the Kaituni obviously only let out as a ploy to sow panic and despair—because of the fourth Unity Warp Point, which was off the beaten path in Orion space and connected to a warp linkage with the Heart Worlds. At least there, the *selnarmic* courier system is still in partial operation."

Trevayne opened his eyes, looked up at her as she stood in the light of Alpha Centauri A, and placed a hand over hers. He managed a very small smile. "Yes. The irony lies in your use of the past tense for the fourth Unity Warp Point. It rather takes one back to that cocktail party in Rome, doesn't it?"

"Yes, and your little conversation with Assemblyman Obasanjo." They had learned some time ago that Obasanjo had been in the Christophon system when an unusually large relativistic object had punched through its sun, and Trevayne hadn't pretended he regarded it as too great a loss. He had his faults, but hypocrisy wasn't one of them.

"And my other conversation, with Dr. Kasugawa," he said. "The PSU government has evidently now had the same conversation with him, since they built a deconstructing counter-generator."

"But, of course, continued to drag their heels about using it," she reminded him.

"Or even issuing clear protocols for its use," he nodded grimly, reflecting on the cumbersome—if not self-paralyzed—nature of the PSU government. Above a certain size, government inevitably became smothered in its own fat. Today's technology, up to and including the *selnarmic* relay, had expanded the envelope of that size limit far beyond that of history's Egyptian, Chinese and Byzantine empires, but hadn't and couldn't eliminate it. The limit was always there, and always would be.

"So," he continued, "the local authorities acted on their own initiative and eliminated the fourth Unity Warp Point just after the news from Zephrain came through it."

"To foreclose any possibility of an attack through it," Magda finished for him. "Not unlike your own action in starting to move this fleet back here without waiting for orders. Seems there's a lot of that going around."

"There has to be. When government becomes too bloated to reach a decision and act on it, individuals have to take the initiative." *Which, of course, begins the devolution of the government into irrelevance,* he didn't add. *But what other choice is there?*

"Well," she said, "at least some of those individuals have come around to your viewpoint about the Unity Warp Points, even if the PSU government is still dithering about destroying the far more dangerous one that leads into the heart of Orion space."

"I've never felt less satisfaction at being vindicated," he said bleakly. Magda waited for him to say something else, but the silence lingered, and his eyes swung back to the viewport.

"Ian," Magda said after a while, "I won't pretend I know to the full what you're feeling. But I do know—"

"Never mind," he said rather abruptly. "That was in another country, and besides . . ." He couldn't bring himself to complete the quotation from Marlowe's *The Jew of Malta* with ". . . the wench is dead." He sighed deeply, once, and then stood up. "We have other things to concern us. He turned to his desk computer and brought up a holographic display of the adjacent portions of the warp network. He traced the route from Alpha Centauri through the closed warp point that led to a whole series of five formerly Arachnid systems to Pesthouse and beyond through Home Hive One to Orpheus-1.

"The heavy units here departed two weeks ago to join Cyrus at Orpheus-1, where he intends to fight a decisive battle. With luck, if we depart without any further delay, we may just possibly be able to get there in time to join him. I want the resupplying we've been doing here completed in forty-eight standard hours. Anything that hasn't been done by then simply doesn't get done."

"Right. I just hope it's not too late. I just hope *everything* isn't too late."

Trevayne looked at his wife and second in command sharply. This wasn't like her. She had held up unwaveringly under the tide of horrific news that had reached them, news of the conflagration that was engulfing the accustomed order of things. But now she continued in the same empty voice. "Ian, is it really all over? Is the universe we've always taken for granted coming to an end? How can we stop these Kaituni from continuing this mad, unlimited destruction?"

As he so often did, Trevayne replied with a quote. He looked out the viewport at the binary suns, so reminiscent of Zephrain, and said the words Stonewall Jackson had once said in answer to precisely the same question.

"Kill them. Kill them all."

CHAPTER TWENTY-SIX

Alessandro Magee glanced at Mretlak, who was in what seemed to be a meditative slouch, back in the avionics and sensors section that was snugged behind the bridge of the patrol corvette *Viggen*. "Anything?" Tank asked the Arduan.

"No *selnarm* of any kind is active in this system," came the mellow response from Mretlak's vocoder.

"Sorry to keep asking you that question." Magee offered a lopsided grin as a good-will gesture. "It's just that once we make rendezvous with this fusion bucket we've been shadowing, we'll be a lot more vulnerable."

"Frankly, I appreciate and encourage your prudence, Captain. I have been on so-called snoop and poop outings with other teams that are nowhere near so careful and it has almost been our undoing. What many humans and Orions do not understand is that the likelihood of a chance encounter with a Kaituni ship is much smaller than triggering one of their sleeper sensor buoys or mines. And we would have little warning, in such a circumstance: the device would emit a short *selnarm* burst to report the contact and then return to silence."

"Let's just hope we don't wake up one of those little sleeping tattle-tales when we dock with this broken-down mining ship." Harry Li was checking his EVA gear; he'd already field-stripped and checked his weapon. "With their docking guide-laser busted, they're going to have to talk us in the last few meters. That means broadcast. And that could mean trouble."

"I share your sentiment," answered Mretlak. "So far, we have been relatively lucky, even in light of Captain Wethermere's decision to restrict our missions to rarely trafficked systems. Frankly, I am glad we are coming to the end of our intelligence gathering operations."

Harry Li raised an eyebrow, turned to Tank, whisper-muttered, "Why do I get the feeling that Mretlak knows something we don't?"

Magee emitted a noncommittal grunt, became more focused on checking his own gear.

Harry stared at him, then grumbled. "Okay, it's only *me* who's in the dark about our next step." He sighed. "Typical. Let's go board this old rustbucket, then."

Two days later, 'Sandro, Harry, and Mretlak wrapped up the mission debrief and summary intel report for Wethermere, Kiiraathra'ostakjo, Ankaht, and Jennifer. In the ensuing silence, the three recon leaders waited. Probably for queries about the reliability of the mining-ship's crew as intel sources, conjectured Wethermere, or data inconsistencies.

After a long silence, it was Kiiraathra'ostakjo who shifted in his seat, signaling an imminent statement.

Which was merely, "It is difficult to believe that such primitive spacecraft are still operating. Reaction thrusters, even those utilizing inertial fusion, are unthinkably slow."

"Slow, but oddly well-suited for the current post-invasion conditions here at the margins of the Khanate's core, Least Fang," Mretlak pointed out courteously. "Consider: because fusion thrusters generate actual physical motion, rather than pseudo-velocity, the captains of such craft can shut down the drives and continue to coast at speed. This allows them to continue to move even if they encounter an anomalous contact that might be an enemy ship—and to be running completely dark when they do so."

"Besides," added Alessandro, "it doesn't take that long at one gee constant to get pretty much anywhere you might want, or need, to go in a stellar system. Some of the intrastellar transits might *seem* long by contemporary standards, but that's because reactionless drives allow us to get almost anywhere we need to go in mere hours. For a fusion bucket like this last one we contacted, they measure their transits in days or weeks.

"And that's not really a big deal for them. They are prospecting, salvaging, mining, shipping goods from one community to the next: all jobs that take a lot of time, anyway. So adding a few days on for travel is not a huge inconvenience: their existence runs along at a much slower pace, to begin with."

"And since their fusion thrusters run on hydrogen, not antimatter," Harry concluded, "they can live off the land pretty easily in any system that has a gas giant. If they've only got liquid water on hand, that makes things a little more difficult: access requires entering the gravity well of the source-planet. And harvesting ice has its own issues. But the bottom line is that these ships get the job done and stay well off the radar of any Kaituni who happen to drift through their systems, looking for traffic other than their own."

Ossian nodded. "Which is why you and the other recon teams have been encountering more and more of these old-tech craft—right down to magnetoplasma-driven robot bulk haulers. Low energy signature and low speed make them harder to find against the routine junk and radiant backgrounds of most planetary systems. And as long as they stay close in among belts, Trojan point rubble clusters, or planets and moons, they are almost sure to see a reactionless ship before it sees them. Our drive signatures stand out like lit flares. By comparison, theirs are guttering candles that can be extinguished with a single puff—well, flick of a switch."

"It's just good to know that some people have survived the Kaituni scorched-earth tactics," Jennifer added glumly. "Which, from what this last crew told you, seems to be pretty much their universal post-conquest pattern."

Tank nodded sadly. "I'm afraid so, Jen. Over the last eight weeks, it's been the same story, again and again. Wherever the Kaituni go, they first obliterate any spaceside defenses, then find the key population and production centers in a system and destroy them. We've only heard of one or two cases where they've used nukes—and we can't corroborate those stories—but between orbital bombardment, HVMs, and long-range seeker missiles that hit outlying communities in asteroid belts and on moons, they've been taking out each system's infrastructure pretty completely. Energy, food, transport, health services, communication hubs: they're slamming every system back to a pre-industrial level before they move on."

"Which is ultimately as destructive as extensive bombing," asserted Kiiraathra'ostakjo. "This was not an uncommon tactic in the Interregnum Strife that followed the war which crippled our homeworld, Old Valkha. Destroying a system's civil infrastructure has almost the same effect in terms of generating civilian casualties, with the added benefit that it preoccupies the survivors far more, keeps them too busy to consider mounting a counterattack." He leaned back, a low growl rumbling at the back of his throat. "The Kaituni have planned well, this time."

"They have," Ossian allowed. "But if your assessment is correct, Kiiraathra, then they've also created a predictable pattern for us to exploit."

Mretlak evidently saw what Wethermere was driving at. "Of course. Now that we are done gathering intelligence, we would do best to keep most of our travel constrained to smaller systems, such as ones in which they have shown scant interest."

"Where are we going?" Jennifer asked.

Ankaht raised tendrils that rippled slowly and—despite their alienness—soothingly. "We shall certainly return to that topic, Jennifer. But first, I want to be sure that I understand the reasoning behind Mretlak's observation." She turned toward him. "You are suggesting that we should keep to smaller systems because they are less likely to have devolved into combative chaos. Having a smaller and more dispersed population that has less reliance on ponderous infrastructures, they are less likely to descend into internecine strife in the aftermath of the Kaituni strikes. Also, because what infrastructure they do have is not likely to be heavily centralized, they will have taken less damage from the comparatively modest Kaituni attacks. Their resources and support systems being smaller and more scattered, they have greater self-reliance and redundancy. And because small colonies are more likely to be technological backwaters, they are more likely to still be using the older, pre-reactionless spacecraft—and so, they are still making interplanetary journeys with greater regularity than modern ships, and yet with less chance of detection."

"Precisely, Eldest Sleeper," replied Mretlak with admiration in his tone. "You have seen it with all three eyes."

Alessandro nodded. "And of course, from a purely military perspective, the Kaituni will continue to be less interested in low population backwaters. At this point, their concern is with forces large enough to upset their overall strategy. Any force *that* large has to be located on or near a sufficient logistical locus—and smaller systems don't measure up. So by sticking to the backwaters, we remain under both the Kaituni patrol radar and strategic focus. But now," he concluded with a change of tone, "back to this matter of 'our travel.' I knew this was our last snoop and poop outing, and that means you folks at the top of the command pyramid have got to be close to issuing new marching orders. But for the life of me—and that might be a really accurate expression, in this case—I can't think of where we'd be going.

It doesn't seem like there's anyplace useful we *can* go—not if we mean to go there *and* survive."

Ossian glanced at Kiiraathra'ostakjo and Ankaht. The Orion's answering nod was a fluid, almost languorous motion; the Arduan's was abrupt, jerky. Wethermere turned back to Tank. "Before laying out our next steps, I'd like one last piece of information about your encounter with the crew of this last ship: the, uh—"

"*Lucky Strike*, sir."

"Right. The *Lucky Strike*. The crew was polyglot?"

"Yes, sir. Humans, Orions, one of the Ophiuchi. About half had been running her for the better part of a decade. The other half were recent additions; refugees with spacer skills, mostly."

"So you feel you had a wide sampling of different intel sources, in terms of what the crew had heard and seen regarding the war to date?"

"As good a selection as we have encountered thus far, Captain Wethermere," put in Mretlak with a puzzled tone, "and their regional experiences are such that we were able to establish a high confidence of corroborative accuracy among the key assertions of their reports. But surely you know this."

Wethermere smiled. "I just want to be one hundred percent sure, because, if the information from the crew of the *Lucky Strike* is as reliable as it seems, then it is an excellent final confirmation of several crucial data points. Some of which you have already reported to us though other sources and earlier contacts."

"And which the other recon groups picked up in the course of their operations, as well, I'm guessing," Harry Li put in.

Mretlak's tone was measured, suddenly certain.

"Which makes it quite clear, now, why we were not allowed to have contact with the other recon groups: so we could not know what anyone else was finding and reporting."

"That is correct," Ankaht affirmed calmly. "Amongst most intelligent races with individual psyches, it is unfailingly observed that groups with similar investigatory tasks subconsciously gravitate toward consensus in their findings—if they can *share* those findings, that is. This process was too crucial for us to allow such behavioral artifacts to skew our data. So we were compelled to structure our recon teams as wholly separate cells."

Harry nodded. "Makes sense. So: what facts have showed up at the overlap points of the Venn diagram you've been building from our reports?"

Ossian leaned forward. "Firstly, it seems that the story of the Zephrain Home Fleet sensitive that somehow escaped the Wasting of Xanadu is *not* a folktale or wishful thinking: it's absolutely true. The woman in question is named Hilda Silverman. And she was watching when the Kaituni destroyed the capitol, and then killed both Amunherh'peshef and Miriam Ortega. All Amunsit's reported assertions were, in fact, also genuine and were recorded. Copies of the recording, as well as transcripts, are being circulated. This means that the *selnarm* morse code that coordinated the Dispersate attacks, the purging of their own *shaxzhu*, their uncertainty regarding the disposition and orders of the Bellerophon Arm fleet, their xenocidal intentions, have all been multiply corroborated. We've encountered three different copies of the transcript so far, all of which are identical in content but were copied at different times, in different star systems.

In short, all the news from Zephrain is genuine and it's spreading."

Mretlak had come to a full upright sitting position. "Did you say '*selnarm* morse code'? Do you mean to say that this was how the Kaituni coordinated their actions across dozens of light-years?"

Ankaht's three eyes closed and opened slowly. "That is indeed what we mean to say."

"But can we trust this claim? Might this be carefully crafted misinformation? I, for one, have always been reluctant to give credence to the notion that Amunsit allowed a number of surviving shuttles and small traders to simply depart Zephrain through several of its warp points after she was done laying waste to Xanadu. It seems—"

"Mretlak," Ankaht interrupted gently. "Your reservations were my own. For many weeks. But I can assure you—personally—that this information, and all it implies, is genuine."

Jennifer was staring at her Arduan friend, wide-eyed. "And does that mean that you—I mean, can you also—?"

Ankaht's voice was slow and deep as it emerged from the vocoder. "Mastering this *selnarmic* morse code is not a simple matter. Not nearly so simple as it is made to sound. However, since we first heard of this claim, I have been—exploring the possibility." Ankaht seemed to take a moment to ensure that her tone remained level. "Two days ago, I made my first contact with Tefnut ha sheri, on Bellerophon, using this method." Her head bowed slightly. "It is an embarrassment that I did not conceive of such a method myself."

The room was still as the gravity of Ankaht's news sunk in, as well as the vastly changed circumstances and possibilities it portended for their small flotilla, to say nothing of the greater war effort.

"Damn." Harry Li uttered that word as a long exhale. "Makes you wonder what the hell Amunsit was thinking when she allowed that piece of strategic intelligence out of the bag."

"We cannot know for sure," Ankaht answered, "but I strongly suspect she felt quite confident that her exact words were not being recorded. And unless she had known about our presence behind her lines, she might have—quite reasonably—conjectured that little harm could come of such disclosures, even if they somehow spread beyond Zephrain."

"I suppose that's true," Jennifer conceded, "But I agree with Mrĕtlak: I still can't think why she let anyone out of the system at all. If it's her sworn intent to exterminate all humans, why leave the system's warp points unguarded for survivors to bolt through?"

Ankaht settled her tentacles in a manner that, to Wethermere's eyes, almost looked prim. "I do not think that factor is so mysterious, Jennifer. I suspect that she wanted the survivors to go forth and spread terror."

"You mean, of what the Kaituni can accomplish, of their power?"

"That too," Ankaht concurred, "but I am thinking more of their ruthless intent. And the anger it will stimulate. Ian Trevayne and Miriam Ortega were once . . . involved, as I understand it. Amunsit may well be trying to inflame his passions, to induce him to hasty action. Indeed, the most senior human PSU admiral, Cyrus Waldeck, is a long-standing associate of Ms. Ortega. I do not know if one could label them as friends, but they served common causes for almost a century, and were both very close to Admiral Trevayne—whose voice and influence in the PSU is almost as great as it has been in the Rim.

"But beside that, I suspect that Amunsit—who is not at the head of the Kaituni, it seems—wished to prove and overtly claim that all the recent calamities caused by the near-relativistic debris from the colony ships of fourteen Dispersates is not, as some have wanted to believe, unintentional or a matter of coincidence. And by releasing the story of what she has done to Xanadu and its people, she is sending a message to all non-Kaituni races, everywhere: 'this is what we shall do to you. It is just a matter of time, and there is nothing you can do to stop us.'"

"But this is where I am still puzzled myself, Councilor Ankaht," Kiiraathra'ostakjo mused through a chesty rumble. "While such a message will no doubt terrify many civilians, it will inflame others, incite them to take up arms or do whatever they may to destroy their would-be exterminators. And insofar as our militaries are concerned, it could not logically have an effect other than to galvanize the will and resolve of our general staffs. It shall lead them to commit just that many more of our largest ships to the great battle that seems to be imminent at or near Pesthouse, from all reports. In all ways, Amunsit's actions remain a mystery."

Ossian leaned forward. "I think I may have an answer to that mystery. Two answers, actually."

CHAPTER TWENTY-SEVEN

Least Fang Kiiraathra'ostakjo leaned toward Ossian attentively. "Today, I have no heart to taunt you, my friend. What do you suspect lies behind Amunsit's actions?"

"Well, as I said, I have two suspicions. The first is, I think, pretty obvious. Since Amunsit knows that we use Arduan sensitives on many of our capital ships, I believe she's trying to reignite the bigotry toward all Arduans—Kaituni or not. The more horrific she is, and the more widely her forces' xenocidal resolve is known, the more it will rekindle racial hatreds and lingering suspicions. And if that comes to pass, it could spark a civil war in the Bellerophon arm and result in having our fleets' Arduan specialists removed—which would mean a severe disadvantage in terms of the speed of our communications and sensor readings."

As most of the heads in the room nodded at the likelihood of that suspicion, Wethermere noticed that Ankaht was still, but staring at him. "And what is the *less* obvious of your two suspicions, Ossian?"

Wethermere resisted the urge to rub his hair briskly. "The hell of it is, it's not a *specific* suspicion, just a general one." Seeing quizzical looks on the other humans' faces, he amplified: "Let's go back to what the Least Fang was pointing out—and rightly so, I think: Amunsit had to know that letting this kind of information get to our populations was tantamount to whacking a hornet's nest with a club. It only stands to reason that we would all be hopping mad to get at her—and not merely to defeat her, but annihilate every trace of the rabid xenocidal campaign she's espousing. So if she *expects* that result, it stands to reason she *wants* that result, that it is somehow key to the Kaituni plans."

Kiiraathra'ostakjo nodded slowly. "This is logical, Ossian Wethermere, but how could our vigor help the Kaituni? Increased ferocity and urgency is our ally, not our enemy."

"I know," Wethermere grumbled, "and that's what bothers me. We're missing something. It feels like—well, like we're being set up for a judo throw."

"I am sorry," Mretlak intruded, "but what is 'judo'?"

"A human martial art," murmured Alessandro, his eyes fixed on Wethermere. "The core principle is that you use your opponent's strength or momentum against them; you find a way to make their own attacks turn into their undoing."

Wethermere nodded. "And that's just what this feels like. The only way I can even imagine that our resolve and rage might work against us is this: that we may be rushing in too quickly, that we may be committing too many of our forces in the effort to score a quick and absolute victory. We've already heard rumors that there's a huge PSU fleet gathering in the vicinity of Pesthouse. Judging from the last deployment rosters, that would logically be Second Fleet, Admiral Waldeck's immense multispeciate armada. And he's got a lot of our best hardware at his disposal.

"It's also true that Admiral Trevayne has a massive fleet under his command, mostly comprised of Terran Republic formations. Until a few months ago, he was hunting down the Tangri raiders—genocidalists in their own right—but who knows if he hasn't started moving to follow in behind his old friend Cyrus? And frankly, he'd be right to do so, from a purely practical standpoint. He'd never say so himself—Ian is a gentleman—but he knows, as does everyone else, that whereas Cyrus is a solid strategist and tactician, Ian Trevayne's battlefield skills are the stuff of legend. And, thanks to the information leak that Amunsit ensured, that same legendary admiral has probably learned that Miriam Ortega was butchered like a piece of livestock amidst the ruins of the city where the two of them fell in love." Ossian shook his head. "Every time I look at this situation, I come away with the same impression: Amunsit is trying to provoke us, trying to goad us to bring every spare ship we've got to annihilate the Kaituni. And that—well, that makes me wary of doing so."

"But the decision is not ours to make, unfortunately," Ankaht soothed. "We must determine what we may do to help, from where we are, with the assets we have."

Harry kicked back from the table. "Well, couldn't we at least send a message? I mean, we have our own *selnarm* telegrapher now, ma'am: you. Couldn't you pass our warnings along to Tefunt ha sheri back in Bellerophon, who could then send it by *selnarmic* courier to Borden and then on to the Terran—?"

Ankaht raised a drooping cluster: a gesture of forlorn futility. "It is not so simple, Lieutenant Li. Firstly, the tortuous *selnarmic* courier route linking Bellerophon to the Terran Republic and thence to Earth itself has been disrupted. According to what I have learned from Tefnut ha sheri, the Tangri raiders have compromised several systems along that path of warp points, so there is no way to know that such a message would ever reach its intended recipients. Furthermore, if Captain Wethermere's conjecture about allied fleet movements are correct—and they are consistent with all the inferential data we have gathered these past weeks—it is almost certain that the persons to whom you would send that message are beyond timely reach. Admiral Trevayne will already be in motion if he is going to come join the effort to meet and defeat the Kaituni along the path leading from Pesthouse to Earth. Admiral Waldeck is almost certainly already in position at Pesthouse. Of course, two such seasoned commanders are almost certain to reflect upon Amunsit's information manipulation and be especially wary. Which is fortunate, because no message from Bellerophon could possibly reach such distant fleets in time to matter."

She paused, and her almost nonexistent shoulders seemed to sag wearily. "Besides, we must now reserve this on-off *selnarm* process to coordinate something much more urgent, much more likely to influence the outcome of this conflict."

"Which would be—what?" asked Jennifer, who clearly heard the pregnant, hanging tone with which Ankaht had concluded her statement.

Ossian folded his hands. "Collectively—meaning the Least Fang, the Councilor and I—have determined that our best use of Ankaht's ability to communicate with Tefnut ha sheri is to coordinate a means of bringing the Bellerophon Fleet through to us."

Magee's eyebrows jumped high. He leaned back. "Sir, with all due respect, I would expect that you'd need to coordinate that with deity. Even if we assumed that we could somehow either sneak or fight our way through the Zephrain system, the path to Bellerophon is blocked. The New India system will be impassable for at least another month, possibly two. And that's for fast, small, individual ships. A whole fleet would—"

Ossian smiled. "Captain, you are absolutely right that what you are projecting would be a suicide mission—in any number of ways. And besides, it doesn't furnish us with the element of surprise—which may be the only decisive advantage to be gained by carrying out the operation we intend."

"Well, sir," Li said, his tone respectful if incredulous, "you certainly have *me* surprised—or at least fully perplexed about how you plan on bringing the Bellerophon fleet here to us."

Ossian rubbed his hair, caught himself doing so, decided not to stop. "Over the weeks, we've had dozens of conversations about how our little flotilla could move faster and hide more easily if we just abandoned the big, cumbersome freighter that the Least Fang was escorting. But we never did get rid of it. Because, every time we had one of those conversations, I thought to myself, 'You never know when it might be handy to have a warp-point generator in your back pocket.'"

Everyone but Ankaht and Kiiraathra'ostakjo stared at him as if he had gone mad. He even saw the Orion glance at him quickly; Kiiraathra had agreed with Ossian's plan, but had yet to become comfortable with it.

"Sir," Mretlak said carefully, deferentially, "I am at pains to point out that it takes *two* generators to create a warp point. And we only have one."

"That's not strictly true," Ossian replied with a grin.

Again, he found himself looking at a row of surprised stares. But before he could expand upon his statement, Ankaht intervened. "We do not have another one here with us, of course. But the other end is available to us—and happily, is located just where it will do us the most good: in Bellerophon."

"Wait a minute," snapped Harry Li, finally forgetting himself and allowing impatience into his tone. "The warp-point generator with us was the one being moved to Bellerophon. The other half is back in Sigma Draconis."

"That is true," responded Ankaht. To Ossian, it sounded like there was a small, coy smile behind the vocoder's rendition of her voice.

Harry threw his hands up. "Look, I give up, okay? Solve the mystery for me. Here in this flotilla, we have one half of a warp-point generator pair, the half that was bound for Bellerophon. The other half is in Sigma Draconis. But now you're telling me that, no, the other half of the generator is actually in Bellerophon *now*. But that's also where *our* warp-point generator was heading. I don't get it."

"Actually, you do get it, Harry," Ossian assured him. "It's not as contradictory as it sounds, if you consider that you might not have all the facts."

Mretlak's largest, central eye narrowed. "Your engineers built another generator on site in the Rim."

"Well, yes and no. Another warp-point generator *was* built in the Rim, but not by our engineers, Mretlak." Ossian smiled. "It was built by *yours*."

All three of Mretlak's eyes blinked so sharply that it looked downright painful. "Our—Arduan—engineers built the other warp-point generator?"

Ankaht touched two opposed tendrils together lightly. "Just so. It is a precise copy of the one we are carrying, and of the one that is still in Sigma Draconis."

Mretlak rose to a formal sitting position. "If this is true—that we were constructing a warp-point generator—then why was I not informed? This is a matter of utmost intelligence sensitivity and importance for our people. It was in my purview to—"

"Mretlak," Ossian interjected congenially, "I'm sorry, but this was out of our hands. It was a policy decision that was taken at the highest level. The *very highest* level. Frankly, the three of us"—he gestured at Ankaht and Kiiraathra'ostakjo—"were all informed about the creation of the Arduan-built generator, but not one of us knew that the other two also knew."

"That's—that's crazy," pronounced Jen with a sudden folding of her arms.

"Actually, Jen, it's not. Frankly, I suspected that Ankaht knew. She's the living repository of the most confidential facts and activities concerning her people, and this was at the very top of that confidentiality pyramid. I suspect Amunherh'peshef knew, and I know that Narrok does. Of course the construction team knows, but they've been sequestered for two years, and were bound for frontier resettlement on

Marathon. And the Least Fang knew because it was necessary for him to understand what was—and what was *not*—at stake when he was escorting our half of the warp-point generator. Which was, by the way, the one that was slated for use, had it arrived in Bellerophon."

"So who told *you*, Captain?" Jennifer, who had long ago declared her low tolerance for the bad faith that she believed motivated all examples of compartmentalization, did not quite sound accusatory. Not quite.

"I had to be in on it from the start, Ms. Pietchkov, for a variety of intelligence and counterintelligence reasons. The entire process was a cooperative effort between engineers of ours who had already built one, and Arduan engineers that had been, at the close of the last war, trying to duplicate our work. Furthermore, the success of this project—on every level—had profound strategic implications for Arduan-PSU relations."

Magee scratched his ear. "Okay, but then why move the one we have with us now all the way from Centauri?"

"To keep anyone from realizing that the Arduans now *can* build a warp-point generator."

Kiiraathra'ostakjo emitted a cross between a grumble and a snarl. "I mean no offense to our Arduan comrades, Ossian, but I remain uncertain *why* the PSU and Rim Federation politicians permitted them to construct a warp-point generator at all."

Ossian turned to his friend. "Kiiraathra, since the Arduans had already figured out most of the engineering by the end of the war, maybe the better question is: what would we have risked by trying to *prohibit* it?" He gestured toward Ankaht and Mretlak. "We are genuinely trying to integrate the Arduans into the Rim Federation—and the PSU, if they want to establish communities there. But how are we going to do that if we selectively prohibit them from sharing in the same technologies we have, particularly those which they are already on the cusp of building for themselves? The diplomatic fallout over an attempt at prohibiting them from building a warp-point generator would have been catastrophic. Besides, it would have been pointless: within a few years, they could simply have built one on the sly—and they'd have rightly come away with the impression that our true interest was in controlling, not including, them.

"Besides, to answer 'Sandro's earlier question, we *needed* a back-up generator in place, just in case something went wrong with the one that the Least Fang was escorting down from Centauri. In the event that one of them failed, then we could have swapped the other one in—they are identical—and no one would have been the wiser, given that the process of activation is a top-secret operation, carried out in deep space."

"Very well," said Mretlak in a somewhat distracted voice, his lesser tentacles slowly switching to and fro, like metronomes measuring the orderliness of his contemplations. "So: we have identical warp generators, one here, one in Bellerophon. And now, through the Elder Sleeper, we have a means of coordinating their activation and, thereby, creating a warp point. But why? To escape to Bellerophon and give them the intelligence they need to defeat Amunsit and break through to this region of space?"

"No," replied the Least Fang quietly, "we shall use

it to bring through Admiral Yoshikuni's fleet. Here into the very den of our enemy."

Again, Ossian and his colleagues found themselves sitting across the table from a rank of stunned stares. "Least Fang," Magee began carefully, "I am ever an admirer of Orion boldness, but this is—well, very bold indeed."

"It is, which is why I like it—although it does, I will admit, border on insanity." He glanced over at Ossian.

Harry Li goggled at his captain. "Sir, this is—is *your* plan?"

"Why Harry, you sound surprised."

"I—I suppose I shouldn't be, sir."

Ankaht extended an imploring tentacle. "On reflection, you may find it is not so outrageous a stratagem as you might first believe. Consider: your own reconnaissance reports, along with the other groups', all indicate that the only nearby Kaituni forces are those which remain in protective postures around and in the Zarzuela system itself. Beyond them, there is only one immense Kaituni fleet still operating in the Orion Khanate: a composite of three Dispersates which arrived from deep space to strike at New Valkha. And they are now said to be advancing upon the growing Orion defenses at Old Valkha. They are not even leaving token occupation forces behind them; they are practicing the scorched earth policy that they demonstrated at Xanadu. We do not know where they might head after the battle at Old Valkha, but two alternatives are logical: that they will either continue to savage the major Orion systems, or will divert and head toward a Unity Point which was used to link the Khanate with the worlds you call the Star Union."

"Which won't have been able to get to a wartime footing yet. So the Kaituni will wipe out the Star Union before it's managed to field a combat-ready fleet, before it can become a problem to them. And besides, if you follow along those systems far enough, you can eventually emerge near Earth." Harry's expression and voice were suddenly grim rather than incredulous.

"Precisely," Ankaht agreed. "So if this Kaituni fleet chooses to move upon the Star Union, perhaps we can follow and intercept them, or intervene in some other fashion which will ensure that they cannot exploit that admittedly circuitous route toward Earth. However, I doubt they will abandon their activities in the Khanate, at least not until they have crippled it. Which will take several years, although, with only one fleet at their disposal, it does not seem that they could accomplish very much.

"If, on the other hand, the Kaituni do not enter the Star Union too soon, it might be opportune for *us* to do so. We could alert the races there, perhaps gather their forces to swell our own, and send word to Earth that we have blocked that unlikely route of approach."

Magee nodded. "Yeah, that's a pretty crazy plan, all right," he affirmed—and then shot an apologetic look at Ossian. "I'm sorry, sir. I meant to say 'inspired.'"

Wethermere smiled. "No, you meant 'crazy.' And in light of the fact that it's unprecedented, you're right. But on the other hand, it might buy us a weapon that can be more decisive than any other: surprise. The Kaituni don't know any of us are here. They don't know we have a warp generator. They don't know a matching warp generator is waiting in Bellerophon.

And they are all busy focusing on the very sizable threats that are closest to them—the PSU fleets near Pesthouse and the Bellerophon Rim Fleet—which they presume will eventually be trying to retake Zephrain. Furthermore, we've now had multiple confirmed reports that the largest Kaituni fleet of all—perhaps the output of half a dozen Dispersates—has arrived in the Alowan system and is heading for Pesthouse, so they clearly mean to fight a decisive battle there. And in order to do so with maximum force, they are not occupying systems. They're simply disabling them and moving on.

"Which means that, given their current lack of routine patrols throughout the space they've blighted, and given their current lack of information about us, they would have to be more insane to suspect such a ploy like ours than we are insane to plan it." Ossian smiled. "So we are going to take advantage of their unimaginative sanity."

Wethermere hadn't meant his summation as a pep talk, but the faces on the other side of the table brightened. Except Harry Li's. "Something still troubling you, Harry?"

"Yes, sir," the diminutive lieutenant shot back. "I want to know one more thing."

Ossian suppressed a sigh. "And what is that?"

"Sir, with all due respect, why the hell are we still sitting here when we've got a campaign to prep?"

Part Four

The Hand of God

CHAPTER TWENTY-EIGHT

Ossian Wethermere managed not to visibly react when the approaching Orion carrier appeared on the viewscreen in maximum magnification. But others on the bridge of the *Woolly Impostor* were not under the same rank-dictated requirement to suppress externalizations of their surprise. At the helm, Sam Lubell inhaled sharply between gritted teeth, sounding like a hissing snake. Katherine Engan let a long, low whistle escape as she alternated between studying the image on the screen and the sensors in front of her.

Commander Knight glanced at her. "How bad?"

"Frankly, sir, I've never seen a ship this badly battered that was still making way."

Wethermere studied the carrier. Her engine decks were leaking hydrogen that must have occasionally been supplemented by vented atmosphere from stricken crew sections: the mix intermittently flared as a diaphanous sheet of twisting yellow-orange flame. One of the ship's two fighter ops hull extensions—both mounted outrigger style—was blackened and lightless. That same side of its hull was almost as cratered as Old Earth's moon, occasionally illuminated by strobing polarity contests between discharges from both damaged railgun mounts and destabilized gravitics generators.

Engan's report detailed the further damage that eyes could not see. "She's only at quarter speed but her tuners are still dangerously hot. Gravity is functioning in about half of the crewed hull. No active sensors or comms of any kind. If she's got any lascom ping-back capability for tight beam alignment, I can't find it, even though I've been sending a wide-beam poll for coordinates. So if we're going to talk to her, we'll have to send by broadcast."

Wethermere frowned, glanced at the tactical-scaled plot. Nothing in it except the *Woolly Imposter* and the stricken Orion behemoth. "Any sign that the warp-point signature is changing?"

"Nothing indicating imminent transit, sir."

Knight stared at Wethermere meaningfully. "Definitely your call, sir. This is a strategic choice."

Wethermere considered, then said, "Mr. Schendler, you are to send a message using PSU cipher Charlie Three, trapdoor protocol Miasma. Two-second squeak. You send our ID, a request for theirs, and their preferred telemetry to receive a gig."

Ensign Schendler complied, listened. Five seconds passed. "Still nothing, sir. I'm not sure they can—"

"Yes, they can communicate," Engan interrupted, smiling at her sensor board. "Energy fluctuations. Precise and repeating. They're replying by juicing their plants to emulate PSU binary, sir. Requesting a meet—and immediate assistance."

✧ ✧ ✧

Wethermere glanced at Kiiraathra'ostakjo, who had changed into his dress uniform pauldrons: colorful, flaring shoulder pieces that were baroque exaggerations of the pre-industrial Orion armor they recalled. When coordinating Ossian's arrival aboard *Celmithyr'theaanouw*, the Least Fang had suggested that Ossian be formally attired as well, but without insignia of rank displayed. When Ossian had asked why, Kiiraathra had deflected the inquiry by asking his human colleague to make haste so that he would be on hand before the master of the battered Orion carrier arrived. And also, to allow any mention of creating an artificial warp point to Bellerophon—now only a week from achievement—to come from the Least Fang himself.

Wethermere was piped aboard his Orion friend's carrier with barely five minutes to spare. The appearance of the ship in the almost uninhabited Oweohar system had been a complete surprise, transiting the warp point just as the *Woolly Impostor* was about to go recon it. The *Viggen*, standing guard behind a medium-sized rock in the far belt near the warp point, had held position while the tense encounter played out.

But once the bogey had been identified as an Orion carrier, and had signaled that allied craft might approach it, the *Viggen* popped out of hiding and sent its own gig forward to make contact. Meanwhile, Wethermere's hasty lascom confab with Kiiraathra arranged a tow for the battered carrier by bringing their one civilian tug out from the flotilla's hiding place behind the outermost gas giant in the system. At the same time, *Celmithyr'theaanouw* scrambled two of her fighter wings, just in case the Orion had pursuers. The Least Fang had then become wholly preoccupied rearranging their irregular battle-group, lest they would have to give fight to intruders as well as assistance to a wounded ally.

Once *Viggen* had launched its gig, it had swung around to pick up Ossian. They had traveled under "need-only" comm protocols: keeping the channels free of clutter and space free of nonessential emissions was *de rigeur* when hanging near a warp point which might start vomiting threat forces at any moment. So until Ossian Wethermere stepped into Least Fang Kiiraathra'ostakjo's ready room, he hadn't been able to ask about the formal dress or lack of insignia. And judging from the shrill, ear-rending wind-chime device that was the Orion equivalent of a bosun's whistle, he wasn't going to have a chance to inquire now, either: the commander of the Orion ship was near at hand.

Kiiraathra'ostakjo glanced at Ossian, nodded approval, stood with his legs very straight, facing the ready-room's hatchway. Ossian decided upon a faint imitation of his friend's stance, not wanting to veer into unintentional parody, and waited.

The Orion who appeared in the hatchway had to stoop—deeply—to duck under the top of the coaming. When he had stepped through and stood straight, it was clear that his body had been every bit as affected by the combat as the hull of his ship.

Missing one eye where a gash had evidently lifted up a flap of his fur from his brow all the way back to the joint of his jaw, the remaining hairs on that side of his face were short and end-crinkled from being singed. A deep wound in his opposite shoulder occupied the spot that one of his two missing dress-pauldrons should have had; the blood leaking through the wrapping was still fresh. The hand at the end of that arm was missing two fingers and stitched in numerous places: it had probably gotten in the way of a hail of highly energetic pieces of his own ship being blasted inward. There was a soft splint on what would have been the left femur of a human, and one of his long, graceful ears now reminded Ossian of a saw-toothed equivalent that he had once seen on a much-embattled tomcat.

But, true to the expectations and toughness of his heritage, the Orion stood straight—all 2.1 meters of him—and presented the closed fist (hence, claw-sheathed) salute of the Khan's military. "I ammmh Small Claww Rrrrurr'rao, captainn ovf the *Tleikh'uu*, and 952nd of my rank. I come withhh honorrrr, to honorrrr you"—his one green eye flicked at Kiiraathra'ostakjo's left dress pauldron—"Leassst Fang."

"We receive your honor and gladly add it to ours for this day," answered Kiiraathra'ostakjo. It was the reply to the ancient guest-right greeting between warriors sharing the same roof, which had been adopted as the formulaic military salute after the Orions' Unification Wars. "I am Kiiraathra'ostakjo, and you may call me so without rank-title. This," he continued, gesturing toward Ossian, "is Commodore Wethermere of the PSU, currently on detached duty to the Rim Federation."

Who just about swallowed his tongue. *Commodore?* Either straight-arrow Kiiraathra had discovered a sudden penchant for lying, or had gone senile. *Or perhaps,* Ossian realized in the very next moment, *I've just been brevetted and that's why he didn't want me to wear my insignia of rank. But that suggests—*

Rrurr'rao offered a human salute. "Greetingss, and I amm honorrred, Commodorrrr."

More out of instinct than reason, Ossian elected to respond casually, and specifically avoid the formal response, which would have revealed him to be well-acquainted with the intricacies of how Orion military personnel dealt with their alien opposite-numbers. "The honor is mine, Claw Rrurr'rao. We're glad to see a friendly face." The concluding idiom was peculiar to human languages and would further suggest that Ossian was far more ignorant of Orion culture and language than he was—which, given Kiiraathra's suppression of Wethermere's actual rank and then sudden promotion, might help further the Least Fang's apparent attempt to misinform their visitor. *But why would he do that to a fellow—?*

There wasn't even the time to complete the thought. Rrurr'rao squinted and then shook his head. "You sshhhall pleassse forgiffe me, Commodorrrr. I amm not ssskilled in your language."

Wethermere half-expected the sudden intervention that Kiiraathra introduced with a wide wave of his hand. "I am sure the commodore shall not be affronted if, therefore, we communicate in the Tongue of Tongues. I have been his occasional tutor in its basics—but fear I was born a warrior, not a teacher."

All three exchanged brief, tooth-hidden smiles that were, collectively, more a sign of polite acquiescence rather than amusement. "By all means," Ossian assured the two of them, "carry on in the Tongue of Tongues. I shall not feel excluded."

Rrurr'rao nodded his thanks, turned to Kiiraathra, and, shifting into the Tongue of Tongues, asked with extraordinary bluntness: "Can the human be trusted?"

To his credit, Kiiraathra'ostakjo managed to express

what Ossian considered to be an optimal mix of surprise and fervor in his response to this wholly unexpected question. "Of course he can. The commodore is a comrade from the Arduan war—the first one, I mean. He is a human of high honor."

"And he does not understand this language?"

"As I said, I am not a good tutor," Kiiraathra'ostakjo answered. Technically a truth, since it did not claim anything about Wethermere's actual conversancy. Ossian silently congratulated his Orion friend on his canniness and was glad for his own study of Orion in the years before they had met, because it seemed that there were secrets Rrurr'rao was about to reveal that he did not want alighting upon human ears. And Kiiraathra had clearly anticipated—somehow—that this might be the case.

Rrurr'rao slowly swept his good paw along the unsinged whiskers on the opposite side of his face. "It is well the human does not know our language. He would not appreciate hearing my thoughts upon his race, at this time."

"The humans? What fault do you find with them?"

"Least Fang, their most recent action—it makes me wonder if the hard-liners have been right all along."

"In what way?" Kiiraathra'ostakjo's voice was almost casual, but, knowing his friend, Ossian could hear the careful, assessing tone beneath it.

"The hard-liners at court have long cautioned that, if we were ever to need the humans to support us at their own risk, they would show themselves to be incapable of—or insensate to—the demands of *theernowlus*."

"You suspect they will not bear the shared risk that

an ally swears to? This is a serious charge, particularly to levy against an entire species, Small Claw Rrurr'rao."

"And I am sorry to make to make such a charge." Rrurr'rao paused, studied Kiiraathra'ostakjo with his one remaining eye. "So you have not heard, then."

"We have heard little, these last weeks. We sheltered in the Sreaor system and gathered intelligence before choosing the waypoint systems—such as this one—which would allow us to approach our new objective with maximum safety. It has been our intention to avoid all contact."

"You were not bound for the defense of Valkha?"

Kiiraathra'ostakjo stiffened. "Alas, I was not. We have—other orders that took precedence."

"Precedence over defending our homeworld, Least Fang? What manner of orders are these?"

Ossian wondered if he had heard a faint tone of rebuke rising up through Rrurr'rao's surprise, a tone which asked, "And what manner of Orion would follow such orders?"

Kiiraathra'ostakjo stood very straight and, although at least four centimeters shy of Rrurr'rao's height, seemed taller than his subordinate. "The orders I am following ultimately came from the PSU High Command—from the polity in which our race enjoys a majority membership. If I were therefore to fail to carry out orders ratified by the political representatives of the Khan himself, I would not merely be *theermish* in breaking the pledge we made to the PSU, but would be guilty of *hiri'k'now* to our Khan himself."

As Rrurr'rao seemed to weigh Kiiraathra legal assertions, Ossian was busy trying to remember what all the terms meant. *Theermish* meant "to shirk risk sharing."

So had Kiiraathra'ostakjo refused to place the warp-point generator where it might bring through the Bellerophon fleet, he would have been derelict in his duty as an officer of the PSU. However, *hiri'k'now* was to break a liege-vassal oath. So by invoking that, Kiiraathra was also claiming that the same violation of orders would have been, by direct consequence, disobedience to the Khan himself. After all, it was the Khan who had approved the orders which his own representatives had supported in the PSU. It all sounded pretty convincing to Ossian.

Kiiraathra'ostakjo's honor-based assertions seemed to have much the same effect upon Rrurr'rao: the large Orion bowed his head slightly. "Then you carry a heavy burden of honor, Least Fang, that your duty carried you away from, not toward, the final defense of the world that gave us life."

Kiiraathra'ostakjo straightened further, stiffening. "The *last* defense—and you speak in the past tense?"

Rrurr'rao kept his head lowered. "I am sorry to be the one to bear this news to you. Valkha is no more."

Wethermere hoped he had suppressed any physical expression of his surprise by forcing himself to look more puzzled at Rrurr'rao's suddenly solemn tone and Kiiraathra's physical reaction to the news.

Ossian's Orion friend remained stiff, almost at attention. "How could this happen? And so quickly? The fleets of the Khanate, collapsing inward en masse upon Valkha, should have given the enemy months of resistance, at the very least."

"This was also the expectation of the surviving members of the *Kimhakaa*—"

—Ossian cast about, snagged the definition for the word: the *Kimhakaa* was the Khan's advisory council—

"—but they could not anticipate what we encountered." Rrurr'rao shook his head. "No one could have. The *chofaki* fleets arrived before we could gather more than half of our forces. They forced the warp point within two days. Their flood of SBMHAWKs, and their strange minesweepers, was almost unending, and so they reduced the forts. Their largest capital ships were a match for our own—monitors, mostly—but they had so many more than we did. And their fighters—"

Rrurr'rao stopped, breathed deep before continuing. "Allow me to show you, Least Fang. I do not trust my composure if I must speak the words."

Kiiraathra nodded, glanced at Wethermere, kept up the charade by informing him in English, "Valkha is fallen—possibly destroyed. Small Claw Rrurr'rao will show us the salient points of the battle."

Ossian felt genuine sorrow and regret when he bowed to Rrurr'rao and said, "I grieve for your race and littermates, both of near and distant blood. We shall avenge them together."

Rrurr'rao returned the bow. As he put his wrist computer into data relay mode, he shifted back into the Tongue of Tongues. "The commodore is a polite human. Does he make this blood oath personally, or officially?"

"I am unsure he understands the full consequence of either, Small Claw. Humans often confuse what they intend as expressions of sympathy and solidarity with our blood oaths of specific vengeance and restoration of honor."

Rrurr'rao emitted a somewhat dismissive grunt as Wethermere suppressed the impulse to smack his forehead: *you idiot. Out of fellow-feeling, and because you forgot the deeper, formal meanings of your phrasing, you made a promise you probably can't keep.*

"Least Fang, you will kindly pay particular attention to the Arduan fighters as they maneuver."

"I shall," Kiiraathra'ostakjo assured his comrade. "You may also wish to know that our adversaries distinguish themselves from the Arduans of the First Dispersate. The ones attacking us now call themselves the Kaituni. They are equally committed to the extermination of the First Dispersate Arduans, who are the only of their species who still retain that label."

Rrurr'rao simply stared at his superior. His gaze was not insolent, but the wounded Orion was clearly unconcerned with the relabeling of a subset of the race that had just killed his own species' homeworld. "I am ready to play the relevant scenes."

Kiiraathra'ostakjo nodded.

The flatscreen was suddenly filled with chaotic images of close, desperate combat. A widely dispersed phalanx of Orion superdreadnoughts, supported by a rear rank of carriers, approached their Kaituni opposites—which, magnification revealed, outnumbered the defenders by at least five to one. On both sides, ships flared and died. The Orion tactics seemed better, but were always executed a little too late, as if they were reacting two beats after the Kaituni had grabbed the maneuver initiative.

The difference between a fleet with selnarmic *relays, and one without*, Ossian reflected. The Kaituni could overextend themselves and still have time to correct before paying too heavily. Similarly, whereas the Orion had a delay between when an opportunity presented itself and being able to see and thus exploit it, the

Kaituni could make preemptive defensive corrections and minimize the consequences. In short, the Kaituni could afford to make mistakes whereas the Orions could not afford to make any. Unfortunately, the Kaituni were not making many mistakes—and there were five times as many of them.

Several minutes into scenes depicting one defensive regrouping of the Orion fleet after another, the camera view shifted to a spot quite close to one of the enemy carriers.

"This image was captured by one of the inert microsensors we kept seeded throughout the system. Watch."

As if summoned to life by Rrurr'rao's exhortation to "watch," a dense flock of fighters launched from the Kaituni carrier—but as they did, they were joined by a second, more numerous cloud of slightly smaller vehicles. The two hordes interpenetrated, as if sorting themselves into a predetermined mixture of medium fighters and the lighter, spindly craft.

"What are those smaller vehicles?" Ossian asked in English.

"Watch more," Rrurr'rao answered in a pained tone.

The scene changed to standard Kaituni fighters pressing home an assault on an Orion cruiser, which was staying light on its heels to shield its aft "blind spot" from this first wave of attackers. But then the second, mixed wave of fighters arrived, and the ship was immediately fighting desperately for its life. Where half a dozen fighters had been troubling the Orion cruiser before, there were now at least half a hundred of them, with two of the smaller vehicles following each of the standard fighters, usually in an offset delta formation.

A flight of Orion fighters arrived to assist the ship, but each time one of them plunged after a standard enemy fighter, one of the smaller vehicles responded by harrying the would-be rescuer's flank. Meanwhile, the second of the small vehicles escorting the Kaituni medium fighter quickly swept into the interposing space, forcing the Orion pilot to attack it in lieu of its original target. The result: the small vehicle between the two fighters was severely hit by the Orion, but the latter was ultimately destroyed: the threat from its flank ultimately drove it into the sights of the main enemy fighter, which had now swung sharply around to launch a counterattack.

The scene returned to the cruiser, where the tidal wave of enemy fighters had so overwhelmed its PDF defenses that significant hits were being scored against its hull. And when the first of the small vehicles finally got close enough to do so, it straightened its course and plunged straight into the ship's bow.

A cataclysmic explosion blanked the screen for a second. Through a minor miracle of terminal intercept counterfire and shields, the savaged cruiser still existed, its bow torn off and scorched. But before it could maneuver out of the line, the rest of the Kaituni fighters—both standard and small—were upon it, launching a fast flurry of missiles. The cruiser endured three or four hits before one reached—probably—the antimatter warheads in its ready rack: the battered Orion vessel became a star, taking along two of the closer Kaituni fighters before the glare receded and left empty space in its place.

The rest of the footage was a montage of the same kinds of fighter attacks destroying one overwhelmed ship after another. Whether a mere destroyer or even one of the few devastators that the Orions had grudgingly adopted, the numbers of fighters involved changed, but the tactics and outcome were always the same. Inundate the target, overwhelm its defenses, and send the first one closest enough to do so on a ramming attack. Then, as the ship staggered beneath that blow, the remaining fighters swarmed it, like a cloud of hornets stinging a bear to death.

In the last scene, the charred remains of the Orion fleet's last line of defense floated just inside geosynchronous orbit, arrayed in a partial arc of shattered hulls. A considerable mass of Kaituni battlewagons gathered and moved through a gap in that hedge of debris, paused as if considering what to do next, and then unleashed a nonstop stream of high-velocity missiles.

Streaking downward at five percent the speed of light, it looked like a planetary beam attack carried out by an electric arc welder: blinding shafts suddenly ran from the orbiting warcraft to the surface of Valkha. Ossian waited for the launches to stop, but after five seconds, realized what he was watching... and was horrified.

He turned to Rrurr'rao. "They're firing until they achieve a core breach."

Rrurr'rao only nodded and turned his eyes back to the screen.

The onslaught of subrelativistic missiles, one after another, into the same few square miles of equatorial terrain on Valkha lasted about forty seconds. Then, like someone switching off the arc welder, the eye-imprinting bombardment was over—and at its base, a deep, glowing hell-pit was growing. The dark ground at its peripheries kept crumbling inward into a brightening molten well that seemed to be slowly gnawing away the walls of its own unthinkably deep shaft. Evidently, some of the Kaituni missiles had worked out from the target point, weakening the mantle at various points to facilitate its continued widening, lest debris choke it and the breach self-seal.

And then with stately ease, Kaituni support craft began pushing the wrecks of the Orion fleet planetside: a multi-million-ton rain of steel to impact on the surface and finish whatever might be left of Valkha's already crippled biosphere if the core breach failed to do the job.

The screen went dark.

Kiiraathra'ostakjo turned toward Rrurr'rao, spoke in English in a very tightly controlled voice. "These new fighters, the small ones, do you have any data on them?"

The tall Orion nodded. "They are very simple machines, and are quite different from prior Ardua—hmmf, Kaituni remote systems."

"How so?"

"It is our belief that they do not utilize *selnarmic* links, are not directly piloted by Kaituni. Rather, they are expert systems that are semi-autonomous, but can also receive conventional communications—and thus, instructions—through the standard, *selnarmically*-controlled fighter."

"So each regular fighter becomes the command-and-control nexus of a small flight wing, comprised of itself and two dedicated robot fighters."

"Exactly. And we hypothesize that, since the robot fighters are so cheap and so fast, the Kaituni are completely unconcerned with losing them. Meanwhile, you saw what happens to our fighters when we attempt to engage them. A situation in which we were already outnumbered became untenable, uncontrollable. Our fighters simply could not get to the *selnarmically*-controlled craft—and of course, their pilots are safely out of harm's way, back in the armored belly of whatever carrier—or even capital ship—they might be housed."

"It is strange that these new robot fighters were not used in the Battle of Zephrain," commented Kiiraathra'ostakjo.

"Maybe not so strange," offered Ossian.

"How so, Senior Commodore?" Kiiraathra asked seriously, while Wethermere almost stuttered in surprise. *Promoting me again? And hoping that our visitor doesn't know that, in conversation among human service personnel, we don't include the specific grade of a rank during personal address? But why go through this charade* at all? *So that Rrurr'rao understands he's third in command? Small Claw of the Khan is about equal to a human commodore, so—yeah, that's probably the reason.*

"Well, Least Fang," Ossian replied, "there was always a chance that if it had been used at Zephrain, news of this new robot fighter might have reached Valkha before the invaders. In that event, the defenders might have—pursued a different course of action." Ossian didn't say "withdraw," but could tell the Orions understood his implication—and had glumly decided not to raise a debate. "Instead, you had all confidence that your superb fighter wings would carry the day, particularly inside the Desai limit."

Rrurr'rao nodded. He turned to Kiiraathra'ostakjo, shifting to the Tongue of Tongues. "The human sees tactics quickly. He is reliable?"

Ossian wondered if Kiiraathra had to suppress a momentary grin. "He is unconventional to the point of madness. He is also the most brilliant human I have ever met. We are lucky to have him with us."

Rrurr'rao growl-muttered, "Even so, in the future, loyalty to his own kind may make him . . . untrustworthy."

The Least Fang straightened again. His voice was stern. "This is twice you have impugned the humans. What have they done?"

Rrurr'rao matched his superior's imposing stare, but did not directly answer his question. "You must understand, Least Fang. We fled. We had no choice. We turned our backs on our last home, our littermates flying to every warp point they could reach. We headed toward V'vettyeao."

"Yes. Logical. The home to Unity Point Five, the one that was just recently forged to link us to the heart of human space. Very near their homeworld, Earth."

"Yes. That warp point. Except it no longer existed by the time we reached it."

Kiiraathra'ostakjo paused. "It had been destroyed?"

"Evidently. I had heard fragmentary reports—rumors, actually—that the humans had begun to develop this warp-point-destroying technology at the behest of their great admiral, Trevayne. But I had not known this could be done, yet. And I never suspected that these humans, these *chofaki*, that these cowardly, *threemish*—"

Kiiraathra'ostakjo stepped forward quickly. "You are injured, and you are my subordinate. It is unseemly that I should challenge you for offending the honor of my friends, for I count many of humanity as such. Similarly, we of the *Zheeerlikou'valkhannaieee* are in desperate need of all our excellent commanders and I am loath to lose another. But if you cannot control such bigotry, I will be forced to—take steps. Whatever those might happen to be."

Rrurr'rao's one green eye glared balefully. But—his eye still on Kiiraathra —he bowed low. "I ask my commander's forgiveness. My first reflex is to identify the enemies—or false friends—of our race. I had thought to do so. I am sorry that it gives offense."

Kiiraathra'ostakjo stared at the bowed head, evidently considering the apology that was not really an apology. "Do not think to remonstrate with me using slanted words, Small Claw, or they shall rebound upon you. Straighten. You are pardoned—this time—but forgiveness will be contingent upon your future actions. Specifically, you must put aside your bigotry. Which is, moreover, quite probably misplaced."

"Instruct me in this, please, Least Fang."

"I shall—and be sure your tone cannot be suspected of insolence or I will make challenge as soon as you are well enough to accept it."

Rrurr'rao evidently heard the aggressive buzz in Kiiraathra's throat and saw the resolve in his eyes. "I—shall earn your forgiveness, Least Fang."

"Very well. Now, consider: have the Kaituni passed through the gate into human space?"

"No, Least Fang."

"And we hold the majority of seats in the PSU, which has its offices of government on Earth, correct?"

"It is as you say."

"Then do you suspect a coup? That our representatives did not approve this order, but rather, were overwhelmed and ousted by the humans?"

"I think it—not impossible, Least Fang."

"That is hardly a statement of reasonable surety, Small Claw, and I recommend you reflect upon, and school yourself in the significance of, that difference."

"But how?"—and now, finally, Rrurr'rao's eyes raised, desperate, along with a wounded-animal catch in his growl. "How would the representatives of the Khan himself shut this door in our faces, condemn their own people to death? Where are their loyalties, Least Fang?"

"To their word and bond, Small Claw," Kiiraathra'ostakjo said quietly, "and to the last surviving holders of those troths: the rest of the PSU. How can you have witnessed the destruction of Valkha, and not realize just what it is you *really* saw, there?"

"And what is that, Least Fang?"

"The decapitation and dismembering of our state, my distant-littermate." Wethermere wondered if the thick tone in Kiiraathra'ostakjo's voice was the sound that grieving Orions made: it was rarely heard among them, and was almost unknown to alien races. "They have annihilated all our fleets in our battles to defend both our homeworlds. They have destroyed—literally, *physically* destroyed—both of those worlds. The Khan was reported dead, along with his vizier and half of the *Kimhakaa* in the first attack. And now the rest of the *Kimhakaa*, probably along with the rest of the senior Fangs of the Khan, are presumed dead on or near Valkha—am I right?"

"You are correct, Least Fang."

"Then tell, me, Rrurr'rao, 952nd Small Claw of the Khan: what was left to save? What succor could Earth have offered? Besides, they face an even greater threat from the fleets approaching their space from Alowan. Are you aware that six, possibly seven of the Dispersates have appeared there?"

"So many more?" Rrurr'rao breathed. "I had heard of the landings, of course, but without any credible data on their numbers. And later, in the weeks leading up to the Battle of Valkha, no further reports reached us from behind the mass of the Kaituni who were approaching."

Kiiraathra'ostakjo nodded. "These are the numbers the humans must contend with. And when the Kaituni fleets are done with our industrial worlds—for surely they shall strike the production centers of the Khanate next—where do you suspect they might go? They certainly have shown no interest in occupation."

Rrurr'rao raised his head slightly. "They will join the other fleets, making for human space. First to destroy the core of their power, near Earth. Or some might move on to Franos and lay waste to the many races of the Star Union before it can add its weight to the defense of the PSU."

"It seems inevitable that they should do one or the other. Perhaps both. Either way, it is our job to do what we may to ensure that the remaining formations of the PSU prevail. Without their victory, the Kaituni will eventually exterminate all of us. Whether they first complete their project of xenocide in the Khanate or in human space is simply a matter of timing: it they are not defeated, we are all doomed to extinction."

Rrurr'rao was standing erect again, and if he felt

any weight of pain in his wounds, it was not stronger than the sense of urgency that was now in his tall, heavy frame. "What is this mission you are on, Least Fang, that I may commit my ship to it? Or rather, may commit what is *left* of my ship."

Kiiraathra'ostakjo nodded slowly. "Well said, and your question about our mission shall be answered soon. But first, let us attend to the needs of your living crew—and consign the dead to space. For I see from the timecode on these data files that, since finding the Unity Point in V'vettyeao to be closed, you have been fleeing attackers. Without stopping."

"For six days, Least Fang."

"And in that time, how many hours have you slept?"

"I-I am unsure, Least Fang. Some. Certainly enough."

"You are a poor liar, Small Claw." He switched to English. "Come, let us share a dish of *zeget* together. There is much to discuss. And to plan."

CHAPTER TWENTY-NINE

It was not the door chime that told Lentsul he had a visitor, but a casual touch of *selnarm*: Mretlak.

"Please enter, Senior Cluster Leader," Lentsul sent, rising.

Mretlak did, preceded by a *selnarmic* bow-wave of (greeting, amity, gratification). "Are you ready to depart for the flagship?"

"Momentarily, Senior Cluster Leader. I am just finishing my report for Narrok on the status of our—"

"Lentsul, you completed that report last night."

"Yes. But. Well, no report is ever so complete that it cannot benefit from—"

"Lentsul," Mretlak sent, along with (approval, assurance, confidence), "do not spend time repairing an unbroken urn. Your report is concise, accurate, and thorough. Do not alter it. It will probably not even be asked for today. It will take the better part of the day for the Bellerophon fleet to traverse the warp point, and its commanders will have much to do before they solicit reports on anything other than immediate security and deployment. However"—Mretlak approached with a data crystal—"I wanted to give you your next assignment before we depart, since it may come up at the meeting."

Lentsul sent (weariness, ennui). "Another of Ankaht's sociological studies of the changing Arduan psyche and its potential impact upon loyalty in our own ranks?"

"No. This is a combination of technical intelligence and cryptography."

Lentsul straightened. "Indeed? This is a pleasant change, Senior Cluster Leader! I shall have read the materials and prepared a preliminary precis for you by the end of the week."

Mretlak's *selnarm* betrayed a thin tissue of amusement. "You shall not be presenting your report to me—any more than I should be the object of your gratitude."

Lentsul paused. "Indeed?"

"Indeed. The assignment comes directly from Capta—well, now *Commodore* Wethermere. He requested that you, specifically, be given this assignment."

Lentsul was so surprised that he could only repeat, "Indeed?"

"He was quite explicit, citing your expertise, excellent record, and impeccable security credentials."

Lentsul was briefly at a loss for words: instead of diminishing, his surprise continued to grow. "I—I am honored. I think. Tell me: what is the focus of this project?"

Mretlak left the data crystal on the edge of Lentsul's desk. "You no doubt recall the briefing we received last week concerning the new robot-fighter designs that make up two-thirds of what Commodore Wethermere and Least Fang Kiiraathra'ostakjo called the Kaituni 'strike triads.' Well, automated sensor and communications recordings made by Small Claw Rrurr'rao's *Tleikhu* have given us somewhat greater insight into precisely how the robotic parts of each strike triad are controlled. Using that information, we may discover a means to thwart their new fighter tactics. Now, follow soon after me: we are leaving presently."

Lentsul tried not to let his excitement show in his rigid clusters or his (eager, vindicated) *selnarm*. "This will be a gratifying challenge."

"Commodore Wethermere and I thought it might be." Mretlak sent (fellowship, congratulations) along with a casual footnote: "You no doubt see the significance: that it was a *human* who suggested you for—and wished to entrust you with—this crucial task." Mretlak left before Lentsul could answer.

Lentsul reflected that, given his deeply conflicted feelings on that matter, it had been singularly wise for Mretlak to have left as soon as he did: a long wait for a change in Lentsul's attitudes toward humans was not in either of their best interests.

From the large gallery viewport in the admiral's private conference room aboard the supermonitor RFNS *Krishmahnta*, Ossian Wethermere overlooked the warp point they had created, and could see distant ships winking into existence with the regularity of silver drops jetting out of an invisible cosmic faucet.

A question—voiced in a brusque alto—roused him from his reverie. "Enjoying the view . . . 'Senior' Commodore?"

Wethermere turned with a smile and a salute, which Admiral Miharu Yoshikuni waved away. "Absolutely enthralled by it, Admiral," Ossian replied. And it was a perfectly true answer: each of those luminescent specks was yet another of the Bellerophon fleet's staggering array of capital ships pouring through to join the rest. Although if Yoshikuni had put any more sardonic emphasis upon the "Senior" qualifier of his "Commodore" title, Ossian suspected that Small Claw Rrurr'rao might take special note. And, in so doing, come to realize that he had, in fact, been conned into believing Wethermere to be his marginally superior officer.

"Well," concluded Yoshikuni, "you'll have the pleasure of watching the fleet come in for at least another three hours. Probably six, if you want to stay and watch all the auxiliaries."

Admiral Narrok, the Arduan admiral who had both protected human civilians from the depredations of Tangri raiders in the last war, and had brought some semblance of sanity to the xenocidal flag ranks in the final weeks of the conflict, emerged from the well-mingled command staffs of both the Bellerophon fleet and the flotilla that had made their transit possible. The ever-composed *Destoshaz* commander approached Wethermere with his clusters raised in formal greeting. "It is good to see you again, Commodore. Particularly under circumstances which put our fleets on the same, rather than opposing, sides."

Wethermere saluted and nodded. "I agree, sir. I am—of all the humans in this room—particularly glad you are on our side, now."

"Oh, and why is that?"

"Because your ships damn near killed me at the battle of BR-02, seven years ago."

Admiral Yoshikuni coughed significantly. "You're not the only one here who can make that claim, Commodore."

Wethermere realized he must have blushed, because Yoshikuni smiled as he added, "Apologies, Admiral. I—well, I forgot that you had a ship shot out from under you, as well."

"Yes . . . well, we'll raise a glass to remember old comrades when our meeting is over. This ship is, after all, the right place to do it."

Wethermere nodded somberly, looked at the hull as if it contained the spirit of the commander whose name it bore. "Admiral Krishmahnta would wish she was here."

Kiiraathra'ostakjo bobbed his head briefly. "She was a fine admiral under whom to serve. But I suspect, were she here, she would rebuke us for dwelling upon past events rather than present challenges."

"True enough," Yoshikuni said, the command-grade brusqueness back in her voice. "Grab a seat, everyone. I don't believe in place-cards or formalities. Least Fang, Commodore, I already have dossiers on most of your team, thanks to the intelligence passed along by Councilor Ankaht to Tefnut ha sheri. Who sends his best wishes—and his frustration, Madame Councilor."

Ankaht's skin seemed to fluctuate slightly in color: a sign of perplexity, Wethermere recalled. Her vocoder's tone confirmed that: "Er . . . the Senior Councilor is 'frustrated,' Admiral Yoshikuni?"

"Absolutely. Tefnut ha sheri charged me to say that he holds you personally responsible that he must continue on in his current incarnation, given all the trouble you've stirred up." The admiral's smile dimmed a bit. "Frankly, he's proven an extremely adept replacement for Senior Councilor Amunherh'peshef, as well as being the new *holodah'kri'at*."

"The new what?" rumbled Rrurr'rao, whose English had improved markedly over the weeks.

"High Priest," translated Jennifer Pietchkov. "He'll make an excellent one, I suspect."

"Indeed: *he* will," Ankaht agreed—but both Narrok and Mretlak glanced at her, confirming the extra gravity Wethermere had thought he perceived in her tone. And he could well guess why: the Arduan dismay over the theological implications of the speciate regression evident in the later Dispersates was growing. Of all the First Dispersate, Tefnut ha sheri had the sufficient age, experience, and gravitas to promote a calm, gradual embrace of those challenges—whatever they might turn out to be.

With everyone seated, Yoshikuni introduced the balance of her staff. "You all know Admiral Narrok, and I apologize if we spooked a few of you by sending his forces through first. But he pointed out that, despite their upgrades, his super-heavy dreadnoughts would be an almost exact match for those of the Kaituni, which—had there been an unexpected threat force here—would have given them pause before attacking. Just the kind of edge we might have needed if things had not gone according to plan."

"Happily," Narrok picked up, "Ankaht's assurances that there would be no opposition were accurate: this deep space warp point, labeled Zheer-Four on the Orion starcharts, has no sign of recent traffic.

An excellent choice for activating your end of the warp-point generator, Commodore—for I believe it was your recommendation, was it not?"

Wethermere paused, not wanting to agree too readily to praise—but Kiiraathra'ostakjo put his own assertion into the momentary silence: "That is correct, Admiral Narrok. It was more circuitous traveling here, compared to some of the other warp-point pathways we could have taken to reach the adjacent Mymzher system and its Unity Warp Point Three. But Zheer-Four—as well as the prior system on this warp-point spur, Zheer Five—are completely unmonitored, being deep space anomalies that do not connect to anything but each other, and one other stellar system, each. If there was anyplace for your fleet to enter unobserved, this was indeed the most isolated and unvisited warp point to choose."

"An excellent choice," Yoshikuni affirmed, with a quick glance down at Wethermere. A glance that lasted a fraction of a second too long, was a little too direct. Not that Ossian minded it: Miharu Yoshikuni was certainly pleasant to look at, even if that extra microsecond of professional attention was perplexing. *Or maybe it was not* professional *attention, but—? No: it's not possible that she's interested—*

But the admiral was moving on. "I believe most of you either know, or have heard of, Captain Chong." She gestured to the silent officer sitting cross-armed to her left. "In the last war, Captain Chong took command of the final attack on Punt City. More recently, he was on site when the subrelativistic hammer came down in the New India system. Immediately after getting his report, I promoted and tapped him to coordinate all flight operations among this fleet's carrier groups. But then we learned of these 'strike triads' that overwhelmed the Orions at Valkha. So I'm shifting him to coordinate and work with you, Lentsul: we need the two of you to come up with a way to undermine that Kaituni innovation."

Lentsul, apparently startled by the direct address from the fleet's senior admiral, and equally startled by the frank announcement of what was expected of him, waved his tentacles in wordless (compliance, acknowledgment).

But Yoshikuni was no longer looking at him. "Least Fang Kiiraathra'ostakjo, to my knowledge, you are the ranking officer among the Orion formations here, and any others of which we have had word, for that matter. So let me start by thanking you. Firstly, for pooling your resources with ours, and secondly, for allowing us to bring a Rim Federation fleet into both Khanate and PSU territory on such short notice and under such extraordinary circumstances."

Kiiraathra'ostakjo inclined his head. "It is we who are honored by your presence. It is a bold move, to bring a fleet so far inside of enemy-held territory, without a supply chain or naval depot to support its continuing operations."

"To say nothing of leaving behind the most powerful ships of your formations," Mretlak added. "Without devastators or superdevastators to serve as the center of your line, or the core of your formation, you are operating in defiance of your current naval doctrine."

Yoshikuni tossed a dismissive hand in the direction of the warp point through which her ships continued to pour. "There was no way to bring them. We don't have any warp-point generators to dredge—which is to say, expand the transit capacity—of any of the warp points we'll be navigating. And sooner or later, we were going to run into a smaller-capacity warp point. So I'd have had to leave all those massive fleet-killers behind, anyway."

Narrok's head lifted slightly higher. "In retrospect, there may even be advantages to this limitation. By leaving the devastators and superdevastators behind, we are adding those forces to the forts that protect the Astria warp point, whereby forces from Zephrain would attack Bellerophon. With the present collection of metal and firepower now guarding that warp point, it would take several fleets of Amunsit's size to break through—and word has it that she was badly attrited by Admiral Watanabe in the Zephrain system. In short, unless the Kaituni turn a great number of their fleets to the task of breaking the defenses at Bellerophon, they will not be able to enter the Arm and wreak havoc upon those well-developed worlds.

"But also, by leaving the largest of the capital ships behind, we increase the maximum speed at which this fleet can move. Both classes of devastators are powerful, but very ponderous, ships. With monitors as our largest capital ships, we may move much more rapidly, and yet our hulls have parity with the largest of our enemy's. And thanks to the repeating energy torpedo batteries, they shall always enjoy a per-hull firepower advantage."

"The question," Yoshikuni mused, "is where to put that firepower to use. Least Fang, I wonder if you could give us a rundown on the most recent disposition of the Kaituni fleets here in the Khanate."

Kiiraathra'ostakjo stood, studied the unfamiliar data control wand for a moment, activated the holographic screen. The Khanate's warp-link network appeared in green, with several dozen systems also ringed in red or pulsing yellow. In the case of New Valkha, both red and yellow designators surrounded the star-system's designating disk. "Please understand that our most recent updates are nonetheless already several weeks old. However, the basic conditions within the Khanate itself have been confirmed with a high degree of confidence. The red-ringed warp junctions are systems that the Kaituni fleets have have attacked and neutralized. However, many of the invaders are still using these warp points to shuffle their traffic in and around the Khanate."

"'Their traffic'?" Chong echoed uncertainly.

"Yes. In addition to expanding their campaign of crippling Orion worlds, the Kaituni have also sent some small flotillas toward their new force concentration that is moving out from Alowan. We hypothesize that these flotillas are relocating command personnel or other persons or technologies that they wish to have on hand for their upcoming—or possibly, already fought—battle with the PSU fleets gathering in and around the Pesthouse salient."

Chong nodded his understanding and thanks, and sat back.

Kiiraathra'ostakjo continued. "The stellar disks surrounded by the yellow, pulsing rings are those which were struck by the deluge of subrelativistic objects. To a lesser or greater degree, they are difficult to navigate and in complete social disarray. Or have been completely depopulated by the bombardment.

"Our best intelligence estimates, updated from contacts we encountered over the weeks we spent traveling from the Sreaor system to Zheer-Four, continue to indicate that three Dispersates entered the Khanate either in the New Valkha system or one of those systems directly adjacent. Each Dispersate has remained a discrete unit of maneuver since its arrival. One is currently in what our race would consider 'reaver mode.' In short, it is striking at both key resources—such as industrial and high-output agricultural worlds—as well as targets of opportunity, simply with the intent to destroy."

"In effect, they are the action arm of the Kaituni scorched earth policy," Yoshikuni muttered grimly.

"Correct," affirmed Kiiraathra'ostakjo. "They also constitute a constant, unpredictable patrol element: to our knowledge, they have already encountered and destroyed two small flotillas of Khanate warships that had been trying to gather enough forces to carry the fight back to the invaders.

"Most of the other two Kaituni fleets have actually begun to follow the path blazed by the Zarzuela fleet. As it turns out, we passed within one warp junction of these units while making our way here."

"Too close for comfort," breathed Jennifer.

"It was a daunting prospect," Kiiraathra'ostakjo agreed. "Our best projections indicate that they are either moving to reinforce Amunsit's attrited fleet at Zephrain, or may be hoping to press up the warp line from Zephrain to Home Hive Three."

Yoshikuni stared at the implications of that move. "That would put them on the alternate route toward Pesthouse."

"Or," Ossian suggested, "if Admiral Waldeck moves forward from Pesthouse to engage, then it puts these two additional Kaituni fleets in a position to cut off his withdrawal from any battle he might fight further along the warp line to Alowan."

Narrok's three eyes squinted at the warp routes. "They are most likely pursuing the strategy Commodore Wethermere has identified. We are descended from creatures that trap prey by surrounding it, it is the preferred method of ensuring kills, of bringing a hunt or battle to a decisive conclusion."

Yoshikuni frowned. "Would two Dispersate's warcraft be enough to stop Cyrus Waldeck if he needed to push them out of the way?"

"Possibly not," Narrok allowed, "but I am not sure that it is necessary to fully block a withdrawal in order to be an effectual impediment. If the seven fleets advancing from Alowan are expecting these two fleets coming from the Khanate to be approaching Admiral Waldeck from the rear, they will know to maintain maximum pressure on any human formation that flees before them. In such a scenario, if Admiral Waldeck is withdrawing, and is also hotly pursued, then the two new fleets in his rear need only ambush and delay him long enough so that his pursuers from Alowan may catch and bring him down."

Yoshikuni nodded soberly. "You mentioned that the majority of these two Dispersates from New Valkha had moved toward Zephrain. Is there word on any elements that might have split off from one or both of them?"

"Possibly." Kiiraathra'ostakjo traced his claw from the doubly stricken symbol of New Valkha through an even longer route that ended at Alowan. "From what fragmentary accounts we have, some of those elements may be moving in the direction of Alowan. At a somewhat leisurely pace, I might add."

"Why?" asked Jennifer Pietchkov abruptly. "Of all the things you've pointed out and hypothesized, that doesn't make any sense."

Yoshikuni nodded. "I agree: that's an odd move. If the Kaituni need all their force up front against Waldeck, I would expect those other elements to be burning through the warp links at maximum speed. Or would simply have stayed attached to the other two fleets that went through Zephrain to get behind him." She leaned back. "It worries me that we don't have better intel or tracking on those lesser elements. They've been sent off on some errand—and I don't like being in the dark about their objective. So, as we go forward, we need to keep one eye looking ahead, and one looking over our shoulder for them. Units without clear locations on the game board have a nasty way of turning up in the most inopportune places at the most inopportune moments. We can't afford those kinds of surprises." She turned toward Wethermere. "And that's where you come in, Commodore."

"Me, Admiral?"

"Yes, you, and the recon methods you've evolved for your group. I want you to keep conducting those advance recon missions, keep walking point. But now, you're doing so for this whole fleet. You've got a Q-ship, a lightning-fast corvette that I understand you've tricked out with some pretty interesting stealth gear, and an Arduan freighter that is very unlikely to be detected as an alien hull or a threat until they get quite close to the OpFor. And, if you need to modify your unit composition by changing your ship mix, you've got just the right collection of dilapidated civilian hulls to choose from." She smiled. "You've done a fine job shepherding your flotilla through enemy territory, Commodore. Now I need you to do it for the rest of us."

Kiiraathra'ostakjo shifted in his seat. "Admiral, in order for me to be able to continue to support the commodore's operations most effectively, I will need my carrier and Small Claw Rrurr'rao's to be retrofitted with advanced stealth systems and—"

Yoshikuni shook her head: her black hair spun and shone. "Sorry, Least Fang, that's the one change I'm making to your current operations. Effective immediately, your warships—even the museum pieces—are being integrated into the Bellerophon Arm Fleet. We'll effect complete repairs to the *Tleikhu* and upgrade your older rustbuckets enough to be able to perform some useful picket and security duties. Maybe even detached missions. But it doesn't make sense to have two carriers lumbering along after the commodore's innocuous little scout group. And besides, I can't spare your carriers from our main van. Your ships—and you commanders—are simply too valuable to put out on the chopping block."

Wethermere swallowed at the image that colloquialism raised, but said nothing.

Kiiraathra had leaned forward sharply. "Admiral, while I understand your reasoning, at least allow me to make the case for ensuring that our recon elements are adequately protected. On several occasions, when surprised by the appearance of a Kaituni patrol, we were able to save the recon grou—"

Yoshikuni held up a palm topped by long, graceful fingers. "Least Fang, your advice and loyalty to your comrades is duly noted and appreciated. But this change is not open to discussion. The risk to the recon element is made greater by the possible discovery of any warships shadowing it, and besides, I need those warships back with us."

Wethermere cleared this throat. "Admiral, a point of order, if I may?"

Yoshikuni's green eyes flicked down the table at him. "I'm listening, Commodore. But don't try my patience: this matter is settled."

"My point of order does not pertain to this matter."

"Very well. Proceed."

"Admiral, if, as you point out, Least Fang Kiiraathra'ostakjo is the highest remaining Orion officer currently known, and since his flotilla of almost a dozen ships has been folded into your fleet, is it not essential that he be promoted—at least for the duration of the conflict, or until a more senior Orion officer is located?"

Surprised looks ricocheted from face to face around the conference table. Yoshikuni leaned back. "You are referring to the regulation that holds that the minimum rank for any flag officer holding command over a species-separate flotilla in a larger fleet is that of admiral?"

"Yes, ma'am, that and a slightly more obscure regulation stipulating the minimal senior command rank for the overall commander of any PSU member state, even in the event that said member state's organized formations are defeated and the polity presently disrupted. Again, that rank is admiral, or small fang of the Khan."

Kiiraathra'ostakjo looked grateful but shook his head. "The Commodore forgets a detail of Orion culture. What in human formations is merely a rank, is, among Orions, a more personal liege-vassal relationship, as well. I cannot be promoted to Small Fang, for there is no liege to whom I may swear my allegiance, anymore."

Wethermere wasn't done. "Understood, but you are also part of the armed forces of the PSU. You can receive sufficient rank through that affiliation, although you could not be titled Small Fang."

Yoshikuni looked both intrigued and bemused. "You could have been a JAG, Commodore, but there's still a hole in your plan. I may be a fleet admiral, but I'm not authorized to promote individuals to just one grade under my own. And besides, I'm a member of the Rim Federation. We are affiliated with, but not in the direct TOO of, the PSU naval formations."

"With the Admiral's pardon, did you note the source of the authorization you agreed to as sufficient for entering Khanate space—since, not being members of the PSU, a Rim Federation fleet requires explicit travel and access permission from a PSU representative of sufficient standing?"

Yoshikuni frowned, then her eyebrows raised. "Why, you—!"

"Admiral, no personal invective, please. As the only individual of sufficient rank present in my flotilla—or your fleet—who is a member of the PSU, and as a representative of the Earth Federation polity component of the PSU holding a clearance and authorization level of One Bravo in diplomatic and intelligence operations, I extended authorization as a proxy for the standing PSU government."

Yoshikuni sputtered. "That does not confer authority sufficient to—!"

"Actually," mused Ankaht, "it does. Commodore Wethermere has, on several occasions, been compelled to make snap decisions on state-level intelligence and counterintelligence matters without waiting for confirmation or consultation with the PSU government on Earth. He asked me to assess his interpretation of those confidential prerogatives as they applied—or not—to this matter. Speaking for the Arduan Council of Twenty, I must say that I find absolutely no flaw in his interpretations or actions. They are consistent with both his written mandate and conditional authority as it has been exercised to date."

Yoshikuni blinked and then smiled crookedly. "Well, hell: I *can* always use another good admiral—'Admiral' Kiiraathra'ostakjo. Congratulations on the strangest promotion I've ever heard of. Well, perhaps that's the second strangest," she finished with a knowing glance at both the Orion and Wethermere. "Now it's time to head home and get to work, all of you. We're going to be laid up here, sorting ourselves out for a few days at least. That means we've got patrol rosters to mount, pickets to set, logistics to coordinate and old ships to start bringing up to scratch. Except you, Commodore"—and Wethermere found himself once again under the scrutiny of those two green eyes—"you are going to walk me through all the dubious legal details of this promotion. In detail. Over a working dinner."

Kiiraathra was exiting the room as the admiral completed issuing instructions to an orderly for dinner to be brought in thirty minutes. Where she and the commodore would be working together. Evidently alone. Hearing that, the Orion's right ear flicked upward, interest piqued, rakishly provocative—and then tucked down again. The door closed behind him.

Wethermere, once again returning the frank and unwavering stare of Admiral Miharu Yoshikuni, reflected that if he'd been an Orion, his ears might have flicked just the same way.

CHAPTER THIRTY

The system still referred to as Home Hive Two was an unusual system indeed: a binary consisting of two type F main sequence stars of very similar mass orbiting each other in a not-very-eccentric ellipse at a mean separation of two hundred and fifty light-minutes. Still more remarkable was the fact that the twin suns, older than average for stars of their mass, had a total of *five* life-bearing planets, three orbiting Component A and two orbiting Component B.

Or, strictly speaking, they *had* been life-bearing planets.

Ever since the apocalyptic battles of 2369, this system had been the graveyard of uncounted scores of billions of Bugs. And it was haunted by the ghosts of hundreds of thousands of humans, Orions, Ophiuchi and Gorm who had died to cleanse the universe of the all-consuming Arachnid abomination.

Those ghosts, thought Cyrus Waldeck, were about to have company.

The slow pace of the main Kaituni armada up the

warp chain from Alowan, hampered by the sheer number of ships that had to be processed through one warp-point bottleneck after another, had allowed him to bring Second Fleet from Pesthouse through Home Hive One and the planetless red giant system of Orpheus-1 and enter this system unopposed. The Kaituni, still in the process of filtering in through the warp point connecting with Bug 06, had of course sent clouds of scout ships speeding through the system toward the Orpheus-1 warp point through which their enemies must come. There had been much skirmishing between those scouts and his own light units, but there had been no prepared warp-point defenses to cope with. Waldeck was glad of that. An assault through a warp point against a strong, prepared enemy on the other side was like . . . well, Ian Trevayne had once compared it to the Somme, leaving most of his listeners none the wiser.

The thought of Trevayne brought a frown to Waldeck's face. He would have liked to have had the Terran Republic/Rim Federation fleet Trevayne had brought back from Tangri space with him, not to mention certain tardy PSU and Ophiuchi contingents that had attached themselves to him, having arrived too late to join Second Fleet before its departure from Pesthouse. That, in turn, brought his mind back to the debate among his subordinates that had still not died down.

He turned back to the holo-pit around which they were all gathered. It displayed the system of Home Hive Two A, with the local sun at the center. Component B was for the moment unimportant, for all three of the system's warp points were here, around A. The Orpheus-2 warp point through which they had entered was at about eleven o'clock, to use the imaginary clock-face conventionally superimposed on the display, at a distance from Component A of twenty-four light-minutes, embedded in an asteroid belt (which had necessitated a degree of caution on emergence). The other two warp points, connecting with Bug 06 and Bug 08 respectively, were both at seven o'clock at about twenty light-minutes, only one light-minute apart—yet another peculiarity of this system. So, although they had cautiously advanced some five light-minutes since the entirety of Second Fleet had completed transit, they were still almost thirty light-minutes from the myriad of monitor-sized-and-smaller ships that made up the Kaituni main body, and positioned so that the gravity well of Component A shouldn't be a factor in closing that distance.

Here and there, crawling about the display, were the icons of the wide-ranging scouts he had sent to probe the system for any forces the Kaituni might have somehow managed to conceal prior to his arrival. Those scouts went in squadrons, with light carriers to provide fighter cover, for there were still running battles with the enemy's similar light units. But he had managed to get a recon probe through the Bug 08 warp point, just in case. That binary system, with its lifeless array of gas and ice planets, had proven empty. (Not that it would have made much difference if it hadn't, given the layout of this system's warp points.) Nor were any crouching threats found to be lurking among the ghosts of Home Hive Two.

Resolution hardened in Waldeck at the thought. "Well, then, are we all agreed?" he rasped.

Most of his task force commanders' faces registered agreement, but Chandra Konievitsky spoke up for the faction of which she was the leader. "Admiral, I still think we should consider waiting for Admiral Trevayne to link up with us here. Judging from our latest communiqués, he shouldn't be much longer."

"We've been over all this before, Chandra," said Waldeck—though not harshly, for he respected her for having the courage of her convictions. "In the first place, while the Kaituni fleet now in this system is certainly an extremely large one, there are indications that it isn't *all* here. In fact, what we're looking at may be simply a very heavy vanguard. If that's the case, we have an opportunity to defeat them in detail. And then, maybe, after defeating them, go on through their warp point of ingress to Bug 06 and present their oncoming forces with a defended warp point to fight their way through."

"Yes!" said Least Fang Tirnyareeo'zhelak, emphatically enough to make his whiskers quiver. "Let us strike now! If their forces are divided, they will not remain so. We may not have this chance again."

"And secondly," Waldeck continued before Konievitsky could try to answer Tirnyareeo, "while Admiral Trevayne has quite a large fleet—especially now, with the additional PSU and Ophiuchi elements he's picked up along the way—the fact remains that he has relatively few devastators and superdevastators. He hasn't really needed many of them against the light, scattered raiding forces of the Tangri. Sort of like swatting flies with a pile driver. Not to mention their deployability problems—all those undredged warp points in Tangri space. In fact, they've been mostly for intimidation value. I grant you, he's got more carriers and fighters than we have—including the majority of the Ophiuchi—and I wouldn't mind having those. But he couldn't greatly add to our total of *really* heavy metal."

Not even Konievitsky demurred on this point. They all knew that even the near-legendary armadas that had battled the Bugs here in this very system would have stood no chance whatsoever against the almost unimaginable—even in this century—destructive power quiveringly leashed inside the Brobdingnagian hulls of Second Fleet's array of devastators and superdevastators. The Kaituni fleet might outnumber them severely in hulls, but it certainly did not outweigh them in total tonnage or exceed them in firepower. Quite the contrary.

"In any event," Waldeck finished firmly, "my decision to implement the plan is final. We will proceed on course and attack on schedule." He manipulated controls, and in the tank the system display was replaced by a three-dimensional array of multitudinous lights, colored to represent various ship types.

"You're all familiar with our formation," Waldeck continued. They were. At its core were the massed devastators and superdevastators, with a fringe of supermonitors—the only smaller class of ship that mounted gee-beams and salvo-capable heavy bombardment missile batteries. Behind that inconceivable phalanx were the bulk of second fleet's carriers—a not inconsiderable total even without Trevayne. Streaming back from its edges were successively lighter capital ships—or at least the monitors and superdreadnoughts and battleships that had once been classed as capital ships. Ranging far afield were the swift cruisers that would have vanished like moths in a flame at the touch of the firepower put out by today's first-line ships. "You also know this formation's rationale. But to recapitulate, the carriers will launch before we get close to the Kaituni, providing a fighter cover for the battle line, which will push ahead toward their warp point of ingress while our lighter stuff sweeps ahead in an enveloping movement. Are there any questions?"

There were none. Nor were there any worried looks, even from Konievitsky. That display reminded them all of the central fact: nothing that the Kaituni had could come within range of that prodigious, unprecedented battle line and live. Waldeck was satisfied at what he saw in their faces.

Only, he thought wryly, *I hope none of you think my planning was influenced by the fact that if Ian Trevayne was here I'd have to turn overall command over to him—that I don't want to share the pleasure of giving the orders that send our battle line smashing into these Kaituni vermin like the hammer of God.*

And, came the unbidden and unwelcome thought, *I also hope it isn't true.*

Destoshaz'at Zum'ref turned away, disgusted, from the limp, quivering captive between the two guards, and gave his attention back to the display screen that showed the course of the enemy fleet: a flat hyperbola across the Home Hive Two system, coming closer and closer to what must seem to them to be a highly irrational formation: a cloud of ships giving no particular evidence of having been distributed to counter that which was approaching them . . . except that the monitors were positioned along the course of the oncoming battle line. It must, he thought, seem to the humans an exercise in futile desperation, for they didn't know that a monitor was the smallest ship that could mount the weapon to which they were about to be introduced. Anticipation quivered within him like a living being long held in check.

"All right, Inzrep'fel," he said over his shoulder to his Intendant as an afterthought. "Take the human away and dispose of him."

They had been fortunate to get this human *zhettek*. In the course of their operations in Orion space, Zum'ref had commanded them to try to capture an officer with experience aboard superdevastators, for although he already possessed the relevant statistics he had wanted certain performance parameters and navigational characteristics clarified. Unfortunately, such officers were relatively rare among the Orions, with their bias toward smaller ships. However, the close association of the two principal races of the pretentiously named Pan-Sentient Union meant that there were a certain number of human personnel on detached duty among them. So they had bagged this—what was his name, now?—Commander James Monetti. Squeezing the desired information out of him had been easy, for all his attempted heroics: a certain drug rendered him incapable of withholding it. The accompanying physical torture had been, strictly speaking, unnecessary, but it had expedited the process by preventing him from concentrating on mental resistance. Zum'ref had thought him to be wrung dry, but then had had certain afterthoughts. So he'd ordered the nauseating *griarfeksh* to be brought here to the control center to answer a few more questions. But now he was done with him and dismissed him from his mind.

Then he heard a commotion behind him. Turning, he saw Monetti, with a sudden surge of what must be hysterical strength, twist momentarily out of the guards' grip. He recalled that the drug wore off quickly . . . and also that he himself was still wearing the vocoder he had used for the questioning.

For a moment, Monetti stood in the bloodstained black-and-silver tatters of his uniform, glaring with eyes that were like burning pits of hatred in his gaunt, battered face. Then the guards grasped him and forced him to the deck. But the human's eyes were still on Zum'ref and he actually managed to smile. "You put yourself at a disadvantage when you let a man know you're going to kill him," he rasped. "He's got nothing much to lose."

"No—although a *zhettek* like yourself has far more to lose than one of the children of Illudor," said Zum'ref in a tone whose mildness the Intendant and the nearby staffers knew to be deceptive.

"So," Monetti went on, eyes wild, "I'm going to tell you that all the information you've gotten from me isn't going to do you a damned bit of good! You see, from all the questions you've been asking me about superdevastators, it's obvious that you're going to be engaging them shortly—probably a lot of them, because surely the PSU has been able to identify you as the main threat and concentrate against you. And once you come into geebeam range of them, you're *dead*, you insane, genocidal piece of filth! You have no conception of what they can do. But you're going to find out." Monetti paused for breath. "I just wish I was going to live long enough to see you realize what a mistake you've made—what a disaster you've brought down upon yourself!"

Zum'ref half-raised an arm to signal the guards to put an end to this annoying *griarfeksh.* But then he paused. Mere death—even the death of the *zheteksh*, who had no reincarnation to look forward to, only eternal nothingness—was too good for Monetti. Instead, he should not be permitted to die before realizing the fate that lay in store for his people. Anyway, he had a few minutes.

So he leaned forward and continued to speak in the same mild tones. "Actually, it wasn't a mistake. This represents the final attainment of our objective. Everything we've done has been *intended* to lure the PSU into sending its heaviest concentration of devastators and superdevastators—the more of them the better—against us, in just such circumstances as these." Monetti's open-mouthed look of incomprehension was deeply satisfying. So Zum'ref leaned further forward. "You are to be honored beyond your bestial imaginings, for I am going to take the trouble to explain it to you before you die, so that you may understand the full weight of doom that is descending upon your race this day.

"In the course of our long journey through normal space, we sought deeper understanding of the quantum physics behind our photon drive. Our delvings led us into the realms of quantum entanglement—and to the realization that it was possible to build a weapon that would hyperaccelerate a particle stream to suprarelativistic energy states.

"As even you humans have been aware for centuries, quantum mechanics is founded on the postulate that, under certain circumstances, particles can 'teleport' from one side of a barrier to another."

"Yes," Monetti said, nodding slowly, as though his incomprehension was beginning to give way to a dawning suspicion. "In Heisenbergian terms, every particle in the universe has a greater-than-zero-percent chance of being anywhere, at any time. We've long since recognized that this must be the basis of *selnarm*—it's the only way to explain the instantaneous transmission of thought over vast distances."

"Then you understand that, without violating the light-speed barrier, it is possible to cause certain particles to exchange one volume of space for another without traversing the intervening distance, much faster than light could travel between the two points—effectively instantaneously, in fact.

"We have exploited this phenomenon of 'focused quantum entanglement' to build a weapon that can cause a hyperenergized matter stream of subparticles such as mesons and neutrinos to experience this 'particle teleportation' effect. The matter stream then reenters normal space in a targeted volume. Perhaps your limited understanding is incapable of imagining the effect on any object occupying the volume where the particles reemerge and multiple bits of matter are forced to do the impossible and occupy the same volume. The result is one hundred percent matter-to-energy conversion. As catastrophic as an antimatter warhead... except that it occurs *inside* the target."

"But," said Monetti in a tone of grasping-at-straws desperation, "how could such a thing be targeted?"

"The targeting is a function of the level of excess energy in the particles and the biasing of the field when they 'jump' out of normal space. These provide the range and bearing respectively. However, your instinct is correct: the weapon is only effective against targets that are big and relatively slow and unmaneuverable. In fact . . ." Zum'ref paused, savoring the effect he knew his next words were going to have. "In fact, the weapon is only practical against devastators and superdevastators."

Now, as horrified realization fully dawned, Monetti's face wore the expression of a man who knew he, and all his world, were in a nightmare from which there would be no awakening.

"Now you understand, don't you?" Zum'ref asked rhetorically. "You understand why our entire strategy has been aimed not at avoiding head-on combat with your monster ships, but at luring the greatest possible number of them to us. And it has succeeded. They have come to us like *bilbuxhati* to the slaughter.

"Our scientists call this new weapon the 'relativistic acceleration weapon.' But our common term for it is 'the Hand of God.'" The term, of course, would translate literally as "the Tentacle-Member of Illudor," but Zum'ref wanted it to have the maximum impact on this cowering *griarfeksh*. "And it is about to strike a blow that will shatter your fleets and open the way to the final purging of your repulsive species, and all the other species of *zheteksh* with the effrontery to pretend to intelligence."

Monetti seemed to have withdrawn into a place where his new knowledge could not pursue him.

"*Destoshaz'at*, it is almost time," said Inzep'fel diffidently.

(Pleasurable anticipation.) "Yes, so it is. Take him away and kill him." Zum'ref turned and walked back to the display screen. The icons of the oncoming, unsuspecting enemy were inching closer to a certain glowing line, marking the range of the new weapon, slightly greater than that of their gee-beams.

It belatedly occurred to Zum'ref that he hadn't made full use of his opportunity. He could have also told Monetti that there was *another* secret he was about to reveal to the humans, here in this system—and he wasn't sure which of the two would horrify them more. But that would have to wait a little longer.

A burst of reports came in. The enemy had launched barrages of long-range heavy bombardment missiles from the massed batteries of their devastators and superdevastators, before coming into gee-beam range. His fleet would have to endure that for a short time. They were also deploying their fighter screen, expecting to have to counter swarms of *selnarm*-controlled suicide fighters. But that, of course, would come later...

Time seemed to crawl as the extended-range engagement raged, with point-defense batteries battling the missile-storm. But then, finally, the enemy icons were almost touching the line.

(Respect behind which quivered eagerness.) "We await your command, *Destoshaz'at*," said the Intendant.

Zum'ref's large central eye, the one that always revealed emotion in his species, gleamed as the line was crossed.

"Let the Hand of God strike," he said.

CHAPTER THIRTY-ONE

There was no warning. None at all.

Cyrus Waldeck was on his flag bridge watching the satisfyingly destructive effect of his battle line's torrential missile bombardment on the Kaituni fleet and the relatively ineffectual response to it. Waldeck was still wondering why no army-ant-like swarm of *selnarm*-controlled fighters was sweeping toward him (as it had toward Yoshi Watanabe's fleet at Zephrain) when the first superdevastator vanished in a boiling cloud of superheated gas that consumed the ship so quickly that its hull did not have enough time fly apart into chunks of wreckage.

As stunned as everyone else on the flag bridge, Waldeck's immediate reaction was, *It must have been an accident*. But then another superdevastator exploded, and then another.

"Aline," Waldeck shouted at his Intelligence officer, a long lifetime of military formality forgotten in the throes of nightmare, "what is it? What's happening?"

Aline Chuan turned a paper-white face to him.

"I . . . I don't know, Admiral. There's no indication that anything was targeting any of those ships. They just . . . blew up. From the *inside.*"

And so the great ships' almost impenetrable energy shields had been irrelevant, Waldeck realized. There was only one thing to do.

"I want maximum velocity!" he commanded his chief of staff. "Whatever in God's name this is, their ships—probably their monitors—are somehow putting it out. We've got to get in close and smash them before they can wipe us out. Get us into gee-beam range! And keep putting out the maximum possible volume of missile fire while you're doing it, targeting the monitors." Then, recalling the intelligence analysis of the data from Zephrain, he added an afterthought. "But don't emphasize the ones with the energy signatures of the heavy assault monitors. Those are designed for warp-point assaults, for taking the lead and early casualties. They won't be the ones we're after."

The order was passed, and, with the fleet flagship PSUNS *Ivan Antonov* in the lead, the battle-line formation surged forward—less raggedly than might have been expected, considering the state of shock that gripped most of its personnel. But Waldeck's orders proved impossible to carry out, for as they strained to get to closer range they simply advanced deeper into the range of the relativistic acceleration weapon—or the RAW, as it was soon to become known. Withdrawal out of that range was the only thing that might have saved some of them . . . but Waldeck could not know that.

Concentration of defense-saturating missile fire on the Kaituni monitors destroyed some of them, but could not alter the outcome. The battle line became defined by a luminous cloud of expanding gas molecules and particulate matter, like a planetary nebula through which shone the stroboscopic glare of exploding superships, like rapid-fire novas.

Cyrus Waldeck's heart was already dead within him when a hyperenergized stream of particles emerged into normal space deep in *Antonov*'s bowels, whose outraged matter instantly converted itself into ravening energy in protest.

At first, Zum'ref could only stand in a state of exaltation, watching the holocaust unfold. And the involuntary *selnarmic* emanation of that (EXALTATION!) bathed everyone else on the command center balcony like the warmth of a nearby sun.

What did the scientists truly know? Their knowledge was shallow and superficial. They knew only the material outer surface of the truth—the quantum physics that was merely a way of putting that truth into terms comprehensible to lesser minds. He, Zum'ref, had glimpsed the truth in its entirety: what was happening was the will of Illudor made manifest, intervening directly in the material universe to cleanse it of the non-Arduan life forms infesting it. It was the Hand of God indeed!

But, he reminded himself, *Illudor helps those who help themselves. And I have been chosen to be his instrument.* So he forced his mind back to practicalities.

Only monitors could (just barely) carry the massive RAW generators. He had, as a matter of prudence, not emplaced those generators on the new heavy assault monitors, whose heavy armor and shields would have given them the maximum protection but whose intended use—leading warp-point assaults—did not tend to increase their life expectancy. Instead, he had distributed them among the other monitor classes, using ubiquity as a form of camouflage. To be sure, it had been necessary to modify the RAW-equipped monitors. They had had to give up most of their conventional offensive armament, while at the same time receiving enhanced energy shields and point defense to increase their survivability. These peculiarities, in addition to the engine output spike that marked the power surge whenever the RAW was used, might make those ships identifiable. But the human admiral—who had correctly deduced that whatever it was that was so inexplicably destroying his super-ships must somehow emanate from the Kaituni monitors, and had accordingly targeted them—had no leisure to analyze his sensor readings and search for such patterns. He had also been correct in his apparent assumption that the assault monitors—specialized warp-point assault ships, according to his best information—were unlikely to be the ones he sought. So he had had no way of knowing which monitors were wielding the new and utterly deadly weapon. Nevertheless, the smashing long-range missile salvos that datalinked superdevastators could administer had gotten a few of the RAW-equipped ships. But only a few. And in his desperation to get within gee-beam range of his tormentors, that human admiral had merely rushed headlong into the mouth of Illudor's furnace.

But Zum'ref wanted no more losses among the RAW-carrying monitors—there would be other devastators and superdevastators to deal with in later battles. And there was no point in risking them. Even the enemy supermonitors weren't massive enough or clumsy enough to allow good targeting solutions for them. So . . .

"Pull all RAW-bearing monitors back," he commanded. "All other elements will proceed with phase two of our plan—the extermination of the remainder of this gutted fleet. Our fighters will concentrate on their supermonitors, which are the only ships they have left that outclass everything of ours. Otherwise, our heavy superdreadnoughts can deal with most of their surviving ships, aided by superior numbers of our lighter hulls."

His subordinates hastened to execute his orders.

Most of Second Fleet's highest officers had been flying their lights aboard devastators and superdevastators, and had died with them. But not all. The vice admirals and rear admirals in command of carrier task groups and the lighter supporting task groups built around battlecruisers survived. And Chandra Konievitsky, whose task force was made up of the latter, abruptly found herself the senior living officer, and in command of a fleet for which escape had now become the best-case scenario.

"Get the fringe of supermonitors back," she ordered in a hoarse voice. "They'll be the next-priority targets for . . . whatever this is, after the devastators and superdevastators are gone."

She could hardly credit that she was saying the last seven words—they had a weird ring of unreality in her ears. All she could do was try to minimize the disaster. And she found herself on the horns of a dilemma. She must try and preserve the supermonitors, the largest ships Second Fleet had left. But they were also the slowest, and would delay the fleet as it retreated to the Orpheus-1 warp point. *But of course,* came the ghastly thought, *if the Kaituni destroy them the same way they've destroyed the devastator classes, that will eliminate the problem, won't it?* She thrust the notion from her mind with revulsion and turned to the nightmarish job of trying to impose smooth tactical coordination on a fleet whose command structure had been more than decimated, whose lines of communication were tattered, and whose collective state of mind was like a choppy sea of uncomprehending horror over which rose whitecaps of sheer panic.

But this was, after all, a professional fleet. Gradually, she and her staff managed to bring order out of chaos, and well-drilled tactical doctrine for a fighting retreat reasserted itself in the face of the Kaituni onslaught: a tidal wave of heavy superdreadnoughts and lesser ships plus a limited number of monitors, spewing uncountable missiles and preceded by *selnarm*-directed fighters in their thousands. (Though not, Konievitsky noted, the fighter "triads" that Intelligence reports from Orion space had described. Perhaps the Dispersates making up this fleet didn't have them. Or perhaps the Kaituni didn't consider them necessary for dealing with a fleet that had just had its heart torn out.)

But as patterns began to emerge, Konievitsky's sweating Intelligence staff discerned two of them quite clearly. In the first place, certain Kaituni monitors were holding back and not engaging in combat. And secondly, none of her supermonitors were simply exploding in that ghastly, inexplicable way. Instead, they were at the center of swarms of fighters like angry bees.

Konievitsky didn't even try to discern any connection between the two. In fact, she barely noticed the first one. She was struggling to cope with the role of fleet command, into which she had been unceremoniously thrust at least two levels below preparation for it. And she therefore fixated on the one datum that seemed very clear in the midst of this maelstrom of space-wracking violence: lesser ships than devastators were *not* turning into miniature novae for no intelligible reason. So, evidently, the Kaituni couldn't do it. She didn't try to understand it. She merely reacted to it.

"Order our fighter screen to concentrate on protecting the supermonitors," she commanded.

Through the disaster-wracked comm channels of Second Fleet, the order was somehow passed, and the fighter screen reconfigured itself in accordance with the new priorities. Those fighters were hugely outnumbered, but by an even huger margin they were individually superior to their adversaries. This was partly because some of them—not nearly as many as Konievitsky would have liked—were piloted by Ophiuchi, whose evolutionary ancestors had traded the ability to fly for intelligence but without giving up millions of years of intuitive sense for relative motion in three dimensions. And partly because even *selnarmic* control could not totally equal the highly motivated instantaneity achievable by a pilot right there in the cockpit. But mostly because of the rapid-fire energy torpedo that had been miniaturized into a viable fighter weapon system. Second Fleet's fighters corkscrewed through the dense swarms of their adversaries, cutting swathes through them. Meanwhile, the supermonitors they protected used their heavier, ship-to-ship energy torpedoes—more effective than standard missiles at the medium ranges to which the Kaituni van was now closing—to lay down a withering defensive fire that would continue as long as their power plants kept functioning.

But the thousands of kamikaze fighters—unhindered even by the natural last-few-seconds' hesitation that must have often gripped the pilots whose suicidal attacks centuries earlier over Old Terra's Pacific Ocean had fixed the label in both memory and lexicon—were too numerous to be insulated against. Konievitsky watched her losses mount as she continued her fighting retreat—always one of the most difficult tactical problems in space warfare, for it could not be a simple headlong flight, lest the pursuing enemy find too easy a path into the sternward "blind zones" created by all reactionless drives. But, she reflected, maybe just such a flight was the only way to save her remaining supermonitors.

"New orders," she told her chief of staff. "All supermonitors are to disengage and get back to the Orpheus-1 warp point. The remainder of the fleet will continue to withdraw in accordance with standard tactical protocols."

The chief of staff stared at her. "But Admiral," he began, but she cut him off with an impatient gesture.

"Yes, I know: we'll lose their firepower. But we've got to get them out of this system. And, as they're our slowest remaining ships, they'll slow us less this way. The rest of us can continue to fight a delaying action, while working our way back to the warp point a little faster than we could with them in the formation." She managed to smile inwardly, for the word *formation* scarcely described her exercise in desperate improvisation.

The order was transmitted, the supermonitors lumbered away, and the battle—now waged by monitor-sized and smaller ships alone—snarled its way across the system of Home Hive Two A.

"As predicted, *Destoshaz'at*, the *griarfeksh* survivors are withdrawing toward the warp point where they intend to escape."

"Naturally." Zum'ref studied the system-scale plot. The local sun still lay well ahead and to the right, as he viewed it, with the enemy's escape-hatch warp point dead ahead, still at a distance of five-sixths the total separation between the two warp points. Given the pace at which they were herding the demoralized rabble that had been a fleet, it would be a while yet before he surprised them by changing his van's course. That surprise would be nothing, he thought, compared to the surprise that would follow.

The plot sparkled with the icons of warp points and planets. The humans, of course, would have similar displays. But his eyes lingered over an icon that would be absent from theirs...

Home Hive Two A now shone whitely to starboard at a distance of only ten light-minutes. Almost directly opposite, though dropping astern, was the system's third planet, once a pullulating mass of Bugs. It was so close—less than two light-minutes—that its moon was a naked-eye object.

Chandra Konievitsky had eyes for neither. She sat slumped in her command chair, worn down by strain and exhaustion and nerve-shattering intervals of battle, bowed under the weight of unanticipated responsibility.

She was struggling to resist the siren song of lethargy when her flag bridge's communications officer spoke up excitedly, in tones she hadn't heard from anyone in Second Fleet in a while.

"Admiral! It's a hail from the Orpheus-1 warp point. Admiral Trevayne has entered the system!"

•

CHAPTER THIRTY-TWO

TRNS *Li Han* had barely transited from Orpheus-1 to Home Hive Two when Ian Trevayne became aware that something had gone horribly, impossibly wrong.

His advance guard had already picked up disjointed, almost hysterical signals that had winged across more than twenty light-minutes, and now Trevayne received a flood of reports. Cyrus Waldeck dead... Second Fleet's awesome array of devastators and superdevastators wiped out... the rest of the fleet trying to fight back in the teeth of unimaginable disaster, under what was left of a decapitated command structure...

"I want the rest of the fleet through the warp point slightly more quickly than possible," he snapped to Captain Elaine De Mornay, his chief of staff, in a voice he hoped would dispel the pall of shock on the flag bridge. "Scrap all safety guidelines for transits except the ultimate emergency ones. And," he added, turning to his Intelligence officer, "Andreas, I want a full briefing as soon as you can sort out all these reports and make sense of them."

"Uh, yes, Admiral," said Andreas Hagen in an unsteady voice that gradually firmed up. "I'll get right on it."

"And," Trevayne continued, turning back to the chief of staff, "have communications raise this Vice Admiral, er, Konievitsky. I want to personally assure her that we're on the way."

There was, of course, no time to bring the various senior admirals aboard in the flesh for the briefing. But *Li Han*'s Intelligence center included a briefing room set up for multiple holographic hookup. So Trevayne, De Mornay, and Captain Hugo Allende, the flag captain, sat as part of an audience otherwise composed of images from other ships.

One of the latter was his wife. There had been much reorganization over the past several months. Originally, *Li Han* had served triple duty: Trevayne's flagship as overall fleet commander, Magda's as commander of Task Force 14.1, and Adrian M'Zangwe's as commander of the Terran Republic's component of the task force. After Waldeck's departure from Tangri space with Task Force 14.2, Trevayne had split off a second task force, with Magda commanding it from the monitor TRNS *Hangchow*, and M'Zangwe commanding a Terran Republic task group under her. The reorganization had proliferated enroute as the Terran Republic/Rim Federation TF 14.1 had collected elements of the PSU navy and its Ophiuchi allies that had been too late to join Waldeck. As the bureaucracy had more pressing matters on its mind at the moment than rearranging organization charts, Trevayne had taken a high hand in doing it on his own, and had taken to referring to his swollen command as "Combined Fleet." At least the passage had given him time to shake it all down into a cohesive fighting force—or so he hoped.

He would have liked to have had Magda, and not just an electronic wraith of her, sitting beside him just now.

Andreas Hagen cleared his throat and began. "Admiral, we've been able to reach certain conclusions about what has happened to Second Fleet—although I frankly can't even speculate as to *how* it happened.

"First of all, Second Fleet's entire complement of devastators and superdevastators was wiped out at an early stage of the battle." He paused to let that sink in. The rumor had, of course, already gotten out, but no one had really believed it. "Whatever destroyed them was undetectable until it stuck, and when it did strike, the target ship was simply consumed by an internal explosion of devastating force."

"Sabotage?" speculated M'Zangwe. Seeing some of the looks he was getting from his fellow holo images, he continued a bit defensively. "Well, Admiral Waldeck *did* have Arduan personnel in his command. And we know about their indifference to death—or discarnation, as they regard it."

"It seems highly improbable, Admiral," said Hagen. "Arduans of the original Dispersate are hardly likely to feel any attachment to the Kaituni—who, as our information from Zephrain makes clear, regard them as traitors and heretics, fit for extermination."

"But," M'Zangwe persisted, "we know there's been an ongoing investigation into the possibility of a fifth column among the First Dispersate *Destoshaz.*"

"True, Admiral. But according to our latest communications, Captain Wethermere is inclined to skepticism about it. Furthermore, the only leads he had pointed to the Rim Federation and possibly the Terran Republic. There was no indication of any penetration of the PSU."

"Quite," said Trevayne firmly. "I'm going to rule that out. Continue, Andreas."

"Secondly, it was *only* the devastators and superdevastators that were destroyed in this manner. All of Second Fleet's subsequent losses have resulted from combat of a conventional nature. The Kaituni evidently have been targeting the supermonitors, our largest remaining ships—but they've been doing it as you'd expect, with their heavy superdreadnoughts and suicide fighters."

So, thought Trevayne, *our largest and strongest ships are also our most vulnerable ones. It makes no sense whatsoever. For now, I must simply accept it as a fact, and try to wring whatever advantage I can from the knowledge.*

"Thirdly," Hagen resumed, "there are indications that in the subsequent fighting the Kaituni have withheld certain of their monitors. From this, we infer that these ships are particularly valuable."

"Or," said Magda, "that they're less useful against Second Fleet's surviving ships. Which suggests to me that they're somehow connected to the weapon that... did what was done to Cyrus' biggest ships."

"That occurred to us as well, Admiral. The data from the battle are understandably somewhat confused and incomplete. But our analysis of those data suggest that the destruction took place when the devastators and superdevastators were within heavy missile ranges of the Kaituni monitors—which, in fact, they were subjecting to a long-range bombardment—but outside gee-beam range."

There was an interval of glum silence. Then Allende turned to Trevayne and cleared his throat.

"Admiral, may I make a suggestion?"

"Certainly, Captain."

"I respectfully recommend, Admiral, that before we come into contact with the enemy you transfer your flag."

For an instant, everyone but Trevayne looked stunned. It was an extraordinary thing for the captain of an undamaged flagship to say to his admiral. But Trevayne only nodded. The thought had been at the back of his own mind for several minutes.

"The point is well taken. I will do so forthwith—to a smaller ship. In the meantime, I have new orders for you, Commodore Allende."

"*Captain* Allende, sir."

"Commodore Allende," Trevayne repeated in the tone of a man who didn't expect to have to repeat himself again. "You will assume command of a special task group consisting of all of Combined Fleet's devastators and superdevastators, and take them back to Pesthouse posthaste, there to await further orders."

A flabbergasted hubbub arose. Trevayne silenced it with a raised hand. "Yes, I know how much firepower they have. But we have to wake up to the fact that their firepower has just become unusable."

"But Ian," Magda protested, "if Captain Hagen is right about them being safe from this . . . superweapon at extended missile range—"

"—Then they may still have a role as stand-off missile platforms in warp-point defense actions," *And what an end for the proudest space warships ever conceived,* Trevayne thought sadly. *Glorified orbital forts!* "But in a fluid action such as we're going to be fighting here, we can't rely on them maintaining that safety margin. And if they transgress it, they're nothing but death traps for their crews." He turned to the almost mutinous-looking Allende with a smile. "Yes, Hugo, I know how it seems: I'm ordering you to turn tail and run. That's precisely why I'm putting it in the form of a direct order. I know you'd never do it otherwise. And it has to be done. Until we learn how to cope with this new weapon, those ships and their thousands of personnel can't be put at risk."

"Understood, sir," said Allende, subsiding a little.

The Terran Republic's *Olympia* class of command superdreadnoughts was one of several classes, in three different space navies, named after historic wet-navy warships. TRNS *Zeven Provinciën* was the namesake of the legendary flagship of Michel Adriaanszoon de Ruyter, one of Horatio Nelson's few challengers for the title of greatest fighting admiral ever to sail Old Terra's seas. At any other time, that thought might have brought a wry smile to Ian Trevayne's face as he was piped aboard her. Under the present circumstances, the only concern he could permit himself was whether her command-and-control facilities would be up to the task of welding the remains of Second Fleet into the already large and disparate force he led, and coordinating the entire agglomeration in battle.

Hardly had he and his staff settled into the flag

spaces—cramped compared to those to which he had become accustomed—when he ordered De Mornay to plan a holding action after contact with Second Fleet was established. The chief of staff—a dark-haired woman in her forties, no beauty but not unhandsome—frowned, and spoke with the upper-class accent of her homeworld of Lancelot.

"Certainly, Admiral. But may I ask: why just a holding action? Between Combined Fleet and the remnants of Second Fleet, they have only a small edge over us in numbers. And even without our devastators and superdevastators, our supermonitors are heavier than anything they possess. And Combined Fleet hasn't expended any of its depletable munitions. This could be a chance to crush them—to snatch victory from the jaws of defeat, as people say."

Trevayne smiled inwardly. Lancelot's nobility produced more than their share of the Terran Republic's military officers, and their élan could never be faulted. Indeed, it sometimes had to be reined in. "Two reasons, Elaine. First of all, the Second Fleet elements are going to be operating below maximum efficiency due to demoralization, weariness, shredded chains of command, and the disruptive fact that they're going to be in the process of being integrated into Combined Fleet's organization. Second, and more importantly, I think Cyrus Waldeck was correct in his supposition that he was only facing part of the Kaituni fleet from Alowan. If there's any truth to the intelligence reports on the size of that armada—seven Dispersates' worth—then there simply isn't enough here to account for it. Less than half, in fact. There must be more of it on the way. A great deal more. And if I were the

Kaituni admiral, I'd feign a retreat to lure us toward the Bug 06 warp point, so we'd be more than thirty light-minutes away from our own warp point of egress when the rest of his fleet arrives. No," he concluded. "At the rate Second Fleet is withdrawing and we're advancing, we should link up with them about here." He used a light pencil to indicate a point on a system display, about twelve light-minutes from the Orpheus-1 warp point from which they'd emerged. "I have no intention of leaving this system until I have to, and I want to inflict as much damage on them as I can while we're here. But I want us to be able to get out if we suddenly find ourselves faced with more than we can handle."

"Understood, sir." De Mornay sounded only slightly wistful.

By the time the leading elements of Combined Fleet joined the running battle, Chandra Konievitsky was dead, immolated when a kamikaze fighter had smashed into her flagship.

Trevayne wished he had known her; she had been thrust into an impossible situation, and had performed as honorably as anyone could have under the circumstances. But he could only make a note to recommend her for a posthumous decoration, and coordinate with Second Fleet's senior surviving officer—a very junior Orion Great Claw of the Khan (rear admiral equivalent) named Threeenow'hakaaeea—as he flung Combined Fleet's assets into the battle.

He had sent his carriers ahead at their best speed, escorted by task groups of equally swift battlecruisers and heavy cruisers. His order of battle in the Tangri

Pacification Force had included an ample carrier component, for dealing with the swift and elusive horsehead raiders. That, and the Ophiuchi task force that had joined him, gave him a very substantial fighter component, and even before his capital ships came up, he ordered it into action. The Ophiuchi pilots lacked combat experience, but their innate aptitude made up for it. And the human pilots of the Terran Republic and the Rim Federation came from Tangri space as battle-hardened as any in existence. Between them, they used their rapid-firing energy torpedoes to slash through the Kaituni suicide fighters. Then he ordered mixed strikes that included heavy missile-armed fighters against the Kaituni ships, with emphasis on the monitors.

By this time, Combined Fleet's capital ships were within extended missile range, and Trevayne ordered the supermonitors to commence barrage-firing with the salvo-capable missile batteries which they, alone among the ships he now had, were the only ships to mount. But he had relatively few supermonitors, for the same reason he had had relatively few of the devastator classes: they hadn't really been the thing for chasing Tangri. So he ordered his lesser capital ships in closer, into the ranges where heavy ship-mounted energy torpedoes were most effective.

It was that word "ranges"—plural—that was the basis of Trevayne's tactical calculations. The repeating energy torpedo had become the dominant weapon for all ships below devastator size precisely because of its versatility. It assumed the functions of standard missiles, medium-to-short-range beams, and point defense, all in one relatively compact package. With modern datanets, the smaller ships were able to coordinate fire without having to juggle different weapon systems.

And Trevayne was almost uniquely able to do so to best advantage, for his "first life" had been spent commanding ships no larger than monitors. To a greater extent than the current generation—or even relative old-timers like Cyrus Waldeck—he was not wedded to the concept of everything other than devastators and superdevastators as auxiliaries to those mammoth bombardment machines. As the battle wore on, and the space between the combatants became trellised with the blinding trails of star-hot plasma packages fired at various and ever-changing ranges, it was almost a homecoming for him. Like a boxer, he "bobbed and weaved," keeping the Kaituni off balance by constantly shifting his increasingly well-coordinated base of unified firepower and engaging from whatever range would minimize his own vulnerabilities.

Whenever a lull permitted, he communicated with Magda, whose appraisal of the situation was cautiously optimistic. "Our losses continue to mount, but the Second Fleet survivors have steadied, and the Kaituni losses are even heavier."

"I know," Trevayne acknowledged. "But something keeps gnawing at the back of my mind."

"What's that?"

"The Kaituni aren't trying to draw Combined Fleet back toward the Bug 06 warp point, through which I'm still firmly convinced that the fleets of at least four Dispersates must eventually come. I keep asking myself why. And I somehow doubt I'm going to like the answer."

✧ ✧ ✧

Zum'ref studied the system plot with satisfaction. The emergence of the second *griarfeksh* fleet into Home Hive Two had occurred much earlier than projected, suggesting that its admiral possessed the seniority and aggressiveness to cut through his species' typical stultifying bureaucratic pomposity and delay. But its premature arrival had not seriously interfered with his plan. The first, ravaged fleet had continued its fighting withdrawal until it could join hands with what it imagined to be its saviors, so his own fleet was now where he had intended it to be at this point. Granted, his fleet was suffering losses at an unanticipated level, but they were expendable. And, Illudor willing, the new arrivals would in the end simply swell the Kaituni game bag.

So his thoughts ran as he gazed at the icon which did not appear in his enemy's system displays. It lay ahead and to the right at about ten light-minutes, forming a scalene triangle with his own fleet and the Oprheus-1 warp point.

His *ha'selnarshazi* Intendant approached diffidently. "*Destoshaz'at*, has the decision been reached? The latest loss figures—"

(Dismissiveness.) "Yes, I have decided." He indicated the icon. "If we send only a few ships, as some have suggested, they might not draw the attention of the *griarfeksh* admiral. Conversely, if they *did* draw his attention, they wouldn't have sufficient strength to prevent him from interfering with the plan."

"Which would only occur if he deduces what the plan *is*, if only in a general way," Inzep'fel demurred respectfully.

"I prefer not to assume any lack of insight on the

part of this particular enemy." (Decisiveness.) "No. The main body of the fleet will change course, leaving only a holding force here. If the enemy yields to the temptation to remain here and overwhelm that force, well and good. But I believe he will follow us . . . which is even better."

CHAPTER THIRTY-THREE

Ian Trevayne muttered a distracted "As you were" as he entered *Zeven Provinciën*'s flag bridge, blinking his interrupted cat nap out of his eyes. Elaine De Mornay and Andreas Hagen nonetheless stood up straight over the system plot of the tactical display they had been studying intently.

"All right," said Trevayne without preamble. "What's this about the Kaituni breaking off the engagement?"

"Well, Admiral, they have indeed discontinued their attacks and opened up some space between their fleet and ours. But since then, something else has happened." He indicated the display, and the swarm of scarlet "hostile" icons. The swarm had subdivided into two unequal parts. And the greater of the two was veering off at an angle of about forty-five degrees.

"They appear," De Mornay continued, "to be leaving a relatively small holding force here and departing with the bulk of their fleet."

"And," Hagen put in, anticipating Trevayne's question, "we have no indication of why."

"Go to system-scale display," Trevayne ordered. "And project the courses of all major formations."

Hagen obeyed, and the white icon of Home Hive Two A shone in the center of the holo tank. Combined Fleet and its enemies currently lay at a bearing of a trifle more than ten o'clock from that star, a little over twelve light-minutes from the Oprheus-1 warp point—a course which a string-light marked, running almost straight "up." But another string-light, forty-five degrees from the first one, showed the projected route of the Kaituni main body, heading . . . nowhere.

Trevayne glared, narrow-eyed, at the expanse of nothingness into which the Kaituni were so inexplicably headed. The second and fourth planets of Home Hive Two A were farther in a clockwise direction around the star, at their present orbital positions . . . and at any rate, there was nothing on any of those charnel-house worlds that could interest the Kaituni. The same went for Home Hive Two B and its retinue of equally dead planets, two hundred and fifty light-minutes away and in an altogether different direction. No matter how far the Kaituni's present course was extrapolated, it intersected with absolutely nothing.

Nothing that we know about, Trevayne mentally qualified.

Were they seeking to rendezvous with an undetected Kaituni force which had entered Home Hive Two earlier and was now lurking in the depths of interplanetary space? No. Waldeck had scouted this system for any such threats, and Cyrus was—or had been—nothing if not thorough.

He sought desperately for meaning, for facts. But there was only one fact he knew for certain—and that fact was surely irrelevant, for it rose from between the dusty pages of history books.

He rejected the thought, irritated with himself. There was no connection with his present problem. There *must* be no connection. How could there be?

No. There could be only one answer.

He became aware that De Mornay was practically fidgeting with eagerness to speak. "Yes, Elaine?"

"Admiral, for some unfathomable reason of their own, the Kaituni have divided their forces. This presents us with an opportunity to defeat them in detail. We can overwhelm this rear-guard they've left almost in contact with us. Let's concentrate on that, and not follow their main body off on some wild-goose chase into the middle of nowhere!"

"There's only one problem with your reasoning, Elaine," said Trevayne. "The Kaituni are, by our standards, stark raving mad—but they are *not* stupid, as we have learned to our cost over the past several months. There is only one rational basis for what they are doing: they must know of a previously undiscovered closed warp point in this system."

That silenced De Mornay. Closed warp points—undetectable until somebody came through them from the other side—were a phenomenon heartily detested by the theorists, who had never succeeded in accounting for their existence, and also by naval officers, for whom they were an ever-present source of nasty surprises from outside the known warp network. When the first Arduan Dispersate had appeared out of normal space—an unprecedented occurrence—in 2524, someone had glumly observed that the entire sky had suddenly become one vast closed warp point. But now the Kaituni had committed themselves to warp-line warfare, and there could be but one strategic reason for what they were doing at present.

"Sir, are you suggesting . . . *another* Kaituni armada, from an unsuspected direction?" breathed Hagen.

"We don't know. In fact . . ." Trevayne paused, with a brief, self-deprecating smile. "There's only one thing that we *do* know. It occurred to me a few moments ago, God knows why. Silly of me. But I couldn't help remembering . . . *we're in what used to be Arachnid space.*"

For a long, silent moment, the air was full of ghosts.

Two centuries before, humanity and its allies had fought the most devastating war in history, and the one with the simplest objective: sheer survival. There could be no peace, no compromise, no reasoning with the Bugs, for every attempt to communicate with their eerily silent hive intelligence had failed. They had been an enemy like no other: an insensate, all-consuming essence of nightmare dredged up from the deepest recesses of childhood terrors, for they had been not merely genocidal but anthropophagous, literally eating entire sentient populations in the path of their seemingly unstoppable advance, and even *breeding* sentient livestock—meat animals that *knew*.

With their backs to the wall of extinction, humans and others had fought the Bugs to a standstill in a series of campaigns almost inconceivable in their scale and intensity, and, in the end, wiped the universe clean of them. But the sheer flesh-crawling horror and loathing they had aroused was seared into the human soul forever.

De Mornay laughed nervously, breaking the spell, and the ghosts vanished.

"Well, sir, fortunately that was a long time ago!"

"Quite," said Trevayne briskly—a little more briskly than was necessary, some might have thought. "At the present time, I am firmly convinced that the main Kaituni body is going where it's going for a reason—to exploit something we can't see, and a closed warp point seems the only possibility that makes sense."

Hagen looked thoughtful. "Also, sir, I recall some of the reports of the investigation Captain Wethermere and Councilor Ankaht had been conducting into Amunsit's machinations. As I recall, they turned up leads that kept pointing back to this region of space."

"So they have. There may or may not be a connection. But whatever it is the Kaituni are up to, we must attempt to disrupt it. I want to interdict that main body if at all possible. As of now, that is Combined Fleet's first priority."

"Yes, sir," De Mornay and Hagen answered in unison.

"And . . . Elaine, have comm raise Admiral Li-Trevayne. I want to consult with her." *Specifically*, Trevayne didn't add, *I need someone I can talk to about this vague, intuitive feeling that won't go away, however little sense it seems to make.*

As the fleets proceeded along the new course, exchanging fire intermittently, it became increasingly clear to Trevayne that even if he was right about a closed warp point he wasn't going to be able to seize it and defend it against entry. The main Kaituni van was too big to be brushed aside. Furthermore, the smaller Kaituni delaying force did just that: it delayed him, even though it was gradually worn down in the running battles. If he paused to wipe it out, as De Mornay had originally wanted to do—and still at least half wanted to do, he suspected—he would be delayed even more. He would just have to observe whatever move the Kaituni van made, whenever it made it, and react as seemed indicated.

They had reached a point eleven light-minutes from Home Hive II A, on a bearing of twelve o'clock, and an increasingly tense Trevayne was sharing his anxieties with Magda. He sat on *Zeven Provinciën*'s flag bridge and gazed at a flat-screen image of her, looking into eyes that reminded him of Han's, although whenever that thought occurred to him he had to sternly remind himself that according to his most current information Novaya Rodina was untouched.

"You realize, Ian," she was saying, "that you're still gambling. You don't know what it is you're trying to prevent."

"I know," he replied glumly. "I just wish I had more to go on than the nagging intuition that I can't quite put my finger on. At any rate, whatever it is, we're just going to have to try to work ourselves into the best position to—"

"Admiral!" rapped Hagen in a brittle voice. He had been living over his readouts of sensor data, and was under instructions to interrupt Trevayne at any time. "What appears to be a small task group—squadron, rather—of cruiser-sized ships is separating off from their van. The rest of the van is changing course—swerving away."

"Tactical," snapped Trevayne, turning toward the holo plot and knowing Magda was doing the same aboard her flagship. Yes, he could see the tiny cluster of even tinier icons speeding ahead of the main Kaituni force, which seemed to be . . . well, he couldn't avoid the impression that they were getting out of the way of something. Whatever it was, the delaying force was still doggedly interposing itself to prevent him from doing anything about it.

But all speculation fled his mind as he watched the cruiser-icons begin to vanish.

"They're making warp transit," Hagen reported unnecessarily.

"Well, Ian, you were right about an undiscovered—at least by us—closed warp point," came Magda's voice from the communicator.

"And now we know where it is," De Mornay added.

"But how the bloody hell did *they* know where it is?" Trevayne demanded. "Since *we* didn't know about it, Amunsit couldn't have passed it on to the coming Dispersates along with all the other navigational data about our warp networks. And why have they sent this tiny detachment of ships into it?"

No one had an answer. For a space that seemed longer than two minutes but wasn't, they all studied the tactical plot as though trying to extract revelation from it by sheer concentration.

Then the icons began to reappear, emerging from the warp point . . . but only half as many as had gone in.

"What the devil—?" Trevayne began.

But then the display suddenly grew brighter as ship-icons began to appear at the warp point—large ships, and appearing in multiple simultaneous transits that seemed to transcend even the usual Kaituni indifference to death. As Trevayne watched, two ships materialized in the same volume and vanished in a space-wracking explosion. But this in no wise caused the new arrivals to grow more cautious; they continued to pour into Home Hive Two system in the same reckless way.

Trevayne forced calm on himself. "Well, at least we're not caught in an awkward position between the force we've been engaging and this new Kaituni fleet. Commodore De Mornay, I want Combined Fleet realigned to—"

"Admiral," said Hagen in a voice whose very expressionlessness demanded Trevayne's attention, "those aren't Kaituni."

"What are they?" Trevayne turned on the Intelligence officer.

"We're beginning to get a lot of detailed sensor readings on these new ships—and they don't match any of the Kaituni classes."

Trevayne had stopped listening. The nagging, tickling intuitive feeling he hadn't been able to dismiss from his mind had suddenly crystalized like a recovered glimpse of a dream . . . and he wanted to reject it, hurl it back into oblivion with revulsion. But he couldn't allow himself to do so.

"Andreas," he cut in, "I want you to run comparisons with *everything* in the ship's database—including all the historical data."

"The *historical* data, Admiral?"

"You heard me. Everything."

It took Hagen only a moment to set up the problem, and even less time for the computer, acting at the speed of molecular circuitry, to run the immense quantity of data through the mill. But afterwards, Hagen said nothing at first.

"Well, Andreas," said Trevayne quietly, not wanting to hear what he was now certain he was going to hear.

Hagen turned haunted eyes to him. "Admiral . . . the only matches in the database date back to the Fourth Interstellar War. They're . . . they're Arachnid ship types, Admiral."

And now Trevayne knew what the dreamlike intuitive feeling had been trying to tell him about an undiscovered closed warp point in Bug space. And he knew the barriers his mind had set up against that feeling, preventing him from grasping it.

"But the Bugs don't *exist* anymore!" he heard De Mornay exclaim.

"It appears they do, Commodore," Trevayne said heavily. "And that the Kaituni have made contact with them. And that they are loose in the galaxy again."

An almost palpable wave-front of shock spread around him, as his listeners found themselves face to face with their culture's ultimate primal terror, only to find that it was real.

Trevayne could feel the paralysis gripping the flag bridge, freezing it into horrified immobility like an ice sculpture which a single word might send shivering into a cloud of panic.

He saw De Mornay start to open her mouth . . .

"Commodore De Mornay!" His voice cracked like a bullwhip of command. "Combined Fleet will disengage and shape a course for the Orpheus-1 warp point. Fortunately, the Kaituni fleet has put itself in a position from which it will not be able to realign itself promptly, and the . . . new arrivals will take time to complete their warp transit." He moderated his tone a trifle. "We will have time later to assimilate this new turn of events and try and account for it. But for now, our duty and only priority must be to get back to Pesthouse without delay. In the meantime, while we're en route, send courier drones ahead of us through the warp point with this . . . new intelligence. Are my orders clear, Commodore?"

De Mornay gulped, took a deep breath, and allowed her tradition to settle over her like a cloak. "Perfectly, Admiral." And she began to give commands, giving people something to think about other than the nightmare which had just emerged into the waking world.

It was, Zum'ref thought, a matter of no real importance that the *griarfeksh* admiral (who, over the course of this campaign, he had almost—not quite, of course—ceased to think of as *griarfeksh*) hadn't placed himself in a position to be trapped here in Home Hive Two. It merely postponed the moment when he *would* be trapped.

So he turned his attention to more immediate matters, and addressed his Intendant. "Be sure no obstacle—even a perceived one—is placed in the path of these *bilbuxhati*." He mentally chided himself for his use of the term—a herd-animal of lost Ardu—for these creatures. The use of that term had become widespread among the *Destoshaz* because it seemed natural to think they were releasing a herd of mindless, maddened *bilbuxhati* before them, to trample their enemies. But it wasn't really accurate. Not at all. One had to somehow imagine ravenously carnivorous *bilbuxhati*. "Remember, the plan is to let them take the casualties for us as they pursue their gluttonous way along the warp chains."

(Distaste.) "In some ways, *Destoshaz-at*, they are

even more repulsive than the humans and other species of *griarfeksh.* It is as though . . . well, their means of hive communication is almost like a dirty joke on us. And on Illudor."

(Indulgence.) "I know what you mean, Inzrep'fel. But they have their uses."

So at last the System Which Must Be Concealed had been escaped. And now the path to the worlds of the Old Enemies was open.

Of course, the New Enemies—the Hive-Killers—must be dealt with as well. And then there were these still newer enemies—distinct from the Hive and therefore, by definition, enemies—to factor into the equation. And, in all the time of isolation in the System Which Must Be Concealed, there had been opportunity to study the technologies of the Hive-Killers. Perhaps even more important, it had been possible to evaluate the survival strategies of the now-dead original Hives. Those had been found wanting. A gradual conquer-and-feed approach had given the Hive-Killers too much time to adapt and innovate—an ability which had been their one great, ultimately decisive advantage. It had been a mistake which would not be repeated.

And because the original Hives' failings and weaknesses had been so fundamental, study of those failings and weaknesses had led into heretofore neglected realms of the biological sciences. Which, in turn, had opened up whole new possibilities for the waging of war, more subtle and insidious than the old brute-force approach. Possibilities which could—and would, when the situation warranted—be turned against the Newest Enemies.

For the moment, however, these Newest Enemies had their uses.

Trevayne had worried that Combined Fleet would be slowed by his supermonitors. But the Kaituni fleet made no move to pursue, and he had been correct about the time it would take the Bug armada to complete its warp transit; Combined Fleet would make it to the Orpheus-1 warp point ahead of them.

In a way, he would have preferred further fighting. As it was, they all had time to brood, to contemplate the abyss which had opened up under their feet, and into which all the comfortable assumptions of their society had fallen, vanishing into the darkness of hopelessness.

He was conferring with Magda when Hagen approached. "Admiral, a report from the recon drones covering the Bug 06 warp point."

"Yes?" As a routine precaution, Trevayne had scattered the drones widely throughout the Home Hive Two A system to provide him with wide-ranging "eyes," with emphasis on the region where the Kaituni had originally emerged, now over thirty light-minutes astern. He was grimly sure he knew what Hagen was about to say.

"While we've been . . . occupied, new Kaituni ships have been entering this system. Our information on their numbers is, of course, out of date because of the communications delay, but—"

"—But now we're starting to see the remainder of the armada from Alowan," Trevayne finished for him. "At least four Dispersates' worth." He sighed. "Well, at least they're in no position to interfere with our departure from this system. And we'll make it well ahead of..." He gestured at the system plot and the red icon that pursued them, unwilling to utter the name of that particular enemy.

So they fled on toward the Oprheus-1 warp point, and it was as though the hounds of Hell were baying at their heels.

Magda looked out of the comm screen, and her eyes held a haunted look that Trevayne had never seen in them, or expected to see.

"Ian...were we wrong to bring a child into this universe?"

CHAPTER THIRTY-FOUR

Commodore Arthur Kim, PSUN, was commander of the fortresses Cyrus Waldeck had emplaced in Orpheus-1 at the Home Hive Two warp point against any unlooked-for eventualities. He had, of course, already received the news from Home Hive Two before Combined Fleet came through the warp point he was guarding, with an armada summoned up out of the blackest pages of history following it. Therefore, having had a little while to assimilate the news, he wasn't quite as shaken as he might have been when he faced Ian Trevayne in the comm screen. Or, if he was, he at least managed a fairly good job of concealing it.

"So, Commodore," Trevayne concluded his terse summary of the situation, "as you see, it is imperative that Combined Fleet get back to Pesthouse to protect the main warp line to Sol. And, while my Intelligence staff is still analyzing the energy readouts from the Arachnid fleet that will be coming through this warp point from Home Hive Two in pursuit of us, it is clear that it is comparable in numbers and tonnage to any of their fleets in the Fourth Interstellar War." Kim earned Trevayne's respect by remaining almost expressionless. "We have no information as to their weaponry. However, despite history's assertions regarding the Bugs' lack of inventiveness, I consider it unsafe to assume that they've been technologically stagnant for the last two centuries."

"Agreed, sir."

"And," Trevayne continued remorselessly, "behind them is a Kaituni fleet seven Dispersates strong. The fleet that annihilated Admiral Waldeck's battle line." He paused, for he had come to a moment which he'd had no desire to reach but which could not be deferred. He met Kim's eyes unflinchingly. "Commodore, Combined Fleet needs every advantage it can get in traversing this system and getting away to Home Hive One and thence to Pesthouse. It is therefore necessary that you fight a delaying action as long as possible."

"That's what Admiral Waldeck put us here for, sir."

Trevayne had never felt more awkward in his life. What do you say to a man you've just condemned to death? Especially when that man knew—and knew that Trevayne knew—that the fortresses could be placed in automated defense mode, and their crews evacuated . . . and that the resulting degradation of their fighting efficiency would reduce the time they could delay the Bug horde. "Thank you" seemed inappropriate as well as inadequate, and under the circumstances "Good luck" would be a banality. "Very good, Commodore," he finally said gruffly. "And keep transmitting reports to us as long as possible. Any information about the weapons and tactics of these . . . latter-day Bugs will be invaluable. For the same reason, I'm going to deploy a lavish quantity of recon drones around this warp point."

"Understood, sir."

Trevayne signed off, not trusting himself to say anything else. He could feel the eyes of De Mornay and Hagen and everyone else in earshot on the flag bridge as he turned away from the comm screen and studied the system display.

The warp point through which they had entered Orpheus-1 from Home Hive Two lay on a bearing of about eleven o'clock from the system primary, at a distance of thirty light-minutes. The Home Hive One warp point through which they must pass to take the most direct route to Pesthouse was at bearing four o'clock, distance twenty-seven light-minutes. Hence, the two were very nearly a light-hour apart—as long a haul between a system's warp points as any in known space, and one which would bring them too close to this planetless system's red giant primary for comfort.

Which facts, of course, formed the altar on which Trevayne had just sacrificed Orphueus-1 Fortress Command. One thing about the Bug fleet had been clear from the sensor readings: it included nothing larger than monitor-size. It therefore might have a small speed advantage over Combined Fleet, with its supermonitors. And this was going to be a long chase. He needed every advantage he could get.

Out of the corner of his eye, he saw De Mornay fidgeting. "What is it, Elaine?"

The chief of staff came to a position of semi-attention. "Oh . . . nothing, sir."

Trevayne smiled at her. "I know what you're thinking, Elaine. You're wishing we could stand and fight at this warp point, alongside those fortresses. I'm sure Threeenow'hakaaeea would agree with you," he added, thinking of the fiery Orion, burning to avenge the multitudinous dead of Second Fleet.

She deflated a little. "It crossed my mind sir," she admitted. "But only to be rejected. I understand why you're proceeding as you are. These fortresses here simply aren't adequate. We're going to need the support of the really massive defenses of Pesthouse when we turn and make a stand."

"That's quite right . . . as far as it goes." Trevayne said, as much to himself as to De Mornay. His eyes went to the icon marking Orpheus-1's third warp point, the one leading to Orpheus-2, lying on the same bearing as the one from which they had emerged but at a distance of seventeen light-minutes, so that their course would bring them within three light-minutes of it. And then he turned and looked at another display screen, which showed the relevant portions of the warp network. As he followed out the warp chain through Oprheus-2 and Orpheus-3 and beyond, he fell into a brooding silence which De Mornay, though puzzled, was disinclined to break with questions.

•

By the time Combined Fleet passed the Orpheus-2 warp point and put it astern, the space around the Home Hive Two warp point fifteen light-minutes behind them was ablaze with battle as the Bug monitors began to transit and the fortresses fought back gallantly but hopelessly. *Zeven Provinciën*'s flag bridge was held in depressed silence, interrupted by hushed reports as that struggle wound down to its foreordained conclusion.

Trevayne reached a decision. He assured himself

that it was rooted in reason, not in guilt. Still, he felt a need to explain it. So he ordered comm to raise Magda's flagship.

"I'm going to have a courier drone sent back through the Orpheus-2 warp point, ordering the fortress commander there to activate his fortresses' automated defense protocols and get his personnel off. They've got some light ships there that can evacuate them to Orpheus-3 or, better still, Home Hive Three."

"But Ian, what if this Bug fleet—and, presumably, the Kaituni armada behind them—go through the Orpheus-2 warp point instead of following us?"

"I don't expect that they will. They'll want to follow us, proceeding by the most direct route to Pesthouse and the main warp line to Alpha Centauri and Sol. But even if, for some reason, they do, it's less vital to slow them down in Orpheus-2 than . . . than it was here. They'd have three more systems to go before they could threaten Bug 05."

"So therefore there's no real justification for sacrificing those crews," Magda nodded. "Not an adequate one, at any rate."

And once is enough, thought Trevayne. *More than enough.* But of course he couldn't say that aloud. Instead, he turned to De Mornay. "Elaine, have Comm prepare a courier drone, to be dispatched to Orpheus-2 Fortress Command. The message will be as follows—"

"Admiral!" exclaimed Andreas Hagen. "We're getting sensor readings from the Orpheus-2 warp point. Ships are transiting through it." He paused briefly and ran his eye over the readouts. "Kaituni ships!"

Trevayne broke the stunned silence. "Cancel that courier drone, Elaine," he said quietly.

Magda stared from the comm screen. "Ian, what—?"

"It's pretty clear what's happened," Trevayne said bleakly. "The possibility occurred to me before, but I didn't mention it because if it was true there was absolutely nothing we were in a position to do about it. Look at your warp-line display." He brought up his own as De Mornay and Hagen joined him. Using a light-pencil, he traced the route from Zephrain through Home Hive Three, Orpheus-3, Orpheus-2 and, finally, Orpheus-1.

"This must be one of the Kaituni fleets that's been ravaging Orion space. It must have followed Amunsit's path to Zephrain, then moved along this route in order to trap us." Trevayne turned even more grim. "It nearly did. If we were still in Home Hive Two, and this new fleet occupied this system, we would have been well and truly trapped, and . . ." He let the sentence trail off. *It would all have been over* was superfluous.

They fled on across the Orpheus-1 system, with the red giant sun growing into a bloated, attenuated, dimly glowing ball to starboard, gradually dropping astern. As they did, they were able to observe certain developments.

First of all, the newly arrived Kaituni fleet had completed its emergence from the Orpheus-2 warp point. (There were, of course, no fortresses there to hinder it. Waldeck had emplaced none since, after all, Orpheus-2 was a friendly system, wasn't it?) According to Hagen's estimates, it constituted the forces of two Dispersates. Combined Fleet could have turned back and overpowered it, especially given the apparent ineffectiveness of the Kaituni's new superweapon against ships lighter than devastator-size, which was all they had. At first Threeenow'hakaaeea had been almost frantic with eagerness to do so. But even he had eventually had to admit it was out of the question to become involved in a battle which was bound to take time—time which would allow that which was coming from the Home Hive Two warp point to catch up.

For they had also been able, by means of the cloud of recon drones around that warp point, to observe as the main Kaituni armada had emerged behind the Bugs. Well behind, in fact—and it remained that way as it followed the Bugs in their pursuit of Combined Fleet.

And finally came an unexpected report from a puzzled Hagen. "Admiral, the new Kaituni fleet is turning away and taking up a course almost at right angles to ours . . . and that of the Bugs."

Frowning, Trevayne turned to the system display. The new arrivals from Orpheus-2 had been in a position to lead the pursuit, ahead of the Bugs. Instead, they were swerving aside.

De Mornay's frown was even more intense than Trevayne's. "You'd think they'd be maneuvering to join their allies. Instead it's almost as though they're getting out of their way."

"I'm beginning to think," said Trevayne slowly, "that getting out of the Bugs' way is precisely what they're doing. And I don't think they are allies."

De Mornay and Hagen both gaped at him. "Not allies?" the chief of staff blurted. "But Admiral—"

"Oh, don't misunderstand me. They're both our enemies. But I don't think they're allies in any real sense. I have no idea how the Kaituni learned that the Bugs still exist, or what their exact relationship—if that's *le mot juste*—is. But I'm certain that the Bugs cannot have—or be—allies. No: I think the Kaituni are somehow *using* the Bugs. And what they're using them for at the moment is to do the work of pursuing and harrying us and taking the losses. In short, the Bugs are what used to be called cannon fodder."

"I shouldn't think the Bugs would be happy about that role," said Hagen drily. "Even assuming they have the capacity for happiness."

"But they seem willing to play the role and be used . . . at least for the moment. That may not always be the case." Trevayne wore a grim smile. "In fact, perhaps one of the reasons the Kaituni are getting out of the Bugs' way is to avoid the possibility of being . . . preyed upon in passing."

"Are you saying, sir, that this is something that might work to our advantage?" asked De Mornay.

"Knowing the Bugs, almost certainly not." Trevayne dismissed the subject with a characteristic toss of his head. "And at any rate, that's not something which we can exploit at the moment. We've got to concentrate on getting to Pesthouse."

As they drove on and the great red sun dropped further and further behind them, it became clear that Trevayne had been right about the Bugs' slight speed advantage. Combined Fleet had to fight a series of rear-guard actions to fend its pursuers off. For this purpose, Trevayne made full use of Threeenow'hakaaeea's carriers from Second Fleet—partly because he regarded fighters as the weapon of choice in this kind of action against this particular enemy, and partly because he realized it was necessary to the morale of those Orion pilots. And indeed they savaged the Bugs' leading elements, taking out their frustration and anger and lust for vengeance against these beings, to whom they would not even allow the title of *chofaki*.

And in the end, it was enough. Combined Fleet passed through the Home Hive One warp point. But just before they departed from Orpheus-1, the drones reported one more datum: the newly arrived Kaituni fleet had curved back (the kind of maneuver made possible by reactionless, inertia-canceling drives) aft of the Bugs to join the oncoming armada from Home Hive Two. As he observed the fleets of nine Dispersates begin to coalesce well aft of the Bugs, Trevayne felt mixed emotions at the confirmation of his suspicions.

But then they were in Home Hive One, and after that the way to Pesthouse was short, for the warp points were only nine light-minutes apart, on a course that brought them nowhere near the system's haunted planets. Trevayne nevertheless had time to evacuate Home Hive One's fortresses—if two times had been more than enough, a third was unthinkable, and anyway he felt sure that even a robotic delaying action would suffice for his passage through the Pesthouse warp point, and allow him time to redeploy to face the inexorable, insensate Bug onslaught he knew would soon follow.

That redeployment fortunately left him little time to brood about the state of the force he was leading back. Only twenty percent of Second Fleet's original tonnage remained, and only sixty percent of what he had brought from Tangri space. The fact that the forty percent attrition in the latter included the devastators and superdevastators he had detached rather than lose was cold comfort—especially considering the now-problematical usefulness of those great ships he had sent out of danger.

But the first thing he did, as soon as *Zeven Provinciën* had made transit, was to inquire as to whether the contingency orders to destroy Unity Warp Point Five had been followed. On learning that they had, he visibly sagged with relief.

Hagen cocked his head. "I know that had to be done, Admiral. But I can't help wondering how the Orion leadership is going to feel about it."

"How will they feel?" Trevayne's gaze was far away, and elsewhere than on the Intelligence officer. "They will be proud that they have followed the honor code of *theernowlus*—followed it down a road their forefathers never imagined."

"I don't understand, sir."

Trevayne turned to Hagen with a smile. "It wasn't humans—and least of all human politicians—who understood the need for that contingency. It took the Orions to understand it. They are warriors and think like warriors: you cannot leave a gate open when the enemy is approaching your walls, even if closing it means some of your own are shut out and can't reach safety in time."

"But what about the rest of the Orions?" Hagen wondered. "Will *they* realize that?"

"I don't know. I hope they do. For I fear what might happen to our alliance if they do not. United, we at least have our backs to each other. Divided, we have no hope."

CHAPTER THIRTY-FIVE

Once the last *Etesh'nrem* class destroyer transited the warp point from Mymzher into Franos to join the rest of the Kaituni ships waiting there, Work Group Manip Hunis'bern reclined further into her control pod. "It is well they have made safe passage," she sent with a tone both (relieved, droll).

Her one companion on the bridge, Jrersh-atr, returned a sense of (shared drollery). "Ah, you already miss the dour chants and high-minded commitment of our *Destoshaz* superiors, do you? Well, I say, Illudor bless and keep them all—far away from us."

Hunis'bern responded with (amusement) but also (faint concern). "It would be wise to refrain from sends that could be claimed as being overtly seditious. Obliquity is our very good friend, Jrersh-atr."

Her navigator blew tired air out his vestigial gills. "Truly, Hunis'bern? And who remains with us in the Mymzher system to tap into my self-incriminating sends? You? You are an informer to the highest caste?"

"I am simply saying that it is difficult to know whom

one may trust these days. And it is difficult to know if one of the *Ssershaz* engine technicians might be on the other side of the bulkhead, *selnarm* alert for faint hints of our own."

"As if those plodders have the *selnarmic* gift to be able to reach through the bulkhead to touch our thoughts? Please, Hunis'bern: you are starting at shadows."

"Am I? And besides, it is improper to denigrate the *Ssershaz* so. How is it that we may share *narmata* with those whom we contemn? The sharing will be distorted by the lack of fellow-feeling."

Jrersh-atr leaned out of his control pod far enough to be able to stare at Hunis'bern where she reclined. "And since when has *narmata* been more than an empty ritual, friend? Whatever it may once have been within and between our castes, it is no longer. And the *Destoshaz* ensure that its importance diminishes with every passing year."

"Given your dangerously open contempt for the *Destoshaz*, I am surprised that their derogation of *narmata* is not enough to prompt you to mulishly embrace it."

Jrersh-atr sent a reflexive wave of (mirth, wry appreciation). "I should know better to spar with you, Hunis'bern. But let us be practical—and practicality is, after all, the strongest trait amongst us *Ixturshaz*. The *Destoshaz* brook no disobedience, and who can best the least of them in a challenge? They have discouraged the practice of *maatkah* amongst the other castes and have made themselves the master of it and every other martial skill. The *Selnarshaz* perform what *selnarmic* tasks they require, we tend to computers and other machinery, and the other castes have all been relegated to the same fate as the *Ssershaz*: dronelike workers. Yes, I know, you've told me: this existence is far inferior that which our race once enjoyed. But, even if that was true at one time, it is the stuff of myths now, and we must live—and avoid execution—in the present. Lest we join the *shaxzhu*, whose passing I would not—"

On the control panel before Hunis'bern, a *vrel*-colored light flashed an alert: an object to inspect in the holopod. She turned to search it, sending a *selnarm* request for all available data on the contact and requiring that the reply be sent as a broad wave so that Jrersh-atr would receive the content also.

In the holo pod, at the middle range of detection, a faint lavender object appeared, emerging from the outer asteroid belt. The data stream from the sensors matched what the faint detection implied: a small object or ship, already at a range of approximately thirty-five light-seconds. Her drive field emissions were intermittent, which suggested damage, as did her speed: she was barely making two percent cee, even when her drives were functioning.

"Is it one of their ships—from the Omnivoracity, I mean?" Jrersh-atr's send was very controlled, anxious. She could hardly blame him: the Omnivoracity—as the Arachnids reportedly referred to themselves in their internal communiqués—were particularly daunting *zheteksh*. Although there was a rude pseudo-*selnarmic* link between each creature and the core of the hive-mind that drove them, they were truly the most alien creatures that Hunis'bern had ever heard of, or imagined. By comparison, the humans were veritable evolutionary cousins—

"Well, is it the Arachnids?" Jrersh-atr pressed.

"No," Hunis'bern sent with a subcurrent of exasperation. "You can read the sensors as well I can, so do so. That is clearly one of our drive signatures, right down to the smallest emission metric. Although it's a little unusual to detect out here, on its own."

"What do you mean?"

"See the low cycle rate? And the close match between total power output and the drive's consumption of it? That's a civilian ship: they don't have the extra energy output to supply weapons, shields, sensors, and reserve power all at once. Judging from the approximate mass readings and that energy output, I'd wager the ship is a freighter or some other bulk-hauler. And a little dated, too." But that was hardly surprising: non-military craft had received scant attention during the hurried movement to war footing that had seized all the Dispersates over the past five years. New classes of military ships, upgrades to the existing ones, as well as to all their support systems and vessels, had consumed the time and resources of the fleets before their arrival in human space. Purely civilian craft had been left unaltered; some had even been cannibalized to provide needed parts for military hulls.

Jrersh-atr scanned his comms board. "There is no communication from them, not even *selnarm*."

"I see that. And it is strange. Although, on second thought, there will not have been a *Selnarshaz* assigned to so small and inconsequential a hull. They might not be able to reach us yet—particularly if their *selnarm* repeater-boosters were either cannibalized or insufficiently maintained."

"True. So do we move to assist?"

Hunis'bern stroked one side of her long, sleek neck with two small tendrils. "If there were any other ships on station, we would clearly be authorized to do so. But if we do not remain in readiness near the warp point, we cannot follow our primary orders: to ensure that if anything approaches, we may transit to Franos and make report."

"We could send one of our courier drones to tell the destroyers that we have had to leave the warp point to assist a ship."

"No," Hunis'bern answered, "that we may not do. Were you not paying attention during the briefing? Any object other than us which comes through the warp point into Franos automatically signifies that the fleet's rear has been compromised."

"What? By one ship?"

Hunis'bern managed to keep the *selnarmic* pulse of (idiot!) out of her reply. "Of course not, because that is not the logic behind the communications and operations protocols. They serve one crucial purpose: to ensure that any transit other than our own functions as an alarm. The transit is the message. That is the beauty, the elegance, of the arrangement."

"Yes, well, while we are debating the finer points of our picket and courier work, that ship is having more problems. Look."

And sure enough, the ship had slowed to a half-a-percent light-speed crawl—well, stumble. It seemed that its drive field was merely an occasional flutter now. Hunis'bern checked the distance: still at thirty light-seconds and barely closing at all. And since a ship equipped with a reactionless drive had no actual velocity, if her drives ceased to function altogether, she would be stranded. Since the ship had not accumulated momentum, it would not coast closer. Which only complicated the situation even further: part of Hunis'bern's orders were to keep the warp point clear of unauthorized objects or sensor contacts. Any anomalous signals could draw increased attention to the spot, and any non-Kaituni attention was unwanted attention.

"So what do we do?" Jrersh-atr pestered. "And look: now it's dead in space."

Hunis'bern switched the two small tendrils against her neck in irritation. This situation had not been foreseen, and so two of her orders had come into profound, mutually exclusive conflict. On the one hand, she had standing orders to provide assistance to all disabled Kaituni craft; on the other hand, her actual mission here was to remain within a few dozen kilometers of the warp point that led into Franos.

Typical Destoshaz *inefficiency,* she thought bitterly, *so ready to give orders and act, but without the patience to ensure that those orders are all in operational conformity with each other, that there are no contradictions or oversights.* As little as five years ago, the *Destoshaz* had still included *Ixturshaz* analysts and procedural auditors in planning, to make sure that such errors did not occur. But that was before the *Destoshaz*-as-*sulhaji* movement began concentrating strategic power and responsibility solely in the *Destoshaz* caste, began diminishing the roles, and even denigrating the worthiness, of the other castes...

"Hunis'bern, we must make a decision!"

No, I *must make a decision since you are incapable of doing so or of offering useful counsel to those who must. You are a cheerful fellow, Jrersh-atr, and it is pleasant enough to stand a lonely post with you, but you are no help in this situation.*

She stared at the motionless freighter, then decided, "Jrersh-atr, bring our engines up to one-quarter. No signals—not yet. If we do this at all, we must do it quietly. That is even more important than doing it quickly, if any Orions happen to be lurking nearby." *Or there are any Omnivoracity stragglers*, she added: *they are at least as dangerous.* "Lay in a course for the freighter and engage autopilot to execute."

"You will not guide the ship yourself, Hunis'bern?"

"I am too busy watching our sensors, Jrersh-atr. If we must turn quickly and head through the warp point, I want to perceive that need and act upon it with all possible speed."

Jrersh-atr sent (understanding, compliance) and engaged the autopilot. There was no perceptible motion since the drive was reactionless and the starfield was changing too slowly to impart any sense of progress.

"ETA?"

"Fifteen minutes. At what point do you wish me to activate the comms array for—?"

Several *selnarm* alerts battered at Hunis-bern's consciousness with sudden urgency. Sensors indicated an object behind them—apparently materializing out of the emptiness of space; an active targeting array had come alive and locked on to them; an energy spike from the ship off the stern signified a beam weapon discharge; *Ssershaz* engine technicians were requesting instructions; the computer recommended an immediate reconfiguration of shields to guard the rear—

Hunis-bern's ship lurched forward violently, throwing

her from her pod. Klaxons—both audial and *selnarmic*—signaled both that the ship had been hit and severely damaged. The hurried inquiries of her *Ssershaz* techs were replaced by death pulses which disappeared almost instantly. The drive and the bridge lights had cut out along with the shields.

"Ill's blood!" blasphemed Jrersh-atr. "What has happened? Have we—?"

"We are under attack—and helpless," Hunis-bern sent back with (calm, coherence, focus) as the emergency lights faded in, bathing the bridge in dim red. "Launch courier drone immediately."

"Trying. Shifting over to battery power; engines are off-line."

And then there was a new send, from a powerful *selnarmic* source, one that seemed somehow very clear and collected and yet quaint—even nurturing. Hunis-bern had never known the touch of such *selnarm* in her Spartan, duty-bound existence of sacrifice and isolation among the stars, but she had imagined it, secretly longed for it—

"Sister," it said.

And she knew she was being touched by one of the Infidels, one of the Deceivers of the First Dispersate. Although she had never wanted anything so much as to return the touch of that kind *selnarm*, she leaned away from it and gave the mental orders to the computer's receivers to self-destruct—

"That will be difficult, sister," the *selnarm* soothed, "since your engines and power plants have been destroyed by a force beam. The type of ship you are in has no means to destroy itself except for self-induced containment failure of the power-plant."

"I shall discarnate myself."

"I trust you shall not."

"And why is that?"

"Because if that was truly your reflex, you would not have bothered to inform me of your intent. You are trying to convince yourself. But before you make your decision, let me show you what it was to dwell on Ardu, and what it is to dwell among those of Illudor's children who have not forsaken his voice."

The *selnarm* which had touched hers opened wide. It was as if she stood upon a promontory from which mists were receding, revealing a dreamscape cornucopia of emotions and relationships and possibilities and acceptance such as she had never imagined.

Not even in her wildest, most secret, and most fervent dreams.

Ankaht entered the conference room and found herself under the unblinking scrutiny of half a dozen pairs of small, beady alien eyes.

"How long do we have?" Miharu Yoshikuni asked sharply.

Ankaht, not accustomed nor receptive to such a peremptory tone without even the scant courtesy of a title, simply stared at the human admiral for a long moment. She was glad—*petty, petty!*—that the honest answer was also one that was sure to rankle the human: "I have no way of knowing—" She let two seconds pass before finishing with, "—Admiral."

Yoshinkuni's brow lowered. But when she spoke, her voice was polite, albeit grudgingly so. "Councilor Ankaht, I do not understand. This ship—a light escort and reconnaissance craft, if I recognize the type—was standing picket duty at the Unity warp point into Franos. It was clearly tasked to carry word of approaching units back through that warp point. But in the event that something happened to it—as is the case now—how long before another Kaituni unit was due to check in on them?"

Ankaht inclined her head in a crude human nod. "I understood the substance of your question the first time, Admiral. But my answer remains: I cannot tell you, because the commanding officer of the ship does not know the answer, herself."

"What?" exclaimed Yoshikuni's Fleet Tactical officer, Rudi Modelo-Vo. "That's crazy!"

Wethermere raised an eyebrow at the reputed *wunderkind*'s unprofessional outburst. Yoshikuni cut her eyes at the fellow. The hatchet-faced Bellerophon native leaned back carefully.

Yoshikuni turned to look at Ankaht again. "It is, however, most irregular."

"I concur, Admiral. However, since the last two Kaituni destroyers departed the Mymzher system just before we sprung our trap, I suspect it will be at least days or weeks before the main van thinks to recontact this element of its rearguard."

"That is not merely unconventional; it is incompetent," Kiiraathra'ostakjo declared.

"It is particular to the modus operandi of the Kaituni, Least Fang," Ankaht replied. "It is difficult to know where to commence my description of the conditions that lead to these answers, so let me start with a frank statement that will put all subsequent comments in context. The Kaituni are utterly and myopically fixated upon the fusion—in their minds—of xenocide and

Destoshaz-as-*sulhaji*, even unto the marginalization of the other castes that are within the populations of their own Dispersates."

"You mean, they are killing their own people?" asked Rudi incredulously.

"Not as such, Commander, although they have done so before. Almost all the *shaxzhu* on the later Dispersates were killed, usually without being roused from cold-sleep. It seems that a few may have been retained, but remain safely slumbering rather than challenging the autocratic dominion of the Kaituni. The other castes are not being exterminated—exactly—but they have been in decline, even as the *Destoshaz* increase in equal and opposite measure. And the other castes' contributions to—and worthiness to be part of—the great xenocidal quest of the *Destoshaz'at* and his warrior cult are derogated more with each passing day, it seems. That is why this ship, commanded by an *Ixturshaz*, Hunisbern, was not given any assurances of recontact from the squadron which has just completed passing through the warp point to Franos. They have been left behind, without any orders or means of securing provisions, like abandoned pets or livestock. Their one job is to stand watch and raise an alarm if needed. No thought has been given to their needs—at all."

Yoshikuni looked around the table, as if to see if the others were as stunned as she was. "They are virtually daring the crew of that ship to mutiny, or at least abandon their post long enough to find provisions."

"Unquestionably, that is what would have happened. But the Kaituni are not 'daring' them to do it; they just don't care. And you must understand, from the Kaituni viewpoint, this is actually quite prudent."

"It's prudent to abandon a unit that is therefore sure to go off station, desert, or die in place?"

"Of course it is, Admiral, *if* you bear in mind the differences between us. Firstly, we do not die forever, but merely discarnate. We conceive of combat losses—even to logistics oversights—as annoyances, not horrific events. Secondly, once regressed *Destoshaz* have joined battle, they will reflexively streamline all their operations to achieve their immediate military objectives. And clearly, rear area security is a minor objective. I suspect that, from their viewpoint, the longer they receive no word from this picket post, the less they care about it."

"Why?"

"Because, as we have seen elsewhere, the Kaituni are not interested in controlling the star systems of their enemies, only in neutralizing them. And then they move on, leaving nothing behind. You may have observed this in the last war." She turned toward Narrok.

Who closed his eyes and opened them slowly. "It is as the Eldest Sleeper says. Our first admiral, Torhok, was so fixated upon *only* attacking that this monomania arguably contributed more to our final defeat than anything else. He was unwilling to leave garrisons or occupation forces behind except in the cases of crucial worlds or warp points. Even so, those were always token forces, incapable of mounting an effective defense or even a significant delaying action. And in that war, he had even more reason to do so than the Kaituni have here."

Yoshikuni studied the tall, golden *Destoshaz*. "How is this war different, Admiral?"

"I do not know if it is different everywhere, Admiral Yoshikuni, but here in Orion space, the Kaituni have decided not to hold on to anything. They travel back and forth to different destinations, yes, but it is not, in any *tactical* sense, a war of maneuver."

Wethermere leaned forward. "I notice you put extra emphasis on the word 'tactical' when talking about a war of maneuver. Are you implying that what we're seeing might be a war of maneuver on a strategic level?"

"It is a possibility," Narrok allowed.

"It is a certainty," Ankaht corrected. Again, all eyes turned toward her. "The commander of the ship confirms what our sensors recorded three weeks ago: that an immense non-Kaituni fleet moved through the Mymzher system to transit Unity Warp Point Three into Franos. And she confirms that, as our covert sensors seemed to indicate, it was an Arachnid fleet, albeit with ships much more advanced than those which faced yours two centuries ago."

Because the fleet's technical intelligence experts had analyzed those onerous sensor recordings almost weeks ago, the news did not come as a complete shock. But still, all of the humans seemed to get a bit more pale.

"And what the hell is *that* about?" Yoshikuni wondered aloud. "The Bugs? Here? And *now*?"

"It is about strategic maneuver, Admiral. You see, it is not coincidence that the Bugs—they call themselves the Omnivoracity, evidently—have appeared at the same time as the Kaituni. Rather, freeing the Bugs was apparently a major objective in the Kaituni strategy of conquest."

"*Freeing* the bugs?" Modelo-Vo exclaimed, his voice cracking on the first syllable. "How the hell did they even know the bugs still existed? Let alone what they call themselves!"

"Fortunately, we have the answers to those questions.

As well as a resolution to the investigation that Commodore Wethermere and I were tasked to undertake years ago regarding Kaituni activity in the systems around Pesthouse and the Home Hive Three. Because the answers to both mysteries are one and the same.

"Firstly, I must stress that we were very lucky to capture the picket ship we did. Having expected the Arachnids to move through Unity Warp Point Three, the Kaituni evidently dispatched a minor fleet element—the one to which the recently departed destroyers belonged—to follow it."

"Why?" Modelo-Vo asked.

"I do not have a definitive answer to that question, since the commander of the Kaituni picket ship does not know. Their orders were simply to ensure that if any threat forces approached the Unity Three warp point to Franos, they were to send an alarm. And that if any further Arachnid forces showed up, they were to, well, show them the proper pathway."

"Madame Councilor, I do not understand what you mean by that last statement." Yoshikuni's hands were folded, her brows very low.

"Admiral, the Kaituni are not in communication with the Arachnids, nor are they even allies. The Arachnids have no such concept. However, they seem amenable to the notion of following a trail of rich worlds while simultaneously avoiding chance contacts with the Kaituni who freed them—and who are now apparently following them."

"Or driving them in the desired direction," murmured Wethermere.

"Yes; that is, I believe, their intent," Ankaht confirmed. "And it is hardly surprising that, once freed, many of the Arachnids moved directly toward Franos. This was the gateway system to enter the Star Union where, as your histories depict in gruesome detail, the Arachnids fed most lavishly during the war with them."

Modelo-Vo raised an unusually high-pitched voice. "So the Kaituni are driving their hounds—well, more like their undomesticated wolves—before them in an attempt to remove yet another potential obstacle to their conquest: the fleets of the Star Union."

Kiiraathra'ostakjo made a throaty sound of demurral. "I suspect they are more concerned with what the Star Union might become, rather than what it is currently. Living along the lengthy expanse between human space and our own, the various star-faring races of that loose polity have had little reason to spend lavishly on defense. Their formations have become small and have not been significantly modernized in the last ten years. But their industrial sector is, collectively, impressive. Given even two years, they could become a formidable force."

"I suspect that is the consideration that led the Kaituni to drive, or entice, many of the Arachnids in this direction. And the crew of the picket was to ensure that any stragglers of this deadly swarm did not go astray, but found the warp point to Franos immediately."

"That's a role that sounds distressingly like 'live bait,'" mumbled Wethermere.

Ankaht smiled. "It is not entirely dissimilar, if that is how the Arachnids need to be guided to the warp point. Fortunately, so that the crew of the picket had some idea of the creatures which they might be dealing with, they were given very extensive data on what the Kaituni have learned about the Arachnids... and how they learned it."

"I'm surprised that data wasn't heavily encrypted," Modelo-Vo said testily.

"With respect, Commander, why should it be? The Kaituni were quite aware that neither humans nor Orions understand *selnarm* recordings. And what was the likelihood that someone such as myself would be here, dozens of warp transits within the zone of destruction they have created? Besides, creating ciphers is properly the province of the *Ixturshaz* caste, and the *Destoshaz* are trying assiduously to reduce that caste's importance."

"So they aren't bothering to put ciphers on intelligence data?"

"Let us say they are being selective about what warrants that measure of protection. And so far as I can tell, the Kaituni would not care that we have uncovered the means whereby they learned of the Arachnids. Judging from the role that ego plays in their new 'society,' I suspect they might derive considerable satisfaction from knowing that we learned of their extraordinary ingenuity—because, truly, their rediscovery of the Omnivoracity *is* a work of genius."

"C'mon, Councilor," teased Wethermere, "you're just dancing around the real core topic, and you know it."

"Which is?" Ankaht teased back.

Wethermere rolled his eyes but smiled as he did it. "Just tell us: *how* did the Kaituni find and release the Bugs?"

CHAPTER THIRTY-SIX

Ankaht rippled her smaller tendrils: the equivalent of a good-natured smile among her own people, but probably lost on aliens, even Ossian. "You might recall that when we finally deciphered the *selnarm*-data that had been carried on the automated couriers, I told you it resembled the forms in which *selnarm* transmits olfactory and tactile sensory information, but did not contain recognizable content."

The human frowned, then his brow raised, evidently along with the memories that provided his answer. "Yes, I do remember. You figured that out just as the subrelativistic barrage was hitting Amadeus."

"Correct. Well, now I know why the *selnarmic* data had that particular structure: because Arachnid communication is apparently partially pheromone based. It is an additional channel of information, much as vocalization and the written word is for us. And that was how the Kaituni field operatives packaged the Arachnid data they found and secretly transferred back to their linguists: in our own analogous format."

Yoshikuni's brow was pinched with the effort of recollection. "I seem to remember reading that we were aware that there was a pheromonic dimension to the Bugs' communications, but had never learned *what* it communicated or how."

"Yes, Admiral, your postwar forensics found the scent organs and receptors on Arachnid corpses, and found some limited presence of pheromone inputting devices on the wreckage of the larger ships. But your experts hypothesized that these systems were simply behavior control mechanisms, following the analogs they noted in many earth insects, which transmit commands for basic actions through just such methods." Ankaht paused. "As it turned out, your experts' reliance on terrestrial analogs could not have been more ill-advised. In the Arachnids, pheromones are only secondarily used for behavior modification; that is primarily determined by coded gestures, including ripple-patterns in mandibular cilia. Pheromones were reserved for a far more rare, but also, more nuance-rich, communicational purpose: cognitive exchange and recording."

Admiral Yoshikuni leaned back, crossed her arms. "Unless I've forgotten all my history—and I haven't—the Bugs had a crude form of writing as their primary means of exchanging data. That's what we found in their computers."

"My statement does not contradict what you read, Admiral. Rather, it expands upon it. You are indeed correct when you assert that Arachnid computers used a binary code that also extended into whole numbers and composite sigils. That was how they exchanged raw data and basic orders.

"But that is not an adequate language for reflective or speculative thought. It is a language of charts, graphs, performance metrics: it is a mechanistic means of communicating largely mechanistic and quantitative information. But when the Arachnids needed to exchange ideas, concepts, alternative plans, they added on the pheromonic component. The subtle distinctions and multiple, simultaneous impressions and qualifications possible in layered scents—or more properly, varied chemical interactions—were only needed by a small number of Arachnids who constituted a kind of 'higher leader' caste. This is what caused the paucity of pheromone-related mechanical systems—which in turn led your postwar researchers to conclude that it was, at best, a secondary method of communication."

Jennifer Pietchkov saw the connection to Arduan communication first. "So because both your people and the Bugs employ special nonverbal and nonphysical communication methods, the Kaituni were looking at possibilities that would not occur to humans."

Kiiraathra'ostakjo's ruff fluffed out. "And this answers the mystery of the dead and missing prospectors that were implicated in your investigations."

"Yes," answered Ankaht. "From what I can determine, Amunsit's researchers became keenly interested in the Arachnids' pheromonic inputs when they learned that, during the early battles between our own peoples, you humans were similarly puzzled by our *selnarmic* repeaters. To you, they were systems that served no discernible purpose. The Kaituni conjectured that the pheromone receptors might have been similarly overlooked and underappreciated.

"On further investigation, Amunsit's researchers

discovered another similarity in the way we Arduans and the Arachnids annotate or attach qualitative commentary to our data exchanges or 'physical language.' Namely, that just as we have sigils which denote either a reference to a *selnarmic* thread or which signify a commonplace *selnarmic* aphorism or observation, the Arachnid binary-coding had similar unprecedented characters which seemed inherently allusive, as if they were pointing to meanings that existed outside the data being presented. This prompted Amunsit's researchers to explore if we Arduans might have success deciphering the Arachnid communication schema where the various races of the PSU failed. But in order to conduct that research, they needed evidentiary materials."

Wethermere smiled. "And so Amunsit authorized some of the factors and consular liaisons she sent to the Amadeus system to commission human prospectors to collect promising Arachnid debris and wreckage."

"Yes," confirmed Ankaht, "all of whom were logically drawn to those systems that were particularly rich in the derelict Arachnid hulks left over from their war with you. And, who—being security liabilities once their task had been completed—were summarily, if gradually, liquidated.

"But before that occurred, they had to relay the information they were gathering in the field, since Amunsit did not wish to create a situation in which her operatives might be intercepted returning to Zarzuela with Arachnid artifacts. That would have potentially led to a more accurate conjecture regarding her clandestine researches and their underlying motives. So the information the Kaituni operatives gathered in the field was added to the courier drones that would ultimately make their way to Amadeus, where Amunsit's handlers received the messages as part of routine *selnarmic* communiqués which were further protected by a variety of trapdoor encryption protocols."

Yoshikuni shook her head. "So the entire suspicion of a *Destoshaz*-as-*sulhaji* fifth column operating within the Rim Federation—and even Republic space—was merely an artifact of our misperceiving what they were up to."

"Not entirely, Admiral. Amunsit had agents pursuing covert and potentially subversive ends, as well. But even there, much of it was just pointless communications—possibly to create the coded traffic expected of a fifth column, which in turn became a reasonable explanation for the mysteries we had at hand. Had Amunsit not provided that stalking horse for us to follow, we might have sooner come to reject that alternative and perceive others."

Kiiraathra'ostakjo shook his head slightly. "Even so, it is not fair to expect that you, or any other investigators, would have ever conjectured such a plot as the one which has now unfolded before us. To have hypothesized the continued existence of the Arachnids would not have been the logical outgrowth of any avenue of reasonable analysis: it would have always seemed a phantasmagoria of past horrors, not present clues. About which: although the Kaituni learned to translate Arachnid communication, how did that lead them to believe that the extermination of the Arachnids had been incomplete? The first condition in no way suggests the second."

Ankaht's clusters expanded briefly in a single pulse; she wondered if even Wethermere would recognize it as her species' gesture for launching into a new topic that was intensely interesting. "This is an excellent question, Least Fang, and it begs one even more fundamental, and for which I have no answer: why did Amunsit—either on her own initiative or at the behest of the new *Destoshaz'at*—commence her researches into the Omnivoracity at all? Alas, that information is not the kind which will be included in the data banks of a humble picket ship. However, their information *did* include an explanatory précis of *how* the Arachnids were discovered—provided to them as a means of familiarizing the ship's commanders with the events which led to their mission.

"Specifically, early in Amunsit's research project, the linguistic analysts detected that high-level pheromonic exchanges between the leadership of the different Home Hives was generally infrequent and terse. However, as the tide of the war turned against them, there was a marked increase in this traffic. This upswing was, in itself, not particularly surprising: a species fearing that its own extinction was imminent would exert every effort to coordinate all its energies against such an outcome.

"However, it was within this fragmentary body of information that the Kaituni first detected signs that, in the very last weeks of the war, this rising trend mysteriously reversed: pheromone communication diminished sharply. And yet, even as the Home Hives were losing touch with each other, there was no longer so absolute a presumption of impending extinction. Indeed, it seemed as if that most dire of all outcomes had been collectively dismissed as a concern."

"Suicidal resolve?" offered Modelo-Vo.

Ankaht wondered how this young human had risen to his current station. "No. Quite the contrary: although Kaituni translation of the Omnivoracity communiqués remains imperfect, it was fairly clear that its leadership had evidently become convinced that this problem was *solved*. This was when Amunsit's interest in the Omnivoracity's end-of-war activities was piqued and she began sending out more operatives with, necessarily, fewer precautions. This change in her methods and narrowed focus of research dates back three years, shortly before we were briefed about the impending need to mount the investigation that we did.

"Amunsit's research also turned toward a detailed inspection of the standard, and more plentiful, binary data that remained in the Arachnid computer banks. And there it was discovered that, in the last months of the war, there had been a modest 'siphoning' of equipment and resources from Hive Two's war production output. Yet, none that materiel ever appeared anywhere else, and there was no evidence that it had been shipped outsystem as cargo or, in some cases, whole combat units. It was as if all this output was swallowed up by the Hive Two system itself.

"Noting the simultaneity of these various irregularities, and then tell-tale signs that the siphoning itself stopped as the human fleets closed in on Hive Two, the Kaituni correctly hypothesized that the Bugs had discovered a new warp point in the system and were establishing a new Hive. And of course, for it to remain hidden, there had to be absolutely no evidence of transits to or from that warp point once the humans began drawing close."

"Damn, but Amunsit is smart," grumbled Yoshikuni. "It seems obvious when you have all the pieces in front of you to look at, but given that she started from a blank slate . . ."

"It may be her researchers that deserve most of the credit, Admiral," Ankaht suggested. "There is much in Amunsit's own handling of her fleets that suggests she may be somewhat rash. Or at least uncommonly bold." *Terms that have both been used to characterize you, as well, Admiral Yoshikuni,* Ankaht added where the vocoder could not read it. She chastised herself for the uncharitable, yet not wholly inaccurate, thought before she continued. "Amunsit's subsequent acquisitions of naval and navigation records of anomalous phenomena in the Hive Two system indicated that, over the past thirty years, local patrols have salvaged some unusual Arachnid artifacts there, and intercepted some odd signals. On the one hand, this was hardly noteworthy. Given the many 'sleeper devices' left behind by the Omnivoracity, most of its former star systems are plagued by just such automated remainders awakening—disastrously—when patrol or salvage craft pass close enough. Also, it was not uncommon that semi-functional wreckage swept into long-period cometary orbits periodically came close enough to the inner system to reveal itself. However, the Kaituni noted with particular interest that, on two occasions, this Arachnid debris in the Hive Two system was reported as being of 'atypical manufacture' and exhibiting surprisingly light wear.

"To human clerks processing these reports, this was simply a mildly interesting anomaly, which was suggestive of the vagaries of the Arachnids themselves.

Their artifacture was not always uniform, particularly when they began employing new systems, and some equipment was no doubt lost or disabled before it saw much use. However, to Amunsit's analysts, these reports were perceived as tantalizing suggestions that an unseen colony of the Omnivoracity might indeed be bordering the Hive Two system and was, periodically, cautiously probing its old haunts.

"Shortly after, the Kaituni undertook a covert mission, staffed almost entirely by *Destoshaz* defectors still in the Arduan community, so that none of the operatives would be detected and trailed emerging from the Zarzuela system to carry it out. The mission was to locate the warp point into this new Home Hive and then tumble a large enough asteroid through it to trigger a transit."

"All that would prove is that a big rock went through a warp point," Jennifer said with a frown.

"Yes," Ankaht replied, "but the asteroid had been specially prepared. Specifically, the Kaituni operatives had embedded a biologically sustained cell chamber it. In that chamber was a very sizable colony of short-lived creatures—those employing what we call *proto-selnarm*—which are similar to the ones we use in what you call our 'stick-hive' minesweepers. The rock's transit to the other system terminated the colony's *selnarmic* link with the *selnarshaz* operator who was still back in Hive Two and, in consequence, the creatures did what they had been bred to do: they released the equivalent of an intense '*selnarmic* scream.' Immediately after doing so, they expired and deliquesced into organic compounds that mimicked those found in the normative interstellar medium.

"At the same time, an immense—well, I suppose you might call it a 'dispersed array'—of *Selnarshaz* sensitives both in Zarzuela and throughout the approaching Dispersates waited to detect that '*selnarmic* scream' and, by having a vague sense of its directionality, discerned its real-space location by triangulating upon the source."

Wethermere's eyebrows rose. "Whoever thought that up is—well, I wish they were on *our* side."

"I agree," answered Ankaht, "it was a stroke of genius. Having thus fixed the real-space position of the hidden colony of the Omnivoracity, the closest-approaching Dispersate dispatched a Desai-drive probe to lurk well beyond that system and examine it for signs of life—specifically, for a burgeoning Arachnid Hive. Which is exactly what they found, and on a scale that dwarfed everything they had ever imagined. It also defined the hidden masterstroke upon which the Kaituni would base many of their strategic plans: to reach and release the Arachnids once again, and, evidently shepherd them against the forces of the PSU."

After a pause, Yoshinkuni sat very straight. "Does anyone have any *good* news to report as a result of today's encounter with the Kaituni picket ship?"

Wethermere nodded. "I do, Admiral." The two humans' eyes met oddly when Ossian uttered her title of rank. Ankaht had the impression that one, or maybe both of them were about to smile. Which was quite puzzling: none of the social cues indicated a source of mutual amusement or—

"Our encounter today proved something we've suspected," Ossian was continuing. "The Kaituni do not possess, and don't seem to know very much about, our stealth technology."

"As I remarked on prior occasions," Ankaht commented, "there was little record of it in your naval communications during the last war. As I recall, stealth technology was still in trials in the Rim Federation when the war started, and the Terran Republic was reserving it for special battlegroups."

Wethermere nodded. "Yes, but there was the possibility of more recent additions to Amunsit's technical intelligence. Specifically, once we learned that she was able to communicate with the Dispersates, and that her agents had been studying our military publications assiduously, it was always possible that they had learned more about our stealth systems than was available during the war with your Dispersate. And if that had occurred, then it was likely that the Kaituni had come up with a set of protocols to detect and counteract it. Instead, as we witnessed in the encounter with the picket and, from what I gather, your debrief of its commander, they have no functional knowledge of it."

"None," Ankaht confirmed.

Modelo-Vo scowled. "Sounds like damned poor technical intelligence work, to me. So poor that it makes me wonder if they do, in fact, know, and have taken steps to suppress that knowledge from their second-tier units so they can trick us into making wrong assumptions later on. *That* wouldn't surprise me at all."

Ankaht made sure her answering tone was calm and unhurried. "Actually, my surprise runs the other direction, Commander. I am frankly stunned at all the technical intelligence Amunsit *was* able to gather. When you consider the small number of agents she was able to field, the fact that they didn't have direct access to any of your classified materials, and that their human contacts and operatives were mostly limited to members of the criminal community, it's rather impressive that Amunsit accumulated the mass of data that she did, and that the Kaituni were able to act on it all so quickly and cannily."

Wethermere was apparently aware that Modelo-Vo's posture suggested an inclination toward continuing the argument. He forestalled that with a comment of his own: "Commander, this is not so much a lucky break as it is the law of averages finally swinging our way—and in relation to a technology that neither Torhok nor Amunsit faced in the last war and which has not been a high-profile news item since then. If you take a look at both popular journalism and the publications of the service academies—and everything in between—their coverage of military technology is understandably dominated by the size, complexity, and expense of the devastators and superdevastators. The emphasis on smaller matters that mostly pertain to lesser ships didn't even make the news—and let's face it: stealthing is never going to be that useful to the larger capital hulls. Their own drive emissions at low speed threaten to overload the stealth field's energy absorption capacity."

"Still," protested Modelo-Vo, "are you saying that Amunsit's agents have never even *heard* of stealthing?"

"Only in passing," Ankaht answered. "The commander of the picket indicated that she had been told that the human mentions of a 'stealth technology' had been presumed to refer to a next-generation improvement upon the cloaking technology which we both possessed during the last war."

"And it's not?" asked Jennifer somewhat hesitantly. "I mean, stealthing isn't simply an extension of cloaking technology?"

"Not at all," Modelo-Vo replied brusquely. "Cloaking was a partial sensor-repelling field that directed both active scans and the ship's own emissions away from enemy sensors. Of course, the success of that was largely predicated upon knowing where the enemy was—particularly in the case of hiding one's own emissions.

"But a stealthed ship is fully surrounded by a sensor-repelling field—which is why it's called 'the black bubble.' Any active sensor emissions get absorbed by it, so nothing returns to the enemy, just like when you scan empty space. Of course, the stealthed ship pays for that. Not only is it blind—remember: nothing comes in—but it can't send anything out. So it can't use its sensors, can't send messages. Which has really limited its applicability. Frankly," he turned toward Wethermere, "I've been wondering how the commodore managed to time getting the *Viggen* in so close behind the Kaituni picket. While *Viggen* was running its black bubble—which I understand takes up most of its old cargo compartment—you shouldn't have been able to coordinate with the *Fet'merah*, and shouldn't have known when the target moved far enough away from the warp point for you to slip in behind it."

Wethermere smiled. "I think it's more accurate to say that no *radiant energy* can get in or out of the black bubble." He aimed his smile at Ankaht, just then. "But *selnarm* isn't radiant. It's a phenomenon rooted in quantum entanglement, which means it doesn't traverse space-normal. It starts in one place, and immediately shows up somewhere else."

Modelo-Vo stared, then shrugged. "I guess I should have figured that out myself." That self-deprecatory statement improved Ankaht's opinion of Yoshikuni's young Fleet Tactical officer considerably. "But I still don't see how it's really going to help us during routine operations, when you need to keep scanning your environment to be able to react to changes in a volatile battlespace."

Admiral Yoshikuni sent a sideways glance at Wethermere—and again, Ankaht was sure she was just barely suppressing a smile—before she commented, "The commodore and I have been working together on that very problem of retaining combat responsivity while fully stealthed. For security reasons, we've kept that work confidential. But when we start shadowing the Bugs, we'll share what we've come up with—and see how it works."

Kiiraathra'ostakjo sat very straight. "'Shadowing' the Bugs? Admiral, do you mean to follow them?"

Narrok answered. "That is precisely what we mean, Admiral. It was our plan to enter the Star Union ourselves, and so move toward Earth. We shall continue to do so, while avoiding the Arachnids. But in order to achieve that end, we will inevitably need to keep abreast of their positions. Hopefully, they will demonstrate the same behavior they did during your war with them: they will attempt to raid the worlds of the Star Union for . . ." Narrok paused, searching for the right word ". . . sustenance."

"You're talking about billions of thinking beings, Admiral Narrok," Jennifer pointed out in a low voice.

"Regrettably, this is true. Regrettably, we are also powerless to do anything to intervene, not if we wish to achieve our prime objective: complete the long journey to the warp line that connects to Earth, and which Admirals Trevayne and Waldeck are surely defending. With any luck, this fleet could be large enough to help ensure victory, there. And if the Star Union has paid any attention to news of the recent events in the Khanate, they will be prepared to defend themselves from aggressors."

"True," Jennifer allowed. "But they weren't expecting aggressors who would stick around to *eat* them."

"At the risk of sounding insensitive, Ms. Pietchkov, I must point out that whether the Star Union was to be invaded by the Omnivoracity or the Kaituni only changes the manner and timing of their demise, not the probability of it. Indeed, were I in their place, I would prefer to be invaded by the Arachnids. Their technology is inferior and they are—or at least, *were*—driven by immediate objectives and appetites: they might decide to bypass strong resistance. Perhaps long enough for us to defeat the Kaituni and return to deal with the Omnivoracity. Conversely, the Kaituni would be determined to destroy strong resistance immediately, wherever they find it, and then lay waste to the resources with which that resistance might be rebuilt. And then, at their leisure, they would return so that they might—scientifically and methodically—depopulate all those worlds."

"Of course," Yoshikuni said, leaning forward to pick up the thread, "even if we did want to attack the Bugs, we'd be fools to do it without the advantage of surprise, and I don't think we're going to get that."

"Why?" asked Jennifer.

"As Councilor Ankaht has indicated, the picket

monitoring Unity Warp Point Three just took over this post from a small collection of Kaituni ships a few days ago. They've since gone through to Franos. I believe that enemy squadron is going to stay right behind the Bugs, herding them toward the crucial targets the Kaituni want removed in the Star Union. So it's almost a certainty that we'd run into that flotilla before we could jump the Bugs themselves—and I suspect the first thing the Kaituni would do is whistle up their Arachnid war-dogs. No, Ms. Pietchkov, as much as I sympathize with your concerns, we've got to stay on course with our original plan. And now we have yet another reason to follow it: so we can double back and the hit the Bugs in the Star Union. By surprise, if possible."

Yoshikuni's eyes moved sideways toward Wethermere. Again. "Speaking of surprises, Commodore—"

"Yes, Admiral?" Wethermere responded when it was clear that Yoshikuni's hanging tone was intentional.

"I thought I told you 'no carriers' on today's operation."

"Roger that, Admiral. None were present."

"Oh no? Then how was it you had four fighters hiding in the belt behind the *Fet'merah*, just in case there was trouble?"

"I'm sorry, Admiral," Wethermere explained, "I may have neglected to inform you that both the *Fet'merah* and the *Woolly Impostor* had their cargo holds modified to hold fighters, or most other forms of small craft. No combat launches or landings at high speed, of course, but so far, we've been able to do without them."

"Evidently," Yoshikuni seemed to stare at Wethermere's carefully expressionless face and Ankaht could not determine if the admiral was going to frown or smile. She actually did both—and then turned to formally bring the meeting to a close.

Ankaht suppressed a stunned tri-blink. What had become of the daunting, indeed ferocious, Admiral Yoshikuni? This person at the meeting did not seem to be her, not exactly. As Ankaht had seen over the past few weeks, Miharu Yoshikuni was not hesitant about tongue-lashing incompetent subordinates or, most especially, those whose deference was anything less than absolute. Of course, Ankaht reasoned, Wethermere would not be a likely irritant to the admiral to begin with: Ossian was anything but incompetent, and he hadn't been insolent in any material way. His tone had been more—well, playful would be the word that came to mind. But still, she was an admiral, and—

Ankaht's mind stopped. Were Yoshikuni and Wethermere…intimate? Granted they knew each other. Granted they were the right age for each other. Granted that they were both extremely intelligent. And granted that, among humans, crisis often proved the catalyst for strange pairings—but this? She turned to Kiiraathra'ostakjo, mentally reminded herself to make sure that the vocoder's volume would remain very low—and stumbled over how to phrase the surprisingly intrusive question she found she absolutely needed to ask.

The Orion glanced over, looked more closely at her when he evidently detected perplexity upon her face—*merciful Illudor, even* aliens *can plainly see my discomfiture!*—and then looked away with one of his closed-lip smiles. "So you have noticed, too."

Ankaht replied. "Yes, I have, if you mean—that is, if you are referring to—"

"Wethermere and Yoshikuni. Yes. I think it began the first time we met on her ship. I suspect, from prior casual conversation with Ossian, that the admiral, as the human expression puts it, has had her eye on him for some time. At least since the war games he participated in at the start of this year. She requested him to work as the Fleet Tactical Officer attached to her flagship for a while. Then she had him delivering personal reports with rather unusual frequency, given the separation between their ships during maneuvers. He suspected she might be assessing him for possible promotion." The Orion's smile widened. "I wondered if she might have been assessing him for different reasons, but elected to remain silent."

"But why?"

"Councilor Ankaht, I am not much learned in the ways of humans, but I have learned this: do not become involved in their counterinstinctual pre-mating rituals of approach and avoidance, beckon and rebuff. It is terribly confusing and gives me a headache. It is doing so even now. You will kindly allow me to take my leave."

Part Five

The Numbers of the Beasts

CHAPTER THIRTY-SEVEN

As Ian Trevayne had been certain they would, the Bugs advanced into Pesthouse from Home Hive One on the heels of Combined Fleet. First came a hurricane of SBMHAWK missiles, streaking through the warp point in a stroboscopic flicker of explosions from superimposed transits, targeting the massive fortresses. Then came phalanxes of monitors, in the inexorable, soulless, seemingly unstoppable way that Pesthouse's younger defenders had read of in history books and the older ones, in some cases, had heard of from their grandparents and great-grandparents.

But those defenders were ready for them, and fueled by the hatred and loathing of the Arachnid abomination that would endure as long as a human or Orion or Ophiuchi or Gorm was alive in the universe.

Trevayne had been relieved to see that Hugo Allende had followed his orders to the letter. He had brought Combined Fleet's now-vulnerable devastators and superdevastators back and positioned them just within heavy missile range of the warp point.

From there they unleashed a datalinked torrent of firepower into the advancing Bug monitors in coordination with the battered but still-fighting fortresses, while Combined Fleet's lesser capital ships poured in the searing plasma bolts of energy torpedoes and its fighters weaved through the holocaust, seeking out the enemy's blind zones and stabbing viciously with their own rapid-fire energy torpedoes. The volume of space around the warp point became an inferno of destructive energy in which the Bug ships vanished into coruscating clouds of debris and vapor almost as rapidly as they appeared.

After a time, Trevayne took a calculated risk. It wasn't impossible that the Bugs possessed whatever weapon had caused Cyrus Waldeck's devastators and superdevastators to so inexplicably explode. But if there was any truth to his assessment of the Kaituni/Bug relationship, they almost certainly didn't—and there wouldn't be any Kaituni ships accompanying them. So he ordered Allende to bring his mastodonic killing machines into the range where they could use the gee-beams powered by their prodigious engines—and Allende obeyed unflinchingly. Within that range of those ships, no monitor-sized or smaller ship could hope to live. And Trevayne heaved a deep but (he hoped) inconspicuous sigh of relief when none of Allende's ships vanished in mini-novae.

Soon, the Bugs sullenly withdrew, and no more came. Trevayne had a breathing space to call his senior flag officers together for an intelligence briefing.

Zeven Provinciën's Intelligence center had no facilities for a phantom holographic staff conference, as

Li Han's did. So Combined Fleet's task force commanders attended in the flesh. Trevayne preferred it that way—and not just because it brought him into physical contact with Magda for the first time in far too long. In fact, he was coming to rather like *Zeven Provinciën*, despite its name's association with a rival of his personal hero Nelson's reputation.

Threeenow'hakaaeea was, in terms of accepted human/Orion rank equivalencies, the most junior task force commander present—in fact, he commanded a task force only by virtue of Trevayne's hasty integration of Second Fleet's remnants into Combined Fleet's organization. But it would never have occurred to Trevayne to not have him there—and not just because they badly needed a representative of his race. No; he was there not just as an Orion but as an officer of the PSU, in the midst of what was by now a predominantly Terran Republic/Rim Federation fleet defending the PSU's human core of the heart worlds. But then, the distinctions between the various polities seemed increasingly irrelevant in the face of the inconceivable calamity that threatened to overwhelm them all.

"In the course of the destruction of the fortresses in Orpheus-1, and in the course of our own fighting retreat from that system," Andreas Hagen began, "we were able to obtain a considerable amount of sensor readings on the Bugs—"

"That's what I call putting the best possible face on things," Adrian M'Zangwe muttered.

"—and still more became available during the recent action here at Pesthouse. We have now had a chance to evaluate these data, and have been able to draw a couple of conclusions about what the Bugs have been up to in whatever concealed system or systems they have inhabited since the Fourth Interstellar War.

"First of all, their ships are no larger than they were two centuries ago. Their most massive classes are still monitor-size."

"Which may not be a bad thing for them, given the . . . new realities," said Magda grimly.

"Secondly, analysis of their combat efficiency, as compared with archival data from the Fourth Interstellar War, indicated that they are making far more lavish use of automation than they were then. This is particularly true of their smaller craft. Simply put, they're reacting faster."

"I wonder," mused Trevayne, "if automation is the only reason for that. I wonder if the Bugs have been able to exploit direct neural interfacing."

Everyone's expressions reflected the distastefulness of the subject. "I know that's been a theoretical possibility for centuries, Ian," Magda objected. "But it's never proven practical for humans or any other sentients outside of controlled laboratory conditions—certainly not in combat."

"That's because of the impossibility of screening out irrelevant mental 'chatter.' But the Bugs . . . well, I think it's safe to say that their individual units are a good deal less complex and more focused than beings like ourselves. Perhaps they, unlike us, could give coherent mental commands—especially if they've genetically engineered a caste with a highly developed nervous system specialized for the purpose, and probably with a rudimentary body permanently hooked into a ship's controls." Trevayne saw the general distaste deepen, and he waved the subject aside. "That's just speculation.

It's not something we need to know at the moment. Andreas, bring up the strategic display please."

Hagen obeyed, and a standard warp-network chart glowed to life on the screen. "The Bugs are in Home Hive One, from which they will undoubtedly continue to fight their way into this system—"

"Let them!" snarled Threeenow'hakaaeea. "We slaughtered these less-than-*chofaki* when they tried it before, and we can do it again!"

"But they have the numbers to waste," Trevayne reminded him. Even the Orion joined in the glum silence that followed. They all knew that this Bug armada exceeded even the legendary proportions of the Bug hordes of the Fourth Interstellar War.

"And," Trevayne resumed, "the combined Kaituni fleets were in Orpheus-1 when we last saw them. If I'm right about where they stand with respect to the Bugs, they're still there. Now, it may be that the Bugs will detach forces from Home Hive One to proceed by way of Orpheus-2, Orpheus-3, and Home Hive Three. Or, it may be that Kaituni forces from Oprheus-1 will do the same thing. But one of them or the other—I rather doubt both, again granting my assumptions—will surely follow that route and go for the jugular by driving along the warp-chain through the old Bug systems in the direction of Alpha Centauri. And if they take Bug 05 . . ." He left the sentence hanging.

"We'd be trapped here in Pesthouse, hopelessly sidelined, and the way to the Heart Worlds would be open to them," said M'Zangwe, voicing what they could all clearly see.

"Admiral," Shang ventured, "are you suggesting that we should abandon Pesthouse and fall back on Bug 05?"

"No." Trevayne was emphatic. "I don't want to write off Pesthouse until and unless I absolutely have to. Its strong defenses provide Bug 05 with defense in-depth. But your basic instinct is correct. We *have* to defend Bug 05. Otherwise, Pesthouse becomes untenable. And, although Home Hive Three is of course lost, as far as we know they haven't entered Bug 03 yet. So, while appealing to Alpha Centauri for all the reinforcements it can send, we will fight a delaying action in Bug 03 to give us as much time as possible to fortify Bug 05 with more fortresses and more minefields."

"And also perhaps the devastators and superdevastators, to be employed as they were here," Magda suggested.

"Only if it turns out that it's the Bugs we're facing there. If in fact it's the Kaituni—and I strongly suspect that it will be—then the risk is simply too great."

Threeenow'hakaaeea rose to his feet, russet fur bristling and whiskers twitching. "Ahhdmiraaaal, I request permission to lead the holding force to Bug 03."

He was somewhat junior for such an assignment. But . . . "Request granted, Great Claw. And . . . may your claws strike deep."

Zum'ref was in a discursive mood.

"Do you know, Inzrep'fel, that when the First Dispersate arrived in human space, the humans' inability to communicate with them in their accustomed way caused something akin to panic, because it aroused memories of the Arachnids?"

The *ha'selnarshazi* Intendant fairly radiated (revulsion). "Do you mean, *Destoshaz'at*, that the humans actually thought we were *those* creatures?"

Zum'ref decided not to reprimand her for her doubtless-unconscious use of *we* to include the First Dispersate. Those Illudor-forsaken traitors were, after all, inescapably members of the same biological species. "Not the Arachnids themselves, no, but perhaps something similar," he affirmed. "Yes, the fact that the humans could have made such an assumption is indeed distasteful. But it serves to illustrate one reason the Arachnids serve Illudor's purpose. The mere thought of them is enough to trigger primitive, irrational fears in humans—memories from their myths and legends of monsters come to eat their children. Actually encountering them, when they were believed to be safely buried in the past, can only weaken their morale."

He dismissed the subject and stood up, walking toward the viewscreen, which was set to view-forward. At its extreme right edge, the yellow sun of Home Hive One shone dimly across seventeen light-minutes.

He had entered this system from Orpheus-1 followed by the fleets of six Dispersates. One he had left behind in Orpheus-1. To the remaining two—the ones from Zephrain, which had so narrowly and frustratingly failed to trap the fleeing *griarfeksh* fleet—he had magnanimously granted an opportunity to redeem themselves in his eyes and Illudor's, for he had sent them to Orpheus-2 to begin the great advance along the main warp chain that led to the already-crippled human Heart Worlds. If they could take Bug 05 swiftly, they might be able to trap their original intended prey after all, in Pesthouse. But Zum'ref wasn't counting on that, for he had come to know this human admiral too well.

In the meantime, there was business to be attended to here in Home Hive One. Which was why his fleet, having emerged from the Orpheus-1 warp point, was now headed directly away from the Pesthouse warp point around which the Arachnids swarmed. Those eerie creatures (Zum'ref could almost understand, if not sympathize with, the humans' feelings) would be left strictly alone, to do the sanguinary work of trying to force an entrance into Pesthouse. And as his fleet moved away from them, it was beginning to separate...

"Have all the subordinate commanders acknowledged their orders?" he asked, still gazing at the Home Hive One sun and contemplating the three now-dead planets that circled it, each of them once a pullulating mass of Arachnids.

"Yes, *Destoshaz'at*." Zum'ref could feel a certain ambivalence in the Intendant's *selnarm*.

"What is it, Inzrep'fel?"

"Well... is it certain that any one of the blocking forces we are dispatching to each of this system's other five warp points is strong enough to hold the Arachnids in if they should make a determined effort to get out?"

(Calm confidence.) "I believe so. Granted, they have a myriad of ships. But our technological superiority should make up the difference."

"Strange that they have advanced so little in all the time they've had to stew in their hidden system. Or, perhaps not so strange. A life form like that..."

"Actually, they have shown more capacity for innovation than the humans' records of them would suggest. But their innovations have, for the most part, been in the biological sciences. Instead of improving their weapons, they've sought to improve themselves." (Firm subject-closing.) "At any rate, it is essential that we keep them here in Home Hive One—staying well behind them, of course—and leaving them nowhere to go but Pesthouse."

"And thus we continue to herd them in the direction we wish them to go." (Fawning agreement.) "And if another . . . herd should come through Home Hive Two—"

"—Then the fleet we left behind in Orpheus-1 will leave them nowhere to go except the Star Union, as has been our intention all along. In the meantime, the Arachnid fleet here will continue to serve our purpose: keeping the *griarfeksh* pinned in Pesthouse by continuing to singlemindedly try to battle their way into it." (Wry amusement.) "In fact, 'singlemindedly' goes without saying in their case. They *are* a single mind!"

So the Newest Enemies had closed off this system's other five warp points. And no doubt they had done the same in the system from which they had come, fearing—correctly—that another fleet would be emerging from the System Which Must Be Concealed.

In the long run, it was unimportant. That fleet would simply proceed to the systems of the Old Enemies, following the warp route that the Newest Enemies had revealed after going into the New Enemies' mysterious artificial warp point. So the Newest Enemies could, after all, be useful.

And eventually, of course, they would be useful as a protein source.

CHAPTER THIRTY-EIGHT

Threeenow'hakaaeea died a death befitting a true hero of the *Zheeerlikou'valkhannaieee*.

Bug 03 was a barren system with a type K orange primary star and a fairly distant red dwarf companion. The Bug 05 warp point was at twelve o'clock, at a distance from the primary of seventeen light-minutes. The Home Hive Three warp point from which they could expect attack was on a nine o'clock bearing, at twenty-one light-minutes. Soon after arriving from Pesthouse with a delaying force comprising everything Ian Trevayne had been willing to spare, Threeenow had come to the glum conclusion that the fortresses guarding the Home Hive Three warp point were hopelessly inadequate, even with the additional ones Trevayne had had time to send lumbering through on their slow maneuvering drives.

But he had also believed that Trevayne was right in his intuition that he would be facing the Kaituni here, not the Bugs. And Andreas Hagen had briefed him thoroughly on the lessons from the fall of Zephrain, learned at the cost of Yoshi Watanabe and his fleet, on the subject of meeting a Kaituni warp-point assault. So he had arranged his defenses accordingly... and, in addition, prepared a certain surprise.

When waves of pinnaces came through the warp point, dispersing microsensors whose readings were gleaned by accompanying survey escorts, Threeenow immediately sent a message drone through the Bug 05 warp point, confirming that Trevayne's instinct had been correct. As those escorts reversed course in the way permitted by reactionless drives and sought to escape with their *selmarm*-acquired data, the fortresses and the monitor-sized and smaller capital ships saturated the region of the warp point with searing energy-torpedo fire—but only from that weapon's maximum effective ranges, and soon ceasing, for Threeenow had a fairly good idea of what to expect next.

Nor was he disappointed. The modular anti-missile superdreadnoughts began to transit, seeking to draw the defenders' energy-torpedo fire away from the SBMHAWK barrage that was to follow. But Threeenow was not deceived, and as per his order the fortresses and capital ships had shifted their energy-torpedo batteries to anti-missile mode, and the SBMHAWKs began to die in great swathes of crackling, flaring antimatter annihilation.

Then the heavily armored Kaituni warp-point assault monitors began to transit, and the battlespace became an inferno of brutal, point-blank ship-to-ship slugging. But with their energy torpedoes back in the offensive fire datanet, Threeenow's fortresses and capital ships were ill prepared to respond when the expected missile-launching framework hulls began to arrive and belched forth their single-shot salvos.

Threeenow watched, heartsick, as the warp-point defenders died faster and faster. And more than heartsick, for it was an affront to his entire warrior tradition of *theernowlus*, or "risk-bearing," that he himself was not there at the warp point with them. But he had to be where he was, in order to implement his plan. Long ago, in the First Interstellar War, the newly encountered humans had taught his race the bitter but valuable lesson that the fiery eagerness of a warrior must yield to the cold practicalities of war.

And soon enough, there would be ample opportunity to expose himself directly to danger as *theernowlus* required.

After his losses had reached a certain predetermined level, Threeenow swallowed another portion of his honor. He sent the order for his mobile forces to abandon their no-longer-defensible position and withdraw toward the Bug 05 warp point and escape. Sullenly, unwillingly, they obeyed, leaving behind those who still lived in the junk-sculptures that had been orbital fortresses. The fleets of two Dispersates completed their warp transit, completed the obliteration of the fortresses, and followed, harassing the retreating survivors.

Bug 03's two warp points were separated by twenty-seven light-minutes. The pursued and the pursuers had only covered a small portion of that distance when they passed within three light-minutes of the system's third planet, a gas giant of more-than-Jovian mass with five substantial moons as well as the usual array of insignificant moonlets. Beyond that, they continued on a course that almost paralleled Planet III's orbit and, about halfway to the Bug 05 warp point, brought them within mere light-seconds of its trailing Trojan point.

Bug 03 A had an asteroid belt, out in the chill darkness of the outer system at an orbital radius of sixty-five light-minutes, where the gravitational perturbation of the red-dwarf Component B had prevented a planet from coalescing. It would have been quite a large planet, for the belt held an exceptional quantity of planetesimal rubble. Over the eons, Component A's gravity had drawn a good many of those rocks inward toward itself. And quite a few of them had collected, as such space-junk will, in the Trojan points of Component A's two gas-giant planets.

Thus it was that the Kaituni, in their singleminded pursuit of the *griarfeksh* delaying force, passed close by, and ignored, a cluster of asteroids. Their rearmost elements were past it when Threeenow finally gave an order that had required all his self-discipline to hold back for so long. His carriers and their escorting cruisers, which had been lurking among those trailing-Trojan asteroids, powered down to minimal life-support and sensor requirements, awoke to ferocious life and swept out, launching their fighters at the Kaituni sterns.

Blood-chilling howls filled the comm circuits as Orion pilots hurled themselves at the *chofaki* who had slaughtered untold billions of their race and turned their old and new homeworlds into deserts. At this moment, the climactic moment of their lives, they were as indifferent to death as their Arduan opponents, even though they anticipated no reincarnation. Their lives simply didn't matter now. All that mattered was vengeance. And, pouring rapid-fire energy torpedoes into the blind zones of Kaituni warships, they took vengeance.

Threeenow wished he could be out there among them. He also wished he could call back the capital ships to turn on their pursuers as his fighters savaged them from astern. But then they all would have died, for the odds against them were simply too great for them to even think of victory or even survival. For that matter, they could all have stood together and fought and died at the Home Hive Three warp point. But Ian Trevayne was going to need every one of those monitors and superdreadnoughts in Bug 05. And he was also going to need all the time Threeenow could give him.

Thus it was that the capital ships continued on toward their warp point of escape while Threeenow fought an action intended to do just what his delaying force was for: to delay. As the Kaituni armada turned to deal with the stinging insects astern, he swung his force aside, forcing the enemy to swerve with him. And, as the fight snarled on, he swerved again and again, drawing the Kaituni further way from their original course.

He was able to keep it up longer than he had dared hope, for the Kaituni fighters had been engaged in pursuit when he had struck from astern, and it took finite time to bring them back and rearm them. But it couldn't last, as he had known it couldn't. They were gradually smothered in sheer, brute numbers of Kaituni. And these Dispersates, coming from Zephrain, were well supplied with the new *selnarm*-directed fighter triads, and very experienced in their use.

But even as he watched his ships die, and the life support of his half-wrecked flagship begin to falter, he knew he had done his duty, and fulfilled the demands of *theernowlus.* And the knowledge was a flame inside him.

He was giving voice to a scream of defiance when the flame in his soul became one with the flame that consumed what was left of his flagship.

"There is no time for us to mourn a hero," Trevayne told a somber conference of his senior commanders. "We must choose between our strategic options—which have now become very limited.

"The Kaituni are now one warp transit away from Bug 05—the system we *must* defend. We are strengthening its warp-point defenses, and have assigned a higher percentage of our mobile forces to it. The question is this: do we continue to try to hold Pesthouse as well?"

"I say pull everything we've got back to Bug 05," rumbled Adrian M'Zangwe. "Including the fortresses, which I realize will take time, and evacuate the station's personnel. If we stay here in Pesthouse, we risk getting trapped if the Kaituni take Bug 05 before we can pull out."

"The same arguments against writing off Pesthouse as before still apply," Magda reminded him. "And now there's a new one. We don't *think* the Kaituni and the Bugs are communicating with each other in any real way, or coordinating their actions except on the very crude level of the Kaituni herding strategy. But we don't *know* that for certain. If we're all concentrated in Bug 05, with the Bugs as well as the Kaituni just one warp jump away, and they *do* mount a coordinated attack so we have to defend two warp points simultaneously..." She let the sentence trail off.

"But," M'Zangwe persisted, "if the Kaituni attack Bug 05 first, and make faster progress than we anticipate, are our forces in Pesthouse going to be able to get out in time? I guarantee the fortresses won't, on their maneuvering drives. And what about Commodore Allende's devastators and superdevastators? If the Kaituni catch them in Bug 05 before they can get away to Bug 17, they're dead!"

Abruptly, Trevayne stood up and walked to the display screen. He brought up a split-screen image of two system displays, with Pesthouse on the right and Bug 05 on the left. No one broke the silence as he studied the arrangement of the systems' warp points morosely. When he spoke, it was half to himself, with his back still turned to the conference table.

"The Home Hive One and Bug 05 warp points here in Pesthouse are only fourteen light-minutes apart. So no matter what happens at the former, it will be relatively easy to get out of this system via the latter. The problem arises in Bug 05. The warp point locations there are very much against us." He pointed to the left-hand display.

Bug 05, like Pesthouse, had a hot young blue giant star as its primary. Even more coincidentally, the astronomers asserted that they were not really all that far apart in the normal space of Newton and Einstein. Clearly, they lay in a region of new star-formation. But Trevayne's attention was riveted on Bug 05's warp points. At a bearing of six o'clock and a distance of twenty-seven light-minutes from the primary was the icon of the Pesthouse warp point. Directly opposite, at a bearing of twelve o'clock and a distance of sixteen light-minutes, was the warp point leading to Bug 17, their only possible fallback position. Finally, at a bearing of ten o'clock and a distance of thirty light-minutes, was the Bug 03 warp point, on the other side of which the Kaituni now lay.

"If the Kaituni attack Bug 05, and look like taking it, before the Bugs attack Pesthouse, we would of course have to evacuate Pesthouse," Trevayne resumed. "But it's forty-three light-minutes from the Pesthouse warp point to the Bug 17 warp point—more, actually, because we'd have to give that damned blue-giant primary a wide berth. And a Kaituni breakout would put them in a position to cut off that retreat."

"Precisely why I recommend evacuating Pesthouse now, while we can, Admiral," said M'Zangwe.

"However," Trevayne continued, "I don't think the Kaituni are going to attack first. I think they're going to continue to let the Bugs go in front and take the casualties, and not try to enter Bug 05 until they can do so behind them."

"But sir," said M'Zangwe in respectful tones, "assuming that the Bugs do attack Pesthouse first, and drive us out of it—a possibility we can't ignore, given the resources we've now had to divert from there to Bug 05—what if the Kaituni attack from Bug 03 while the withdrawal is in progress? If they catch Commodore Allende's command—"

Trevayne turned to face them. "It is for that reason that I'm going to order Commodore Allende to take the devastators and superdevastators out of Pesthouse forthwith and station them in Bug 05 just short of the Bug 17 warp point. That way, if the Kaituni do break in, they'll be able to get away ahead of them. And if, as I believe, the Bugs attack Pesthouse and subsequently attack Bug 05, they'll be in a position to cover our retreat to Bug 17 before exiting."

Magda looked very thoughtful, even though Trevayne was agreeing with her about staying in Pesthouse, at least for the time being. "You realize, Ian, that without the firepower of the devastators and superdevastators, holding Pesthouse against the Bugs becomes very problematical."

"Let's call a spade a bloody shovel! The defense of Pesthouse will become a delaying action. But I believe delay is worth it. It gives the Heart Worlds and what's left of the Corporate Worlds more time to rebuild our forces. Nevertheless, I will evacuate Pesthouse without hesitation, writing off the fortresses, the instant it appears that the system can no longer hold. We have to conserve our forces for the defense of the main warp line to Sol."

There was no further discussion. No one present envied Trevayne for being the one who had to make such decisions, and such terrifying choices.

Zum'ref sent (satisfaction) and settled into a relaxed pose after hearing the last of the reports from Bug 03.

"Very well. The operation was somewhat more difficult and protracted than we anticipated, but the point is that we are now in a position to threaten Bug 05 directly. So we can proceed to make a series of probing attacks."

(Perplexity.) "But *Destoshaz'at*, it was my understanding that—"

(Irritation.) "Of course, Inzrep'fel, of course. These attacks won't be pressed home to the extent of taking the system, even if our forces in Bug 03 could do so at this juncture, of which I'm far from certain. No; these attacks will be for the purpose of forcing the human admiral to siphon off more and more of his forces from Pesthouse, thus enabling the Arachnids to take it and press on to Bug 05 from their direction. Only when they have entered Bug 05 will our fleets enter the system—from both directions, forming up behind them. I'm sure this will come as no surprise to this human admiral."

(Smugness.) "By this time, he probably thinks we have no surprises left."

"Very likely. Little does he know what we have left—a very major surprise."

CHAPTER THIRTY-NINE

The moment Alessandro Magee stepped down onto the turf of the Star Union world of Tevreelan Three, Harry Li's voice was loud in his helmet earbud. "Tank, have you deployed into the target zone?"

'Sandro, weapon still at the ready from habit rather than immediate necessity, surveyed his surroundings. "Yep, Harry. We sure have."

"Well, Boss—how about a report?"

Harry sounded impatient and more than a little annoyed. He'd been the one to point out that the two of them, as the most experienced ground-pounders in Commodore Wethermere's recon detachment, should not both be risked in the snoop and poop missions to each of the worlds the Bugs had hit. But whereas Harry's surreptitious intent had been to keep his large friend out of the field, 'Sandro had ordered a fifty-fifty split of the landing missions. The two of them now alternated between dirtside landing team leader and spaceside operations controller, planet by planet. Li had still not forgiven him for subverting his initial intent.

"My report," 'Sandro said finally, "is that Tevreelan Three is damned weird."

"Weird how?"

"You'll see. I'm adding video feed to the laser-com now."

Tank toggled through the HUD's secondary selection matrix with his chin, selected the video icon, and held up his left fist, signaling his squad to stop. He did not motion them down, although in other environments, that would have been the doctrine. Instead, he moved his head slowly from side to side. "You getting the feed, Harry?"

"Yes, I—I guess I am. What the hell are those?"

'Sandro looked down at his feet, where a radially symmetric, six-legged arthropod lay in what seemed to be torpor. Its pencil-sized legs were mostly folded underneath a body that resembled a flattened ostrich egg. The only sign that it was alive was a faint dilate-constrict cycling of respiration ducts, one of which was snugged into every gap between leg joints, all around the periphery of its body. The faint bull's-eye marking, imparted by concentric back plates, seemed to bulge a bit, as if the creature was swollen or gorged. "They're Arachnid creepers."

He heard Li hiss out a surprised breath. "That doesn't look much like the ones we've seen on the other worlds. Are there any others nearby?"

By way of answer, Tank tilted his head back up to give Harry the same horizon-line view that had confronted 'Sandro and his team when they first exited the *Viggen*'s armored gig. They had been, as per their unofficial motto, ready for anything.

But not for this. Scattered across an overgrown

lawn like a plague of immensely large mushrooms, the crop of torporous creepers stretched right up to the PSU consular compound's walls, into the fields behind it, and the woods that rolled up toward hills beyond them. 'Sandro turned slowly to his rear. Behind the *Viggen*, the town identified on their maps as Lelraen lay motionless beneath aqua skies and a yellow star called Tevreelan. The streets were filled with the motionless humps of still more creepers.

"Damn," breathed Harry. "Where they hell did they all come from?"

"The Bugs. Where else?" The creepers had been a common sight on all the worlds they had visited as they moved in the wake of the Arachnid fleet: Franos, Telik, Reymiimagar. But on those planets, the creepers had been lean, agile, speedy, and much flatter, skittering toward intruders with utter abandon—and utter disregard to their own losses. A veritable horde of them had streamed toward 'Sandro's landing team on Telik, emerging from the savaged buildings of one of the few cities that had not been wholly incinerated by the Bugs. Like a rolling carpet of hyperactive severed hands, they had not posed a credible threat to the battle-armored humans who blasted them with incendiary grenades and flechette rounds. But the mere thought of being buried under that writhing mass of senseless attackers had made the team edgy, particularly as, despite staggering losses, the creepers closed through the last few meters—

—and then abruptly stopped and ran the other way until the bipedal intruders stopped firing at them. Some returned to their prior shelters, others, still restless, seemed to circle about, seeking more satisfactory prey until they, too, ceased to be agitated and sought new cover.

A few specimens had been stunned and transferred to the dilapidated civilian packet that Yoshikuni had designated an all-purpose quarantine and observation ship. There, fleet med-techs—wishing they had one true xeno-biological specialist among them—had observed and ultimately dissected the sample creepers. Their common origins with the Bugs were immediately evident: they shared approximately ninety percent of the same, simple and almost totally nonmutative genetic material. The creepers' peculiar shift from extreme aggressiveness to avoidance was explained fairly quickly, also. Initially attracted by the motion of the landing team, the arthropods' terminal approach had failed to furnish them with the final stimulus to press home an attack: prey scent. The sealed suits made the encased humans no more interesting to the creepers than a patrol of robots would have been.

But the unanswered mystery posed by the presence of the creepers was why the Bugs were bothering to seed infestations of them on worlds they had already shattered. Certainly there were likely to be survivors of the withering blanket bombardments, which had been a mix of nuclear weapons and simple kinetic penetrators and impactors launched by rail guns. But there was no credible hope of those survivors rebuilding the savaged planets back to the point where they might offer resistance again—not for many years, at least.

"Okay, Tank," Harry sighed. "Enough time staring at the creep-show. Time to advance."

Alessandro Magee's one great failing as an officer asserted itself as, given the eerie and onerous environment into which they had to advance, he took point himself and announced, "Hound One, on me. Harry, we are moving to waypoint one. Shall observe and report."

Harry didn't even bother to argue with 'Sandro; he just released a long, exasperated sigh. "You know, you're setting a terrible example for every man in the team who might become an NCO or officer, one day."

"Yeah, well, on *this* day, I'll take that chance. I don't like the vibe down here. Too many ways we could be surprised."

"All the more reason for you to have your senior NCO on point. And for you to always run ops, up here."

"Drop it, Harry. You can pester me off the clock, but not when I need to stay sharp."

"Acknowledged. Look-down sensors show no movement in your area. No bio-grade thermals in the open. Can't tell about the heavier buildings of the consular compound."

"Roger that. Am now at the outer wall of the compound. Is my video feed still good?"

"All transmissions are five-by-five. Give me a corner peek and a pan-around, Tank."

"Will do."

The compound gate—ornamental rather than a serious defensive barrier—was ajar. There was no evident damage to the structures, or even the electronic surveillance equipment, but again, there was the same ghost-town appearance, and the ubiquitous, inert creepers. The grass was long, the gardens gone to seed, the main doors wide open, as were several windows. No lights were showing anywhere, not even on the security and communication control panels at checkpoints or liaison stations—

—a silhouette lurched past an upper story window, was gone as quickly as it had flitted into view.

Li had evidently seen it too. "Tank, recommend you deploy a microbot to—"

But Tank had already signaled the closest fire team to stick on him and was charging the front entrance of the consulate. "No, Harry. That takes too long, and we don't know if some of these damn creepers might activate." He charged into the consulate's lobby, scanning, saw the stairs, started up. "I need to get a battle-suited human wall up around whoever, or whatever, we saw. And I want a medical skiff down here as soon as you can—"

'Sandro reached the top of the stairs, saw motion, swung his gun in that direction, keeping the barrel high since he had not yet identified the source as friend or foe—

And for a moment, was not entirely sure which he was looking at. A human—a woman, perhaps in her thirties—was staggering toward Magee's fire team. It was unclear if she was aware of them. But it was quite clear that she was emaciated, distracted—and adorned with creepers.

Behind 'Sandro, Corporal Anasi Uhatu brought her coil gun around to bear on the woman. Magee intercepted it with his hand. "Belay that, Corporal."

"But sir," Uhatu objected tensely, "she's—infected. Or something."

"Yes, and we won't find out what that 'something' is if you blow her apart. And don't be so quick to kill one of us, Uhatu."

"Uh . . . okay, sir. But are we really sure she is *still* one of us?"

Good question, but—"Until we know differently, that's what we assume. Now, let's get her back to the LZ. Commander Knight should be sending the med skiff down from the *Woolly Impostor* any minute, now." He grazed a power-suited paw at the thigh of the woman, who had come to stand before them in a dull-eyed daze: one of the creepers fell off at his touch, tried to wallow off into the shadows. "Uhatu: that creeper—"

"You want me to burn it down, Captain?"

"No, I want you to capture it, Uhatu."

"Yes, sir. But to tell the truth, I just wanna understand how to kill them."

'Sandro took the dazed woman's shoulder in a gentle grip, began to steer her toward the stairs. "Understanding how they live will also tell us how best to exterminate them wholesale, Corporal. And possibly, much more."

In the admiral's conference room aboard TRNS *Krishmahnta*, Ossian Wethermere nodded approvingly at the conciseness of 'Sandro Magee's presentation. "Thanks, Alessandro. Any other pertinent facts—or observations or hunches—that don't fit into an after-action report?"

"Well, sir, I've got an observation, but I'm sure it's something you've already noticed. Along with half of the ratings in the fleet."

Admiral Yoshikuni leaned forward. "Commodore Wethermere tells me you're a very direct man, Captain. Start proving it. What is this observation?"

"Yes, Admiral. Well, it's simply this: the Bugs aren't behaving at all the way history paints them. According to what I learned in school, they had only two discernible traits, both strategically and biologically: they were perpetually ravenous and they were absolutely xenocidal. Every other intelligent species was both a threat and a food source, which elicited the same response: when it came to other races, 'defeat 'em, eat 'em, and move on.'

"But this time? Sirs: we've followed behind them into four systems now—five, if you count C-4, which had no population to speak of—and so far, they haven't even bothered to land. All they do is bomb the hell out of everything that looks half-important, seed these creepers, and move on. And if fleet scuttlebutt is right, they didn't even pause long enough to take a small detour to hit the Telikans' most populous world, Myschtelik."

"I don't see how fleet scuttlebutt would provide you with that information, Captain," observed Kiiraathra'ostakjo.

"Well, sir, common sense helped. After all, we didn't go to Myschtelik ourselves to find out how the Telikans were doing, did we? And we could hardly afford *not* to confirm that, since if the Bugs had gone into the dead-end Myschtelik system, we would be risking going past them and having them appear on our tail. So I tend to suspect that the rumors about Commodore Wethermere's arm's-length meeting with a Telikan ship patrolling the warp-point into Myschtelik are accurate."

"And just how did you come by those rumors, Captain?" Modelo-Vo asked sharply.

"Commander, it would have been hard to avoid them. They were flying thicker than jack flies around a camp lamp. Not that the contact with the Telikans could have been hushed up, anyhow. Shortly after arriving in the Reymiimagar system, and just as we starting drawing abreast of the warp point into Myschtelik, the fleet stopped and then dressed its formation for battle. That was the first and only time since we started shadowing the Bugs that the fleet adopted a formation other than the extended van pattern that is best for maximum traveling and warp transit speed. And as for what had caused that change of formation—Well, some of us work regularly with the commodore's recon element and spacers drop hints, even when they don't exactly mean to. If you get my drift, sirs."

"No, I don't," Modelo-Vo snapped at the same instant that Wethermere drawled, "Oh, I certainly do get your drift." Before Modelo-Vo could recover, Ossian followed with, "So, 'Sandro, did those rumors tell you anything more specific about this ostensible meeting between my recon element and the Telikan ship?"

"Not much, sir," Magee admitted with a shrug, "except that they didn't want to let our fleet enter their system and they weren't willing to send any of their units along to help us. Which has a lot of us wondering, sirs."

"Define 'a lot of us,' Captain," ordered Yoshikuni.

"Well, ma'am, pretty much the whole fleet. At least all the parts that I have any contact with."

"I see. Anything else?"

'Sandro looked cautiously at the flag officers in the room. "Permission to speak freely, Admiral?"

"Granted. On this occasion, encouraged."

"Yes, sir." Magee was silent for a moment, apparently choosing his words very carefully. "Sirs, I'm very well aware that you won't and can't tell me—or anyone beyond the flag ranks—exactly what's going on, or all the information you've gathered about the Bugs thus far. But fleet morale suffers, particularly at the enlisted level, when the scuttlebutt points to some significant developments—like the fleet readying for battle, or like contact with the crew of that Telikan ship—but then zero information is shared, and no rumors leak out."

Yoshikuni folded her hands. "Captain Magee, as you said, and as I would expect from a long-service officer with a number of medals, you anticipate that you cannot and will not be kept abreast of all of our intelligence. So I'm going to presume that you also understand our need for absolute secrecy about key developments until, and unless, it is prudent to share them with all our personnel." Yoshikuni's tone bordered on being severe.

"Absolutely, ma'am. And I repeat that I am not trying to tell flag officers how to do their jobs. However, I feel it *is* important that I report on the conditions among the ranks. And I must, in good conscience, report that morale is being impacted by both the severity of our situation and the upper echelon's silence about it. Frankly, sir, the troops are scared."

"Scared? Of what? We haven't even joined battle—yet."

"Well, that's just it, sir. Sometimes, skulking about is more nerve-wracking than a straight-up fight, particularly for those of us who are accustomed to being on the sharp end when things get bad. And out here in the Star Union, with every passing day, there's more secrecy—which enlisted men tend to interpret as meaning more danger. And without any information to limit the scope of that danger, their imaginations begin to run wild."

Kiiraathra'ostakjo nodded slowly. "Some truths are particularly difficult to speak to superiors, Captain. Every one of my race, every *Zheeerlikou'valkhannaieee*, knows this because our leaders are often—mercurial—in comparison to your own. You have performed your duty—apprising us of fleet morale—well and faithfully, and with bravery that not all captains possess when confronting a room of frowning admirals."

"Agreed. You've discharged an uncomfortable duty admirably," said Yoshikuni with a sharp nod. "Now, anything else?"

"Well, sir, while we're on the topic of morale—"

Wethermere was fairly sure he heard Yoshikuni slowly exhale through a suppressed sigh. "Go ahead, Captain. Much as I hate hearing troubling news about my personnel, I'd rather have the information than stay ignorant."

"Well, sir, it's not exactly about *your* personnel." Magee glanced at Kiiraathra'ostakjo. "It's about his."

Eyes shifted to the Least Fang. Who nodded slowly. "I have heard some rumors from my own officers. It is true, then?"

"Is *what* true?" Yoshikuni insisted, an edge rising in her voice as she looked back and forth between the Marine and the Orion.

Magee nodded back at Kiiraathra'ostakjo, then turned toward Yoshikuni. "Admiral, the word in the bunkrooms is that there's some significant resentment growing among the Orion crews."

Yoshikuni's eyes were hard as she turned toward Kiiraathra'ostakjo. "And just when did you plan on telling me this, Least Fang?"

"When I had ascertained that the scope of the problem was both wide enough and severe enough to warrant the attention of this already overburdened command group," the Orion answered. "I received decisive reports just this morning and planned to present the results as soon as we finished hearing the captain's after-action report. However, his comment now tells me that the resentment among my crews is continuing to grow and becoming more widely known. It must be dealt with—harshly, if necessary."

Narrok's smaller tentacles writhed in a muted, slow-motion chaos-dance. "I do not understand: what, exactly, is the source of your crews' resentment?"

"I suspect," Wethermere interjected, "that the Orions blame the rest of the PSU, but particularly the human contingent, for abandoning their homeworld—well, both homeworlds—at their hour of need."

"But . . . that's absurd," Modelo-Vo sputtered with his customary lack of tact.

Kiiraathra'ostakjo's response gave the lie to all the stereotypes about Orion temper and impetuosity: he merely nodded in response. "It is irrationality compounded upon irrationality. I am quite sure that it was not a sudden choice, but rather, compliance with worst-case contingency planning, that led the PSU's High Command to rightly determine that it would have been strategic suicide to leave Unity Warp Point Five open. Indeed, the remaining fleets of the PSU—which remain only because they were not committed piecemeal to a battle that had already been lost—are now the only hope my people have to be rescued from the depredations of the Kaituni. But accusations of 'human treachery' cannot be dismissed by countervailing facts."

Admiral Narrok's central eye blinked slowly. "I do not understand; how can facts lose their rhetorical power among reasonable beings?"

"Because the accusations are not driven by specific reasons, and so, cannot be reasoned with. Moreover, our Khan and his advisors are all dead. Every public edifice or social institution that mattered has been vaporized. Our fleets have been annihilated, both in the great battles fought at our homeworlds, but also, because the fury and disorganization that was rampant among the remaining elements led them to engage the enemy piecemeal. They were a pride of hunters that, had they worked together, could have defeated their immense adversary, but instead, were stomped into oblivion—one brave, futile element at a time.

"In short, we *Zheeerlikou'valkhannaieee*, who derive all our honor from risk and success, have failed. We risked all and lost all. And so a pain and fury rises up that many of us cannot contain, that must be discharged before it drives us mad. If we were fighting the Kaituini actively, they would be the sure and just targets of the rage of all my crews. But since we are not engaging the ones who actively killed our worlds and our way of life, those emotions will, for any who lack the mastery of their passions, turn upon those closest who also, in the more uncritical minds of my heartsick crews, most deserve it. It does not matter that logic does not support the narrative of human betrayal that they have constructed to validate their rage. They cannot be talked out of their resentment any more than they can be talked out of the deep wound that is the well of their fury.

"For now, I must drive them back from that well, even as I grieve with them for all that we have lost. But before I take up these grim matters aboard my ships, I must urge you, Admiral Yoshikuni, that we engage the enemy as quickly as is prudent. Although I am well aware"—he finished with a glance at Wethermere—"that it will be some time before such a course of action is practicable and wise."

"Practicality and wisdom notwithstanding, Least Fang, we may be taking the fight to the Bugs sooner than you expect," replied Yoshikuni. "If the morale and cohesiveness of this fleet is at stake, I might forego our current policy of waiting for the right moment to strike." She glanced at Wethermere. "Patience is not always a virtue."

"Patience can certainly devolve into lethargy and inactivity," Wethermere obliquely agreed. "However, Admiral, our waiting and watching has hardly become apathetic habit. Every system through which we shadow our prey, shows us more—both by direct evidence and inference—about the Bugs' numbers and capabilities. And besides, if Least Fang Kiiraathra'ostakjo does intend to crack down on his crews within the near future, then it would send the wrong message to also head straight into battle, as well."

"That doesn't make any sense," Modelo-Vo blurted out.

Ossian was rapidly coming to the conclusion that, when dealing with Yoshikuni's upstart Tactical Officer, patience had indeed ceased to be a virtue. However,

Kiiraathra intervened: "No, the commodore's assertion actually makes a great deal of sense. You must understand my people. If I punish them and then, immediately afterward, give them what we all know they want—battle with those who slaughtered their kith and kin—I, and all the flag officers of this fleet, will be perceived as weak. You do not punish a *Zheeerlikou'valkhannaieee* and then give him what he wants. It suggests you are irresolute and that you are uncertain that the punishment you meted out was both just and effective. You could not undermine your credibility, your *Vrr'rakhshee*—or 'command-honor'—more. So we should wait for several weeks after the punishments before we attack the Bugs."

Yoshinkuni frowned but nodded. "Very well, Least Fang. You know your own people best, and we shall follow your recommendations in this matter. But even so, I am getting pretty tired of surveying one Bug-slaughtered world after another. We'll be bringing the battle to them soon enough." She let her eyes graze across Ossian's on the way to Kiiraathra's, and Wethermere could read them clearly enough: there was going to be yet another debate about the advisability of trailing so far behind the Bugs—or about trailing them at all. Yoshikuni had been, from the first time he had seen her on her command bridge almost eight years ago, a fighting admiral in the classic style. Show her the enemy and she wanted to head straight at them, or at least make immediately executable plans to hit them as hard as possible. But the situation here in the Star Union was arguably not one for which a fighting admiral's temperament was well-suited. There were disturbing reports from survivors—and from the cloaked Telikan patrol ship that he had found standing overwatch on the warp point to Myschtelik—that the Bug Fleet was either larger than thought or had an immense number of auxiliaries moving along behind it. Furthermore, other than one *selnarm* buoy per system, there had not been any sign of the Kaituni squadron that had been dispatched to follow along behind the Bugs. And that was particularly worrisome, since, unless Wethermere found them first, they could arguably alert and mobilize the Bugs—and thereby destroy the profound yet fragile advantage of surprise held by the Bellerophon Arm's renamed "Relief Fleet." But beyond that quantifiable concern, Ossian was uneasy because the precise role of the vanished Kaituni was conjectured, not known, and so their objectives remained an unsolved variable in the overall tactical equation. And in Wethermere's experience, that made the Kaituni squadron a possible source of unpleasant surprises. Which the fleet could ill-afford.

Yoshikuni had turned back to Magee and was nodding. "Captain, I'm almost scared to ask, but—is there anything else?"

"No, sir. I think I've caused enough trouble for one day."

Yoshikuni—known widely as the Iron Admiral—answered him with an uncharacteristically broad smile. "Thank you, Captain. That will be all."

The big Marine stood, saluted, turned smartly, and was gone.

CHAPTER FORTY

When the door had slid closed behind Magee, Yoshikuni turned toward Ossian. "Given what the captain just told us about the rumored contact with a Telikan vessel that was blocking the warp point into Myschtelik, I think you need to check the security in your recon element, Commodore."

"I agree, Admiral—but I'll point out that unless you want to keep all the personnel in that element nonrotating, then the security issues become a matter of fleet intel, as well. Every rating—or pilot—who is on rotation with me moves out of my security bubble when they leave the recon unit. And the nature of our work is such that complete compartmentalization between my various ships is impossible. Witness the conjectures about the Telikan picket ship. No details, really, just a report that one had been encountered near the warp point to Myschtelik. Which suggests that the leak was not from the standing crew of the *Woolly Imposter* or *Viggen*."

"Then what are you suggesting?"

Kiiraathra leaned forward. "I believe Wethermere is

suggesting the rumors probably came to the fleet via the pilots who were on rotating assignment to man the fighters that the commodore's recon element hides in the cargo bays of both the *Woolly Imposter* and the *Fet'merah*. And I suspect that the commodore is probably correct in that assumption: the running crews of those two ships have had no rotation in or out since the encounter near Myschtelik, only the flight wing."

Yoshikuni looked simultaneously relieved and miffed. "Very well, but Commodore, I need you to push further ahead of the main body. Attack or no attack, I want to get, and stay, closer to the Bugs. We don't even know how many systems ahead of us they are, by now."

"I still advise against that, Admiral," Wethermere recommended, matching her contentious, not entirely professional, stare. "And, relevant to that, I have some updates from the research being conducted on the creepers which might underscore the caution I've been recommending."

"I'll take those reports under advisement, but for now—"

Narrok raised two of the larger tentacles on his right cluster. "I would like to hear what the commodore has found. In part, because I agree with him: it would not be propitious for us to press our foes any more closely than we are now."

Yoshikuni turned to Narrok—the second most senior fleet commander—with widened eyes. "Unless I am mistaken, Admiral, you were also of the opinion that our posture might be too cautious."

"You are correct: I shared your opinion that we could afford to be somewhat more aggressive in following the enemy."

"And now you *agree* with Commodore Wethermere? Why?"

"Because, Admiral Yoshikuni, we have begun decoding the static *selnarm* report-buoys left behind by the Kaituni squadron that is trailing the Arachnids. What we have been learning from them has left me—uneasy."

"Why? What's their content?"

Narrok straightened. "Firstly, I cannot tell you all their 'content' yet, since *selnarm* can be coded almost as effectively as lexical communication. So the Kaituni exchanges are not transparent to us, nor are they even using a single code. We have access to some uncoded data—routine housekeeping is what you call it, I believe—but my misgivings arise not from what is in the messages, but from how many of them there are. And from how much housekeeping is being relayed. In short, it is out of all proportion for any mere squadron of ships, Kaituni or otherwise."

"Could it be caused by their need to report on the star systems, and what the Bugs did to each, in detail?"

"No, Commander Modelo-Vo, although that is a useful question. Frankly, there is only one factor which generally tends to necessitate this exponential of increase in communications volume."

Yoshikuni frowned. "Increased fleet size."

"Precisely. Multiple reports from each hull, and all attached logistics—including how maintenance induces constant variations in drive signature, readiness rating, crew and section reports—are the only explicable sources for this density of traffic. It would be different if there were civilian communication packets included—they can dwarf even fleet reports—but out here, where all the star systems behind us, and presumably several in front of us, have been rendered functionally inert by the Arachnids, there is no reasonable source or destination for civilian-grade Kaituni comm-traffic. And besides, the structure and security protocols on all the messages are definitively military in nature."

"So you think there's a whole Kaituni *fleet* ahead of us?"

"It is a distinct possibility. And it makes tactical sense."

Kiiraathra'ostakjo passed a paw at his long whiskers. "How so?"

Narrok allowed his spine to relax slightly. "I am familiar with the records of your encounters with the Omnivoracity, since the First Dispersate needed to ascertain if the accounts of your war with them was fabricated or genuine. In consequence, I may assure you that if the Kaituni learned what I learned, they would not believe a small squadron of their ships could reliably influence the movement and probable path of so large an Arachnid fleet. Since the Kaituni cannot apparently communicate with the Omnivoracity, they would have to establish and exert such influence through force."

"You mean, you think the Kaituni are ahead of us in greater force, and are nipping at the heels of their own war-dogs?" Modelo-Vo asked.

"Actual confrontations might have occurred once or twice, but I suspect that the Arachnids learned that moving toward the Kaituni was infinitely less productive than moving away from them. At the same time, they probably discerned that the path left open to them was filled with food-rich target worlds. Like any reflex predator—even a sophisticated one—they saw no risk in avoiding the negative stimuli projected by the Kaituni, and saw gain to be had by pursuing the positive stimuli that lay in the opposite direction. I am sure they considered this at length, mindful of a trap, but found none. At least, not so far."

"Admiral Yoshikuni," Wethermere injected into the silence that followed Narrok's statement, "this actually conforms to a number of the statements made by the Telikans who waved us away at the warp point to Myschtelik. Their reports of a second fleet moving through the Reymiimagar system after the passage of the Bugs' main body now seems a great deal more credible than the other explanations we'd been hypothesizing, such as the Telikans seeing two different parts of the Bug fleet because they had very intermittent safe windows during which they could scan the system. They might, instead, really have seen two different fleets: one Bug, one Kaituni."

Yoshikuni tossed down her stylus. "Unfortunately, I am compelled to agree. But here's what I want to know: if there *is* a whole Kaituni fleet between us and the Bugs—and that is a very big 'if'—then how the hell did it get there? Our sensors saw the Bug fleet move through Mymzher to the Franos warp point. There was no other notable traffic in the whole time we had it under observation, only the small Kaituni squadron that left Mymzher the same way, just before the commodore's recon element put the bag on the single picket ship they'd left behind. And from that point on, nothing else moved through the system. But according to the warp-line map"—she gestured at the holo-flat at the center of the conference table—"there's a single pathway without external connections from Franos all the way to here. So how did a whole Kaituni fleet get ahead of us?"

"With respect, Admiral," Modelo-Vo pointed out

meekly, "there is another point of access to that warp line through Reymiimagar." He pointed. "There's the warp-point to the X-2 cluster."

Yoshikuni shook her head. "No, I think that's an extremely unlikely avenue of arrival for the Kaituni. Firstly, that whole cluster is still beyond Unity Point Three, so how would the Kaituni get to it, given all their Dispersates touched down in or very near Orion space? Secondly, the most militarily capable race of the Star Union, the Crucians, have a considerable colony in that cluster, and from what we heard from the Telikans, the Crucians haven't been attacked yet. So I very much doubt that this hypothetical Kaituni fleet emerged from X-2 into the warp line we're looking at." She stared at the map again. "No, something doesn't add up."

Wethermere nodded. "I quite agree, Admiral. And here's another, but probably related mystery to add to the origins of the possible Kaituni fleet ahead of us." He manipulated his control wand. Two timelines, superimposed on a single grid, supplanted the warp-line diagram.

"What are we looking at, Commodore?" Yoshikuni asked, folding her hands.

"The red timeline is a pretty solid estimate of when the Bugs began their attack on the main world of Tevreelan, the third planet."

"That's an extraordinarily precise 'estimate,' Commodore. How did you get it? I thought you didn't find any persons dirtside who were still capable of communicating reliably."

"That is correct, Admiral. But we were fortunate enough to know that one of their primary space-habitats was actually in a geostationary orbit with a rotational rate of .8 rpm. We also had detailed mass data on it. That gives us an excellent starting point for the debris that was ejected from it when the station was disabled by a single, center-of-mass railgun projectile."

Modelo-Vo was nodding approvingly. "And so once you located the leading edge of that debris cloud and measured its velocity, you had all the mathematical components necessary to calculate how long it had taken for it to travel from the point of impact to the point where you discovered it."

"Correct, although we had to guess at the energy imparted by the impact of the rail gun projectile. But, given that the Bugs only use two types, we were able to narrow it down pretty quickly. So the Bugs attacked the Tevreelan system thirteen days ago."

"And what is the other timeline?" Narrok asked.

"That, Admiral, is a timeline of the maturation cycle of a creeper. We've now had samples of them under observation since we surveyed the aftermath on Telik."

The gathered officers stared at the timeline. Glances were exchanged. "Commodore," observed Modelo-Vo with what sounded like embarrassed solicitude, "I think your chart is wrong."

"Why is that, Commander?"

"Because it shows that the creepers take twenty-two days—at a minimum—to reach the maturity state of those you found on Tevreelan."

"Yes, that is correct."

"But—but that would put them on Tevreelan almost ten days before the Bugs attacked it."

"Again, that is correct."

Yoshikuni saw it first. "Wait a minute. Are you telling us that the creepers were planted on the planet *before* the Bugs hit it?"

Ossian nodded. "Yes, Admiral, that is precisely what I'm telling you."

Narrok had sat up straighter once again. "That changes many of our assumptions—and explains much of what we've seen since entering the Star Union. Particularly the ease with which the Omnivoracity devastated the main worlds in each system. This means that the infestation did not follow the bombardments: it preceded them, and its effects upon the local population and infrastructure probably degraded all their defenses and ability to organize evacuations."

"So the Bugs sent advance units—possibly quite small and innocuous—to pre-seed the creepers," Kiiraathra'ostakjo growled. "And their primary purpose was not to reduce the population, but to incapacitate it with the neurological disease they spread among each planetary population as they bred and grew."

"And the bite-transferred pathogen responsible for that disease is proving to be most unusual," Wethermere added. "Tevreelan Three is the first planet we've encountered in the Star Union that had any permanent human habitation at all. Namely, that's the consulate to which we sent Magee, and which was established in a fairly small, remote city as a kind of xenocultural experiment in alternative diplomatic contact. So that gave us our first chance to see what the creepers' disease does to an intelligent life-form. Before Tevreelan, we landed near major cities and so never got a look at how these creatures affected the local Telikans or Crucians, who had all died or fled into the country. Where we assumed the creepers had hunted them down and consumed them." Wethermere brought up a collage of images, depicting the various humans who had been discovered in or around the consulate's precincts. "But as you can see, we're revising that theory in light of what we found here."

Yoshikuni's eyes were hard as they scanned across the pictures. "The rest of the survivors were all covered with creepers, like the pictures you're showing?"

"No, only the persons who were still routinely ambulatory. After that, the creepers apparently drop off, gorged. They then enter into a reproductory hibernation, which we currently have under live observation in the fleet quarantine ship. We'll have dissection studies to confirm the data we've been gathering before the day is out, but confidence is high that the creepers are not designed to kill their prey. Rather, they draw enough sustenance to breed. And while attached, they introduce a microorganism into the circulatory system of their victims that broadly interferes with the operation and production of neurohumors in most carbon-based biologies."

Modelo-Vo narrowed his eyes at the images. "Leading to the lassitude, disorientation, aimlessness, and intermittent activity."

"Yes. Infected humans fade to the point where they are just barely able to eat, drink, and eliminate before becoming utterly exhausted. The persons we found in the consulate reported that the Telikans were affected differently: seizures that completely wiped their short-term memories. We didn't encounter any Telikans, but they were evidently wandering around the woods, lost, just trying to survive day to day."

"What an odd disease," Narrok mused.

"Unusual, yes, but maybe not exactly odd, Admiral," Wethermere offered. And waited.

"Please, Commodore. Share your thoughts."

"Yes, sir. There is one perspective from which this

particular malady and its aftermath—both in terms of the creepers and their victims—might be quite ruthlessly pragmatic. You will note that although the victims are rendered helpless, they are not destroyed. Also, the succeeding generations of creepers range further to attack animals and any communities that were spared during the Bugs' orbital attacks."

Kiiraathra'ostakjo reared back. "So you are suggesting that, both by breeding more creepers and allowing survivors to live—albeit barely—that the Bugs are creating food caches. And, unlike the first war we fought with them, they do not delay themselves, nor diminish their offensive force by tasking it with either occupation or . . . provisioning."

"Precisely," finished Ossian, shutting off the holo-projector and the ghastly images.

"Yes, but why?" asked Yoshikuni after a brief silence. "Why not stop and—feed—the way they did last time? Because a Kaituni fleet is behind them, pushing?"

"Possibly, Admiral,'" Wethermere allowed. "But I consider that unlikely."

Narrok nodded. "Yes. This organism—this 'creeper,' as you call it—is not something the Kaituni gave to the Arachnids. It is a pre-evolutionary form of the Arachnids themselves, is it not?" Seeing Wethermere's nod, he continued. "So the only reasonable conclusion is that, before the Omnivoracity had awareness of the Kaituni, they had elected to weaponize this precursor organism. They may have been intending to do so at the end of your first war with them; that may have been part of what Amunsit's agents learned. But either way, it reflects a changed perspective on how the Omnivoracity means to wage war."

Yoshikuni nodded. "They were too slow, last time. Every time they stopped, we had enough time to regroup, throw up defenses, start building for a counterattack. The survivors in their hidden system must have resolved to analyze their failures in the war with us, and if they did, they would naturally discern that their strategic pace was too slow. They had to get and stay inside our decision cycle in order to hit us with one staggering blow after another and so prevent us from ever having the time to recover and rethink our prosecution of the war."

"So now they intend to carry through their assault in one long rush and then return to the conquered worlds, one after the other, to reap the bloody crops they have sown," Kiiraathra'ostakjo spat.

"So it seems," Wethermere commented.

"Your tone suggests some reservations with that conclusion—even though it is your own, Commodore." Narrok's three eyes were upon him, unblinking.

Ossian shrugged. "I do have reservations, Admiral. But not with the conclusion. I just—well, I think we're still missing something. Call it a hunch, but when we zoom back and consider all the special strategies and force-shifting required to get the Bugs back in position to lay waste to the Star Union a second time, I've got to wonder: is it all worth it? Couldn't this effort and these resources have been dedicated to a more crucial objective? Because while the Star Union is significant, it really could not have hoped to disrupt any of their other plans that we've seen up until this point." Wethermere shook his head. "No, they—the Kaituni, and maybe, separately, the Bugs—are up to something else. I just wish I knew what it was."

"Well," announced Yoshikuni, standing abruptly,

"we're not going to figure it out sitting here. We've all secondary briefings to attend and ships to get to. Least Fang, do you need to meet with me and Admiral Narrok about your morale issues?"

"Admiral, since those issues are now generally known and must be addressed, I would prefer to put off a further briefing until I have formulated the necessary disciplinary action for my crews, and so report all items at once."

"Excellent. Then everyone here is done. Except for you, Commodore. You've got some early lab results on a possible cure for the creeper virus, I believe?"

"That is correct, Admiral." By the time he said it, he and Yoshikuni were the only two people left.

"Then let's get out of this cavern of a room. We'll work over dinner. My quarters?"

Wethermere smiled. "Suits me fine, Admiral."

On the table in Miharu Yoshikuni's reading room, the bio reports lay forgotten next to a pair of cold, untouched dinners.

Wethermere put a hand on the base of Yoshikuni's spine. Curled up on the other half of the unfolded hand-crafted futon, she emitted a catlike sound that reminded him of the ones many Orions made just before they drifted off to sleep. "Hey," he said.

"Hey what?" Miharu's voice was unconvincingly brusque.

"Hey. We have to talk."

She had rolled around to face him before he could blink. Her face was all at once severe and worried. "Talk about what?"

He smiled. "No, not 'that talk.'" And they both

knew the one he meant. As a commodore, Ossian just barely passed the propriety test governing fraternization between different ranks. She was flag rank; he was almost. Sort of. Commodores occupied a gray zone between flag and field ranks—and different boards of inquiry had expressed different opinions about their actual status across the history of both their navies.

She smiled back, through which he could detect a faint annoyance at herself for allowing herself to appear concerned. Iron Admiral Miharu Yoshikuni was a supremely confident commander but was less than comfortable when it came to navigating the slalom course of a relationship that necessarily altered between professional and private spheres. "Then what do you want to talk about?" she asked almost flippantly.

"Admiral, I wish to discuss our rules of engagement."

She had evidently heard the intimate leer in his tone. She pressed herself closer to him. "Here's my one rule of engagement, Commodore. No plan survives first contact with reality."

"I'm serious, Miharu. I'm not sure you should be having me come to all the flag staff meetings."

"Well, I am. Maybe you forgot you're the ranking PSU officer in this fleet? And that you're the CO of what is both our tactical recon and strategic intelligence element? And that you have commendations for innovative strategic and tactical thought as long as my legs?" Which she moved languorously. "So, yes, you keep coming to the meetings."

"Then I think we have to watch our eye contact and—exchanges."

"Ossian, do you really think anyone *doesn't* know that we're, well—an item?"

"No, but I don't want that to impact morale."

Miharu raised up on one elbow. "How would it impact morale?"

"You know how people can be: they may say otherwise to themselves and each other, but deep down, they assume that a personal relationship undermines objectivity, creates favoritism—if only subconsciously."

She pulled back, surveyed Wethermere with surprisingly detached eyes. "Well, if they think that, they don't know *me*."

"No, some of them don't—and that's my point. This fleet, and its recent additions, *don't* know you, Miharu. They don't know that you're more likely to be *harder* on a person with whom you have a personal relationship."

"Commodore, are you suggesting that I'm guilty of overcompensating?"

"Admiral, such a thought never once crossed my mind."

"No, it's probably crossed it twenty times, knowing you." She smiled.

A hell of a lot more than that, he thought. And smiled, too.

"So stop worrying about our rules of engagement, Commodore," she murmured. "I've got matters well in hand." Her voice and eyes conspired to form a profound leer.

"As you say, Admiral, you have matters well in hand."

"I'm glad you've noticed. Now stop calling me Admiral."

CHAPTER FORTY-ONE

Junior Cluster Leader Jathruf-jem stared at the contact which had just appeared in his bridge's holopod and considered his options.

"Do you wish to launch a courier drone, Cluster Leader?" his Second, Brem-sheef, sent anxiously.

Jathruf-jem returned a *selnarmic* wave of calm, with an invocation of (patience, reflection). Technically, he should launch a courier the moment he had any unexpected contacts whatsoever. As the rear-guard element patrolling the crucial warp-point access zone in the Bug 29 system, his would be the first warning of approaching danger.

Except it seemed impossible that this sensor contact could represent any danger. Firstly, the signal came from the opposite direction of the warp point over which he stood watch, the one into the system the humans had designated Bug 28. If, in fact, there were any enemies following them, they had to come from the system's only other warp point: the one that led to Pajzomo, and which was located on the opposite side of this system. The sensor contact, had, by comparison, come from an oblique angle *behind* Jathruf-jem's two ships and the warp point he guarded.

And then there was the matter of this sensor contact's intermittent signaling. Its communications protocols were a match for the combination marker/*selnarmic*-relay buoys that the forward units had left behind in this very system, and which typically lay still and dark until signaled to awaken, usually to replace a similar unit that had been destroyed by enemy action.

But apparently this buoy was either malfunctioning or damaged and had started signaling without provocation. And worse still, it was active not merely on *selnarmic* channels—that would have been bad enough—but broadcast as well. If it went on signaling, it would call *any* intruder's attention to the region near the warp point into Bug 28. And that was unacceptable.

But otherwise, it hardly seemed a threat. And that put Jathruf-jem on the horns of a dilemma his commanders had never considered: if he followed his orders to the letter, he would send a *selnarmic* courier through the warp point into Bug 28, contrary indicators notwithstanding. And the moment the courier arrived there, every Kaituni unit available would begin to reconfigure into a formation to hold that warp point against all intruders. Meaning that whatever other operations they were undertaking would be immediately and completely ruined.

Jathruf-jem flexed his smaller tendrils in vexation. It would not matter if he explained that he had just been following orders. His fellow *Destoshaz* would deride him as wanting self-assurance and boldness, since he had summoned all their ships to repel—what? A single, malfunctioning buoy that couldn't even move under its own power?

No, Jathruf-jem decided with a straightening snap of those same, smaller tendrils. To send the courier drone was not in keeping with the intent of his orders. It was merely a nervous—not to say slavish—compliance to the letter of them. "The courier is not needed in this circumstance, Brem-sheef."

"But our orders—"

"Do not mean for us to spread panic and interrupt our pod-mates' operations because we have come across a malfunctioning buoy."

"Well—at least we must do something about the buoy itself. Its transmissions—"

(Agreement, accord, promptitude) "Yes, we must silence it. Dispatch the *Degruz-pahr* to investigate. Once they have completed their approach, they are to send an EVA team to examine the buoy for tampering, and, assuming it is deemed safe, take it aboard."

"Group Leader, is it prudent to send our only other hull off-station merely to deal with a buoy?"

(Impatience, decisiveness) "Second, that buoy is no more than thirty light-seconds out from our patrol coordinates. This will be, at most, a brief change in our defensive posture and well within the operational latitude that has been entrusted to me." *I hope.* "During this maneuver, we will move our own hull to a more central overwatch position to protect the warp point behind us."

"In order to provide the same coverage arc, we will need to not merely center our ship on the warp-point access route, but move it slightly outward. And deploy our fighter triads."

"All of which we shall do, as per contingency. And we will have recovered to our prior, two-hull defensive posture within forty minutes at most. Do our sensors show anything within even a light-hour?"

"No, Group Leader. Sensors are clear."

"Very well. Execute your orders, Second."

Brem-sheef responded with a *selnarmic* flourish of (accord, confidence, compliance). In the holopod, the smaller of the two ships in Jathruf-jem's detachment—the destroyer *Degruz-pah*r—broke away from its patrol position on the spinward side of the warp-point's entry path and began angling toward the malfunctioning buoy. His own ship, the *Meftr-bak*, drifted slowly from its trailing-side position to the center of the navigation funnel that led into the warp point, while also moving slightly further away from the anomaly to provide a wider arc of defensive coverage. Small blips emerged from the icon denoting his light attack cruiser even as the he felt slight tremors in its deck: the *Meftr-bak's* small flight wing of both *selnarmically*-controlled and ROV/semi-autonomous fighters were deploying in their triads. They began moving to take up evenly dispersed picket points along the defensive frontage.

"Cluster Leader, the *Degruz-pah*r is requesting permission to target the buoy with active arrays, in the event that it has been weaponized and programmed to attack."

Weaponized by whom? Jathruf-jem was tempted to ask, but only sent (prudence): "Confirm sensors show no possibilities of enemy contacts that might detect our active sensors."

"None, Cluster Leader."

"Then *Degruz-pah*r may commence using active arrays to acquire a targeting solution for the buoy."

"Yes, Cluster Leader. Fighters are now in place and all circuits testing as—Cluster Leader! (Surprise, panic.) Behind us—contact; no, *contacts!*—bearing—"

"I see it, Second." But seeing the unfolding situation in the holopod did not aid understanding it. From out of nowhere—literally—enemy fighters, both human and Orion, were emerging from the sheer vacuum of space.

A split second later, Jathruf-jem's sensors showed their source as if an intervening shroud had dissolved: a massive Orion fleet carrier had somehow emerged out of the vacuum also, situated directly between his ships and the warp point into Bug 28. *Degruz-pahr* was not only too far off to help, but would stand no chance against either the fighters or the carrier's own considerable armament. Meanwhile, the carrier continued to spew out a steady stream of fighters that would surely overwhelm Jathruf-jem's—if given time. "Second, order fighter triads One through Four to conduct an immediate frontal counterattack. Triad Five is to make for the warp point at all speed."

"Group Leader, how will Triad Five be able to transit—?"

"Shift the robot fighters to automated courier mode: they will make transit and sound the alarm that we will not be able to."

"Yes, Group Leader. I will—" Brem-sheef halted in mid-send and, except for a series of *befthels* that kept all three of his eyes blinking rapidly at the holopod's display, was motionless.

Jathruf-jem glanced at the holopod himself, and restrained the impulse to do just what his Second had done—

—upon seeing the unthinkable become reality: Triad Five's two robotic fighters had, contrary to orders, veered away from the warp point. And were headed directly back toward *Meftr-bak*, weapons charging. . . .

The mood in the corridors of TRNS *Krishmahnta* was very close to jubilant. Having destroyed a Kaituni attack cruiser and battered a destroyer so severely that its crew no longer had sufficient control to scuttle it, was not, in the scheme of the greater conflict, a significant victory. Even the satisfaction of finally striking a blow against, rather than simply skulking after, the enemy did not answer to the almost electric mood that had suffused the flagship and was rapidly spreading through the fleet. No, realized Alessandro Magee as the decontamination protocol ended and he stepped out into the ready bay for returning ship's troops, the excitement was generated by *how* the victory had been won.

He removed his helmet, nodded to acknowledge a few pats on the back—he had led the first boarding team personally, despite Harry Li's wet-hen neuroses—and strode out of the bay.

And straight into Jennifer's arms.

"Jen!" he exclaimed, shocked to see that she was already on the flagship. "How—or why, did you—?"

"Yoshikuni brought all the command and intel staff over as soon as we heard the news four hours ago."

"Oh, right. You got the results by *selnarmic* courier."

"Well, we got *some* results. We know that the Kaituni went for the buoy that the *Viggen* deposited while running under stealth, that our ships beat theirs without taking a single loss, and that we captured what was left of the smaller of their two ships. But how did you manage to keep them from getting at least one courier, or one robot fighter, through the warp point to warn the rest of their squadron?"

'Sandro smiled. "Jen, I hate to disappoint you, but you already know as much or more than I do. I just know that whatever technical wizardry Chong and Lentsul have been cooking up in secret for months was given its trial run today—and apparently it worked. The com chatter I heard about it was in code, and I'm pretty sure it didn't function at one hundred percent spec, but it was decisive. I just wish I knew what it was."

"Well, maybe that's what they're going to tell us in the briefing."

"Don't bet on it, Jen. Hell, I'd bet against it. We've got a lot of Arduan ships along with us; if any one *Destoshaz* on any one of those hulls was to decide to defect to the Kaituni, we'd lose whatever edge this new device could buy for us." He shook his head. "I can't see any of the senior command staff deciding to share out *that* kind of info."

"Well," Jen asked, "why the big confab, then?"

"I think," 'Sandro said, cupping her chin with his hand, "they're going to tell us what happens next—and maybe some of what they've found out about what's going on further up the warp line. Come on; let's get good seats."

As if seating at such meetings was ever a matter of choice.

✧ ✧ ✧

Mretlak glanced at Lentsul, whose *selnarm* was like a self-perpetuating supernova of insufficiently shrouded (gratification, pride, accomplishment). And its continuing reignition was sparked by praise from a human he still inherently distrusted: Miharu Yoshikuni.

"Group Leader Lentsul and Captain Chong's work made it possible for us to interrupt the command and control links between the *selnarmically*-controlled Kaituni fighters and their robotic wingmen, and so, kept the engagement entirely contained to the Bug 29 system."

"I don't suppose we are going to learn any more about how that command-and-control disruption was achieved?" drawled Modelo-Vo.

"I am afraid not," Admiral Narrok replied. "The need-to-know classification for that project is both very high, and very limited, at this point. We anticipate sharing it more broadly in the coming weeks, as we finalize plans for conducting a larger assault against the Kaituni elements in this theater of operations. But until that time, we will be maintaining the current secrecy protocols while working to perfect the system in question."

"Then can someone at least explain how today's attack was carried out?"

"What do you mean, exactly, Commander?" Kiiraathra'ostakjo asked.

"Admiral, with all due respect, you *must* understand what I'm getting at. Your fighters emerged from the *Celmithyr'theaanouw*'s stealth field and already had targeting solutions. But you can't see or scan anything from inside a stealth field, so how did they have a lock already?" Modelo-Vo sounded particularly sour, probably since, as Yoshikuni's Fleet Tactical officer, he felt he should have been included in the need-to-know circle that Narrok had referred to. But as the weeks had worn on, Modelo-Vo's role had become limited to what Mretlak thought of as "conventional tactical" concerns. The unusual and innovative activities had become Wethermere's province, along with nearly autonomous control over the increasingly essential Fleet Recon element.

The Orion smoothed his mane. "I believe Commodore Wethermere was the one who devised the strategy you are inquiring about, in concert with Admiral Narrok." Kiiraathra glanced over at Wethermere.

Who took the cue. "A stealth field is indeed opaque to everything in the electromagnetic spectrum, limited only by its capacity to absorb energy. But as we demonstrated when we captured the Kaituni picket ship in Mymzher, *selnarm* is unaffected. So the buoy—one of the several left behind by the Kaituni from here to Franos—was not only modified to appear to be malfunctioning, but equipped with a very acute passive sensor package."

Modelo-Vo saw the rest of it without prompting. "So when the Kaituni took the precaution of targeting the buoy with active sensors, the buoy acquired a reciprocal lock with its passive sensors and relayed that data by *selnarmic* link to an Arduan operator on board the *Celmithyr'theaanouw*."

"That and a little more. The passive sensors were sensitive enough to detect the drive of the two Kaituni hulls. The one that approached the buoy become consistently stronger and so the sensor was able to interpolate a trajectory by tracking back along the approach of that energy return."

"Which," Narrok concluded, "indicated the ship's approximate starting point. By inference, this also gave a very close estimate of the coordinates of the second hull, which repositioned itself according to our conventional doctrine for adapting to reduced perimeter defenses. Consequently, the fighters that came through the *Celmithyr'theaanouw*'s falling stealth screen had a fairly small footprint to scan, and they acquired lock within two seconds."

The mood in the room was not merely satisfied, but truculently exultant. Even Lentsul—*Lentsul!*—radiated an eagerness to move his work to the next level of success, even if its final battle-proofing came at the cost of destroying millions of Illudor's children, however misled they might be. Mretlak kept his glum ruminations to himself, fearing how it might seem if anyone sensed that he did not share in the same measure of jubilation. It was, it seemed, unavoidable that the Arduans of the First Dispersate would have to provide many of the tools whereby the great majority of their living brothers and sisters would be discarnated. And that was a grim business, more properly evocative of mourning than celebration.

Worried that his reservations might escape the margins of his *selnarm*—and Ankaht was acutely perceptive of such nuances, even for a *shaxzhu*—Mretlak raised an inquisitive tentacle. "Admiral Yoshikuni, I suspect that if your only topic was the success of the two experimental attack protocols that were validated in today's ambush, you would simply have informed us so by lascom. Yet here we sit. So, I wonder: is there something else you have called us together to hear? Something, perhaps, that has come to light through the analysis of the computers on board the disabled Kaituni destroyer?"

Yoshikuni smiled at Mretlak. "You are absolutely correct, Senior Group Leader Mretlak. And it was important to begin our meeting with a report on how successful today's trial runs were—because we are going to have desperate need of those tactics, and every other conceivable advantage, in the weeks to come."

As Yoshikuni's eyes made the circuit of the round conference table, her smile faded. "We'll start with the least ominous news first. It's pretty much a certainty that two separate Bug forces split off from the main fleet that we've been following since it passed through the Mymzher system. Here in Pajzomo, we found evidence that the Kaituni had to exert some force to keep the Bugs going on the main warp line, through to Bug 28 and Bug 29. And the Kaituni weren't fully successful: at least a few Bugs made transit. In fact, the naval combat spoor we found here is a close match to what we found when we passed through the Skriischnagar system, just a few weeks after Tevreelan."

"So," growled Kiiraathra'ostakjo, "our conjecture—that the Bugs intended to move off the main warp line and down through the prey-rich worlds of the line that runs down to Menkasahr—has been confirmed."

Yoshikuni nodded. "Sure looks like it. Here in Pajzomo, it's pretty clear that the whole Bug fleet was headed toward the warp point to Jzotayar, the other entrance to that same target-rich cul-de-sac. But before more than a few of their lead elements could make transit, the Kaituni came in and headed them off—hard, just like they did in the Skriischnagar system. The Bugs got the worst of the exchange, shifted course, moved toward the only other reasonable course open to them: the warp point to Bug 29."

Chong nodded. "And if our guess is right, those first few Bugs that entered the cul-de-sac were the ships best equipped to seed creepers and follow up on the aftermath of their infestation."

Yoshikuni chopped her hand at the warp-point map. "Our biggest problem is that we have no way of knowing how large a squadron the Bugs slipped away down each of those warp line shunts into that cul-de-sac. And here's why that ignorance is dangerous: if the Bugs go through those worlds quickly, link up, and come out as a unified force, we could have them on our own tail if we continue to follow the fleet we're shadowing right now. And we can't afford to leave any squadrons behind to plug up the cul-de-sac access points in both Skriischnagar and Pajzomo. So we need to understand that by pressing forward, we are potentially putting ourselves between two hostile forces."

Modelo-Vo looked at the map. "Should we break off, head into the cul-de-sac ourselves, find the Bugs and beat them there? Even joined together, their two squadrons won't match us in quantity, and certainly not in quality. And if we find them separated, that offensive would be just that much easier and decisive."

Narrok's clusters flattened into a negation. "There are too many uncertainties to entertain that course of action. How long will it take to find them? Will we have the advantage of surprise, or will they detect us first? Will we find ourselves having to assault a warp-point held against us? If we do, that could severely offset our advantages in both quantity and quality of ships. No," he concluded with an expressive trailing of tentacles, "as much as I dislike doing so, we must press forward without assured rear area security. Indeed, pressing forward has become more, not less, urgent."

Mretlak looked at the map and closed his eyes slowly. Now that the Bugs had been shepherded past both entries into their traditional feeding zone, there was only one logical strategic objective which explained the course upon which the Kaituni were keeping them. "Yes, I see the urgency," Mretlak said calmly. "They are heading toward Sol."

CHAPTER FORTY-TWO

Wethermere glanced at Mretlak, struck—as always—at just how far-sighted and clever the Arduan was, and how fortunate it was that they were allies, not enemies. "Yes, Mretlak. It's pretty clear the Kaituni are pushing the Bugs toward Sol. Or to express their immediate strategic goals more narrowly, they mean to emerge into Admiral Trevayne's rear area at Bug 15." Ossian used a light pencil to draw the almost ineluctable path. "Let's assume that the Bug fleet is in Bug 27 right now. Their logical route of advance—and they have only one, weaker alternative—is through Bug 26, Bug 25, Bug 24, and on into Bug 15."

Jennifer Pietchkov sounded as if she was trying not to swallow her tongue. "My God. Bug 15 is right next to Alpha Centauri. And that's right next to Sol."

"Yes. But Bug 15 is also several systems behind where Admiral Trevayne is probably trying to hold the main concentration of Kaituni fleets that will be coming up at him through Pesthouse. If the enemy fleets in front of us can get in behind him"—Wethermere snapped off the light pencil—"Sol's primary defensive force will have been cut off from it and Trevayne has no route of retreat. Instead, he'll be ground down between one set of millstones rising up the warp line and another set descending from higher up."

"What doesn't make any sense to me, sirs," Alessandro Magee said quietly, "is that a single squadron of pretty light Kaituni ships can steer a huge Bug fleet around so easily." The hanging tone with which he finished invited comment.

Ankaht let breath sigh out of her vestigial gills. "You are most perceptive, Captain. The answer, as you no doubt suspect, is that the Kaituni force we've been trailing is no mere squadron. It is a whole Dispersate's fleet."

Modelo-Vo, who'd been kept out of the most recent confidential strategy discussions, jolted as if he'd been stuck by a pin. "A—whole Dispersate? And how the hell did they get past us? We've been over this: the Kaituni couldn't have reached Franos ahead of the Bugs, and we'd have seen that kind of unit if it moved in behind them. Granted, there's been a lot of anomalous comm traffic back to the intermittent pickets the Kaituni have left in their wake, but—"

"That communication traffic is no longer anomalous, Commander," Ankaht explained. "We had hints of this when we examined some of the Kaituni wreckage left behind from their Bug-herding skirmish in Skriischnagar, but the destroyer we captured today confirmed our suspicions: a Dispersate was present in the Star Union ahead of the Bugs because this is where it ended its journey from Ardu. This is the landing site of yet another Dispersate."

"So they were setting up for this maneuver for years?"

"They would have had to, Commander. And I suspect they did so the moment that their leader, the *Destoșhaz'at*, received confirmation that the Omnivoracity still existed. With that knowledge in hand, and so many Dispersates approaching this region of space on so many different trajectories, I suspect he was able to redirect one to a system here in the Star Union. To be specific, this Dispersate arrived undetected in the Riikfahryn system, the one we arrived in after Treveelan. From there, they evidently avoided Treveelan and Reymiimagar by traveling to Skriischnagar and heading into Rehlkohr. Their data suggests they then pushed through the populated systems of Gytohkiir and Omm-Ajaar and followed the shunt warp-line over to X-2, where they awaited word that the Bug fleet was passing through Reymiimagar. I suspect the squadron following the Bugs from Franos sent a *selnarmic* courier to alert the fleet they correctly expected to be waiting in X-2, which transited into Reymiimagar and made sure that the Bugs did not assault the Myschtelik warp point. That would have been a pointless waste of time and resources, from the Kaituni perspective."

Modelo-Vo nodded. "So that's why the Kaituni were able to herd the Bugs past their favorite feeding grounds: they had a whole Dispersate's worth of persuasion with which to enforce their will. But damn it," he said almost as though he were arguing with himself, "the Bugs may be pretty direct, but they're not stupid. They *have* to realize that they are being shepherded forward to work as eventual cannon-fodder for their Kaituni drivers."

"I am sure they understand, Commander," Narrok offered quietly. "But I suspect they are willing to trade the risk for the implicit opportunities. It seems a certainty that had the Kaituni wanted to prevent all of the Bug armada from entering the cul-de-sac, they could have done so. But instead, they allowed a sufficient formation to enter at each of the two access points. From the Kaituni perspective, that is sufficient to ensure the demise of the Star Union as a credible strategic threat. However, from the perspective of the Omnivoracity, it is an opportunity: free time in which to start converting all the worlds in the Star Union into new Home Hives with all possible speed. I suspect that the Arachnids will be shuttling more forces into the Star Union from what they call 'The System Which Must Be Concealed' to achieve just that end. It is only five warp points from there to Franos, and their Kaituni herders have abandoned the area. The Omnivoracity will not fail to seize all those opportunities for reexpansion, any more than they shall obligingly commit suicide for their Kaituni shepherds.

"However, the Omnivoracity and the Kaituni have one—and probably *only* one—thing in common: they are absolutely xenocidal. Which means that even though they may be affecting a rough symbiotic cooperation presently, they both know that, when all is said and done, each will relentlessly work to extirpate the other."

Jennifer was perplexed. "And the Kaituni don't care about all this activity behind them?"

Narrok rippled his tendrils. "Why should they care? The systems that are arrayed between the points of Pesthouse, Alowan, and Franos are not particularly attractive to our people. Furthermore, the Kaituni seem to be consolidating along the warp line between Zarzuela and Zephrain, which boasts far more green worlds. But with all the Dispersates at their disposal, these strategic nuances will hardly matter, particularly if the PSU and Omnivoracity fleets reduce each other to tatters first. The Kaituni have created what your military analysts call a multiple overkill situation: they have arrayed such a superiority of forces in such superior positions, that they can suffer numerous setbacks and reversals, and still they will prevail."

Yoshikuni leaned forward. "So, that's where we stand. The squadron that we thought was herding the Bugs was just rear area security for the Kaituni fleet that touched down here in the Star Union to work as the real herders. It also means that, because we took some of their pieces off the game board today, the Kaituni are going to become suspicious sooner rather than later. Not too soon, because like the picket we nabbed that was left guarding the Unity warp point between Mymzher and Franos, the two ships we hit today were assigned to the warp point as an almost permanent force." She smiled ruefully. "We're not the only ones concerned that the Bugs currently in the Star Union cul-de-sac could come raging out again—right on our tails."

"Which works to our advantage, somewhat," Kiiraathra'ostakjo observed. "The Kaituni are most likely to ascribe the disappearance of the two ships in Bug 29 to Bug activity—very possibly by a small unit that exited the cul-de-sac on a scouting mission."

"Exactly," Yoshikuni agreed, "which is why we have a little time to ready ourselves for what has to come next: engaging the Kaituni fleet. But that's only step one. We have to push on through them, through the Bugs, and either destroy or get ahead of them, now. Because if we don't get to Bug 15 first or wipe them all out trying, Admiral Trevayne is going to be cut off. And the warp line to Sol will be wide open. We can't let that happen. And not just because of the size of these enemy fleets, but because of what some of the Kaituni monitors are carrying." She glanced at Ossian, nodded: on this occasion, there was no twinkle in her eye.

Wethermere surveyed the room. "I have the dubious honor of presenting the worst news last. The Kaituni have a new weapon that they employed at the Battle of Home Hive Two, a weapon which absolutely decimated our devastator and superdevastator formations. Here's some footage of the battle." The room became very still as he narrated over scenes which gruesomely depicted how the strategic and naval assumptions of the past century had been dashed in a few short hours. "We found references to the weapon in the dispatches carried by the Kaituni destroyer. Its technical name is the Relativistic Acceleration Weapon, although the Kaituni leadership prefers the label 'The Hand of God.' In brief, it directionally energizes subatomic particles to the point where, leveraging quantum entanglement and the uncertainty principle, they essentially teleport to a space inside a sufficiently large and slow target. The result is essentially a matter-energy conversion, with the results that you have now witnessed." Wethermere discontinued the stupefying montage of one supposedly impregnable ship after another being turning into wreckage-streaming stars of blue-white energy. "The possible use of such weapons against forts further complicates our overall strategic picture. With the devastators and superdevastators either destroyed or withdrawn from the line of battle, that places increased importance on forts as means of holding a warp point. However, while forts are not as large as devastators, they are much, much slower. So forts, too, could be at considerable risk. And if we presume that most of Sol's ready naval elements were rushed forward to join Admiral Trevayne's fleet, then all the Heart Worlds will have put themselves in a position where they are relying disproportionately upon forts for their local security. If they have done so, they may have put themselves in grave danger indeed."

The eyes around the table looked not merely haggard, but desperate.

"However, as chance would have it, we are arguably in a position to deal the Kaituni a particularly nasty surprise. Indeed, our fleet's need to accept what started out as a tactical disadvantage, has now, oddly, transformed into an advantage. Specifically, when Admiral Yoshikuni's Rim Fleet arrived from Bellerophon, there was concern that it had to leave its primary firepower—devastators and superdevastators—at home. So, accordingly, Admiral Yoshikuni took the step of replacing those leviathans with almost every smaller capital ship in the Rim Fleet's lists. And that is exactly the kind of ship we need to fight the Kaituni. To whatever extent they have assigned RAW-equipped monitors to the fleet just ahead of us, the Kaituni have further weakened their conventional firepower by burdening a sizable portion of their tonnage with a special weapon that is essentially harmless to us."

Yoshikuni nodded acknowledgment. "Thank you, Commodore." She turned back to the table, looked at every face before she continued. "That's our situation. We have some excellent advantages and surprises on our side, but the enemy in front of us has the advantage of both numbers and position. Furthermore, for them, a stalemate is a victory. Whereas, even if we defeat both fleets, we must emerge from those victories strong enough to be decisive in the defense of Sol.

"If we succeed, all our species might have a reasonable hope of surviving long enough to stabilize the strategic situation and turn back the combined Kaituni and Bug tides. If we fail—well, then we will each come to some moment in which we know that our peoples are doomed to extinction." She stood. "I, for one, don't want to experience that terrible moment. I'd rather die fighting, uncertain of the outcome, than live long enough to know that my species is being relegated to the dustbin of history, a footnote for conquerors to sneer at. If you revile and reject that outcome as much as I do, then carry your bloody resolve against it back to your command staffs and every last member of every crew. This is a fight for survival—for the survival of everything we have, we knew, or we hope for. Dismissed."

The table and room emptied silently. Ossian hung back; for the first time, he had not waited to see what subtle signal Miharu would or would not send.

When he looked at her, she was still standing straight, her face strained, her eyes very bright.

Ossian moved toward her slowly. Miharu Yoshikuni was not, in any sense of the word, a tender person. She was, through and through, the Iron Admiral. But she was also human through and through, and he could see the terrible price that uttering those grim words had exacted from her own stores of hope, of courage, of tenacity.

He kept his voice soft. "Miharu."

She blinked; none of the bright liquid in her eyes escaped them. "I don't know if we're going to make it, Ossian."

"I know," he said. "None of us do. But as you said, we're not beaten until the last of us die. And we have some pretty promising tricks up our sleeve."

She smiled faintly, her eyes finally drifting over to meet his. "Always the optimist, aren't you, Commodore?"

"At this moment, Admiral, I'd like to think of myself as a realist," he lied.

She shook her head. "Sometimes I think you may be the tougher of the two of us. I just put on the harder face: the gnarled old oak. But you do a pretty fair impression of the willow."

Ossian felt his own anxiety trying to fight through the calm he'd learned to cultivate since he was very young. "I'm a pretty tired willow, right now," he admitted. He looked at her frankly, not giving a damn about her rank or any of the other shibboleths of professional propriety.

She blinked and returned his stare. The smile on her face became less despairing, more tinged by rue and poignancy. "I suspect both of us have had stronger moments, Commodore. I wonder if you'd stay behind a while before returning to your ship. To discuss—well, a change to our rules of engagement."

Ossian smiled back. "The fleet's rules of engagement, or our own?"

"Both," she answered with the suggestion of a laugh at the back of her voice.

He felt renewed by that sound of mirth and hope, and wondered if his eyes looked as desperate and needful as hers did.

CHAPTER FORTY-THREE

"It's time, Ian," said Magda sleepily.

"Is it?" mumbled Trevayne, who knew perfectly well that it was but didn't want to face that disagreeable fact.

"I'm afraid so. I've got to get back to my flagship."

"Are you sure?" he persisted, reaching for her. "Maybe we could just—"

"No!" She gave his hand a playful slap and swung her legs out of bed. She walked a few steps—*Zeven Provinciën*'s flag quarters weren't particularly large—and created a spurious "morning" by activating the viewscreen and admitting the harsh bluish light of Pesthouse's primary, only nineteen light-minutes from where they lay near the Home Hive One warp point.

"Sadist!" He blinked his eyes repeatedly until he could see clearly. Her form was silhouetted against the light, which didn't help. He got up and embraced her. She didn't resist.

"I wish we could prolong this," she whispered into his ear.

"I know." It was what they said every time they were able to snatch a little time together, always in connection with some admirals' conference. But, Trevayne realized, he shouldn't complain. These opportunities might be all too rare, but they had been nonexistent during the entire campaign in Home Hive Two and the flight from there through Orpheus-1 and Home Hive One. Only here in Pesthouse were they able to occasionally touch each other.

They could have had more spacious quarters on the great space station that was the heart of the Pesthouse navy yard. But with the ever-present threat of the inevitable Bug onslaught hanging over them, Trevayne felt obliged to remain aboard his flagship. Also, the space station had a hollow, depressing feel these days, for Trevayne had gradually been evacuating its personnel to Bug 05. By now it was almost deserted, and those remaining tended to talk in hushed tones, as though oppressed by gloom and despair. Over the entire ponderously massive structure hung a heavy air of impending tragedy that had passed beyond the ability of human effort to avert. Trevayne had no desire to breathe that air.

But the same miasma was beginning to seep into the warships as well, and for much the same reasons. A series of Kaituni probing attacks on Bug 05 had forced Trevayne to shift more and more of Combined Fleet's mobile forces there, and by now no one had any illusions about Pesthouse's ability to put up more than a delaying action when the Bugs came through from Home Hive One in earnest. Indeed, the only reason Trevayne himself was still in Pesthouse was to lead a fighting retreat.

As far as Magda was concerned, that wasn't a good enough reason.

"I still wish I could talk you into pulling back into Bug 05," she said as they dressed. "You should take direct command of the defenses there, and leave me here to—"

"We've been over all that. Alistair M'Zangwe is quite capable of directing the defense of Bug 05. My duty is to—"

"I know, I know," she sighed. "The captain has to go down with the ship."

"The Royal Navy never had any such idiotic tradition! The captain was merely required to be the last one off the ship. Gave him a bloody good incentive to make certain there were enough lifeboats for everyone, y'see."

His attempt to jolly her fell flat. "I think," she said somberly, "that we may be running out of lifeboats."

"Well," he replied, meeting her eyes and holding them, "I'm going to make it a point to see there's always one for you. If there weren't, there wouldn't be much point in there being one for me. Who do you think has made it possible for me to keep going through all this?"

"Oh, Ian . . . !"

They were barely in each other's arms when the end-table communicator came to life with the nerve-grating screech of the emergency circuit that required no "accept" switch.

"Admiral," came the tension-tight voice of the flag captain, "one of the few probe drones that lasted long enough to transmit a report—"

"Yes, yes," said Trevayne impatiently. He had ordered, as a matter of routine, that the drones be dispatched through the warp point, sometimes in clusters. Most of them were promptly vaporized, but the occasional exception had yielded valuable—if discouraging—data on the vast Bug armada they faced.

"Well, sir, it reports a stirring of activity, and a spike in energy output, and . . . Excuse me, Admiral." The flag captain paused, and a muttered background colloquy was audible. Then he resumed in a tightly controlled voice. "Sir, AMBAMMs are emerging from the warp point."

Trevayne and Magda exchanged a split-second's wordless eye contact, then left at a run.

It soon became apparent that Trevayne's most pessimistic assumptions were—as was all too frequent these days—being triumphantly confirmed.

The previous attack, shortly after Combined Fleet's arrival in Pesthouse, had been a mere headlong dash by the leading elements of the Bug pursuers, on the chance that they could break in and establish a bridgehead against the tatters of a debacle, a defense that hadn't had time to organize itself. They had underestimated that defense—and they hadn't been expecting the devastators and superdevastators that had already been in position, waiting to blanket the warp point with murderous firepower.

So they had learned their lesson. This attack had been so long delayed because they had been bringing up their entire fleet and preparing with great thoroughness. And this time they were not going to stop.

Trevayne, knowing he would not be facing the Kaituni "stick-hives" here, had mined the warp point as densely as his resources permitted. But now antimine ballistic antimatter missiles, spewed forth by the AMBAMM pods—fairly old technology by galactic standards, but not ineffective when employed in these lavish numbers—thinned out those minefields in a stroboscopic wave of explosions. There followed a flood of SBMHAWK missiles, targeting the fortresses, for the Bugs had been doing their own probing. The fortresses fired back desperately with energy torpedoes, and the mobile forces added their own rapid-fire plasma bolts. But enough of the missiles got through to rock the fortresses, even before the phalanxes of sullen monitors began to emerge.

And this time there were no devastators and superdevastators here, where they might be cut off by Kaituni invaders as they withdrew across the long stretch between the Bug 05 warp points. In fact, by this time Trevayne had nothing larger than a monitor in this system. His supermonitors had already been dispatched to Bug 05, lest they slow the inevitable evacuation of Pesthouse.

The battle was space-wrackingly intense, and the technologically superior defenders took a heavy toll. But the Bugs had the numbers to waste, and as the sheer tonnage of their ships on the Pesthouse side of the warp point gradually built up it became clear that there would be no miracle. A grim Trevayne ordered his ships to withdraw across the relatively short expanse of space to the Bug 05 warp point, while transports took the remaining shipyard personnel to the same destination. His only consolation in abandoning the warp-point fortresses was that very few of their crews were still alive anyway. And they would fight to the death. Capture by the Bugs was something better not thought about.

And the decision, though hard, was one which Trevayne made without hesitation. He was coldly certain that Pesthouse must be evacuated without any further attempts to fight a delaying action, because he had a pretty definite idea of what was going to be happening in Bug 05 all too soon.

"*Destoshaz'at*, matters are progressing as anticipated," Inzrep'fel reported. "Our drones confirm that the Arachnids are continuing to transit the Pesthouse warp point in waves. Our tactical analysts deduce that they have broken into the system." (Flattery.) "As always, your order to dispatch the message drone in anticipation of this, shortly after the Arachnid offensive commenced, showed an order of wisdom that outstrips the rest of us."

(Complacent satisfaction.) "True. Did the drone get off on schedule?"

"Yes, *Destoshaz'at*."

"Excellent." Zum'ref glanced at the strategic display and visualized his message speeding on the wings of *selnarmic* relay, flashing from Home Hive One where they lay observing the Arachnids and keeping them on the intended path, through Bug 04, Home Hive Three, and finally Bug 03, to the Kaituni forces there, ordering them to immediately commence their well-prepared attack on Bug 05. That attack, he estimated, ought to go in while the *griarfeksh* were still in position at the Home Hive One warp point, locked in battle with the Arachnids—or, possibly, when they had already withdrawn from that battle and were in retreat toward the Bug 17 warp point.

He turned and studied the Bug 05 system display,

and pleasurably imagined the dilemma in which that attack would place the human admiral, who by this time had probably deduced the Kaituni's intent to stay behind the advancing Arachnids, but couldn't be absolutely certain of it.

"Excellent," he repeated. "Now, summon a conference. I want to make sure all our subordinate commanders are clear on my guidelines for how long we wait after the last Arachnids have left this system, before we begin to follow them into Pesthouse."

It was Pesthouse all over again. After Trevayne's forces transited to Bug 05, the leading elements of their Bug pursuers came through precipitously, in the hope of turning a retreat into a rout by not allowing a breathing spell. They were disappointed. Trevayne had emplaced a fair number of fortresses and dense minefields around the Pesthouse warp point, and once again a Bug attack that lacked careful preparation and full concentration of force was blunted.

It was then that Trevayne received word from Adrian M'Zangwe at the Bug 03 warp point that the Kaituni were attacking . . . and that this time they were doing so in earnest. They had learned better than to waste their "stick-hives" in profusion, but a storm of SBMHAWKs was being followed by waves of heavy assault monitors.

"They must be coordinating it!" gasped Elaine De Mornay.

"*Selnarmic* courier, of course," said Trevayne absently. "You see, it isn't really a case of the Kaituni coordinating with the Bugs; of that I'm pretty certain. No, it's a matter of the Kaituni activating a well-prepared plan to take advantage of the Bug movements." He dismissed the subject with an impatient gesture. "Have comm raise Ma . . . Admiral Li-Trevayne. I want her and Admiral M'Zangwe on a split screen."

While the order was carried out, Trevayne glared at the system display. Bug 05's three warp points described almost a right triangle, with the longer of the two sides opposite the hypotenuse a vertical forty-three light-minutes between the Pesthouse and Bug 17 warp points. Off to the left of the Bug 17 warp point, at a twenty-two light-minute distance, was the Bug 03 warp point and the embattled Adrian M'Zangwe.

"We have no alternative," he told them bleakly. "I'm still convinced that the Kaituni are going to get behind the Bugs and keep their distance. But in case I'm wrong, we can no longer risk being trapped in this system. And this time I'm not going to sacrifice the fortress crews here at this warp point. We'll put the fortresses on automatic defense mode and commence a fighting retreat to the Bug 17 warp point. Alistair, you must hold the Bug 03 warp point until we're at . . . about seven o'clock from the local sun, at a distance of five light-minutes, which is as close as I want to approach this blue giant star." They all knew even that would have been far too close without energy shields. "Then I'll signal you, and you will commence withdrawal, to rendezvous with us at the Bug 17 warp point." He met their eyes in turn, lingering longer over Magda's. "I'm going to risk leaving Hugo Allende's command at that warp point for now, to help us fight a delaying action with Bugs as long as possible."

It was impossible for M'Zangwe to go pale, but he

looked apprehensive. "Is that wise, Admiral? Whatever the Kaituni's policy toward the Bugs is, such a prize might tempt them to join the battle, and if they do, and get in a certain range—"

"—Then the devastators and superdevastators are doomed," Trevayne finished for him with merciless finality. "In case of such an eventuality, I'm going to keep them close to the warp point, and if—no, when—the Bugs get much closer to them than heavy missile range, I'm going to order Hugo to transit to Bug 17 immediately."

"Which he'll do under protest." Magda managed a small smile.

"He and anyone else can protest as they like. But everyone has to recognize one thing: we've reached the point where even delaying the enemy and inflicting the maximum losses on him—important though those are—have become secondary to preserving a fleet in being. In Bug 17 we're going to be all that's standing between the Bugs and the final approaches to Alpha Centauri, the gateway to all the Heart Worlds and Sol itself. I want those words—a fleet in being—branded into everyone's brain beyond any possibility of forgetfulness. And now . . ." He turned away from the screen and addressed De Mornay. "Let's start getting those fortress crews off."

The evacuation of Pesthouse went about as well as could be hoped. M'Zangwe was compelled to pull back from the Bug 03 warp point somewhat earlier than planned, to avoid unacceptable losses. But he was still able to link up with Trevayne's forces just short of the Bug 17 warp point, for the Kaituni attackers made no attempt to pursue him and cut off Trevyane's retreat. Instead, they followed the kind of now-familiar course that would bring them around behind the advancing Bugs, whom they followed at a distance of several light-minutes.

So Combined Fleet reunited at the Bug 17 warp point, then turned at bay and struck back against the leading Bug elements. In the absence of Kaituni attackers, Allende's devastators and superdevastators poured out a torrent of heavy bombardment missiles, and fighters slashed through the stolid Bug formations. But as more and more of the pursuing armada piled up, Trevayne knew he could delay no longer. Combined Fleet made its escape to Bug 17, then prepared to face the expected Bug pursuit. But in this case the latter was little more than a probe, of short duration. Turning about in accordance with long-established tactical doctrines, the retreating forces turned and blazed away at anything hostile that emerged from the warp point, and the fortresses Trevayne had pulled back from Bug 05 (which he had known he could not count on holding) added their fire. The Bugs, clearly aware that another well-prepared attack would be necessary here, drew off. The fire and fury of battle died away, leaving Trevayne and Magda to contemplate two things they had observed before leaving Bug 05.

The first was the sheer numbers of Bug ships. The relatively uneventful retreat across the Bug 05 system had given them the opportunity to gain a fuller appreciation of what they faced, and even with the losses Combined Fleet had inflicted it was even worse than their previous estimates.

The second was that, as the Bugs had doggedly

pursued Combined Fleet past the blue Pesthouse sun, Kaituni ships had begun to emerge from the Home Hive One warp point behind them, keeping well astern of the seemingly oblivious Arachnids. And the other Kaituni fleet which had entered from Bug 03 swung about in a course clearly intended to coalesce with the new arrivals.

Thus Combined Fleet stood in Bug 17, facing a Bug swarm that exceeded even those of the history books, and, following behind it, what might well amount in the end to the total fleets of seven Kaituni Dispersates. And Trevayne could not permit them to disguise from themselves the probable implications.

CHAPTER FORTY-FOUR

Bug 17's primary was a Sol-type class G2v main sequence star. But the system was lifeless, for its second planet—orbiting at eight light-minutes, precisely in the "Goldilocks Zone" (not too hot and not too cold but just right)—was a dustball too small to hold a useful atmosphere. So once again Combined Fleet, in its stubborn retreat through the old Bug systems, was spared the strategic complication of having a planetary population to defend.

They were, Ian Trevayne thought bleakly, not likely to remain much longer in that happy state.

He ran his eyes over the haggard faces around the conference table. Combined Fleet's command structure, after all its vicissitudes, had shaken down to something not too different from the old Allied Tangri Pacification Force. Adrian M'Zangwe commanded the Terran Republic component, Rafaela Shang the Rim Federation one. Magda exercised an overall command of both. Second Fleet's remnants had by now been integrated with the PSU elements

Trevayne had picked up on the way to Home Hive Two and the Ophiuchi carrier flotilla, all under the command of Admiral Mario Leong. He, like Magda, reported directly to Trevayne, who had, as a kind of political afterthought, been appointed Grand Admiral of the alliance.

Trevayne had taken this probably fleeting opportunity to summon his senior officers to *Zeven Provinciën*—and not just the most senior ones. The compartment was packed, for everyone down to task group commanders was there, as were Elaine De Mornay, Andreas Hagen, and the flag captain, Janos Thorfinnssen, a massive Beauforter. It was not just the standing-room-only overcrowding that made the atmosphere oppressive. Everyone knew this would be a somber conference indeed.

"All right, this is the situation," Trevayne began using a light-pencil to indicate locations on the system display. They lay near the Bug 05 warp point, at a bearing of six o'clock and a distance of twenty-six light-minutes. Fourteen light-minutes away was the Bug 21 warp point, on a five o'clock bearing, but no one paid attention to that one. Far across the system, at a bearing of eleven o'clock and a distance of twenty-three light-minutes, was the system's third warp point: the one leading to Bug 16, one step closer to Alpha Centauri.

"We would, of course, prefer to hold this system against the Bugs," Trevayne continued. "However, we must face certain facts. The first, of course, is the sheer size of the Bug armada we're facing. Now, given their technological inferiority, and our ability to use the devastators and superdevastators for defensive fire, it is within the bounds of possibility that we may be able to hold them—"

A low collective growl filled the packed room. It held no bravado, no false optimism, nothing at all but grim determination and refusal to accept defeat.

"But," Trevayne resumed remorselessly, "as we are all aware, the Bugs have an indifference to losses that seems suicidal to us. Actually, they're not suicidal at all; their hive consciousness is in fact extremely tenacious in protecting its own survival, as we've learned to our sorrow. But individual units mean nothing, and will be sacrificed unfeelingly in pursuit of an objective considered obtainable. The point is, even a successful defense of this system might well entail unacceptable losses for us."

"Whereas they have no such concept as 'unacceptable losses,'" M'Zangwe grunted.

"Which leads me to the final fact that we cannot conceal from ourselves. While still in Bug 05, we saw a very formidable Kaituni fleet beginning to coalesce in that system behind the Bugs. Captain Hagen is of the opinion that it may, in the end, amount to the total resources of seven Dispersates." Trevayne paused to let that sink in. "Now, by this time I think it can be taken as established that the Kaituni strategy is to let the Bugs go ahead of them, bearing the brunt of the fighting and taking the losses. So far, they have held to this policy with great consistency. But this is the system where that could change. If they decide the Bugs have served their purpose, and have suffered too much attrition to advance any further unaided, they may decide to intervene directly. And I need hardly tell you the danger—no, not danger; certainty of destruction—our devastators and superdevastators will face if they do."

There was a long silence, for Trevayne was reluctant to continue and many of his listeners had already guessed what was coming next. Finally, he spoke. "Therefore, given the paramount importance of preserving a fleet in being for the defense of the final approaches to Alpha Centauri against the fresh Kaituni fleets following the Bugs, it will be necessary for us to avoid an attritional struggle here. We will put ourselves in a position to conduct a fighting retreat to the Bug 16 warp point. This, of course, will be a lengthy process, given the distance: more than fifty light-minutes. Furthermore, the navigational hazards posed by this system's asteroid belt, at a radius of thirteen light-minutes and in the same plane as the warp points, mean we'll have to pass through it twice. Commodore Allende's command will commence withdrawal now. The main fleet elements will follow when it becomes indicated."

For an instant, Allende stiffened and seemed about to speak. But he subsided under Trevayne's gaze, and the latter resumed after a brief pause.

"In order for the withdrawal to be safely carried out, a covering force will have to be left here at this warp point to delay the Bugs. When the main fleet begins to pull back, it will swing away and take up position at the warp point. Without the support of the devastators' and superdevastators' firepower, this is all such a rear guard can realistically hope to accomplish. And it must expect to suffer . . . serious casualties.

"This is why I asked the task group commanders to be present. I want to keep Combined Fleet's task force organization as intact as possible, so the covering force will be composed of task groups detached from various task forces. And those task groups will be selected on a volunteer basis."

After a moment, a hubbub arose as task group rear admirals and commodores urged the qualifications of their commands. Trevayne called for order, and made selections on the basis of suitability. For example, he wanted to keep his invaluable Ophiuchi carrier formations intact, so the rear guard would be almost all human, save for an almost token contingent drawn from the Orion elements that still remained to Combined Fleet after Threeenow'hakaaeea's self-sacrifice in Bug 03.

"Thank you, ladies and gentlemen," he said when it was done. "All volunteers among the task group commanders will remain here aboard the flagship for the present, as we will need to hold at least one further briefing concerning the necessary reorganization. Captain Thorfinnssen, please arrange for temporary quarters. Are there any questions?"

"Yes, Admiral," said Magda, looking him straight in the eye and speaking in level tones. Too level. "You haven't said who will personally command this covering force."

"I will," Trevayne said briskly. His tone invited no discussion. "You will command the main fleet in its withdrawal. And now, if there are no further questions, the meeting is adjourned."

The ones lucky enough to have chairs stood up, and everyone milled about in the usual manner of a meeting breaking up. All but one. Magda rose to her feet into a posture of frozen erectness, turned on her heel, and marched out, cutting a path through the crowd.

Trevayne sighed inwardly. *May as well face the music.* He proceeded toward his and Magda's quarters.

"—So you're going to risk yourself—no, throw yourself away!—just out of some misplaced notion of heroism? Is that it?"

Trevayne held onto what was left of his temper after half an hour of raging argument that had gone around and around in fruitless circles, as domestic quarrels will. "We've been over this . . . and over it, and over it, and over it. For this rear-guard action to have any hope of success, it's going to have to be led by someone with . . . well, symbolic value. It goes to some very deep-seated traditions."

"But that's the whole point! You're indispensable. If a, well, symbol is necessary, that's all the more reason why I should be in command of the covering force. Remember, I've got 'Li' in my name, and this force is going to be predominantly from the Terran Republic." Magda stopped herself just short of adding, *where* I *was born rather than naturalized*, for that would have been too low a blow.

"And just how useful would I be as a symbol—or anything else—if I was seen to run away and leave my wife to—"

"So *that's* what this is all about! Just because I'm a woman—"

The leash on Trevayne's temper finally snapped. "That is *not* the issue at all!"

"It is . . . and you know it!"

Trevayne drew a deep breath, drew himself up,

and spoke in a carefully controlled voice, his face set and hard. "At the moment, the point is not that you're my wife but that you are my subordinate. My decision is made, and it is final. And I will tolerate no more insubordination."

She blinked as though she had been struck. For a moment, the silence reverberated. Then she stood as rigidly as he, and spoke in as tight a voice. "Very good, Admiral. Have I your permission to return to my flagship?"

For a segment of frozen time, they stood with eyes locked, each one wanting desperately to reach out—no, to cry out to the other. If a single word had been spoken, they would have been in each other's arms. But neither could yield.

"Permission granted," Trevayne finally said through a constricted throat.

She left the flag quarters and proceeded along *Zeven Provinciën*'s passageways. A young man fell in behind her. As she brought her seething emotions under control, she remembered that he was a new aide her chief of staff had assigned to her. For the first time, she noticed that his space-service grays had the black-and-silver trim of the PSU. It was typical of the way personnel had become more and more interchangeable in Combined Fleet with less and less concern for the services to which they belonged.

"What's your name?" Magda asked, because she needed to talk to someone.

"Lieutenant Menocal, sir. I was assigned—"

"Yes, yes, I know." She indicated his PSU colors. "How did you happen to end up with the Terran Republic fleet?"

"Well, sir, I was originally with the PSU Fortress Command, but I transferred to the Battle Fleet after... well, my homeworld of Orphicon, which my fortress was orbiting, was hit by one of the Kaituni kinetic projectiles."

Magda stopped short and actually looked at him for the first time. He was slender, of medium height, with a light complexion and features that seemed to hold a suggestion of Slavic origin. She spoke to him in a voice of sincere compassion. "So you had to watch your homeworld die?"

"Not altogether die, sir. It got off rather lightly compared to some: an ocean strike by a fist-sized object. But at two-thirds lightspeed..."

"Yes, of course."

"But I did watch a tsunami consume the coast where my old family home stood," he continued, his eyes growing haunted. "The home where my maternal great-grandmother lived. Irma Sanchez," he added, as though she should recognize the name. And, indeed, it had a certain familiarity. "She was a hero of the Bug War—"

"Oh yes, I remember now! I've read the story. She saved the life of Admiral Prescott."

"Yes, sir, and was awarded the Wounded Lion of Terra. My grandmother, her adopted daughter, always remembered that her mother had promised her that Bugs were never going to come..." He could go no further.

"As far as she knew at the time, that was true," Magda told him gently.

Their eyes met across the yawning gulf of rank that separated them, and the young man's voice steadied.

"Yes, sir. But now I suppose we have to do it all over again. I don't know if we're as good as they were then, in my great-grandmother's day. But we have your hus . . . that is, Grand Admiral Trevayne. Thank God for that. We need him." He stopped abruptly, as though feeling he had said too much. But she only smiled a distant smile.

"Yes, we do, don't we?" Suddenly, her features hardened into mask of irrevocable decision. "Lieutenant . . . uh, what's your first name?"

"Victor, sir."

"Victor, I have a special—and highly confidential—job for you. I want you to personally find the following officers in the temporary quarters they've been assigned on this ship." She reeled off the names of the task group commanders who had volunteered for the rear guard and been selected, and he repeated them into his wrist computer. "I want you, without speaking to anyone else about it, to ask them to meet with me at . . . oh, twenty-two hundred, to give them an hour." She recalled the name of Miyoshi Santana, a particular friend of hers. "And ask Rear Admiral Santana if we can use her quarters for the meeting."

Victor frowned with puzzlement, for it all seemed just a bit irregular. But he hastened to obey.

CHAPTER FORTY-FIVE

For a few moments, the silence in Miyoshi Santana's quarters wasn't even a stunned silence, because what Magda had said had not fully registered on her half-circle of listeners. Then it did, and the silence somehow deepened, descending into the realms of shock.

Commodore Nathan Harding, RFN, was the first to find his voice. "Do you have any idea what you're asking of us?"

"I do. I should, since I'm asking the same thing of myself." Magda smiled grimly. "Only more so. Unlike the rest of you, I'll also be betraying—and I suppose there's no other word—my husband as well as my commanding officer."

"Betraying more than that!" Santana's voice quavered. "What you're proposing is . . . is . . ." She swallowed hard and, with a physical effort, released the word into the air of the compartment. "Mutiny!"

Silence fell again, and this time it held a psychic undercurrent of horror. All three of the space navies represented in the group prided themselves on the fact that they had never experienced a single mutiny in their histories. Nor had the old Terran Federation Navy that was ancestral to them all . . . except, of course, for the mass mutinies at the beginning of the Fringe Revolution that had given birth to the Terran Republic. (But that was history, and the passage of time had caused it to take on the more respectable, if not glorious, patina of revolution.)

"Maybe we could call it 'defection' or something, instead," Magda suggested.

"Is that supposed to make me feel better?" muttered Harding.

"I've got a pretty good idea what a court martial would call it," growled Commodore Lavrenti Trofimovitch Korypatkin of Novaya Rodina.

Magda gave him a tight little smile. "Frankly, Lavrenti, at this particular moment in time I think a court martial is the very least of our worries. In fact, the possibility is all too likely to become academic." Korypatkin subsided uncomfortably and didn't reply, for this was inarguable.

"But Magda," Santana pleaded, "you can't ask us to do this. This isn't just mutiny. It would be Admiral *Trevayne* we'd be disobeying and even deceiving!" There was a general rumble of agreement.

Magda leaned forward, and her eyes were black fire. "The fact that you're all reacting this way is precisely why we have to do this! Can't you see? He's special, and not just—or even mainly—because he's an acknowledged tactical genius. It runs far deeper than that. His . . . his legend, as I have to call it, taps into the very wellsprings of human myth. Nathan, you're from the Rim—you know what he means to the people there. Their great defender and lawgiver when he was cut off there during the Fringe Revolution." Harding nodded, remembering the statue of Trevayne that had stood before Government House on Xanadu before the Kaituni had come. Magda pressed her advantage. "And afterwards, the way he slept in cryo suspension, as if healing his wounds, and came back at exactly the time when his people were threatened... it's simply mythic. And by now the PSU and the Terran Republic share in the myth as well." She allowed them a moment to assimilate the truth of her words, then resumed with even greater intensity. "We can't conceal the facts from ourselves. Combined Fleet may very well find itself with its back to the wall at Alpha Centauri, or even Sol itself. When that happens, the mythic aura that surrounds him may be one of the few things Terra has left to believe in. He *cannot* be allowed to throw away his life here, even though his nature requires him to do it." She looked each of them in the eyes in turn. "I said earlier I'd be betraying him. And I will, even though it will be harder for me than it could be for any of you—to save him from himself. Are you with me?"

Slowly, one by one, heads began to nod.

People got out of Ian Trevayne's way as he strode onto the flag bridge.

"All right," he demanded of Elaine De Mornay. "What is this nonsense?"

She spoke in tones of perplexity. "Well, Admiral, as you know, we've been gradually pulling back and keeping the fleet together, except for—"

"—Commodore Allende's command. Yes, yes, I know." The devastators and superdevastators were already on the way across the Bug 17 system to the Bug 16 warp point. "And we're waiting to detach the covering force, to swing back and take up a close defensive position at the Bug 05 warp point. But if I understood your rather disjointed call correctly, they're *already* deploying at that warp point! Who the bloody hell gave that order?"

"No one, sir."

"Well, have comm raise them!"

"We've tried, sir. No one acknowledges. And sir . . ." If possible, De Mornay's misery deepened. "*Ark Royal* is also deploying with them."

Magda's flagship, shot through Trevayne's mind. He sought for some rational explanation of all this, but found nothing. "Well, keep trying to raise someone in the covering force!"

"Admiral," the communications officer called out, "we're being hailed."

"About time!"

"Uh . . . it's not from the covering force, sir. It's from *Ark Royal*."

Trevayne swung around and faced the comm screen, on which Magda's carefully controlled face appeared. Everyone nearby made it a point to look somewhere else.

"Admiral," she said in a voice that matched her features, "I would like to report that the covering force is coming into position as planned."

"Magda . . . Magda, for God's sake, what is this all about? What are you trying to do, upset the plan?"

"No, the plan for Combined Fleet's withdrawal will be carried out to the letter—with you in command of the main body. I have assumed command of the covering force." Her face softened a bit. "Don't blame the task group commanders, Ian. I talked them into it . . . more or less bullied them into it."

Trevayne had to try several times before the word would come. "Mutiny," he croaked.

"You're not the first one I've heard that word from lately." Suddenly, she smiled. "I've been waiting for years to be able to pull a quote on *you*. 'If this be mutiny, make the most of it.'"

"That is *not* a quote! At most it's a paraphrase!"

"Whatever." She turned aside, as though receiving a report, then turned back to him with renewed seriousness. "Ian, we haven't much time. On my own initiative, I've been having probes sent through the warp point, and enough of them got back to make it clear that the swarm is stirring over there. That's how we timed this move. And now—" She glanced aside again. Behind her, Trevayne could see a flag bridge crackling with tension. "And now it's out of our hands."

"Admiral!" Andreas Hagen called out. "Sensors detect—"

"I see it," said Trevayne in a flat voice, as he watched a tactical display of the Bug 05 warp point light up with a typhoon of SBMHAWKs.

"So you see, Ian," said Magda gently from the comm screen, "it's begun—the final Bug attack on this system. You're always talking about 'a fleet in being.' Well, now it's up to you to preserve one. And to preserve *yourself*, which may be even more important. Do you finally understand what I'm doing?"

He did. He just didn't want to. "Magda . . ." He hesitated. He couldn't tell her that he needed her, truth though it was. He began again. "Magda, Han needs you."

She gasped, but then recovered herself. "Han and billions of other children need you, Ian. As for Han, she needs both of us. And I don't intend to die if I can possibly avoid it. This isn't a suicide charge. We're going to hold this warp point as long as possible, then begin a fighting retreat to join you. But whatever happens . . . remember that I love you. And if you love me, as I know you do . . . *go!*" She made a quick, savage motion with her hand, and the screen went dead.

For a long moment Trevayne stood rock-still, staring into the depths of the blackened comm screen, and no one dared disturb him. Finally he turned and spoke in a voice of cold iron. "Captain De Mornay, Combined Fleet will continue on course. The covering force will be following us when the situation at the Bug 05 warp point warrants it."

The rear guard held out longer than anyone had anticipated under the Bugs' characteristically relentless onslaught. Too long, as it turned out.

The covering force's composition, plus the fact that it was just coming into position, threw off the SBM-HAWKs' targeting. Thus Magda was able to let the fortresses bear the brunt of dealing with them, and when the Bug monitors began to make their quasi-suicidal multiple transits her energy-torpedo batteries were already in ship-to-ship mode. And she had held her carriers back and ordered them to launch early. An intense blaze of plasma bolts and a hurricane of fighters tore the first Bug waves apart. But they kept coming, and more and more of the defending ships signaled "Code Omega," the traditional death-cry of space warships.

The main body of Combined Fleet was sixteen light-minutes from the scene of Magda's battle, with Bug 17's Mars-like second planet a ruddy speck four light-minutes to starboard, and the covering force was still holding out, when Andreas Hagen approached Trevayne, who had never left the flag bridge. What he saw in the Intelligence officer's face caused him to tear his attention from the continuing stream of reports.

"Admiral . . . excuse me, but . . . well, we naturally have been concentrating on the Bug 05 warp point, and . . ."

"What is it, Andreas?" Trevayne's attention was now entirely focused. Hagen's stammering urgency was utterly unlike him.

"Admiral . . . *Bug ships are emerging from the Bug 21 warp point!*"

"Show me."

The system display told the tale. The ignored, unguarded warp point, fourteen light-minutes from the Bug 05 warp point in a direction almost at a right angle to Combined Fleet's course, was vomiting forth ships as fast as the Bugs could make transit. And as they emerged, they were shaping a course that would take them around behind the covering force.

"Admiral," Trevayne heard Elaine De Mornay's voice, "what's *happening*? Where have they come from?"

Without immediately answering her, Trevayne turned to a strategic display. He expanded it to cover more of the warp network. His unblinking eyes drilled into it for several heartbeats. Then he spoke without turning.

"I think it's pretty obvious. After the Bug armada we've been fighting emerged into Home Hive Two, and we withdrew to Pesthouse, a *second* armada emerged from their hidden home system, unknown to us. And the Kaituni let it come out . . . but only allowed it one direction in which to go." He traced the warp lines from Home Hive Two to Bug 06, Sharnak, and the stars beyond. "All that time, this second armada has been rampaging though the Star Union, the Bugs' old enemies. And now it's come around *this* way." He indicated a route that terminated in Home Hive Four, then Bug 21, and, finally, Bug 17.

"My God!" De Mornay breathed. It was a prayer, not a curse.

"Admiral," said Hagen, "a signal from the covering force. They're commencing their fighting retreat."

"If only they'd done it sooner," De Mornay muttered . . . then clamped her mouth shut as she saw Trevayne's features contract as though in pain.

For they could all see it was too late. The newly arrived Bug ships continued to pour from the Bug 21 warp point in as steady procession, and they were in a position to approach the covering force from its rear left flank, trapping it between the two hostile armadas.

Trevayne turned back to the system display. From somewhere deep in his mental turmoil came the vagrant thought that it would have been easier if this had been the centuries-ago age of reaction drives. Those earliest spacefarers had been blessed more than they'd known by their limited options. Without reactionless, inertia-cancelling drives that allowed a course to be reversed, there would have been no decisions to make, no alternatives to choose between: he would have been locked into his present course by the laws of physics. As it was, if he so ordered, Combined Fleet could turn about and join the death-struggle in which Magda was about to find herself. There was nothing to prevent it . . . except for the fact that it was utterly out of the question. His own words, *a fleet in being*, came back to mock him. And now it was more vital than ever.

"It has become clear," he said in an emotionless voice, speaking to no one in particular, "that the problem of defending Alpha Centauri and the Heart Worlds, including Terra, is even more desperate than we had thought. The reserve fleets are being demothballed and mobilized, and construction is proceeding as expeditiously as possible given the damage to the Corporate Words from the kinetic strikes, but for the present it is still up to us. We must complete our withdrawal to Bug 16 as expeditiously as possible. Having done so, we must immediately dispatch a force back through Harnah to Bug 15, to close off the other route from Star Union space."

De Mornay blanched. "Sir, does that mean you think there's a *third* Bug armada?"

"Not necessarily. But this second one could turn back around and come through Bug 24 to Bug 15. Thank God they took the route they did instead of that one—we'd be well and truly trapped. And they'd be one warp transit away from Alpha Centauri."

"Then why didn't they?" De Mornay asked no one in particular.

"They must have wanted to make rendezvous with the first armada," Hagen speculated.

"Perhaps. Also . . ." Trevayne took on a look of faraway concentration—farther away than most people were capable of concentrating. "It actually makes strategic sense, if you think about it. After all, they don't know how strongly or weakly held Sol is. For all they knew, they might have bitten off more than they could chew. Here, on the other hand, they had a chance of cutting us off in this system. We've seen the Kaituni try this strategy before, you know: herd a Bug force in behind us that may prevent us from withdrawing in time. As it is, what's their worst-case scenario? We escape, but this new Bug fleet provides more cannon fodder for the Kaituni push up the warp line to Sol. And the 'herding' Kaituni fleet that must be behind this new Bug armada now comes into communication link with the mastermind who must be directing things from behind the first Bug armada." Trevayne brought his mind back to the immediate tactical situation, and his emotionlessness seemed to waver—but only momentarily. He resumed in the same tone. "At any rate, there is no possibility of our being overtaken in this system on our present course. And now . . . I'll be in my quarters for a short time."

It was practically the only time Trevayne was absent from the flag bridge for the duration of the withdrawal. With little else to do, he followed the increasingly outdated—eventually almost a light-hour old—reports of the covering force's desperate attempts to extricate itself from between the two swarms of Bug ships enclosing it.

Finally the last of Combined Fleet's major formations completed their transit to Bug 16. *Zeven Provinciën* was one of the last ships remaining, and was preparing for transit when De Mornay and Hagen approached Trevayne. Their expressions told him all he needed to know.

"Sir," De Mornay spoke with desperate steadiness, "we have a Code Omega from *Ark Royal*."

"Thank you, Commodore," Trevayne replied with a nod, after a moment that seemed longer than it was. He stood up and looked at the viewscreen that showed the view aft. The sun of Bug 17 was a small yellow glow across twenty-three light-minutes.

"Admiral," said De Mornay in a voice that was unsteady with her desperate need to reach out to this man, "please let me express my condolences and deep sorrow for your—"

Trevayne turned and faced her. "Thank you, Elaine, but that's premature. I don't presume anything concerning Admiral Li-Trevayne's status until more conclusive evidence is forthcoming."

They stared at him and said nothing. He turned back to his last sight of the Bug 17 system.

Magda, thought Trevayne, who had never been even remotely religious, *I know that you still exist in the universe. And somehow, I'll find you.*

Then the warning sounded, and the little yellow sun vanished into the vortex of warp transit. The viewscreen showed a new starfield, the starfield as seen from Bug 16.

With a deep sigh, Trevayne departed the flag bridge. It was night, by ship's time, and the passageway lights had been dimmed. He strode off into the darkness that seemed to engulf them all, toward a glimmer of light that only he could see.

Arduan Terms and Concepts

Terms rendered in the Arduan tongue throughout the novel are shown here (and in the body of the text) ***in italics***. The transliterated forms of the terms are presented here **without italics**.

'ai: the way (or path or calling or discipline or spiritual domain) of something; used solely as a modifying suffix.

almgr'sh: an Arduan scavenger that was capable of both self fertilization and fertilization by a wide number of related species. It gave forth litters of ten to twelve young, amongst which there was often arresting genetic and physical variation. Its unusual combination of pronounced concupiscence and plentiful, chaotically diverse offspring made it a natural object of ridicule and contempt for Arduans (who despise both disorder and sexual indiscriminacy). The term, applied as an epithet, has a meaning roughly equivalent to "skank-whore."

Anaht'doh Kainat: Star Wanderers.

assed'ai: zen balance/yin-yang ("the way of balance").

Asth: a continent on Ardu; later, a new star system.

'at: senior, prime, or first.

at'holodahk: insult to enlightenment.

befthel: a "triple-blink," or instant of reflexive and complete eye-closing. It can be a sign of impending, possibly debilitating, shock.

bilbuxhat: a kine-like draft animal of Ardu.

crivan: a color in the ultraviolet range invisible to humans.

dest'ah: conflict (arising from the root concept of discarnation, or *dest*).

dest: to be discarnated; the death of a person.

desta'tuni: literally, "Death-Vowed." A ritualized, sanctified "suicide mission" for the good of the Race.

Destolfi montu shilkiene: a philosophical statement—"death is but a tiny thing."

Destoshaz: warrior caste. Literally, "the caste that traffics in (or is habituated to) discarnation" (of self, others, or both).

Destoshaz'ai: the way (or path or calling or discipline) of the warrior.

Destoshaz'ai-as-sulhaji: literally, "the way of the warrior as (the path to and attainment of) true enlightenment." Originally, the caste's delineation of behaviors and values that made their warrior ethos the acme of racial perfection and service to Illudor. By the time the First Dispersate had arrived at Bellerophon/New Ardu, it had become both the creed and name for a militant supremacist movement (rather than genuine "philosophy") among the *Destoshaz*. In this movement, the traditional desiderata of the caste became secondary to a blend of authoritarianism, hero-worship, pre-Enlightenment ritual and values, a distrust of *shaxzhutok*, a presumption of both speciate superiority and speciate exclusivity of personhood, and aggressive militarism.

discarnate: what a sentient does when it expires.

erzhu: nimble, dextrous.

Erzhushaz: the artificer caste, in which the presumed challenge of such artifacture would be associated with manual dexterity: e.g.; pottery, smithing, glassblowing. Ultimately, "makers."

flixit: a small, songbird-like creature that superficially resembles a cross between a bird and a lizard.

griarfeksh: a bald, semi-aquatic scavenger with nasty habits.

herrm: a color humans cannot perceive.

holodah: a *satori*-like state of enlightenment.

holodah'kri'at: senior high priest.

holodah'kri: high priest.

holodah-ra-nekt: honor carriers/bearers (honor surrogates); the term is used exclusively by the *Destoshaz*, since in the formulation, the concept of *holodah* ("enlightenment") is conflated with the principle of "honor."

Hre'selna: a category of simple biots—most akin to Terran jellyfish—that radiate a weak form of protoselnarm. These creatures employ the protoselnarm as their only sense and cannot swarm for mating season without it. Early in their electronic age, the Arduans recognized that the ability of these creatures to detect and react to changes in *selnarm* could be exploited so as to provide instantaneous-relay command circuitry. In the *Urret-fah'ah* minesweeper, *Hre'selna* biots were used to obviate the need for the weapons to wait upon post-transit reorientation of their electronics. Instead, the moment each specially-bred *Hre'selna* biot completed warp transit, it sought the correct electronic signal. Failing to find it—since the electronics were not functional yet—it sent a *selnarm* pulse to other *Hre'selna,* which, upon receiving that pulse, actuated piezoelectric launcher-initiators. The result: the ship's missiles were deployed almost 1.5 seconds before its command electronics had sufficiently recovered from warp-point transit to perform the same task.

hwa: a prefix denoting junior, lesser, apprentice, aspirant. It never carries a negative connotation; it simply indicates one who is still being mentored to assume the title modified by the *hwa*. So *hwa'kri* is "aspirant priest," or, in conventional English usage, an acolyte. It tends to be a formal term, used for traditional roles. It would be idiomatically perverse to apply it to something like a technical competency: one would not call a gunnery trainee a "*hwa'*gunner" because there is no alteration of social status or role intrinsic to one's skill in gunnery.

Ill'sblood: equivalent to the early Modern English "god's blood" or "s'blood" (now simply "bloody"). A profound profanity.

Illudor: the name of God.

incarnate: can be used either as a noun or as a verb. As a verb, it means to have one's soul returned to physical existence. As such, it is distinct—both as a concept and a term—from the purely physical phenomenon and context of "birth" and is, in Arduan metaphysics, presumed to precede the physical processes of returning to material form. Thus, Arduans believe that only after their souls are selected and sent forth for incarnation, are they then conceived, gestated, and born.

'ix: a collection of incidents or objects (however, it cannot be used to designate a "class" of objects, only their multiplicity). Cannot be used as a referent for persons.

ixt: numbers.

ixt'un: to calculate, mathematics.

Ixturshaz: the calculators, a caste that is held to be slightly less important than either *Selnarshazi or shaxzhu*. This is because their skills are considered more trainable than the first two (which are, respectively, largely or wholly innate) and so less individually crucial to the function of the community.

Ixturshaz: a thinker, one who calculates, uses logic/deduction.

'kai: a sanctified quest or holy way or path or calling. It can signify divine favor, inspiration, or character—without referring to or partaking of godhead itself. The divine tenor of this word is never vernacularized into a purely mundane usage: it always invokes the presumed presence, consecration, or will of Illudor. So a *'kaiKri* would be the closest Arduan synonym for a saint: a divinely touched, favored, and/or selected priest.

kreevix: an insect like a mayfly.

kri: priest.

maatkah: a form of Arduan hand-to-hand combat.

maatkahshak: training in a particular school or style of *maatkah*.

matsokah: training of the soul.

murn: a color invisible to humans on the infrared end of the spectrum.

Myrtak: the Arduan Einstein.

narmata: group harmony or harmonious action.

***nerjet*-motleyed**: the *nerjet* was a common, small lizard on Ardu reviled and renowned for its horribly clashing colors. For the Arduans, whose sense of smell is very restricted (being registered through the mouth), the concept of "stink" is not particularly significant. However, their powerful visual dependency and acuity renders certain color- or pattern-combinations as almost nauseating. The *nerjet* was Ardu's visual equivalent of a skunk. The epithet "*nerjet*-motleyed" essentially translates, into human terms and senses, as "shit-reeking." It is a common, crude, but nonprofane, curse. By comparison, "Ill'sblood" is quite profane and strongly frowned upon.

ranarmata: chaos, disharmony in action; willful disarray.

Sekahmant: a blue giant star 1.973 parsecs from the Arduan sun.

seln: to sense with great precision, almost at "connoisseur."

selnarm: the empathetic sense.

Selnarshaz: sensitives, those who have profound *selnarmic* talents. This is often, but not preponderantly, associated with superior intellect. They are communication facilitators, many are teachers, psychologists.

shaxzhu: one who has many, detailed past-life memories.

shaxzhutok: the state of having past-life memories.

shotan: sense/taste.

skeerba: a three-bladed knife that sits on the tentacle like a set of brass knuckles.

soka: life force; the tangible/lived soul (as against the potential soul when discarnate).

sokhata: soul building.

ssers: flexible, pliant.

Ssershaz: the versatility caste, or "those who may do many things." Now the "free safeties" of Arduan society, they have diminished almost as greatly as the *shaxzhu*. They were originally the Arduans who possessed no particular casted skills of any other area; they were a default set, and comprised the menial or mass labor of pre-industrial Ardu.

ssersxhu: versatility.

sulhaji: true vision.

threem: nautilus shell, reddish, of Ardu.

tun: promise, vow, or oath.

tuni: promised, dedicated to, or reserved for.

urm: the seven senses; particularly the sense of touch, tactile quality.

vrel: a color invisible to humans.

xen-narmatum: forever outside order.

xenzhet-narmat'ai: literally, "the place of eternal death beyond order or hope." (Where "place" is taken to mean a nonphysical domain that preternaturally and ultimately exemplifies the principle which is vested/sited there. Hence the suffix, "ai.")

yihrt: a large murn- and black-colored predator on Ardu.

zhed'bid: "terminal drone"; an automated transponder, jettisoned from an Arduan ship when destruction is imminent.

zhet: to die; what a nonsentient does when it expires.

zheteksh: that category of being which may truly (i.e. permanently) die. Consequently, this word also meant "nonsentients." Since Arduans traditionally linked personhood to the possession of *selnarm*, not to thought, they had a tendency to lump all non-*selnarmic* creatures together.

zhetteh: to kill; specifically, to cause to permanently die, as distinct from causing to become discarnate (i.e., *dest*).

zifrik: a colony-complex of ant-bees of Ardu. They created sophisticated structures but were not intelligent (either by human or Arduan standards).